CONFLICTED HOME

A. AMERICAN

Conflicted Home

First Edition: December 2017

CHAPTER 1

We stood for a long time and watched as the mushroom cloud climbed above the horizon. It was evil, malicious, malignant even. Being one that grew up in a time when the Berlin wall fell, I could remember what the tail end of the Cold War felt like. It was a constant fear of this very image. A mushroom cloud rising over an American city.

Little Bit came up and gripped my hand tightly. I looked down at her as she stared wide-eyed at the spectacle. She had no frame of reference for what she was looking at. But even this little girl could sense the horror she was witnessing. It didn't help that there were others in the park positively losing their minds.

When the cloud first became visible, some people panicked. Many began screaming about fallout. Others thought it was simply the first salvo in a full nuclear exchange, became terror-stricken, and ran, screaming. This was something I never understood, screaming. What good does that do? It was something I always talked to my girls about. Not screaming per se, but also crying.

When something happened that would scare them, and they would cry, even at an early age, I would tell them to stop crying. I would ask them, what good does crying do? It may sound harsh, but I wanted my girls to keep their heads when others were shitting themselves. I wanted them to maybe have that couple of seconds or minutes that could make the difference between life and death. And while I often felt these lessons were falling on deaf ears, it looked as though they may actually be listening.

My family stood silent as we watched what unfolded before us. We hugged one another a little tighter. But each was left to their own thoughts. I looked at my girls and my heart sank. This was something I could do nothing about. Tampa was a long way off, but the winds could certainly carry fallout this far. But hopefully, the way the converging sea breezes worked over the peninsula would prevent it. Hope is all we have now. But I'll never say that to anyone.

"What are we going to do?" Mel asked.

I looked down at Little Bit. She was looking up at me. Scanning my girls' faces, they were all waiting for an answer. I shrugged and tried to keep a stalwart outward appearance. "There's nothing for us to worry about. It's very far away from us."

"What about fallout?" Taylor asked.

I looked at Thad, who was standing close by. He too appeared to be waiting on good news. But what could I say? Tell them the truth? No. Instead, I decided to lie. "I don't think we need to worry about it. The Gulf breeze should keep it away from us." And it was a bold-face lie that was laid bare on Thad's face. But he didn't counter my statement. Nor did he try to bolster it.

In the Florida summer, a unique weather phenomenon takes place. The Gulf is a large warm soup bowl of water that warms during the day. Rising water vapor climbs high into the atmosphere. The westerly breezes carry it inland where it meets with equally warm moist air moving westward from the east coast over the center of the state. When these air masses collide, it creates intense thunderstorms. And it was these winds I was thinking about when I lied to my wife and daughters.

Sarge's voice pulled me out of my mental stupor. "I was going to give this to you in the hospital. I had some smart-ass comments I was going to say." He paused and looked west. "But nothing seems very funny right now." He held a small silver revolver out. "Here."

I took the small short-barreled pistol from him. It was a ridiculous looking thing. Hammerless, it sported mother-of-pearl grips. Holding it in my hand, I examined it, turning it over and over. After a moment, I said, "Looks like a damn pimp gun." I opened the action, breaking the pistol over and looked into the cylinder. There were two live rounds and three spent. Shaking my head, I said, "I can't believe this thing almost killed me."

In an attempt to be humorous, the old man replied, "Could'a been worse. Could'a been a Hi-Point," and he smiled.

I grunted as I tucked the little revolver into my pocket. "Yeah, I guess."

Sarge turned back to the west again. He stared for a long time at the cloud that was now very plainly visible even at this distance. Mel pressed in close to me. Little Bit did as well. I put my arm around each of them and looked at Lee Ann and Taylor. Lee Ann was standing off a little from everyone. It pained my heart because I could imagine what was going through her head.

She'd come a long way since that day on the side of the river so long ago. She was harder. But maybe that was for the better. It was a different world now. And for better or worse, she was adapting quickly to it. Her sister, however, was a different story.

When I first came home, I thought she was handling things way better than her sister. And she was at the time, for sure.

That is until that day on the side of the river. But now she stood alone, and I could sense the fear in her, though I couldn't see her face. Taking Mel and Little Bit with me, I walked to her and folded her into our embrace. I hadn't seen it, but she was crying. Quietly, softly. And when we touched, there was a release for her; and then I could feel her pain.

It hurt; and all I wanted to do was to get her and her sisters home. I wanted to get all my girls back where I knew they would be safe. Even if there was an invisible threat I couldn't see, smell or defend them from. But at least I'd feel safe, and maybe, just maybe, that feeling would make it through them as well.

"You guys ready to get back? There isn't much more we can do here," I said.

Thad and Mary stood silently, facing west, as we all were. Sarge inhaled deeply and slowly let it out. After a short pause, he said, "I reckon we should get back." He looked around the park and added, "We ain't doin' no good here anyway."

Thad looked at me; and the expression of fear mixed with uncertainty pained me. He was holding Mary close. It was the first time I'd seen such an open expression from him towards her. He must have sensed what I was thinking. I could see it on his face. It added to the emotions he was already going through, as though he were somehow betraying a wife and son he'd buried with his own hands. This big man, my friend, seemed almost on the verge of tears. I turned to him and wrapped my arms around him.

It was almost humorous when he returned the hug. I felt like a child in the arms of his father because Thad was so huge and I was so small. But in that moment, I was offering support. Though neither of us spoke a word, we said a lot to one another in that brief embrace. When it was done, he looked back to

Mary, who was clearly in need of more. And I went back to my girls. We all walked back to the truck together in silence.

Mel was pressed in close and it hurt my side, but I wasn't about to complain, and I kept her there. With Little Bit and Taylor in front of me, it made it hard to walk, but I wasn't about to shoo them away either. I could feel the weight of the little pocket piece. It was odd in that it was the only *hardware* I had on me. It's kind of funny how fast you get used to something. Like carrying weapons and wearing body armor.

I was surprised when I saw the old Suburban sitting in a parking place, in the park. I looked at Mel and asked, "You drive that here?"

She nodded. "Yeah. Danny had to help me get it started. The battery was dead, and we had to jump-start it."

"Yeah. I was going to rejuvenate those batteries. Just haven't done it yet. Hope it starts now."

"It did when I parked it. I restarted it before leaving it." She replied.

The girls quickly climbed into the truck. Little Bit got into the front, demanding to sit between us on the big bench seat. As I was getting in, Sarge stopped by my door and said, "See if this thing'll start."

Putting in the key, I turned it over. The drive from home must have been enough to bring the batteries back to life because it cranked right up. The old man slapped the roof of the truck and said, "Alright. We'll follow you back."

We had a string of trucks headed out of town. It felt kind of eerie not seeing anyone on the streets of Eustis. Just a short time ago it appeared everyone that lived in town was at the park. Now, it was a ghost town. I grunted to myself when I thought of all the people that must at this very minute be trying to dig a bunker or otherwise engage in futile preparations to survive fallout.

We rode in silence through Umatilla, which was likewise deserted, as we crunched over the remnants of the storm debris still on the road. It's one thing to ride through the town you live in and the power be out, like after a storm. It's another thing entirely to do so when darkness after sunset is the norm. Little Umatilla was totally dark. I didn't' see a single light anywhere. Even now, you could generally spot a window with a faint glow coming from inside. But this night everything was blacked out, as though the remaining residents of Umatilla expected an air raid.

The little market in Umatilla was abandoned, as well as the one in Altoona. I was greatly relieved when we pulled into the neighborhood, even though it was just as dark as everything else. Perez and Ian were at the barricade when I pulled up.

Perez came up and leaned in the window. He started to say something but looked at Little Bit and stopped. He smiled and asked, "How you feeling?" His breath wreaked of cigarettes.

I nodded. "Better, I guess."

"Well, I'm glad you're feeling better, amigo."

Ian pushed Perez out of the way and patted my shoulder as well. "Glad to see you back on your feet, Sheriff."

I looked at him and smiled. Then I looked down at my lap, "But I'm not on my feet."

"Whatever, smart—," he paused abruptly and finished with "guy. You're a smart guy, aren't you?"

I laughed at him. "Yes, I am. Thanks, buddy."

He rapped the door and I pulled away. I drove straight to the house. I was ready to get home. Little Bit held my hand as we walked to the house. The dogs swirled around us, jumping up on me. I patted them and actually smiled. No one said a word. I could feel the apprehension everyone felt, and I wanted to do something to try and lift everyone out of it. As we stepped up on the porch, I asked, "Who wants to watch a movie?" In reality, all I wanted to do was to go to bed.

Little Bit perked up immediately. "I do!"

I patted her head. "I bet you do. What do you want to watch?"

She started to jump up and down. "Lion King! I want to watch The Lion King!"

In my head, I groaned. But I smiled and said, "Me too. Let's go watch The Lion King."

Opening the door, the girls went in and Mel grabbed my arm and asked, "You sure? You don't want to just go to bed?"

"I do, babe. I really do. But everyone seems so bummed. I think a movie will take the girls' minds off the situation."

She nodded. "You're probably right." She stopped and shook her head.

"What?"

She chuckled and said, "I was just thinking about picking through the five-dollar movie bin at Wal-Mart. Never imagined just how important those movies would be."

Putting my arm over her shoulder, I said, "Yeah. But that movie didn't come from there. We paid full price for it."

She looked at Little Bit who was already putting the disk into the laptop, and said, "Maybe so. But it was worth every penny we paid for it, whatever it cost." Then she looked at me and asked, "You want a glass of tea?"

"What kind of question is that? Hell yes, I want a glass of tea!"

"Sit here, dad!" Little Bit shouted as she climbed up onto the couch.

I plopped down beside her as Lee Ann and Taylor both

came from their rooms with pillows under their arms and arranged themselves a place on the floor. Mel came in with my tea and handed it to me before sitting down. So, for the next eighty-nine minutes we all forgot about the flash in the western sky. Gone from our minds was the cancerous cloud that climbed ever higher into the atmosphere. Instead, the magic of computer-generated animation took us all to a happier place and time. Even if it was a little annoying.

When the movie was over, everyone went to bed quickly. Little Bit wanted to sleep with us but we convinced her she was going to sleep in her own bed, and I followed her to her room and tucked her in. Lee Ann climbed into the top bunk as I was kissing her little sister goodnight. She was way too big for such nonsense. But when I stood up, she stuck her arms out and I stepped up onto the rail of the lower bunk and gave her hug.

"I'm glad you're here," she whispered.

"Me too," I whispered back and kissed her head. She smiled and I turned off the little battery lantern they were using in their room.

Going into Taylor's room, she was sitting in her bed reading, using a small triple-A flashlight to see the print. "You alright?" I asked from the doorway.

She looked up from her book but didn't reply. After a moment of thought, she asked, "Are we going to be alright?"

I went in and sat on the edge of her bed and patted her leg. "Yeah. I think so. It was far away."

She thought for a minute and said, "I'm glad you're OK. Mom was so worried. She was mad too." She paused as though she'd said something she shouldn't, then continued. "She said you do too much, that some of the other people around here should be helping out."

I half chuckled. "Yeah, I know she thinks that. But I'm just doing my little part. Other people are helping. Aric was there when it happened. We all have to do our part, you know." She nodded and I asked, "You think I'm doing too much?"

She shrugged and rocked her head, "No. Not really. I mean. I don't want you to get hurt."

Now I laughed. "And on that I think we can all agree. 'Cause I don't want to either!"

She smiled. "Goodnight, dad."

I leaned in and kissed her forehead. "Goodnight, baby."

Mel was already in bed when I got to our room. I sat on the side of the bed and pulled my socks off. I felt kind of grungy and said I was going to take a quick shower.

"I bet it will be. That water's going to be cold," Mel replied.

Laughing, I replied, "I bet it is."

She was right. It was damn cold! But it felt good to scrub myself clean. In the process of so doing, I realized our piece of soap was nearly gone. We needed another piece and I hoped that there still were some pieces to be had. After toweling off, I went back to the bed and sat down. While drying my hair, I asked, "Where's my stuff?"

"What stuff?" Mel asked.

"You know, my gear. My rifle and pistol and stuff."

She pointed at the closet, "Your guns are in there. That vest thing had a lot of blood on it."

"Ok. Where is it?"

"You're not going to wear it again, are you?"

I rolled over on my side and looked at her. "Hell yes. It's my armor."

"Lot of good it did you."

"This time, maybe. Next time, it could save my life." As soon as the words left my mouth, I regretted them.

Her eyes narrowed, and while she already wasn't in a good

mood, me saying *next time* was a really, really bad idea. "Really? Next time, huh?" She shook her head. "You're not going to be happy until you're dead, are you?"

I held my hand up. "Babe. Bad choice of words, I know. Not what I meant."

She nodded very animatedly. "Oh, it was? So now you don't think it'll save your life next time?"

I dropped my face into the pillow and shook my head. I've been married a long time and know when I'm beat, so I sat up, smiled and leaned over and kissed her cheek. I wasn't about to try and kiss her on the lips. After resting my head on her shoulder for a moment, I said, "Goodnight, babe. We'll talk about this tomorrow."

I lay back and got comfortable and reached over without looking and turned the little lantern off. Mel sat in the dark for a minute before she got herself comfortable. I knew she wasn't as mad as she wanted me to think when she said, "Turn the fan on. I'm hot."

I got up and turned it on and got back in bed under the sheet. Pressing my luck, I said, "You should just sleep naked like me." But she didn't reply, and I could see her rolling her eyes in my mind. But at least that was the end of it for the night.

I woke in the morning before Mel and sat up in the bed, rubbing my eyes. I was sore all over. Partly from the wound, partly from lying in a bed for a couple days. The latter was something I hadn't done since the Event. In the Before, I had done so when down with a bad cold or some other such illness. As it was, I realized I hadn't had so much as a sniffle since things changed. Maybe it wasn't all bad.

I reached back and touched my ribs. Tender was an understatement. Any kind of a deep breath was very painful. The thought of a sneeze racked me with terror. Another hand touched my side and I looked back to see Mel leaning on an elbow.

"Does it hurt?" She asked.

I nodded. "Very much."

She ran her hand over my back and I heard her fall onto the bed. I looked back to see her staring at me. "I don't want to argue with you," she said.

"There's no reason we should start now," I replied. Mel and I had been married for over twenty years when things changed. Sure, there were times in the past when we argued loudly. But those days were long gone. Even before this happened, we seldom disagreed; and when we did, it was a quiet affair, settled quickly. Life was simply too short to get your blood up with the person you love and live with.

"I know. I'm sorry I was mad last night. I'm just so afraid you'll leave here one day and not come back."

I lay back and put my arm around her. "Me neither, babe. But at the same time, I don't want anything to happen to you. Or the girls. And that requires action on my part and that of others. I'm not doing it alone and I'm not doing it recklessly. I promise you that."

She nodded but said nothing. She raised a hand to her face and I assumed she was wiping away tears. We lay in the bed for a few minutes, not saying anything. After a short time, she asked, "Are you hungry?"

"Famished," I replied.

She sat up in the bed, the sheet falling away and I saw she was naked. I smiled, and as she stood, I reached over and slapped her ass. "I see you took my advice."

She looked back as she got into her robe, saying, "It's cooler. Come out when you're dressed and I'll fix you some eggs." And she left the room.

I sat up and slowly dressed so as not to aggravate the wound. In clean shorts and a t-shirt, I headed for the kitchen. Mel already had the Butterfly stove lit and was going through the motions of cooking. Getting myself a glass of tea, I took a seat at the table. "What was with the lanterns last night? Why was everyone using those?"

She shrugged. "The girls just wanted to. I didn't care and let them."

I nodded as I sipped my tea. "What's going on around here?"

"Thad's getting worried about the garden. He said we're going to have more produce than we can eat and there aren't many ways to store it. We went on another scouting mission looking for vinegar for Kay. She and Mary are going to can and pickle everything they can."

"Did you find any vinegar?"

She nodded as she a banged a spoon full of butter on the side of the cast iron skillet. "Some, but not much. Not nearly enough."

"Guess we'll just have to make some."

She looked up from the stove. "You know how to make it?"

"Yeah. It's not that hard. I'll get with Kay about it."

She smiled and shook her head as she turned her attention back to the stove. "What?" I asked.

"I've known you for nearly twenty-five years, and yet I learn something new about you nearly every day." She looked back up at me, "When did you learn all this? When did you find the time?"

I laughed. "It was in all those books you complained about so much."

"It wouldn't have been so bad if they weren't left lying everywhere in the house."

"Guess it was a good thing now, huh?"

She cut her eyes over to me. "Maybe."

In didn't take her long to slide a plate of fluffy eggs in front of me and set out another for herself. We ate breakfast and talked about nothing particular or unpleasant. When breakfast was done, I told her I was going over to Danny's to see what was needed for the day. She said she would hang out around the house and wait for the girls to wake up. I kissed her and hugged her, maybe a moment longer than I normally would have, before going to the door.

I was so used to picking up my vest and rifle when I went to the door that I stood and stared at the empty place it should occupy. The vest wasn't hanging on its hook and the carbine wasn't in its place in the corner. I looked back at Mel about to ask when I remembered. *Fuck it,* I thought. Instead of putting my shoes on, I slipped my feet into a pair of flip flops and headed out the door.

The dogs were unusually happy to see me. All three of them followed me, nosing at my hands and demanding I rub their heads. Maybe this was just their way of saying they were glad I was back. I remembered reading an article about dogs being trained to sniff out tumors in people. And another that would go through an assisted living facility and climb up onto the bed of one close to death or in failing health. And that not long after doing so, the soul would slip away from them. They claimed the dog had a way of knowing. I wondered, rather morbidly, if it wasn't the dog that was actually the cause of their deaths. As though it was the harbinger, and had it not visited, they would have gone on a little longer.

But these mutts obviously knew something was different and were eager to show their happiness at my return. It made me smile though, and I happily indulged them as I walked. It wasn't common for them to follow me all the way to Danny's.

Hell, it wasn't common for them to follow me off the damn porch. But today, they did follow me. Rounding the corner, I saw the porch was full. The old man looked as though he were holding court.

Seeing me, he smiled, "Glad to see you among the living, Sheriff."

I nodded. "Me too. Beats the alternative all to hell."

Kay was sitting beside him and started to rise from her chair, asking, "Are you hungry, Morgan? I can fix you something."

I waved for her to stay in her rocker. "No thanks, Miss Kay. Mel already fed me up with a skillet of eggs."

She smiled and settled back into her chair. "Well good. I'm glad you're back." Then, wagging a finger at me, she said, "You gave us quite the scare!"

I smiled sheepishly. "I didn't intend to. You can count on it."

As I replied, Aric came out of the house with Fred. Seeing him, I stepped up on the porch and held out my hand. "Thanks for looking out for me, buddy." He took my hand and I pulled him in, putting my other arm around him and patting his back. A gesture he reciprocated. I said, "You saved my life, buddy."

Releasing the embrace, he said, "You saved me once. It was the least I could do."

When those inside noticed my presence, there was a flurry of hugs and kisses. Well wishes as well as admonitions. Jess stood on her toes and held me tight for a long time. She whispered in my ear, "You scared the shit out of us. I'll kill you myself if you get yourself killed."

I couldn't help but smile, and I whispered, "You already tried once." She stepped back and gave me a look that told me what I could go do to myself, making me smile even harder before leaning in and hugging her one more time, which she did not return.

Instead, she pointed at me and said, "You're an asshole." Then she smiled and said, "But you already know that."

I cocked my head and said, "You aren't the first to tell me, and probably won't be the last."

"Not by a long shot!" The old man barked.

When Mike and Ted came out, Mike had a shit-eating grin on his face. He stepped up in front of me and stood there for a second, just staring at me as he rocked on his heels with hands behind his back. "What?" I asked. He reached into his cargo pocket and pulled out a small black case and handed it to me. "We think you've earned this."

Opening it, I saw a Purple Heart lying on the silk. I shook my head and snapped it closed, "No. I didn't earn that." And I held it out for him to take back. "It's not for the county Sheriff that takes a little-ass bullet for being stupid. It's for you guys that go out and defend our country."

"You were doing the same thing, bro," Ted said. "Keep it. You've earned it."

Seeing they weren't going to yield on the issue, I nodded. "Ok." But I held it out to Mike. "But I don't want to take your medal."

"Shit!" Sarge barked. "That thing ain't his!"

Mike looked over his shoulder and said, "Some of us don't carry all of them around everywhere we go."

"You keep that, Morgan." Sarge said. "You deserve it as much as any man ever has. You're giving your life to your community."

I still disagreed with them but gave up on the argument. I motioned with it in my hand and said, "Thanks, guys," and shook Mike and Ted's hands. Sliding an old milk can over, that was nothing more than decoration, I sat on it and asked, "So what's up?"

Sarge leaned back in his chair, as an old man will do. "We've got a lot to do. I talked with those engineers. They're already at work on the line going into Eustis. The focus at the moment is to get power to the armory and then to the county building."

I nodded. "That's good. I want to run that line down here too. We're going to get power back in here too if it kills me."

"I don't know if Sheffield will agree to that," Sarge replied, shaking his head.

"He can kiss my ass," I snorted. "I'm also going to try and get power back to some of the houses in town. The power plant is small and can't run the county, but it can run quite a bit, and we're going to use it."

The old man smiled. "I told him you'd say that. He seems to think the plant is somehow under his control."

Shaking my head, I asked, "Why the hell wouldn't he want others to have power?"

"I don't know. Don't really matter none."

As we talked, Thad and Mary walked up on the porch. He dropped down to hang his legs over the edge of the porch and smiled. "Glad to see you up and about."

I patted his leg and replied, "Thanks, buddy. Good to be back. We were just discussing what needed to be done."

"The garden is coming along good. We're going to be able to start picking soon."

Kay was sitting beside Sarge. She piped up, "We need more vinegar. I don't have enough."

I nodded. "Mel told me. I'll get to work on making some soon."

"Making some?" Kay asked.

I nodded. "Yeah. You can make it. I just need some fruit of some kind. It's pretty much like making wine, you just let it go longer. I want to make a still so we can distill it and get pure vinegar."

Kay clapped her hands in front of her face. "Morgan, if you could make vinegar, that would be amazing."

"I'm going to go see Gena and see what she has in the way of fruit." I looked at Thad and asked, "How's the farm coming?"

He sighed, "It's been a hell of a battle. Horn worms got into the tomatoes and the only thing we could do was pick them off one at a time. They did some damage but not that bad. The squash had to be checked every day and the flowers pinched off or they would rot. But it's coming along."

"Have we had anymore run-ins with armor?" I asked Ted.

He shook his head. "Not yet."

"We've set some pickets up on 441. Just observation posts. I figure if they come this way, they'll come through there." Sarge said, "We're using Sheffield's people for it."

I nodded. "We should probably put another one up on 44. That's the other route into this area. They could bypass 441 and get right into downtown Eustis."

The old man nodded. "Already done." He laughed at me and said, "Leave the military stuff to us. You handle the law and order business."

"Guess I should go into town," I said.

"That would be a good idea. Let folks know their Sheriff is still around."

I rose to my feet. "I'll get my stuff."

"I want to go with you," Jess said.

I shrugged. "Fine by me."

I walked back over to the house to collect my gear. I again asked Mel for the vest. She finally brought it out. The side did indeed have a large stain. But it wasn't nearly as bad as she made it sound. I took some time getting my equipment put back into the various pockets as the girls sat chattering away at the table. They were having their breakfast.

Mel came into the bedroom and leaned against the door. She watched for a few minutes before asking, "Where you going?"

I was slipping magazines into their pockets when I replied, "Just to town. I'm also going to stop by Gena's and see if she has any kind of fruit so I can start making the vinegar."

"I know I can't stop you. Just promise to be careful."

I finished stowing the gear and slipped the rig over my head as I walked towards the door where I paused and kissed her. "I will, babe. I promise. What are you going to do today?"

"Bobbie said the kids' clothes are getting small. We're going to go through the houses and see if we can find anything for them."

"I say, take any clothes you find. Little Bit will need new stuff soon too, probably."

"I've got her covered for a while. You know we bought a lot for her and put it away."

"Good," I replied. "I'll be back later. I won't be long."

She kissed me and I headed out the door. The dogs were gone now. Probably off hunting or something, I imagined. Walking back over to Danny's house, I saw Jess, Aric and Fred waiting beside the smaller of the two buggies. "All of you going?" I asked.

Fred nodded. "Yep."

"Good," I replied. "You can drive, Aric."

He hopped into the driver's seat and the girls climbed into the back. As he pulled out, I told him I wanted to go to Gena's place before going to town."

"Roger that, boss."

At the bunker, we stopped when Dalton and Danny walked out into the road. Dalton looked me up and down and said, "You look alright to me. I don't see what all the fuss was about."

I patted my side. "Pretty much. That little .32 stung though."

"Hmmm. I bet. Better to just shoot 'em next time. Don't let 'em get so close."

"You guys going to town?" Danny asked.

I nodded. "Yeah. Just to fly the flag you know." Then I asked, "You don't know where there's a big crock do you?"

Dalton pointed at me and replied, "Yeah. It's sitting right in front of me."

I gave him the finger. "Thanks. But I need something to make vinegar in."

"I've got one in the shed," Danny replied. "It's nearly five gallons."

"Perfect. Can you dig it out later?"

"You're going to make vinegar?" Dalton asked. I nodded and he added, "Why would you want to ruin wine like that? If you have the stuff to make vinegar, you have the stuff to make wine. Let's make wine."

"You can't pickle with wine," I replied.

"Like hell!" Dalton shouted. "Give me five gallons of wine and I'll get thoroughly pickled!" Getting Fred and Jess to laughing.

"Me too," Aric said, holding up a hand.

I pointed at Dalton and said, "No," then at Aric as well, "and no. I need to find some copper to make a still out of so we can get pure vinegar."

"Just take it from that church they were building on nineteen," Danny said. He was referring to a large church that was under construction before things went south. It was one of those perpetual construction projects that was being built as the money was raised. A large stack of copper roofing was sitting on the site, the last delivery before things changed.

"That's a hell of an idea!" I replied.

"Yes, it is!" Dalton shouted. "We need a still!"

I laughed and shook my head. "For what? You can't make anything in it. We don't have grain or sugar."

"Oh, where there's a will, there's a way," he replied. I shook my head again and waved Aric on. We left Dalton and Danny as they were trying to devise a plan for sour mash.

Gena and Dillon were out back tending the canning stove. The relief valve on the pressure canner rattled as Gena filled jars with tomatoes. It was hot work in the stifling heat of a Florida summer, and sweat poured off Dillon's forehead as he added wood to the fire, despite the bandanna tied around his head.

"You two look busy," I said.

"Gotta get it all put up before it spoils," Gena replied.

"Glad to see you up and about," Dillon said as he removed jars from a large kettle of boiling water.

"Thanks. Good to be up. I was wondering if you guys had any kind of fruit. Even skins, rinds, anything at all."

"If you want skins, you're in luck," Dillon said as he reached down and picked up a five-gallon bucket and set it at my feet. "We made jelly from the muscadines yesterday. Here's all the skins."

I looked into the bucket and smiled. "That's perfect."

Gena wrinkled her nose. "What on Earth are you going to do with those?"

"Make vinegar," I replied.

I could see she was thinking that statement over. After a moment, she said, "Huh. I never thought about making vinegar. If we had some, we could make some pickles! How long does it take to make?"

I shrugged. "Depends. Down here though, in this heat, probably not more than two weeks."

"Well, if you get it made, I want some," she replied.

"Not a problem. We got to get to town. I'll see you guys

later." I said and picked up the bucket. Holding it up, I said, "Dillon, I'll bring your bucket back later."

A five-gallon bucket with a handle and no holes was a commodity to be coveted today. Sure, they used to be everywhere, and we always took them for granted when you could use one as a shopping basket at Lowes or Home Depot and take it home with you when you were done. They were left outside to fill with water and become little ecosystems, or blown out of the bed of trucks to be smashed on the highway. But not now. Now, it was very difficult to find one, as they were infinitely useful.

He waved me off. "Whenever is fine. I've got more."

"Wait," Gena said. She went into the house and came out with several small jars piled into her apron. "Here," she said, handing the jars to Jess, "take some jelly home with you."

Jess held one of the jars up to the light. It was a pretty light purple. "Thanks, Gena. That's very sweet."

"We've got more than we can eat."

"I'll say!" Dillon shouted. "Not to mention, there ain't no toast to put it on anyway!"

Jess's eyes rolled back. "I would give anything for a loaf of bread!"

"Maybe if we lived in Kansas," Dillon replied.

"Well, we ain't in Kansas, Dorothy," I replied with a grin.

Dillon laughed uproariously. Pointing at me, he replied, "You're funny, Morgan. But keep your day job."

I laughed and shook my head. "I don't know, buddy. My day job is killing me."

Jess kicked me in the shin and scowled at me. "Don't talk like that!"

Gena agreed with her, "That was not funny, Mister Morgan."

"Okay, okay. It wasn't funny." I agreed in surrender.

Saying goodbye, we climbed back in and headed for the market in Altoona. As we rode, Fred said, "I don't feel so good."

Looking back, I asked, "What's wrong?"

"Nothing. Just an upset tummy," she replied and turned to look out the open side of the buggy. I looked at Aric, but he just shrugged and kept his eyes on the road.

Aric swung into the market and stopped beside Mario and Shelly's booth. This time though, Shelly wasn't there, and I asked Mario where she was.

"She's back at the house with Garrett." He nodded across the market and added, "John's here helping me today."

John was Mario's lifelong best friend. Seeing me, he waved and smiled, which I returned.

"Damn," I said. "I haven't seen him since…" I thought for a moment, "before all this started, I guess. Where's he been?"

"He's been keeping an eye on our place. That and working the bees to keep us in honey."

"I'll have to go say hi to him."

"Hey, Morg, me and the girls are going to walk around," Aric said. I nodded, and they headed off to wander the day's offerings.

"Heard about what happened to you," Mario said. "Glad to see you up and around."

"Me too, my friend. Thanks."

"What are you up to today?"

"I need some honey. I'm going to try and make vinegar so we can pickle some of the crop from the garden."

I could see he was thinking about it. "That's a pretty good idea. But I've never heard of anyone using honey to make vinegar."

"Me neither, honestly," I replied. "But all you need is sugar, and honey is sugar."

"That's true," he said as he picked up a gallon jug and held it up. "Best sugar there is." And he held the jug out to me.

I took it and asked, "What do you want for it?"

He waved me off, saying, "Don't worry about it. If it works, show me how you do it."

"Thanks. I really appreciate it."

"Just doing my part for the community," he replied.

"It's a lot," I replied, smiling.

I said goodbye and carried the gallon over to the buggy. Aric was there, sitting on the front of it with his feet on the bumper. He was leaned on his knees looking at something in his hands. I dropped the jug into the back seat and leaned up beside him. He was turning a small velvet box over and over in his hands.

"You still haven't given that to her yet?" I asked.

He shook his head before looking up at me. "Not yet. But I need to. Soon."

I looked out across the parking lot of the market at the girls. Jess was holding a little sun dress up as though she were modeling it. Fred was laughing at her. "Soon, huh?" I asked and looked over at him.

He nodded nervously. "Yeah."

"Why?" He shrugged and looked at the box. I smiled and asked, "How many months do you have?"

"What?" He quickly asked.

"Well. You said you needed to give it to her soon. And she wasn't feeling good earlier. I didn't think anything of it until you said that. But now, well, even I can do that math."

"Please don't say anything," he pleaded.

I smiled and asked, "Why? What's the big deal?"

"Well," he hesitated, "We're not married or anything. She doesn't feel right about it."

I laughed. “What the hell does that have to do with anything? So, you didn’t go to the county courthouse and buy a license. Big damn deal. You two love each other, right?” He nodded. “That’s all that matters. It’s not like you’re going to be filing your taxes married, or adding her to your health insurance. All that matters is what you two think of it. No one around here is going to think anything less of you. Hell, all those hens back at the ranch will probably be excited as hell for you!”

“You don’t think anyone will say anything?”

“Hell no! Who would have the right to say anything to you two anyway?”

“I guess you’re right. I just don’t know what to do.”

I stood up and patted him on the shoulder. “What you need to do is give her that ring. I mean, shit, you’ve had it long enough.”

He looked up and smiled. “I guess you’re right. But what about the baby? She’s kind of scared. You know, no hospital and all.”

“Don’t worry, buddy. When it’s time, it won’t matter. Babies are born all around the world every day without hospitals. Nature will take care of that. Besides, we’ve got Doc and the clinic as well. Not to mention, Miss Kay and Mel. She knows a thing or three about having babies.”

The girls were walking back towards the buggy now, without the dress. Aric gripped the little box in his fist. I saw it out of the corner of my eye and elbowed him. As Fred walked up, I said, “Go ahead. What are you waiting for?” He looked mortified, but Fred asked, “Go ahead what?”

Aric stepped down off the buggy. He looked at Fred, the box was still wrapped in his fist. “What?” Fred asked.

“Well,” he started. Then Jess squealed and cupped her hands over her mouth.

Fred looked confused and asked again, "What?"

Aric held the little box out in front of him. Before he opened it, Fred covered her mouth and took a step back. He opened the small velvet box and took the ring from its satin setting and held it out. "I've had this for a long time."

Fred looked at me and I nodded. "He has. I was with him when he traded for it."

Aric reached out and gently took Fred's hand. "I want our child to be born to parents that are married." He slid the ring on her finger. She held her hand up and looked at the stone in the sunlight.

After a moment, she said, "But we aren't married."

I smiled and asked, "Do you want to be?" She looked at Aric and smiled, nodding her head. I shrugged and said, "Then you're married."

Fred let out a squeal and fell into Aric's arms. He caught her, and they hugged one another for a long time, then kissed. Aric looked as though the weight of the world had been lifted off his shoulders. Personally, I found the whole thing funny. People were so stuck in the old ways that even now they were worried about not being *properly* married. What did that really mean though?

When they finally let go of one another, Jess pulled Fred away, drawing her hand out so she could see the ring. "Oh, that is so beautiful," she said with a tear in her eye.

Fred held her hand up again and replied, "Isn't it, though?" Looking at Aric, she asked, "Where did you get it?"

"He went to Jarred," I laughed.

Jess scrunched her face at my joke. Before saying, "We need to have a party for them!"

I nodded. "That's a fine idea. We'll have a party for you two."

"Really?" Fred asked.

"Of course! It's not every day two people get married," I paused and smiled, "and we find out there's going to be a baby."

Fred looked at Aric in surprise. He held his hands up, "He guessed it! I didn't say anything, I promise!"

"He didn't tell me Fred," I said in his defense. Then I asked, "How far along are you?"

She put her hand over her belly and said, "Five weeks, I think."

"I say six!" Jess interjected.

"Five, six, it doesn't matter," I said and leaned in and hugged her, then kissed her on the cheek. "Congratulations. This is going to be big news. Everyone is going to be so excited."

"You don't think anyone will be mad?"

"Mad at what? No, sweetheart, no one will be mad," I smiled.

Now, she too looked relieved, and I watched in amazement as she took on a glow that I would never have expected. She went to Aric and they stood side by side with their arms around one another. He looked happy, on top of the world even. And she was radiant. It was a moving thing to see. They'd kept it in and hidden this wonderful news from everyone as though it were something to be ashamed of. But they were two consenting adults, and I knew looking at them, they would be together for the rest of their lives.

"We got work to do first, newlyweds. We got to make this run to town then we'll go back and tell everyone the good news. Why don't you two sit in the back," I said.

"You ride shotgun. I'll drive," Jess said.

I looked at her with raised eyebrows. "Really? You're going to drive?"

With her hands planted on her hips, she cocked her head to the side and replied, "Yes! I can drive!"

I reached for my side and said, "I don't know if I'm well enough for this," trying not to smile.

She rolled her eyes. "Get in, old man."

"Now that hurt!" I mocked her.

As she climbed into the driver's side, she pulled herself up to look over the roll-bar at me, "Bullshit."

I nodded. "Yeah. You're right," I said as I got in on the passenger side.

We left the market in Altoona behind us. Jess was getting a thrill out of driving the big war wagon and took the old saying, *drive it like you stole it,* to heart as she flew into Umatilla. It was mid-morning and starting to get hot already. The sky was clear and bright, and the hot air blew over us as she roared into town. As we passed the old Ace Hardware, she asked, "You want to stop at the market?"

I nodded, "Yeah. Just for a minute."

She did manage to slow the wagon down as we got to the market. I was beginning to think she was going to come in sideways. As she shut it down, I looked over at her and said, "Good driving there, Andretti."

She gave me a dismissive look over her shoulder, replying, "Told you I could drive."

As it was high summer, there were a few things coming into season in the Florida wilds for those that knew where to look. One thing, that most anyone could find, was blackberries. Florida blackberries are not like their northern kin. They are smaller, usually tarter and heavy with seed. But they were still good. I'd been keeping my eye out for the patches I knew of, and marking their progress. Waiting to see the bushes go from the bright red of young fruit to the nearly black that would signal ripe fruit. Even when passing at speed down the highway, they were easy to spot.

So, I wasn't too surprised to see fruit in a couple of the stalls at the market. It reminded me to look in Altoona next time to see if there were any there. But one stall caught my eye. Sitting on the table were two large glass jugs of black liquid. I walked over and picked one up, "Is this what I think it is?" I asked.

The man behind the table was thin and bearded. He wore overalls with no shirt and only one strap buckled. "Blackberry wine," he nodded.

I held the jug up to the light and asked, "How'd you get wine already?"

He pointed at the jug and said, "That's from last year. I been savin' it. Now that I can get more berries, I figured I'd trade it."

"What'cha trading for it?" I asked. It was the standard question and was met with the most common reply, "What'cha got?"

I reached into the pocket on my vest where I kept a few silver dollars and pulled a couple out and held them up. He eyed them, then shook his head. "Naw. Them ain't gonna do me any good."

"What are you looking for, then?"

"Something to eat!"

I nodded and walked back over to the buggy. We kept a case of MREs in the back for those times we may be caught away from home unexpectedly. They were starting to become scarce and I assumed that with Tampa now out of the picture, the chance of us receiving any more was slim. But I also figured that a wedding party would be better with a little blackberry wine too!

I took four meals out and carried them back over to the table and laid them out. The old man looked at each one, reading the menu printed on the front.

"Chili Mac," he said as he rubbed his chin. "I ain't had nothing like that in a long time."

"It's one of the better ones too."

Still scratching at the scruff on his face, he started to nod his head and reached out for the meals, "Alright. You got a deal."

I put my hand on top of his, pressing it to the table. He looked up and I smiled and said, "First. I gotta sample it. Could be anything in that jug."

He smiled a toothy grin, "Sheriff, you ain't gonna find no better wine, I promise you that. Besides, what fool would try and cheat the damn Sheriff?"

I unscrewed the cap and said, "A damn fool." And with a smile, I took a quick sip. It was an explosion of flavor unlike anything I'd tasted in a long time. I slowly capped the jug as I savored the elixir.

"We got a deal?"

"Oh, we got a deal. That is damn fine wine. As a matter of fact, I want the other one too. I'll be right back." I went to the buggy and got four more meals and carried them back to the table. The old man collected them up and turned to leave.

"Where you going?" I asked.

"I'm done for the day. I'm going home to eat!"

Aric walked up and leaned over my shoulder, asking, "What's that?"

I looked at the two jugs and replied, "Oh. Just a little something for a party."

He reached out for one of the jugs and I slapped his hand, "You will have to wait."

He looked at me, then at the jugs. "But what is it?"

I smiled. "You'll see at the party." Picking the jugs up, I headed back towards the buggy. "But what is it?" He called out as I walked away. I just laughed and shook my head.

The market was uneventful aside from my dealing in liquor, and we left and headed for Eustis. I was sitting in the passenger seat as Jess pulled out onto 19. Aric leaned forward and asked, "You want to put those back here?" Inquiring about the jugs sitting in my lap.

"Nope. I'm good." He lingered for a minute. I could feel him wanting to ask. "You'll see soon enough!" I shouted, and he slumped back into his seat. It was killing him, and I was loving it.

Jess was headed to Eustis when I called for her to pull over at a most unexpected sight. A bucket truck was sitting on the side of the road with its bucket up in the air and a man in it. As we got closer, I could see it was Scott, one of the engineers. We rolled to a stop beside the truck and I got out to a smiling Baker.

"Like my new truck?" She asked.

I was slack-jawed and nodding. "Where did you find it?"

"Cecil actually found it. I think it belonged to the city of Eustis. It took the mechanics over at the armory about an hour to get it running."

"No shit? That's going to make the job of getting power back up so much easier."

She looked up at Scott working in the bucket and nodded. "You like this better than climbing those poles?" She shouted.

He looked down. "Hell yes! We've already done more work today than we did in three days prior."

I looked at the lines they were working on. "What are you doing? Cutting the side lines?"

Baker nodded. "Yeah. We're just trying to get a solid line into town. We can always come back and add sidelines in later."

"Good call. This is awesome. Is there anything going on in town? I don't really want to go in there if I don't have to."

She shook her head. "No. Shane is doing a pretty good job.

Between him and Mitch, they keep everything under control. That, and it's so damn hot, no one is doing anything. During the day, the town is virtually deserted."

"Good. That's how I like it. I guess we'll drive by the farm for a minute before heading back home."

"They're pretty busy over there right now," Baker said. "Crops are coming in and they're trying to harvest it as fast as they can."

Terry was standing at the rear of the bucket truck, acting as Scott's ground man. "They need to hurry or the people in town will get it before they can."

"What the hell are they stealing it for?" Aric asked. "It's for them!"

"It's the whole bird-in-the-hand argument."

I shook my head. "Everyone is just out for themselves. I imagine it's even worse now since they all saw that mushroom cloud. I'm sure panic is probably pretty high."

Terry snorted. "Some people have gone bat-shit crazy."

"You guys need anything from me?" I asked.

"No," Baker replied.

I waved Jess on and we headed towards the farm. Since I wasn't driving, it gave me time to really take in the scenery. I'd driven this road many times since the Day, but it was like I was seeing it for the first time. As though I'd been away for a long time and just now returned.

Grass was now growing quite far out into the road. The roadsides were a tangled mass of vegetation. Some of it so tall it was falling over on itself. You couldn't see far off either side of the road because of the tall weeds and even small trees that were now crowding the roadside.

I tapped Jess on the shoulder and pointed to a church that had been under construction before things changed. Jess pulled onto what was once the dirt driveway, but now was nearly indistinguishable from the rest of the field surrounding the construction site. All manner of building supplies was still stacked as though it were waiting for the crews to return to work. But it didn't look new now.

Time had taken its toll on the materials. Rust and dust covered every surface. Vines creeped their way up from the ground and were taking over pallets that were now unrecognizable. But I could see what I was looking for and pointed it out to Jess, and she weaved in and around the piles and stopped.

"That's a lot of copper," Aric said, looking at the long stack of copper roofing intended for the church.

Climbing out, I said, "Sure is. And it'll make a great still."

Fred and Aric got out and walked over to the stack. "What are you making a still for?" Fred asked.

"We can use it for a number of things. But right now, I'm going to use it to make vinegar."

"That's why you got those grapes from Gena," Aric said.

I nodded. "And the honey from Mario. I'm going to give it a shot."

"Are we going to take this now?" Aric asked looking at the war wagon. He was clearly wondering how in the hell we would load a twenty-foot-long three-foot-wide sheet.

"No. I'll come back with some tin snips and cut it up so we can get it out of here."

"I want to go inside and look around," Jess said.

"Go ahead. I'm going to hang out here," I replied.

Fred chased after her, saying, "I'll come with you!"

The girls ran off and Aric and I climbed up on top of the stack of copper. While he sat dangling his feet, I stood up and looked around. It was a bit of a vantage point over the tall weeds and I could see all the across the field behind the church. To the west ran the train tracks that used to serve the orange juice plant. I was shocked to see the field full of corn.

"Holy shit. Who planted that?" I asked as I looked across it.

Aric stood up. "Wow. That's a shitload of corn. It's funny how early on no one wanted to work in the fields. Now look at it." He sat back down.

I sat down beside him. "From the sounds of it, there's plenty of people wanting to get into the field now."

"Yeah, so they can grab as much as they can carry and take it home." Aric shook his head in irritation. "Why can't they just wait? The food is for them. All they have to do is wait for it to be harvested and they'll all get some."

"Hunger is a powerful motivator. Especially if you have kids," I leaned in and bumped him, "as you're about to find out."

He nodded. "I'm worried about that. What are we going to feed the baby?"

"I think Fred has the necessary equipment for the first year," I replied with a smile.

"I know that. I mean later. When he's ready to eat real food. What are we going to feed him?"

With mock surprise, I asked, "So it's a son, then? And you know this how?"

He looked at me, "Of course it's a boy!"

Laughing, I said, "Well, we can always use another strong back. Don't worry about the food. Baby food in little glass jars is a relatively new thing. Not to mention, most of the children the world over have never seen it."

"I guess you're right," he replied as we heard the girls making their way back to us. "I just want the best for him."

I patted his leg, "Of course you do, dad. And you're not alone. You'll have plenty of help."

The farm was a flurry of activity. Cecil looked like a mad

conductor leading the strangest orchestra ever seen. A number of tractors had been pressed into service. Both conventional large tractors and even smaller yard versions. Wagons and carts of all sorts and sizes were being pulled behind them as the vast amounts of vegetables were being picked.

We parked by the camp for the security personnel and walked out into the field. I found Cecil standing at what had become a main road, directing tractors and even people who were pulling hand carts.

"Looks like you got your hands full, ole buddy," I said by way of greeting.

He turned and smiled the toothy smile of an old man. "It's getting a little sporty!" He reached out and shook my hand. "Good to see you up and about. It's good for the people to see you up too."

"I appreciate it. But I don't think they much care either way."

"Not so," he replied and nodded with his head towards the field where a couple of people stood looking in our direction. "There was a lot of talk here about what happened to you and whether you'd make it or not."

I laughed. "What were the odds?"

Shaking his head, he replied, "Six to one in the beginning."

"And which side did you take?"

With a grin, he replied, "I took the long. I knew you'd be back."

I gripped his shoulder and gave it a squeeze. "I'm glad I didn't let you down." Looking out at the hustle and bustle going on, I asked, "I see a lot more security folks. I heard there was a little pilfering going on."

He nodded. "There was, but we got a handle on it. It's just hungry folks. Shane took the ones we caught and turned them over to Mitch. He did the same thing you've done in the past.

He made them stand in the market with a sign around their necks that read, *I stole food from you.* It had the desired effect."

"It's difficult to deal with hungry people stealing food. Being harsh would just cause problems. Hey, what's with that field of corn over off nineteen?"

He smiled a sly smile. "You found that, huh?" I nodded. "I planted that myself. I found an old planter and hooked it to my tractor. I didn't tell anyone about it. But there is a squad over there watching it."

"What kind of corn it is?"

"I had two fifty-pound sacks of feed corn. It ain't fit to eat like regular corn, but we went over to Renniger's and managed to come up with a couple of grist wheels. My plan is to grind it all into meal."

"Good idea. But I'd like some whole corn. I have an idea."

Cecil cut me a conspiratorial grin, "You going into the shine business?"

I nodded. "Purely medicinal of course."

"Of course," he replied with a smile. Then, changing the subject, he asked, "You heard anything more on what happened over Tampa way?"

"No. Nothing yet. You?"

Cecil shook his head. "Sheffield isn't saying anything. Actually, haven't seen much of him. I think it rattled him."

"Hell, it rattled all of us. But there isn't shit we can do about it. I wasn't going to go to town, but maybe I should take a ride down there."

"It'd be a good idea, I think."

I thought about it for a minute. "Looking at him, I asked, "So, you digging a bunker yet?"

Cecil laughed. "No. But there's plenty of it going on. A lot of folks are scared shitless."

"Plenty of that going around at the moment." I pointed at the field. "Good luck riding herd on this chaos."

With a big smile, Cecil replied, "This is the fun part!"

I waved and walked back to the war wagon. As I approached, I could see Aric set a basket in the back. "What's this?" I asked, looking in.

"They told us to take this. Wanted us to take more but I said no." He shrugged, "You know, with Thad's garden and all, I didn't think we needed it."

"Good call," I said as I climbed in. Looking at Jess, I said, "Let's go to town."

I laughed to myself when we passed through the barricade at the edge of town. Sheffield's paranoia shown through here. More cars were added to the defenses as well as two of the captured MRAPs. There were also several men manning the position. With one notable change. All of them were wearing gas mask carriers strapped to their legs.

"This looks different," Jess commented as we pulled through.

"Yeah. I think that blast rattled ole Sheffield."

As we headed towards the armory, she glanced sideways at me. "What do you think is going to happen?"

I shrugged. "Doesn't really matter. There isn't much we can do about whatever may happen. We're just along for the ride. We'll just deal with it as it happens."

She laughed. "So, like usual then."

"Like normal."

At the armory, I found Sheffield in his office. He and Livingston were standing in front of a large wall map.

"Well, how goes the war?" I asked as I walked in.

"That's what we're trying to figure out," Livingston replied.

"You guys really think those things are going to help?" I asked, pointing at the gas mask strapped to his thigh.

Sheffield looked down at the one he wore. "They can't hurt. If we think there's fallout, we can at least put them on."

"And then what? You won't be able to eat anything. Drink anything. You don't have a fallout shelter."

"What's happened to you?" Sheffield asked. "This doesn't sound like the Morgan I know. The guy that works his way through everything. No problem too big."

"I'm just saying, it's a waste of effort. Besides, I don't think we'll be seeing any here. I hope, anyway. Do you guys even have measuring equipment?" Livingston looked at Sheffield and he shook his head. "Then how do you propose to know when to wrap that thing around your head? The frickin government did away with Civil Defense and screwed us all. If that were still around, then we'd have the equipment to sample the air. But we don't and there isn't shit we can do about it now."

Livingston glanced down at the bag strapped to his leg. "I guess it is a little silly."

"All I'm getting at," I replied, "is we have plenty to worry about that we *can* do something about." The two men looked at one another then at me. "I heard there are pickets out on 441. Have they seen anything yet?"

"Fortunately, no," Sheffield replied.

"Good. That's good."

"We've made contact with command again. It's been moved to Eglin," Sheffield said. "They said it was only one missile and was in response to the sinking of the majority of a Chinese fleet off the coast of California."

"If that's the case, why Tampa?"

"MacDill," Livingston replied. I gave him a *no-shit look.*

"CENTCOM and SOCOM were there," Sheffield replied.

"*Were,* is right."

He shook his head. "*Were,* as in they were dispersed. Yes,

losing the base was bad. But not nearly to the level it could have been. There wasn't much left there by the time they nuked it."

"So, it was the civilians that paid the price then." I shook my head. "That's the way these things usually work out. You survive all the shit going on and a damn rocket falls out of the sky and incinerates you in a fraction of second."

"If you're lucky," Livingston replied. "From what we hear, there are still a lot of wounded. The Red Cross is actually just outside the exclusion zone trying to help."

That surprised me. "No shit? The government is actually doing something now?"

"Not the government," Livingston said as he looked at Sheffield, who nodded and said, "Go ahead and tell him."

"Tell me what?" I asked.

Livingston took a deep breath and started. "This sounds worse than it is. There's been a military coup. The President has been useless from the beginning. They've done nothing to help people."

"Not to mention inviting foreign invaders into the country," Sheffield added.

Livingston nodded, "That too. So, the military decided it was time for them to intervene. We are now officially under the control of the military. They've quickly organized some NGOs, you know, non-governmental organizations to help."

"I know what NGOs are. Personally, I don't see it as a bad thing. Someone needs to take control of this shit sandwich. And who better than those used to working in chaos such as this. How long ago did it happen?"

"A couple weeks ago," Sheffield answered. "It's not like it was a big deal. There wasn't any shooting or anything. We've got troops stationed outside the bunker that useless piece of shit is hiding in."

Livingston smiled. "Not for much longer though." Sheffield gave him a look and he said, "What? How's telling him going to change anything?"

"What are you talking about?" I asked.

"The President doesn't know it, but we're in talks with his protection detail to bring him out," Sheffield said.

"Doesn't really matter," I shrugged. "I don't care what happens to him. Won't change anything for us. But, why haven't you guys said something?"

"It's been classified," Livingston replied.

I laughed out loud and turned in a circle holding my arms out, "Who the hell are we going to tell around here?"

"We're still the Army. It's just the way it works," Sheffield said.

I laughed again. "Whatever works for you guys." Curious, I asked, "Does the old man know?" Sheffield shook his head. That made me laugh again. "Oh, he's going to be pissed!"

"It was *need to know*."

"And you don't think we needed to know? You don't think he's got contacts as well? You've seen that stack of radio equipment he's got."

"It doesn't matter now who knows. It's a done deal."

I nodded and dropped into a chair. "Ok, so what's the plan?"

"We're still working on it. There's a bunch of Chinese troops running around on the gulf coast and we've got a rather significant contingent of Russians and Cubans moving up from the south," Sheffield said.

"Have you seen others since the incident over near Apopka?"

"We've heard some radio traffic from south of Orlando about seeing some armor running around. But we don't know what they saw."

"For now," Livingston added, "we're just keeping a careful eye out for them."

"Do you guys have the weapons to deal with armor?"

"Not much," Sheffield answered.

"That's concerning. What are the odds of getting some?"

"We're trying," said Livingston.

I had a feeling what their odds were. I wanted to talk to the old man. "Alright guys. I'm going to leave you boys to it."

"Alright," Livingston replied. "Glad to see you back on your feet."

I paused at the door and nodded, replying, "Thanks," before heading out.

I rounded everyone up and got them back to the war wagon. "I'm driving," I told Jess as I climbed into the driver's seat. An exaggerated pout formed on her face as she got in the passenger seat.

"Any news?" Aric asked.

As I wheeled out of the armory, I replied, "There's been a coup. The military is in charge now."

CHAPTER 2

THE OLD MAN WAS STEWING. He was sitting in a rocking chair on Danny's front porch, rocking slowly and staring at an indeterminate point in the yard. I was watching him closely, waiting for his response. It was kind of funny that I actually saw it first.

When Linus Mitchell gets mad, really mad, if you're paying attention, you'll see it. A crimson line would slowly rise out of his collar and creep up and envelope his ears. Then those two furry caterpillars would start inching towards one another. Usually, when they met, the valve would pop. He glanced into the coffee cup sitting on the armrest of the chair; it was empty. *Pop.*

He jumped to his feet shouting. "Those rotten, gutless, spineless, panty-waisted, snot-nosed, fucking fucktards! Who the hell do they think they are to keep this kind of information from me? Need to know! Security? Bullshit!" He bellowed. "I got my top-secret clearance when those two twats were still shitting yellow and sucking on their momma's tit! I'm going to wring their fucking necks like the chicken shits they are!"

Inwardly, I was smiling. "What's it matter?" I asked.

He paused and looked at me as though I'd just proclaimed myself king of Egypt. "What the hell do you mean, *what's it matter?*" He practically spat the last part.

"Just that. What difference does it make to us here, now? If there was a coup, it has no effect on us here. We still have to find food. We still have to get the power plant up and running. We still have to sniff around for Russians or Cubans. Doesn't change anything for us."

He stood there for a minute. Obviously, he heard what I said; he was looking right at me. But he stared at me like a man hearing one speak in a foreign language.

"The point is those two cocksuckers didn't tell us! I don't give a shit if there was a coup. It's about damn time! Needed to happen a long time ago if you ask me."

"So, you're pissed you weren't told? Are you fucking serious? Don't you have your own back channel communications? You've got all that radio gear over at your place. Go find someone to talk to!"

It was like I slapped him in the side of the head. The old man stood there for a minute blinking. Then he spun on his heels and stomped off into Danny's house. Ted was sitting on the porch and heard the entire exchange. "He's pissed," he said.

"No, he's butt-hurt, and shouldn't be."

"He's probably going to stomp Sheffield's ass when he sees him."

I shrugged. "Those two have been at one another since day one."

The door flew open and the old man stomped out, coffee cup in hand and thermos tucked under his elbow. Ian was sitting on the barrel saddle and offered some conciliatory words, "Fuck 'em, Top. We don't need those assholes anyway."

Sarge stopped and looked back. "Look here, you self-propelled sandbag. When I want your opinion, I'll damn well give it to you!"

Ian laughed. "Holy shit, ain't heard that one in a long time.

But coming from a PX Ranger trench monkey, I'll take it as a compliment."

"PX Ranger my ass!" Sarge boomed. "I earned this tab!" He gave Ian the finger before turning and walking off.

"That should keep him occupied for the rest of the day," I said, getting a laugh out of Ian. "Where are the rest of the guys?"

Ian nodded towards the road. "They're up at the bunker or off in the woods jerking off I guess."

I shook my head and laughed. I could hear the laughs of children coming from the backyard and stood up. "I'm going to see what sort of trouble those youngins are getting into back there."

Walking around the porch, the laughing grew louder. Thad and Danny were back there with the kids. One of those old harp-style lawn sprinklers was going, slowly sweeping its arc of water into the air. Thad had little Edie on his shoulders. Danny had Jace on his, and they were running and jumping through the streams. Little Bit was running between them as they all laughed and squealed. I smiled and shook my head as I kicked off my shoes and pulled my shirt off.

"You better hurry up and get out there. That little girl needs her daddy," I heard Kay say.

I looked over to see her relaxing on a chase lounge. She was holding a glass glistening with sweat in the heat of the day. "That's just what I was thinking," I replied.

Going out the screen door, I ran into the maelstrom of water and bodies and grabbed Little Bit up and swung her up onto my shoulders. She squealed with delight while I winced at the pain of my complaining ribs. But I ignored it and joined in on the fun. We formed a pinwheel as we ran after one another, jumping through the water and trying to catch the one in front of us and escape the one behind.

"We're going to get you, Morgan!" Thad called from behind me.

"Get the Sheriff!" Jace called out.

"Run, daddy, run!" Little Bit shouted.

It went on like that for a long time. Far longer than I personally wanted, as I was sore. When Danny turned and ran into us, Edie and Little Bit grappled for a moment as they giggled. There was a small play pool set up and I headed for it, where I dumped Little Bit with a splash. It wasn't long before the other two kids were in it as well.

I walked over to a shady spot where several folding camp chairs were set up. Thad and Danny soon joined me. We sat in the shade and relaxed, still wet from the fun. It was cool as the water dried from our bodies. We laughed as Little Bit pulled the sprinkler over to spray on the pool.

"Looks like they're having fun," I said.

"Oh, to be a child again," Thad replied.

"Anything going on in town?" Danny asked.

I told them about the engineers working on the power lines and about my visit to the farm and the frenzied harvest going on there.

"It's about time," Thad said. "We need that food."

"I brought some home. They made me take it."

"Good; we should get some too." Danny added.

"There's more. Looks like there's been a coup. The military took over and is trying to drag the President from whatever hole he's hiding in."

Neither of them thought much of it. Like me, they said it didn't really matter who claimed to be in charge. We agreed it was up to us to take care of things. No one was coming to help.

"But it sure pissed the old man off," I said.

Thad looked surprised. "I wouldn't have thought he cared."

I laughed. "He's pissed he wasn't told. I guess Sheffield knew about it but didn't tell him. That's what he's pissed about."

Thad smiled broadly. "I bet that did stick in his craw. What's he doing?"

Shrugging, I replied, "He stomped off towards the house with a thermos of coffee under his arm. I'm guessing he's burning up the radios trying to talk to someone."

"Good," Thad said, "He needs a way to vent all that hate he's got in him."

"Indeed," I replied. Then I looked at Danny and asked, "Did you find that crock?"

Nodding in the direction of the shed, he said, "Yeah, it's sitting over there. You find what you needed to make it?"

"Well. I think I have. But we'll see." I stood up and added, "I'm about to go find out. Hopefully, in a week or two we'll have some vinegar."

"That'd be good. We'll have plenty to pickle here soon," Thad said.

I looked at the garden. It was lush and green. "How's the tomato crop looking?"

Smiling once again, Thad replied, "Oh we're going to have a bumper crop. It ain't been easy. I've had to check the plants twice a day and pick the horn worms off them. But we're going to have a bunch."

"Good. Miss Kay will be able to can a bunch and we can store fresh ones in ash."

"I can't believe that works," Danny replied.

I shrugged. "I know. But it does."

Danny looked at me and changed the subject. "You know. You're full of ideas. You know of any way we can cool the house? Even a little? We keep the windows open and all, but it's just so damn hot."

I thought about it for a minute before replying. "Well, there is something I've been wanting to try. We'll need a bunch of two-liter bottles and some plywood or something. No, I have a better idea. We just need the bottles. I'll get the girls to find as many as they can and bring them here. Then we'll build it."

Laughing, Thad asked, "How you gonna cool a house with two-liter bottles?"

I gave him a big smile. "I'll show you later. Well, looks like I got work to do." Standing up, I added, "I'll see you boys later."

I left them to watch the kids play and made my way to the shed where I found Dalton sitting on the steps with the crock in his lap examining it.

"Don't get any ideas. That thing is mine and I've got plans for it," I said.

He looked up. "I've always liked these. Never had a use for them really, just always appreciated the form." He looked at it again, turning it over. "What's your plan for it?"

"I'm going to make vinegar with it."

"No shit? You're still going to ruin that wine?" He stood up holding the crock. "I'll help. What do we need to do?"

"Wait here. I'll get the other stuff and we'll get started."

I went to the war wagon and got the grape skins and honey, then we walked over to the house. Stepping over the lazy-ass dogs, we went inside. The girls were lying around the living room, reading or otherwise wasting time. "Hey, you two. I've got a job for you."

Lee Ann rolled over to look at me. "Awe, come on, Dad, it's really hot out."

"Off your butts. I need you two to go check every recycling bin in the neighborhood and bring back every two-liter bottle you find."

Taylor was obviously confused. "What for?"

I pointed at her. "Don't worry about that. Just go get them." I clapped my hands, "Let's go; on your feet!" With absolutely no enthusiasm, they got up. "And take a weapon with you too."

"No one's going to mess with us here," Taylor said.

"It's that kind of thinking that gets people killed." Dalton replied. "You should never be more than an arm's reach from your weapon."

I turned my hip out and pointed to my pistol, adding, "I was just playing in the sprinkler with the kids and I had mine on. Take yours."

Mel came out of the kitchen. "Hi, Dalton." Then she looked at me. I know she hates unexpected visitors, even now. "What are you doing?"

I held up the bucket of grape skins and the jug of honey. "We're going to make vinegar."

She looked back at the kitchen. "Don't make a mess in my kitchen."

"I'll make sure we clean up, Mel," Dalton said.

Reluctantly, she replied, "Alright. I guess I'll go over and see Bobbie."

Mel left and we carried our ingredients into the kitchen. Dalton suddenly stopped in his tracks and exclaimed, "Holy mother of God, man! What in the blue hell is that?"

He was pointing above the sink. I looked over and smiled. "That's my Biltong."

Setting the crock down on the island, he walked over to the sink and inspected the meat hanging there. "What is it? Jerky?"

"Kind of. But better, I think." I reached up and took a piece down. I bent it to test the moisture content. The meat flexed but didn't crack. Taking out my pocket knife, I cut it in half. The outside was dry, but the inside was the consistency of taffy.

I popped a piece in my mouth and chewed. "Not bad," I said, offering the other half to Dalton.

He took it and sniffed it, then took a bite. With a very serious look, he chewed the dry meat for a long time. Once he swallowed it, he looked at me and said, "That's the best damn jerky I've ever had! How the hell do you make it?"

Taking another bite, I replied, "It's pretty easy. I soak the meat in vinegar overnight. Then I salt it with coarse salt. Add a little coriander and hang it up to dry. Wait a couple weeks and you've got jerky."

He eyed the piece of meat in his hand. "This stuff has been hanging here for a couple of weeks?"

"Not quite," I replied. "The longer you leave it, the drier it gets. I like it like this."

He pointed at me with the piece of meat. "If this gives me the squirts, I'll have your head." Then he took another bite.

Laughing, I replied, "It's the oldest preservation method there is. You'll be fine. I promise."

He was still chewing when he replied, "Well, if you need vinegar to make this stuff, let's get to the chemistry!"

I washed the crock out and dumped the grape skins in. Dalton leaned over the crock and sniffed. "Smells like it's already starting to ferment."

"Good," I said as I turned to the cabinet and took out a precious jar of Braggs Apple Cider Vinegar. It was the only one around, that I knew of anyway. Opening the bottle, I dumped about half of it in.

"What's that for, mother?" Dalton asked.

Nodding, I replied, "Yeah, we don't have a mother, but this will add the necessary bacteria to get it started. We really need juice, but don't have any, so we're going with this. I'll just add water and mash it around a bit to make a juice of sorts."

"Then what?"

"Well, we cover it with a cloth and wait. After I mix this up, if it isn't sweet enough, I'll add the honey. I was thinking about distilling it as well. Just depends on how it comes out. This won't be like your normal white vinegar. That shit's actually made from natural gas in some cases."

"Natural gas?"

I nodded. "The beauty of having the FDA in bed with the food industry."

I took a large wooden spoon and stirred and mashed the skins. We took turns on it, working it for a long time. We mashed and stirred for what seemed like forever, stopping from time to time to taste it.

"I don't think it's going to get any sweeter," Dalton said after sampling it.

"Me neither."

"You think it's sweet enough?"

"It's not real sweet. Let's add the honey." I poured about a quart of honey into the crock and thoroughly stirred it in. This dramatically increased the sugar levels. "I think this is better."

Dalton tried it. "That's not half bad. The vinegar adds an interesting note to it."

I laughed. "Didn't know you were a sommelier."

He shrugged. "I was young and needed the money."

Since the sliding glass door had been shot out and replaced with plywood, the dining room was very dark. I carried the crock over to the corner beside the now defunct door and set it down. Then, I covered the top with cheese cloth, securing it with a big rubber band I'd made by looping several together. Standing up, I looked down and said, "Now we wait."

"How long?"

I shrugged. "I don't know. I'll check it after a week and see what it's like."

"I want in on that. I want to see how this all works."

"Cool. We'll keep an eye on it then."

Dalton looked at his watch. "I have duty here in a bit. I'll catch you later."

He left and I wandered into the living room and fell onto the couch. It was nearly supper time and I wanted to enjoy the quiet for a while. The house was hot though, really hot. Even with all the windows open, it was probably ninety degrees inside. But you kind of get used to it. At least in the way that your mind accepts that this is the reality and there isn't much you can about it. But now that I was thinking about cooling houses, I sat for a while thinking about the project to do just that. While noodling on this idea, I came up with a better way to do it. It would require a trip to the Save-a-Lot.

I looked at my watch and got up to head to Danny's. I smiled, thinking about the response from everyone when Aric and Fred made their announcement. If it made me smile, I'm sure it was going to bring joy to everyone else. Thinking of this, I headed out the door. It felt cooler outside than it did in the house. Jamie and Perez were on the front porch when I walked up. Naturally, Perez was smoking. I just can't imagine how he still had any, but he did.

"How's tricks?" I asked.

"It's hotter'n the Devil's ball sack," Jamie replied.

"Muy caliente," Perez added.

I laughed. "That's weird. A Spanish echo." Perez took a drag off his cigarette and shrugged.

Looking around, I asked, "You seen Aric and Fred?"

Jamie shook her head. "No. Why?"

"Oh, no reason." I went inside. Mel, Bobbie, Miss Kay and

Mary were all in the kitchen. A warm scent filled the house. I don't know how they did it, but they always managed to cook something that smelled amazing.

"You didn't mess up my kitchen, did you?" Mel asked.

"Nope. It's clean." I just didn't mention the vinegar flies that were sure to arrive in a few days.

"Did you get your vinegar started?" Kay asked.

"Sure did. Shouldn't take too long. Vinegar likes heat."

She mopped her brow with the bottom of her apron. "Well, Lord knows we've got plenty of that!"

"What's for supper?" I asked.

"You just go out there on the porch. You'll find out soon enough," Kay replied.

I did as instructed and went out to the porch. The kids were all sitting at one table with towels wrapped around them, their hair still wet. I went over to Little Bit and ran my hand through her wet hair.

"Did you have fun out there?"

She looked up, smiling. "Yeah, we did! The little pool was really fun!"

"So was the sprinkre!" Little Edie tried to say.

I patted all of them on the head and took a seat at a table with Thad. He was working on a large pot of snap beans, stringing them. I reached into the pot and pulled out a handful and went to work. "This is quite the haul," I said.

"This ain't nothing," he replied.

"This is really good to see, these beans."

Thad smiled as he snapped a bean in several pieces. "The summer has its blessings as well as its tribulations."

"Well, this heat is damn sure a test."

"You come up with a way to cool the house off?"

Reaching for another handful, I replied, "I think I have."

"Well, anything'll help."

"I need to go up to Save-a-Lot for some materials."

Taking another handful, Thad replied, "I'll go with you."

"You seen the old man?" I asked.

He shook his head. "No. Not since this morning."

"I guess he's off stewing someplace."

Thad reached for another handful and replied, "I think he is."

We heard more voices and I leaned over to look into the back door. Mike, Ted and Sarge were coming into the house. He didn't look like he was angry and the guys were carrying on in their usual manner. Everything looked normal.

"He looks alright to me," I said.

"Time will tell," Thad said with a smile.

The guys came out and took a seat. Mike was smiling in his usual smartass manner and I asked what he was grinning about. "You'll find out soon enough."

"What's the old man doing? In there sniffing around Miss Kay?" I asked.

Mike rolled his eyes. "Enough already. I don't need the visual."

Sarge came out the door, "Alright, the grownups are here, knock off the bullshit. Follow me. We need to talk." He continued out the screen door and into the back yard. I looked at Mike and he shrugged.

"Ted, what's this about?" I asked.

He got up from the table and slung his rifle. "Come on. You'll hear it for yourself."

We all got up and went outside. Danny was out there puttering around the well house and Sarge called him over too.

"What's this about?" I asked.

Sarge rocked on his heels for a minute before speaking.

"Since those chicken-shit bastards in Eustis don't want to share communication with me, I went over their heads."

I shook my head. "You just can't get over it, can you?"

"Hell no, I can't! Who the hell do those weekend warrior want-a-be shits think they're fucking with?"

"Why don't you three just get together and hate-fuck already? Just get it over with," I replied. Naturally, this got Mike to howling. It even got to Thad a little.

He stifled a laugh. Shaking his head, he replied, "I swear, Morgan you is a mess!"

"Oh, my God!" Mike shouted. "Hate fuck! That's it! That's exactly what they need to do! Just rip each other's clothes off, oil up and hate fuck!"

"You done?" Sarge asked.

Mike held up a finger, "One more time. Hate fuck!"

"You know the problem with you?" Sarge asked. Mike smiled with anticipation. "You're still here. No one's killed your dumb ass yet."

"That's cause I'm the baddest man alive! No one can kill me!"

Sarge looked at him seriously and in a quiet voice, said, "No, that's not it. It's that your mother didn't have the fortitude to do the right thing and drown your stupid ass when you were a baby."

"Or eat him when he was a baby. When his bones were still soft," Ted added.

Mike held his hands up, "Haters gonna hate. Don't hate the player, hate the game."

"Would you just shut the fuck up for a minute so the grownups can talk?" Sarge spat.

"Whatever. Go ahead."

Shaking his head, Sarge said, "We're going to Eglin."

"The Air Force base?" Thad asked.

Sarge nodded.

"And just how the hell do you plan on doing that? It's got to be four hundred miles up there!" I asked.

Sarge looked at me like I was stupid. "We're going to drive. Unless you've got a plane up your ass." Mike started to make a comment, but the old man shot him a look and he let it pass.

"You know what kind of risk that is? How much shit can go wrong on a trip like that?"

Sarge shrugged, "We just have to be careful. We're going to take two trucks and plenty of fuel and even extra tires."

"How are you going to haul all that?" Danny asked.

"Sheffield has trailers up there. We'll just get two of them. And the fuel from that bladder tank. We're going to be bringing back a bunch of stuff as well, so we'll need the trailers."

"Like what?" I asked.

"Ammo, rockets, mortar rounds. That kind of stuff. The general isn't too happy with Sheffield's lack of desire to go out and engage the enemy. We have foreign troops in the country. We need them gone."

"What about a Geiger counter? Can they give us one of those?" I asked.

He nodded. "We're going to get some NBC stuff too. They're already sending the 20th CBRNE command towards Tampa to evaluate the situation. We're getting equipment to monitor the situation as well."

That made me feel a little better. "That's good. When do you plan on making this kamikaze trip?"

"Soon as we can get the equipment together. We'll be gone for a week or so."

"We who?" I asked.

He pointed at me, "You're part of we. I need you, and the

General wants to see you. You're the civilian head here, so you gotta go."

"Like hell! I'm not going on what will surely turn into the Bataan death march. You can kiss my ass. I've already done that once and I ain't doing it again."

Sarge took a deep breath. "Look, we both know you're going. I know you don't want to, but I know you will. We're also taking Dalton and Ian."

"Who the hell is going to guard this place?" I asked.

"Just calm down. I'll tell Sheffield we need a few people for a few days. His guys won't mind getting out of town for a while and it'll be less mouths for him to feed, so he won't give a shit."

"I couldn't care less what he thinks!" I shot back. "You're missing the fucking point here. I'm not leaving my family to go on some wild-ass goose chase across Florida."

"It's not a goose chase." Sarge said. "This is a very clearly defined mission."

I folded my arms over my chest and asked, "And just what is this mission?"

Sarge gestured with a hand, "I already told you what we're doing."

"Going to get a bunch of ammo? Rockets and shit?" I pointed at him and said, "I think you're just pissed at Sheffield and this is your way of rubbing his nose in it. You giving any of the crap we bring back to him?"

"Hell no!" Sarge shouted. "I've got my orders and this material is going to be used to fulfill that mission."

I nodded. "Yeah. Just pissing off Sheffield. That's what I thought."

"Sounds like he's onto you, boss," Mike said.

"Shut up, Mikey," Sarge barked.

"Look, Morgan. It's on the up and up," Ted said.

I looked at him and he nodded. "Under one condition."

"You name it," Sarge replied.

"I want to get some stuff while we're there. I want some things we don't have now. Things to make everyone's life around here better."

"Done."

"You don't even know what I want!"

Sarge held his hands up. "Maybe not. But knowing you, you're not going to be asking for anything crazy, and I'm sure Fawcett will do it for you."

"He damn sure better," I replied. "Oh, and there's one more thing."

"What?"

Jabbing my finger into his chest with every word, I said, "And-**you**-tell-Mel." I looked up onto the porch and saw her sitting with Mary and Bobbie. She was going to be pissed.

The old man saw me and looked back over his shoulder. The look on his face was priceless. "That's just not fair." He said, "She's going to hate me."

"She's going to hate both of us, so you won't be alone."

"She can't be first, but she can be next," Sarge replied with a sigh. "Come on, supper's ready."

Mike leaned in close as he walked past me. "It's a long-ass list. Like, taping the pages of a phonebook end to end. Like a Manhattan phonebook."

I laughed and slapped him on the back as we walked towards the house. "Maybe. But now he's going to be on Mel's bad side."

"Don't sweat it, Morg. This'll be a milk run," Ted said.

"Your optimism is refreshing, if misplaced," I replied. Ted laughed and shook his head.

The porch was now crowded. Everyone was there and in good spirits. We'd taken to running a large fan during meals. It helped to make it bearable between the airflow and the natural cooling the onset of evening brought. The fan was loud, but it couldn't be heard over this crowd. The kids all sat together at one table, laughing as they ate.

Miss Kay was at the head of the picnic table, ladling stew into bowls and handing them out. Mike took his bowl and went to the kids' table and sat with them, eliciting loud giggles when he took his seat. Sarge looked at him as he waited for a bowl and said, "That's where he belongs."

Miss Kay looked at him, shaking her head, saying, "Oh, be nice, Linus."

As he reached for his bowl, he added, "I'll nice him to death."

Kay pulled the bowl away, saying, "Keep talking like that and you'll go hungry."

He smiled at her and replied, "Yes ma'am."

She handed him his bowl, saying, "That's better."

I saw Fred, Jess and Aric all sitting together at one table. I stepped up to Kay and she handed me a bowl. Holding it up, I took a long sniff. "This sure smells good, Miss Kay. What is it?"

"Just a little stew. Thad fixed up a selection from the garden and I browned some beef. It's quite good."

"It always is. You ladies never cease to impress."

She gave me a swat and gushed, "Oh, Morgan, go sit down!"

I walked by Aric and bumped into his elbow as he was taking a bite, spilling it onto his shirt. He looked up at me and I said, "Sorry. *I thought you said something.*" He looked around the room then back at me. "You do it, or I will."

He looked at Fred, who had a look of excited anticipation on her face. Then looking back at me, he said, "Would you?

I leaned down and whispered in his ear. "If I do it, I'll start off saying you were too chicken shit to say it yourself."

"You wouldn't!" Fred said.

I stood up and smiled. "You willing to bet?"

Fred slapped him on the arm. Her eyes narrowed, and through clenched teeth, she said, "You better not let him say that!"

It made me smile. I looked up and said, "Hey, everyone…" Aric was immediately on his feet, with Fred helping push him out of his seat.

But he didn't hesitate. "I have something to say," he said. Then he looked down at Fred, holding his hand out. She took it and stood up with him, blushing. "We have something to say." He looked at her for a moment before continuing. "Fred is pregnant."

All the ladies on the back porch began to pour out their excitement. They all came over to her and hugged her. It was exactly as I pictured it. Mel asked how far along she was and Fred said she wasn't sure.

"I say six weeks," Jess said.

Kay put her hand on Fred's belly. "Oh, you sweet thing. A baby! This is amazing news!"

Even the guys hugged her. They shook Aric's hand. It totally interrupted dinner, but in a good way. Bobbie was giving her a hug when she noticed the ring on her finger and asked, "What is this?"

Fred held her hand up so everyone could see the ring. Saying, "Aric and I are married."

This seemed to cause a little confusion. "When did you get married? And how?" Mel asked.

Aric and Fred both looked at me. Aric asked, "You wanna take this one?"

All eyes were now on me, waiting for an explanation. I chuckled. "They're married because they say they are. We don't need a judge or someone to say so. They say they're married. So, they're married."

There was more excitement. More hugs and handshakes. Miss Kay started to cry. Sarge went to her and put his arm around her, concerned. But she shooed him away. "These are tears of joy, Linus. You men just don't understand these kinds of things. I'm just so happy." She got control of herself and added, "You two are married. But that doesn't mean we can't have a ceremony." She started to cry again. "I've been saving some flour for a special occasion. I didn't know why, just being a silly old woman. But now I know why. It was for your wedding cake."

Fred's eyes lit up. "You mean we could have an actual ceremony with a cake?"

"Of course, dear, of course."

Then Fred's expression changed a little. "What about a dress?"

"I still have mine," Mel said. "You're more than welcome to wear it."

"Mom!" Taylor nearly shouted. "We found wedding dresses in some of the houses!"

"Yeah," Lee Ann said. "We'll get them all, so you can take your pick."

As discussion about the wedding dress continued, Doc walked out onto the porch. He saw everyone bunched up and Miss Kay and now Fred crying. He stopped in the doorway, taking it all in, then cut his eyes at me. He walked over and asked, "What the hell's going on?"

"Fred and Aric are getting married."

He looked up and smiled. "That's awesome."

"And she's pregnant," I knew that would get the Doc in him going.

He looked back at me wide-eyed, "What? How the hell did that happen?"

I laughed out loud. "Really, Ronnie?"

He shook his head. "You know what I mean. It's a big risk."

I stood up and gripped his shoulder. "She'll be alright. She's got you. No pressure."

"Kiss my ass." A look only describable as nausea came over him. "God, I hate deliveries. The crying, the screaming," he shuddered.

"Not to mention all the racket the mother makes," I replied. Naturally, that got me a *fuck you* look. "Now go congratulate the bride and groom."

He pulled it together and walked into the chaos that was happiness overflowing from the porch. Thad hugged Fred, lifting her off the floor. She squealed and Kay admonished him to be gentle with the soon-to-be mother. Back on the ground, Fred smiled at him and said, "You're going to make a terrific big uncle." Hearing the words, tears welled up in his eyes.

He smiled and wiped them away. "I'll love her like my own."

"Him. Love **him** like your own," Aric corrected, getting a laugh from Thad and a playful swat from Fred.

"The baby will have all kinds of uncles!" Mike shouted.

"Yeah," Sarge replied, "Every kid needs a crazy uncle."

Mike didn't miss a beat. "Glad to see you volunteer for the job!" This got a roar of laughter from everyone, even the old man. He nodded, replying, "Touché."

Kay broke up the festivities. "Alright, everyone, sit down and eat before your supper gets cold! There's plenty of time to plan this out."

All the women gathered at one table. I think Aric was relieved for the chance, or excuse to escape. He joined the rest of us at our table, where he naturally received a fair amount of good-natured ribbing.

"Go ahead, Doc. Tell him what you told me about how much you enjoy delivering babies," I said.

He gave me the finger, but Aric was looking at him expectantly. Doc rolled his head, "Ok, it's not my favorite thing to do, admittedly."

"But you do it so well," Ted said.

Sarge pointed at him with his spoon. "If I remember right, you delivered a baby in Iraq in the middle of a firefight once."

"No shit?" Aric said, surprised.

"Yeah, he did. Like a boss!" Ted shouted.

"Don't let Ronnie fool you. He's much better at bringing life than he is at ending it," Mike chimed.

"Some things are more rewarding," Doc replied.

Mike gripped his shoulder, rocking him back and forth. "Well, buddy, in about eight months you're going to get a hell of a reward."

Doc slapped Mike's hand from his shoulder. "I'll make an exception for your ass."

"You ain't the only one," Sarge added, getting everyone to laughing.

"How long you known about this?" Thad asked me.

"I found out today. They were all nervous about what everyone would think."

"What do you mean?" Danny asked.

"You know, they're not married and worried that we," I circled my finger around the table, "would judge them for some reason."

"What a load of hog wash," Sarge said.

"They got nothing to worry about," Thad said. "It's

wonderful news. With all the loss of life we see, seeing one start is a nice change."

"With all this in mind," Danny said, "Can you guys get medical stuff for her when you go to Eglin?"

Doc nodded, "Yeah, I'll round up what I need."

"It don't take much," Sarge said. "I've seen them dropped in the dirt in Africa."

"Where they have one of the highest infant and maternal mortality rates," Doc replied.

"Yeah, but that ain't happening here," Thad said.

"No," Sarge replied. "Between Doc and all them henpecks over there, I think there's more than enough help."

Looking to change the subject, Aric asked, "What's up with Eglin?"

"We're going to make a run up there. I need to go see the general and pick up some supplies for us," Sarge said.

"It's your lie. You tell it," I replied.

"Who's going?" Aric asked.

"Not you," nearly everyone at the table said in unison. Causing all of us to laugh, except Aric of course.

"Sorry, son. You're about to get married and have a baby coming. You're staying inside the wire," Sarge told him. It was not what Aric wanted to hear.

"I can still do my job. This doesn't change anything."

"It changes everything, buddy. But you'll still be doing your job. Just not on this mission," Ted said.

"Give it a little time, man. Things will get back to normal," I said. Then I asked, "You don't have any kids do you?" He shook his head. "I didn't think so. Fred's going to need you around."

"Welcome to crazy town," Mike said as he stuffed a spoon into his mouth.

Aric looked at him, "Fred's not like that."

Sarge, Thad and I all laughed. "They're all like that when they're pregnant," I said.

"And in this heat?" Thad added. "Yeah. You gonna have your hands full."

"We'll see about that," Aric replied. Once again causing us to laugh.

"Let's take care of cleaning up the supper so the ladies can continue on with their planning over there," Danny said as he stood up.

I looked over my shoulder at the table of women and said, "Plotting. I think the word you're looking for is plotting." This again got a laugh.

Perez walked up to the table. He'd been on the far end of the porch. He tried to keep away from the kids when he smoked, and he was always smoking. He looked at Sarge and held out a cigarette, "When you go to Eglin, find me some of these."

"Are you *trying* to smoke yourself to death?" Doc asked.

He shrugged. "Every boy needs a hobby."

He held his hand out to Aric, "Congratulations, my friend."

Jamie left the table of chattering ladies and walked over. Perez looked at her and asked, "So you next? When you get a bunch of women together, these things seem to happen at the same time."

"Fuck you, Perez," she replied.

"Where is Ian, anyway?" Sarge asked.

"Fuck you too," she replied before storming off.

Watching her go, Mike said, "You sure she ain't pregnant already?" Getting another laugh out of us.

Thad and I collected the dishes from the porch. "Well, look at you guys being all domestic," Mel said.

"Maybe you should get Aric out here so he can start

learning how to be domestic too," Bobbie said, getting the ladies to giggling.

"He's inside washing dishes," That replied with a smile.

"He's learning already!" Jess shouted.

"Oh, leave him alone," Fred said, feigning sympathy.

"You gals keep on with whatever it is you're doing. We'll clean everything up," I said.

"I see you have him trained too," Kay said with a smile.

"I beg to differ!" I laughed. "Keep it up and we'll go find something else to do!"

"No, no. You just keep at it," Kay replied. Looking back to the conversation at hand on wedding planning, she added, "We have important things to do here."

Thad was smiling. "We'll take care of it, Miss Kay. Ladies, thank you for supper." He looked at Fred and added, "And congratulations again, Fred. I'm really happy for you."

She smiled back and I saw Thad make eye contact with Mary, who had been quiet all through dinner. But she was always quiet. Mary smiled when he looked at her and quickly looked away. As we carried the bowls into the kitchen, I glanced up at him and asked, "Is this going to be a double wedding?"

Thad was such an incredible guy. I loved him like a brother. His natural response to everything was to smile. And here again, he smiled. Big, warm and infectious. "Morgan, you a mess!" He replied laughing.

I shrugged. "Just asking." I said as I set a stack of bowls on the counter. "It wouldn't be a bad thing, ya know." When he looked at me, I added, "Or wrong."

His smile faded. I could see he was thinking about it. He glanced around at the other guys.

"What wouldn't?" Danny asked.

"A double wedding," I replied with a grin.

Danny was obviously surprised. "What?"

"Jus' sayin'," I replied.

"Of course, it wouldn't be bad. It' be awesome!" Aric added. "Did you ask her?"

Thad was embarrassed, something easily done. He shook his head. "No. No, I didn't ask her. I don't think it's right."

I shook my head and gripped his enormous shoulder. With a little laugh, I said, "What in the world would be wrong about it, old buddy?" He lowered his head and looked at the counter, fumbling with the bowls. I leaned down and looked him in the eye. "You deserve to be happy too, my friend. You wouldn't be dishonoring them. You know that, right?"

A tear ran down his cheek and he wiped it away. Looking up, he said, "I really care for Mary. But I feel so guilty."

"I've asked you this before, but I'll ask it again. If things had been different, would you want Anita to spend the rest of her life alone, feeling guilty? Or would you want her to find happiness?"

Wiping his eyes again, he said, "I'd want her happy. More than anything in the world. I'd want her to be happy."

I smiled and said, "Then honor her the same way."

He looked up and was met with a face smiling back at him in anticipation. He looked back down at the counter again. "It would make you both happy," Danny added.

"More than just the two of you," I replied with a nod.

He looked up again and smiled. "I know you're right. But I don't have a ring, an—" he paused and looked down again.

"And you're embarrassed," Aric said.

Thad shrugged. "Kinda."

"Sure, it's scary, brother," Danny said as he went to a small cabinet in the dining room and took out a small wood box. "When we left here for the river, I took this with me. It isn't a practical thing to keep in today's world, but it meant a lot to me." He carried it back over to the counter and set it down. Opening it, there was a piece of silk rolled up inside. He took it out and handed it to Thad. "But just like Miss Kay holding back some flour for reasons she didn't understand, I also kept this."

Thad unrolled the piece of silk to find a diamond ring inside. It was a silver setting with three stones on it. Thad held it up and looked at it. The stones were high quality and sparkled brightly in the light. "I can't take this," he said.

"It was my great grandmother's. But it's yours now," Danny said.

"No excuse now," I said.

Thad smiled and flushed. He looked at us, saying, "I'm scared."

I gripped him by the shoulders and turned him around, pushing him towards the door. "Best way to handle fear is head-on, brother!"

I could hear the guys in the kitchen scrambling to get out onto the porch. Sarge and the guys were still sitting at the table talking over their plans for the road trip. When I pronounced, "We have an announcement!" everyone stopped talking and looked up. The guys came out of the house, bumping into one another as all eyes were on me. Thad stood there looking at his hands, so I gave him a push.

"What is it?" Kay asked.

Thad looked up, hesitating, so I said, "Thad has something he wants to say."

He looked at me and I smiled, giving him a nod. He looked at Mary and I could see she knew something was up. Thad made his way around the table to where she sat, all eyes were on him. When he got to her, he took her hand and lifted her from her seat and pulled the chair out of the way.

"What's this?" She asked.

Kay gasped and covered her mouth as Thad knelt down in front Mary. Realizing what was going on, Mary started to cry. Down on one knee, Thad looked up at Mary. He unrolled the piece of silk and took out the ring. Holding it up, he said, "Mary. I thought I would never find happiness again. But I met Morgan," he looked back at me and smiled, I returned it and nodded. "And in doing so I found my way here. Then you found your way here." The ladies were starting to cry, and truth be told, I had to wipe my own eyes. "But I did indeed find happiness. That happiness was made brighter when you arrived and has only gotten brighter with every day." He held the ring up and asked, "I want it to keep getting brighter. Will you marry me?"

Mary dropped to her knees and wrapped her arms around him. Crying, she replied, "Yes! Yes, I will!" Thad took her hand and slid the ring on her finger.

A cheer erupted from everyone as they shot to their feet. I shouted, "It's a double wedding!"

Little Bit ran over and wrapped her arms around Thad and Mary. "You're getting married!" She shouted. "I'm so happy! Can I be the flower girl?"

Thad smiled and patted her head, "Yes you can, Miss Ashley." She smiled and hugged him tight, then hugged Mary as well. They were all smiles.

While everyone was celebrating, I snuck out and went to the house. I grabbed one of the jugs of blackberry wine and carried it back to the porch. "A day like this calls for a proper celebration! I picked this up and I can't think of a better time for it. Who wants some blackberry wine?"

There was a round of approving shouts and Bobbie went into the house and returned with glasses. I started pouring drinks and passing them out. I handed one to Mike and he started to take a drink from it. Sarge cuffed him in the back of the head, saying, "Wait for the toast, dipshit."

"I was just smelling it. Calm down, ya old prick."

After taking a glass of his own, he put his arm around Mike and said, "Sure you were." They both laughed and walked back to the table together. Sarge got up on a chair and announced, "Everyone get a glass and I'll make a toast!"

The porch was electric with happiness and excitement. It didn't take long to get everyone a snort of the wine. I handed a glass to Doc and Taylor stepped up. "You're not old enough," I said.

"Oh, come on dad. What's it matter? Just a sip so we can do the toast." Lee Ann was standing behind her with an expectant look on her face as well.

I shrugged. "What the hell." And I poured them about a finger each into a glass. Once everyone had theirs, I looked at Sarge and held my glass up.

Still on the chair, Sarge began. "Alright, everyone, quiet down!" He gave everyone a moment to quiet, and once everyone was looking at him, he started. "With everything going on, today marks a new dawn for all of us. I couldn't imagine anything better than these two beautiful couples committing their lives to one another." There were some coos from some of the ladies as Sarge continued. "And the fact that Fred is pregnant is the only way it could possibly have been any better. Aric, you're a good man and I'm glad to call you friend. Fred, you're a beautiful young lady and you're going to make a wonderful momma."

He looked at Thad. "Thad, you've been a friend for a long time and I am so thankful you're here with us now. It's an honor to have you in my life." Looking at Mary, he smiled and said, "Mary, you're a beautiful person inside and out. I'm so happy to know you and Thad are about to embark on a new chapter in your lives. I couldn't be happier." He held up his glass and said, "To the health and happiness of the new couples!"

"Health and happiness!" Everyone shouted back as they drank to the toast. Mary whispered in Thad's ear. He smiled and nodded and stepped over to whisper to Aric and Fred. Fred smiled and her eyes brightened. They both nodded their heads.

"Before you sit down," Thad called to Sarge, "we have a request." The old man looked up and Thad said, "We'd like for you to give both of the brides away at the ceremony."

The old man paused and looked around at the faces staring back at him. His expression was unlike any I'd ever seen. It was nearly expressionless. But he straightened his back and wiped his eyes, saying, "I'd count it as one of the highest honors of my life." He looked at Fred and Mary. "I've never had a daughter and never imagined I'd give a bride away." He paused and smiled. "Let alone two."

Everyone began to talk and clap at the same time. Sarge sat down at the table and Mike looked at him with a sly grin and said, "You old softy."

CHAPTER 3

THE REVELRY WENT ON LATE into the night. A guitar was produced from somewhere and Mike and Thad took turns at the strings. When Mike started his chords, everyone fell silent. It had been a long time since we'd heard music. Of course, the girls often played music from Jeff's iPad, but this was different. This was live music and, surprising to all of us, Mike was a skilled player. He started to thumb the strings and we were all surprised again when Thad started to sing, staring Mary in the eye.

"Beauty queen of only eighteen……." He continued to sing Maroon 5's "She Will Be Loved" to cheers and catcalls. The rest of us joined in on the chorus. It filled the place with an unimaginable feeling. Gone was our daily reality and thoughts of the recent attack we'd witnessed. The next several hours were filled with a forgotten sense of happiness as Mike and Thad passed the instrument back and forth and requests were shouted at them.

Smiles, laughter and even dancing took over as the sun began to sink. I was dancing with Little Bit and Lee Ann as Mike wore the strings out on a rendition of "The Devil Went Down to Georgia". He played the fiddle parts, both sides, like I wouldn't have imagined. Everyone was singing and stomping on the porch till the entire house was shaking.

When he finished it, he set the guitar down. Everyone was hot and thirsty. Miss Kay carried pitchers of ice water out and we all had a cold drink as we talked even more and laughed and poked fun at each other's dance moves. It was getting late and I was about to leave when Sarge stood up.

"Alright," he said as he reached out and gripped the neck of the guitar. "I don't want to hear any shit. One more song, I think," he said as he slipped the strap over his neck. He thumbed the strings as he adjusted the tuning knobs. "I'm going to do this for the brides," he said and looked up, "and the first one of you that says something smart will get this thing over their head." Silence fell over the porch.

He started into the chords, cleared his throat and began to sing. Everyone fell silent as we watched the old man sing with eyes closed and his head tilted slightly back. He did the best acoustic rendition of Paul McCartney's "My Love" I'd ever heard. But there was something more than the mere words he sang. Like something lost, but not forgotten. Or something longed for and never found. When the song was nearly done, he opened his eyes and looked at Miss Kay, singing that last line to her. She sat blushing as he did.

Oh I love oh wo, my love
Only my love does it good for me

Yet again, cheers, shouts, whistles and catcalls erupted as everyone jumped to their feet. The old man gently set the instrument down. He motioned for everyone to quiet down, shaking his head, but the applause kept coming. Miss Kay got up and walked over to him and wrapped him up in a hug. This renewed the clapping and whistles. You couldn't help but smile. Old Linus was very obviously uncomfortable with the attention and I could tell all he wanted at the moment was out. So, I went over and whispered in his ear that I needed a word. He nodded, told Kay he'd be back and followed me out through the front of the house as he was patted on the back and hugged repeatedly.

Outside, I sat in a rocker. Sarge came and fell into another. I sat rocking and smiling at him. "So, we going to make this a triple header? You going to make Miss Kay an honest woman?"

He looked as though he'd just tasted something bad. "You're as bad as that little asshole Mike, you know that?"

"Hey, hey, hey! I thought we were friends!"

"Stop acting like a dickhead and I'll stop calling you one."

I cocked my head to the side. "You feeling alright? You take your Geritol today?"

He pointed at me and hissed, "See? Right there. You're just like that little fucker. Keep your shit up and I'll stomp a mud hole in your ass and kick it dry." He shook his head as he sat stewing for a minute. "What'd you want anyway?"

"Nothing. I could tell you wanted out of there."

He nodded. "I appreciate that."

"On a serious note though, it really was a good song and I think it's fantastic the girls want you to give them away."

"Too many years spent in karaoke bars in Japan. They have the best karaoke over there."

I laughed. "I could just see you getting shit-faced and singing, *It's Raining Men.*"

He laughed. "I saw a big black Marine sing it once." He laughed again. "It was fucking awful. But no one was about to say anything to him. I think he did it just to start fights. Didn't get one that night."

I laughed at the thought. "I could just see Thad's big ass all drunk up and singing it." Sarge leaned forward, slapping his knees as he laughed and snorted at the mental image. After we laughed it out, I said, "On a more serious note. You really think we'll be gone a week?"

Sarge wiped tears from his eyes. "No. I like to under-promise and over-deliver. So, we tell everyone we'll be gone a week and when we're back in four days, they'll all be happy."

"You really think we'll be able to just drive up there with no issues?" I asked.

"Why the hell not? Things have calmed down a lot. We'll need to be on the lookout for commies. But I don't think there'll be any problems from the locals."

I thought about it for a minute. "It used to be a nine or so hour dive. It'll probably take twelve or better now. What about driving it at night?"

"We could. But it would take a lot longer. You just can't drive as fast. We'll start out driving during the day. If things get hairy, then we'll switch to driving at night with night vision. But honestly, Morgan, I don't think it'll happen." He smiled, "Should be a milk-run."

"How are you going to convince Sheffield to give you a couple of MRAPs?"

He gave me a conspiratorial smile. "*I'm* not going to. *You* are."

"Me?"

"Yes, good Sheriff. You're going to tell the honorable Captain you need some of his men and a couple of trucks to handle something up this way. He won't question you. He'd probably tell me no. Not that he doesn't have the bodies or equipment. With all the trucks we seized from the DHS camp, there's more than enough. But we only want one MRAP. And we're going to need one of his five-ton medium transports with a five-ton trailer. That way we can bring everything back with us."

"What are we getting?"

"More ammo. Fuel, food, and medical supplies. Some heavy weapons. We don't have anything to deal with armor like the last encounter. I want something that will handle that. Plus, new commo gear, batteries. That sort of thing."

"He's going to be pissed when he finds out what we did," I said, referring to Sheffield.

"Let him. I don't give a shit. Part of this is for him and his people anyway."

"Why don't you just tell him what you're doing?" I asked.

He leaned forward and sneered. "If he won't share his info with me, why the hell should I share anything with him?"

I leaned back and shook my head. "You know, if you two worked together, we would be more effective."

He waved dismissively. "There's nothing going on that needs coordination. When the time comes for that, I promise you we'll work together. I'll just tell him what to do, and he'll do it."

I leaned back, shaking my head. "Oh yeah, he'll do just that." Cocking my head to the side, I asked, "You think this trip will interfere with the weddings?"

He shook his head. "Naw. Them ladies need time to plan anyway. They won't be ready any time soon. They'll want to sit around and cluck about it for a while."

"You better not let them hear you talk like that. They'll have your head." I laughed. "So, when do we go see Sheffield? When do you want to leave?"

"Let's go see him in the morning. I want to leave soon."

"Alright," I said as I stood up. "I'll be right back."

"Where you going?"

"Just hang on," I said as I went through the door.

I made my way back out to the porch. Everyone was still sitting around talking. It was much quieter now, but there was still a lot of chatter going on. I went to Mel and whispered in her ear to come with me. She got up and followed me into the house. "What?" She asked.

"Hang on, Sarge wants to talk to you."

"Me?" She asked. "What's he want with me?"

Opening the door, I replied, "You'll see."

Sarge looked up when I came out. Then he saw Mel. I could see on his face he wanted to kill me, but he held his tongue in check. Though I was certain I'd hear about it later. Mel stepped out onto the porch and looked at him. He stared back, and she looked at me and asked, "Well?"

I looked at Sarge and said, "Go ahead."

She was getting irritated. "Someone better say something."

"Have a seat, Mel," Sarge said as he pointed to a rocker. "I know you're not going to like this, but—"

She cut him off, "But what?"

"We're going to have to take a road trip and I need Morgan to go with us. It's important." She looked at me with an ice-cold glare. "Look, he doesn't want to go. But I need him to. We won't be gone long."

"How long?" She asked.

"We should be back within a week."

"A week!" She shouted. "Where are you going?"

He reached out to pat her leg, but apparently, he got a look that stopped him. "We're going up to Eglin Air Force base."

"Where's that?" She asked.

"It's up near Pensacola," I replied.

"Why do you have to go?" She asked.

Sarge took a deep breath. "You remember what we saw at the park. We have to go meet with the general over the state. There are foreign troops here and we need to be prepared to deal with them when they come."

She looked at me. "There's soldiers coming here?"

"I don't know," I replied.

"It's not like they're on their way right now," Sarge said. But even I knew he had no way of knowing. "But if they do come here with tanks, we have no way of dealing with them. So, we need better weapons. We also need supplies for the clinic in town and some other things. We're going to pick up a load of supplies."

Mel looked at me, then back at Sarge. "Why does Morgan need to go? He's not a soldier."

"No, he's not. But he's a big part of things here and the general wants to see him. I promise this won't be a big deal. We'll be back before you know it."

"But if you guys are all going, who's going to look after things here?"

"We're going to have some of the Guardsmen from town come out here while we're away. You'll be safe," I replied.

She threw her hands up. "I know it doesn't matter what I say. I know you're going."

"It has to be done, Mel," Sarge said.

She shrugged. "Just be careful and come back home."

I gave her a hug and a kiss. "I will. Promise."

"I'll get him back home to you, Mel," Sarge said. I promise"

She looked at me. "You walked home from there once before. I just hope you don't have to again. But I know you'll come back. I'm going back to the fun. Because this just isn't."

"Could you ask Mike, Teddy and Doc to come out here?" Sarge asked. She nodded and went back inside. The old man cut his eyes at me, "That was some underhanded shit right there. You're an asshole."

I shrugged, "Learned from the best."

It didn't take the guys long to come out. Sarge got up

and said, "Come on. Let's walk down to the bunker and talk to Dalton."

We filed out and headed into the darkness. Walking down the road, we discussed the upcoming nuptials. Everyone agreed it was a happy thing. Mike even managed to not show his ass, which kept the conversation going in a positive direction.

"Y'all make more noise than a gay pride parade," Dalton said from the darkness at the side of the road.

"Personally, I wouldn't know what one sounds like," Sarge shot back. "Come on up to the bunker. We've got business to discuss."

He emerged from the black and we all walked up to the pile of logs and dirt. Ian and Jamie were sitting on top of it. Jamie was smoking a cigarette.

"You know those things are bad for you," Mike said as he climbed up and sat down beside her.

She flicked the butt at him and it bounced off his chest, the dim cherry cartwheeling in the air. "Alright, folks," Sarge said. "We've got a mission."

"What are we doing now?" Ian asked.

"We're going to make a run up to Eglin for some gear and face time with the general."

"I thought they were turned to ash in Tampa," Jamie said.

"No. They'd all pretty much unassed that place prior to the attack. He's back up north. We're going to get a couple of trucks from town and make a run up there."

"Who's going?" Jamie asked. You could hear in her voice that she expected to be told she wasn't making this run.

Sarge was quiet for a minute before replying. "All of us here."

"What about Perez?" She asked.

"No. He can stay here. I love the beaner. But he's about as worthless as a menstruating nun."

From somewhere in the blackness, Perez replied, "Fuck you too, old man." Then the cherry on his smoke flared as he took a drag.

"Who's going to provide security here?" Dalton asked. "You're taking most of the shooters. That's going to leave this place vulnerable."

"We're going to have some of the Guardsmen come out and stay while we're gone. I don't expect any trouble any time soon."

"That's when it usually happens," Dalton countered.

"You are correct. But we need to get up there and grab some stuff for the job ahead."

"And just what is that job?" Ted asked.

"Good ole infantry work," Sarge replied. "Locate the enemy. Close with him and destroy him. But we need some heavy weapons to deal with armor. I don't want a repeat of our last encounter."

"It's about time for a proper fight," Mike said.

"Careful what you wish for, Mikey. These aren't a bunch of Joe the lob cob can kicking Feds. We could very easily come up against Russian Spetsnaz or even Cuban SF."

"Ah," Dalton said. "Comando tropas especiales. I'd like to talk to both of them."

"You've got some kind of gay ass man crush on those commies, don't you?" Mike asked. "Especially those Russians."

"It's more of a respect. I've interacted with the Russians before. They're tough bastards."

"Maybe so," Sarge interjected, "but hopefully we only have to deal with the Cubans. Their people are alright, but they've lacked equipment and other materials to train with for a very long time, so it'll be like going up against the JV team. Spetsnaz on the other hand, will be like playing in the NFL."

"I don't care either way. I want some commie scalps," Mike replied.

"You ain't scalping shit," Sarge shot back. "We're going to town in the morning for the trucks. Everyone be ready first thing tomorrow. Once we're back with the trucks, we'll get everything ready to go and probably head out in the afternoon."

"You going to try and drive straight through?" Ian asked.

"I don't see no reason to stop unless we need to. Things have settled down a lot, so we shouldn't have much in the way of trouble."

"Everyone get some rest. It's a long ride. I don't want anyone falling asleep driving," Doc said.

"I'll be fine," Jamie replied. "I'm driving one of the trucks."

"That's fine with me," Sarge replied. "We'll sort out duties tomorrow."

"You going?" Dalton asked me.

"Looks that way."

"Alright then. You guys all go get some rest. Me and Morgan will stay here for now. Danny and Thad will be down later to relieve us." Sarge ordered.

Everyone wandered off without much more said. Once the old man and I were alone, I looked at him and said, "Thanks for volunteering me to hang out here all night."

"Dry up," he replied. "You'll be able to sleep in the truck. I need these people ready for the job."

"Didn't know you were going to have Ian and Jamie go."

He scratched his head. It was still warm out, but there was a breeze blowing that thankfully kept the mosquitoes away. "I wasn't going to originally. But with them, we can take the Hummer too. Just in case."

"Do these trucks have the range to get up there?" I asked.

"We'll take some extra fuel with us. In the morning, we'll

round up some fuel cans. There's plenty of them lying around. We'll fill them from Sheffield's bladder."

"He's going to get suspicious."

"Then you better sell it to him."

We hung out in the dark. Off in the west, lightning lit up the horizon from time to time, followed by the low rolling rumble of a heavy thunderstorm. It was nice to watch, though I dreaded the rain that was sure to follow.

Thad and Danny showed up a couple hours later. Thad was in good spirits and I felt kind of bad that he had to leave Mary on this night to stand watch.

"You should be at home with Mary," I said.

"She's still at Danny's house. We're going to pick out our own house soon, so that when we're married, we can live together."

I patted him on the back. "I'm really happy for you. Both of you, buddy."

He smiled in reply. "Thank you, Morgan.

"You guys leaving tomorrow?" Danny asked.

"We have to get the trucks in the morning. Once they're loaded, we'll head out," Sarge replied.

"You guys have fun and stay safe."

"I'm going to leave you guys to it," I said. "I'm tired and tomorrow is going to be a long day."

"Me too," Sarge said. "You fellers stay safe out here tonight."

They said goodbye and we left. I headed back towards the house in the dark. I had the NVG in a pocket on my vest, but chose to take in the darkness. I heard the dogs coming up the road, their tags jingling. When they got to me, they all stopped for a head rub. I knelt down and rubbed their ears and scratched their backs. Tails wagged and tongues lolled from their mouths. They licked my face and arms, and it made me smile. They were utterly useless. Unless you counted putting a smile on your face.

Once they were satisfied with their attention, they continued on their way. I wondered where they were going. They moved as though they had a plan, knew exactly where they were headed and what they were after.

Sitting in front of the porch were several large trash bags. I kicked one and the sound of empty plastic bottles inside replied. The girls had collected quite a number of them. I guessed when we returned from our trip to see the Wizard I'd get on that project. There was always something to do.

Inside, I went to the kitchen and cut a piece of Biltong and chewed it. Going into the bedroom, Mel was lying in bed reading a book. She looked up briefly when I came in, then returned to her book. I took off my gear and laid it beside the bed before stripping down.

"I'm going to take a shower," I said with a piece of meat dangling from my mouth. She didn't reply.

I took a quick shower. The piece of soap was small, but sufficient. Shampoo was a thing of the pastpast, but I washed my hair with the homemade soap as well. The water was cool, not cold, or maybe it was and I didn't care. Either way, I enjoyed the shower and lingered for a bit, letting the water cascade over my head. Getting out, I dried off and walked to the bed naked.

I adjusted the fan so it was blowing across us and slid between the sheets. We used only a top sheet as anything more was just too hot. I longed for fall and winter to arrive. I looked forward to sleeping in the cold, the colder the better as far as I was concerned.

I reached over and rubbed Mel's thigh. "Goodnight, babe." She closed her book and looked at me. "I know you're not happy," I said.

She patted my hand. "I'm not. But I also know that you

have to go do these things. You'll be riding in an armored truck with plenty of people. I'm sure you'll be fine."

"I can't tell you how happy it makes me to hear you say that. I will be alright; we all will. Is there anything you need? I'm going to be trying to get some things like flour and soap."

"We need feminine pads. No one has any and they're all using rags. It's really gross."

"Why didn't anyone say anything? We could have figured something out. How about you? What are you doing?"

"You remember we bought those Luna pads. The girls and I have been using those."

I remembered ordering those. They were reusable pads. I'd forgot about them until now. But I guess that was a really good idea. "I'm glad we did."

She snorted. "You are? You have no idea how happy I am. I couldn't imagine what we'd be doing. So, get some pads for everyone else."

"Have you thought about making any?"

"Any what?" She asked.

"You know, something like those Luna pads."

She obviously wasn't into the idea. "Out of what?"

"The outside of the ones you have are like felt and the inside is some kind of cotton batting. I'm sure we could find something."

"You just see if you can get us any real ones."

I lay back on my pillow. "That's not a long-term solution."

"Everything doesn't have to be a long-term solution."

She lay back and I rolled over, putting my arm over her. "Everything does need to be long-term. That's how we need to think. Love you, babe, goodnight."

She pulled my hand up and kissed it. "Goodnight."

I woke up early to the sound of rain. Getting up, I tried not to wake Mel. But she woke up anyway and asked if I wanted breakfast. I told her no. "Just stay in bed, babe; it's early."

She rolled over and pulled the sheet up over her head in reply. I quietly dressed and pulled the armor back on and slung my rifle. Before leaving, I went to the fridge and poured myself a mason jar of tea and ate another piece of Biltong before heading out. The dogs were back on the porch, asleep of course. The rain was heavy under a slate sky. It was early, but darker than it should be for the hour. Not a good omen for the start of the day.

Setting my tea on the handrail, I pulled my poncho over my head. Tea in hand, I left and headed for Danny's. The porch was empty but I could see light through the front window and went in. Sarge, Mike, Ted and Jamie were sitting in the kitchen having a cup of coffee. Seeing me, Miss Kay asked if I wanted a cup. I help up the mason jar and replied, "No thanks, Miss Kay. I already have mine."

"One of these days, you'll have to learn to drink coffee like a grownup," Sarge jabbed.

"Oh, I will. About November when it's fit weather for a hot drink."

Sarge looked around and said, "Well, now that the good Sheriff is here, we can go." He got off his stool and walked around the island to where Miss Kay was making herself busy. He leaned in and kissed her on the cheek. It was the first public expression from either of them, and it felt kind of weird. Like when you were a kid and saw your parents kissing. But no one said anything. Because, while it was a little strange to us, it was also a good thing. A change was coming over our little community. A good change.

We all climbed into the Hummer with Ted at the wheel. Mike wanted to drive, but Sarge put the kibosh on that idea. Saying he wanted to enjoy his coffee, not wear it. We rode in silence as rain beat down. Apparently, windshield wipers were an afterthought in these military trucks. While they technically functioned, they did little to keep the windshield clean.

The markets in both Altoona and Umatilla were deserted. The roads were totally empty, except for us. Since the roads saw so little traffic, usually just one of our vehicles and the occasional bicycle, the water was pooling up heavily in places. In others, heavy streams of water flowed along the edge. At times, depending on the grade of the road, these flows would cross the road to the other side. The Hummer splashed through these, sending sheets of water into the air.

We pulled through the barricade at the edge of town. The men standing watch there had no appreciable shelter and simply stood in the rain, wearing ponchos or Gortex jackets. They looked miserable.

"Why haven't they built something to shelter them up here? They stand in the sun and they stand there in the rain." Mike commented.

"Conditions are what you make them," I replied as I watched one of the guardsmen watch us pass, a rivulet of rainwater running off the front of his Kevlar helmet.

"That's exactly what I'm talking about!" Mike acknowledged.

"Their leadership lacks creativity," Sarge said. "As a result, they do too. Poor bastards." Sarge looked over his shoulder at me and asked, "What are you going to tell him?"

I shrugged. "Haven't really thought of it yet."

"You better well hurry up and figure it out!"

"Quit yer bitchin'. I'll figure it out."

We pulled through the back gate of a nearly vacant armory. Sarge turned in his seat and looked at Mike. "Go find the best trucks. We're not taking any broke down shit and I ain't letting him decide what we're taking."

Mike nodded and Ted said he'd help. Jamie also volunteered for the job and the three of them got out and headed to where the trucks were parked. Sarge and I went inside. We found Sheffield and Livingston leaned over a radio in their comm shack. Someone was giving a report.

Just seems odd for these civilians to be moving in this weather. Something is pushing them out.

Sheffield keyed his mic and asked, "Have you made contact with any of them?"

Negative. We've just been observing.

"Alright. Don't contact them. Wait and see what's behind them."

Roger that.

Sheffield laid the mic on the table and turned around.

"What's that all about?" Sarge asked.

"Our pickets are seeing a bunch of folks on the road. Kind of weird for them to be moving in this weather," Sheffield replied.

"Where at?" Sarge asked.

"Up on the 441, just east of Mount Dora," Livingston replied. "We moved them out there to give us some warning if something were headed this way."

"Well, let us know if something comes up."

"What are you guys doing up here on a day like this?" Sheffield asked.

"The Sheriff here needs something," Sarge replied and looked over his shoulder at me. Sheffield looked at me expectantly.

"I need a couple of trucks and trailers and a few of your people for a few days. We've got a little issue I want to address up our way," I said.

"What is it?" Livingston asked.

"This may be a good thing for all of us. There's a group of bandits holed up out in the woods. They've got vehicles and a rather large stash of fuel from what I understand. They raid people's houses and waylay them on the road. I want to take them out. Whatever supplies they have, I'll bring up here for the folks in town. The fuel too." It was a total lie, but it sounded good.

"What do you need?" Livingston asked.

"I need one MRAP, one five-ton truck and a trailer for each. We're going to haul our small buggies in the trailers to the AO to save on fuel and such. The MRAP will be used in the assault and the trailers are for whatever we find."

"Wouldn't just the truck be enough?" Sheffield asked.

I lied some more, telling him we'd already done a recon on the place and saw large fuel tanks. Sarge helped me embellish the details to the point Sheffield and Livingston were excited at the possibility of all the loot they'd get. When we were done, they were offering to go on the raid with us.

"No, this is just a law enforcement issue. Wouldn't be right for you guys to be involved."

"I'll go get you a couple of trucks," Livingston said.

"Just round up a half dozen of your people. We're going to use them for security for the trucks, since they are yours," Sarge said. Laying on the ass-kissing pretty heavy. I was happy he did it with a straight face.

"Alright. You know which trucks to get?"

Sarge nodded and waved him off. "Oh yeah. We'll get with your motor pool NCO and get it sorted."

Livingston nodded and headed off to volunteer some of their people. Sarge and I left the building and went to find the guys. They already had the trucks ready to go, with the trailers connected. The two big vehicles sat idling with Mike behind the wheel of one and Jamie in the other. Some of the Guardsmen were busy filling three fifty-five-gallon drums in one of the trailers with fuel. The transfer pump was manual and it was taking some time to get them topped off.

"How much longer to get those drums filled?" Sarge asked Ted.

"They're filling the last one now. Won't take long."

As they were talking, a group of men walked up. Each either wore or carried a large pack as well as their weapon. Sarge told them to hop into the back of the MRAP, that we'd be leaving soon. When the last drum was full, Ted grabbed the pump and tossed it into the trailer, telling the motor pool folks we'd bring it back with the trucks. We quickly got back into the Hummer before anyone could say anything and were out of the yard and headed back towards the ranch.

Once again, Ted drove the Hummer, leading the three-truck convoy. I sat in the backseat, looking out the window at the rain. I leaned forward and said, "We need to go see Mitch. I want to check the weather before we head off on this little adventure."

"That's a good idea," Sarge replied and picked up his radio to tell the other trucks to head on to the ranch while we took care of this side mission.

Mitch wasn't at the courthouse, so we drove out to his place. I could have just called him on the radio, but I wanted to see the most recent SAT image myself. There was a storm out there that had the potential to cause us real trouble. Mitch was standing in the backdoor with a steaming mug in his hand when we stopped.

He saluted us with it as we got out. "Morning, guys." We replied in kind and he shook everyone's hand as he invited us in.

We wiped our feet at the door and followed him into the kitchen where he set out mugs for everyone. "Coffee?" He asked as he poured one for Sarge, knowing his answer before he asked.

Ted and I both nodded in the affirmative and he filled our

cups as well. Then he set out a tub of sugar and, to my surprise, a canister of powdered creamer. "Oh wow. Where'd you find this?" I asked as I shook it into my cup.

"I had a bunch put away. It's a luxury now," he replied.

Stirring my coffee, I replied, "Well, I appreciate the hospitality."

"If you drank it like a grownup, you wouldn't need that crap," Sarge admonished with a scowl on his face. Then he added, "Ruining a perfectly good cup of coffee."

"Yeah. Sucking dick is an acquired taste too. But I prefer not to acquire it," I replied. Then realizing what I'd said, looked around for Michelle.

Mitch laughed at me. "She's upstairs."

"Whew," I replied. "Sorry about that."

"Don't worry about it."

"Mind your manners," Sarge barked. "I can't take you nowhere."

"So, to what do I owe the pleasure of this visit?" Mitch asked.

"I wanted to see the latest SAT image. We need to take a little trip. But I wanted to see what that storm looks like first," I replied.

"I have one that's a couple hours old," he replied as he got up. "Looks like it fell apart. It's not nearly as well formed as it was." He returned with a stack of images and started laying them out in chronological order. Pointing to one of the older ones, he said, "You can see here it looked like an eye was about to form. But it hit this black area here that's high pressure, dry air. That really put a damper on it."

"That's good," Sarge said as he inspected the images.

Pointing at the newest one, I said, "Maybe. But look at this mess coming off the coast of Africa."

Mitch nodded. "Yeah that one's pretty nasty. But it's ten days or so away."

"Maybe that high pressure will stick around and turn it," Ted said.

"No," Mitch replied, pointing at the image again. "The high pressure is moving to the west, pulling this storm with it. We're going to have this rain for about three days, I'm thinking. If this ridge moves on off further to the west, it'll open the door for the next one."

Sarge looked at him, "You some kind of meteorologist?"

Mitch smiled, "It's a hobby."

"He's the only weatherman we have," I added.

"So, aside from the rain, we should be good for at least the next week?" Sarge asked.

Mitch nodded in agreement. "Looks that way."

The old man got to his feet. "We appreciate the hospitality. Tell your lovely wife hello for us. But we've got work to do and need to get going."

Mitch asked what we were doing and we shared it with him, making sure he understood not to share the info with Sheffield.

"Oh, I never talk to him. I usually work with Shane and Shawn. He stays out of our business," Mitch replied.

"As it should be," Sarge replied with a nod.

Mitch walked us out to the truck where we said our goodbyes, with handshakes all around. He told us that if anyone up our way needed anything to please let him know. I thanked him for the offer and told him I'd pass it on. Then we were back in the truck and headed home.

"We'll drop you off at your place, Morgan," Sarge said. "I'll get those Guardsmen sorted and we'll get loaded. You pack a bag and we'll come pick you up."

"Be sure and let those guys know where to go to eat. Tell

them if they need anything to get with Thad. He's jefe as far as they're concerned"

"Leave the Army shit to me," he replied dismissively.

I snorted and shook my head, turning my attention back to the rain outside. It was a miserable day, though it was a reprieve from the heat. But that would be compensated for when the sun came back out and began to burn the water off. It'd be like living in a sauna.

We rolled into the neighborhood and Ted took me to my house. Pulling into my driveway, Sarge turned his head and said, "Get your shit together. We'll be back in a little while."

As I opened the door, before the truck even stopped, I replied, "I'll be ready."

I pulled my poncho off on the porch before going in. No sense in making a mess inside. Mel was lying on the couch. Little Bit was on the floor with paints spread out in front of her and papers scattered around her. Taylor and Lee Ann were on the floor in front of the fireplace watching a movie on the iPad. They were sharing a set of earbuds, each having one stuck in an ear.

I leaned over the back of the couch and kissed Mel on the head. "I have to go pack. They'll be ready to go soon."

She scrunched into the pillow she was lying on and replied, "I already packed you a bag. It's on the bed."

I looked into the bedroom to see my bag sitting at the foot of the bed. "Thanks. Then I can just chill out with you guys for a little while."

"Where you going?" Little Bit asked.

"To see some Army people."

"How long you going to be gone?"

I got down on the floor beside her. "Not long. What'cha painting?"

"A school. That's the teacher and that's the blackboard."

"It's a nice-looking school." I looked at her and asked, "You miss school?"

She shrugged. "A little, I guess. I miss my friends. I miss having kids to play with."

I roughed her hair. "You will again, someday."

"Hey!" She shouted as she patted her hair back down.

I sat up and leaned against the couch. Mel put her arm around me and I rested my head on it. I fell asleep there and woke up when I heard a horn. Little Bit was patting my leg saying, "Daddy. Mister Sarge is here."

I smiled at her and pulled her into my lap. "I guess I have to go." I hugged her tight. "I love you."

She wrapped her arms around my neck and squeezed as tight as she could, grunting as she strained. "I love you too!"

"Aahg, you're going to pop my head off!" I cried. She laughed and I tickled her. "Be good for mommy."

"I will," she replied and kissed me on the cheek.

I crawled over to the girls and lay in front of them, putting my hand on the iPad. When they looked up, I said, "See you two later."

"Can we come?" Lee Ann asked.

"No. You're going to have to help out here."

"We never get to do anything fun," Taylor replied.

"Be good for mom and help out."

"We will," Lee Ann replied.

Mel was waiting by the door with my bag. She handed it to me and said, "Get back home in one piece."

I kissed her and replied, "I will. Promise."

"I put a bunch of that jerky in there for you."

I leaned in and hugged her, giving her another kiss. "Thanks, babe."

CHAPTER 4

Sarge was standing on the porch when I came out. "I was about to knock on the door."

"I was coming. Calm down."

He pointed to the Hummer and said, "You drive."

Grunting, I replied, "What happened to sleep on the way?"

"Improvise, adapt, overcome."

"What? You a Marine now?"

As I got in on the driver's side, he replied, "Question my heritage like that again and this'll get ugly."

Dalton was sitting in the back seat and in his famous cockney accent, shouted, "Top of the mornin' to ya guvna!"

I looked over my shoulder at him and asked, "What the hell are you so chipper about?"

"Just glad to be alive."

I asked Sarge, "Which way are we going?"

"Let's try and take I-75. It'll be a lot faster; and with this weather, maybe it'll keep the slow thinking types from trying anything."

"That just means any we do come up against are committed to their endeavors," Dalton added.

Sarge pointed and I put the truck in gear and pulled out as he replied, "We'll just have to show them the flaw in their logic then."

As we passed the bunker, I saw it was manned by the Guardsmen we had picked up yesterday. At least here they had a tarp to get under out of the rain. They waved as we passed and it made me wonder if they were unhappy at not getting to go, or relieved they got to stay behind. Or if they even knew what we were up to for that matter.

"You tell those guys what we're doing?" I asked.

Sarge shook his head. "Nope. They don't need to know."

I drove down 19 and hung a right onto 42. It was a straight shot to highway 441 in Summerfield. Just like 19 that we drove often, this one was clogged with debris. Nothing the trucks couldn't handle, but the absence of traffic and maintenance was obvious. Tree debris littered the road. Piles of leaves, twigs, sticks and some large limbs were everywhere. Dirt was also piled in places where it had been washed in by the rains. This was magnified by the rain we were currently experiencing, as rivers of water ran along the sides and crossed anywhere the pitch of the road changed.

But it was an easy drive and I wasn't particularly worried about being waylaid. The rain, this volume of rain anyway, would surely keep people inside. It'd rained all night and only the most dedicated would be watching the roads. And it wouldn't be particularly profitable for them either as their potential victims would also be seeking shelter. So, I relaxed and settled into the drive. The fact the Hummer was up-armored certainly helped.

We made it to Summerfield without seeing anyone on the road. I spotted a couple of faces watching us from porches as we passed by, but that was the entire sum of people, and they made no effort at action of any sort. It was an odd sensation to turn out onto highway 441 with no traffic. It was a major artery and had always been busy. But today, it was empty, save the abandoned cars lining the sides of the road.

"Wonder who pushed all the cars out of the road," I asked no one in particular.

Sarge was looking out his window and dismissively replied, "Who cares. But I'm glad they did."

As we passed the Camping World on the left side of the road, I noticed something. "There isn't a single towable camper over there," I said.

Sarge looked over. "Makes sense. People with trucks that still ran came up here and cleaned them out. Probably sitting in the Ocala Forest now with dead bodies inside of them."

"I'm sure some are," Dalton added. "These woods down here aren't very hospitable to man or beast."

The only things on the lot were the RVs, most of which sat with their hoods and doors open to the elements. Doomed to rot away from exposure to wind, rain and critters. I could just imagine bird nests being built in them. Or worse yet, wasp nests in profusion. Waiting on some poor unsuspecting soul to make the mistake of poking their head in.

But there was one with the awning pitched. Maybe someone was living there. Though in the heat of the summer, it would be hell stuck out in the middle of an asphalt lot. But our ideas of comfort had changed. No longer could we so radically alter the environment to suit us. We were now as much a part of the natural world as the wild animals. If it was hot, we sought shade. If it rained, we sought shelter. But there was no air conditioning. We could still make heat, but we could not make cold except in very limited amounts, such as the fridge. The thought of keeping an entire home at seventy-two degrees was as likely as walking on the moon at this point.

After making the turn onto County Highway 484, it

wasn't long before I-75 came into view. The truck-stops lining the approach to the interstate were a sad sight. Trash of every kind filled their parking lots. The doors either stood open or shattered. Sometimes both. Windblown piles of paper and plastic bottles formed heaps at the edges of curbs. Litter was everywhere. I guess the first thing to go in a crisis is the concern for one's trash. But then, without service to haul it away, where's it supposed to go? The apparent answer is, wherever you drop it.

I swung onto the on-ramp and looked in the mirror to make sure everyone was still there. Of course, I'd have known if there had been any trouble. I-75 was lined with cars. Fortunately, the drivers of most of them had made their way to the side of the road when their cars stalled and weren't blocking the travel lanes.

"Keep it at about forty-five," Sarge said as he leaned back and put his foot up on the dash.

"You know, the only people I've seen do that are teenage girls," I replied.

Sarge grabbed his crotch. "I've got your teenage girl right here."

Then Dalton's leg shot out between the seats and thumped down on the tunnel cover between the us. The old man cocked an eye at it briefly before seizing the foot under his arm. Dalton nearly kicked me into the windshield when he used the back of my seat as leverage in order to snatch the trapped foot from the old man, all the while laughing uproariously.

When he finally got it free, Sarge said, "Stick it up here again, Gulliver, and I'll cut it off!"

The radio crackled and Mike said, "We need a piss break."

"Go ahead and stop," Sarge said.

I stopped the truck in the middle of the road. Not bothering to pull over. Getting out, I stretched and pulled my poncho on. It was still raining pretty good and I looked back at the MRAP, which was at the rear of the column. I could see the Browning M2 swiveling around as someone inside scanned the road.

"Set up security!" Sarge barked

I walked to the front of the Hummer and leaned against the fender. Rain pelted the poncho as I tried to look out to the tree line at the edge of the road. It was obscured by the rain, low cloud ceiling and dim light. All I could see was a gray haze. But the way I figured it, if I couldn't see over to it, anyone there couldn't see me either. But looking up, it was obvious that the odds of anyone being out were slim.

"Saddle up!" Sarge called out.

I looked back to see everyone headed for their trucks and made my way to the driver's door and pulled the poncho off. Getting in, I wadded it up and laid it on the floor in front of my seat. That's the problem with these things. When you take them off, they're soaked and you're only somewhat drier.

We continued on our way, making decent time. Although, I was continuously doing the math in my head about how far we had to go and how we were doing. It was going to take forever to get there. And that's provided there were no issues.

And everything was fine until we came to the outskirts of Gainesville. Just south of town on I-75, the interstate is bordered on both sides by a rest area. They sat just past the Paynes Prairie Preserve and made a good buffer for traffic coming north. And it was at this point that we encountered the first roadblock. Several cars were pushed into the travel lanes and some of the trees in the rest areas were dropped to block the shoulder. With guardrails bordering the center median, it made it virtually impassable.

"Stop here," Sarge said. "Get up on that minime, Gulliver." Dalton wedged himself up into the turret. Sarge keyed the mic and said, "Teddy, get on that electronic eyeball and let me know what you see."

On it, boss.

I squinted to see. But it was futile. The rain battered the windshield and the anemic wipers could hardly keep up. Sarge reached over and pushed my face, saying, "Look out *there*, numb nuts. Teddy's got an eyeball up ahead."

I looked out the side window and replied, "You need to stop being a dick."

"I second that!" Dalton called from the turret.

After what seemed like forever, Ted called back. *Looks deserted, boss.*

Sarge sat for a moment, tapping the mic on his leg. "Pull around and go check that rest area out. We'll cover you from here."

Moving. Ted replied.

The MRAP came around us and headed towards the exit. The truck rolled slowly up the ramp as we sat and watched. The big truck would move up a few feet and pause, then move up again. It did this repeatedly until it was finally sitting in the parking lot.

"What's the word, Teddy?" Sarge asked.

We had a couple of bodies squirt out the back, but it looks like this has been abandoned for some time now.

"Safe for us to move up?"

Looks that way. We'll drive out the other side. I'll let you know if we see anything.

"We'll wait for your call."

It didn't take Ted long to call back with the all-clear. We had to go up the ramp and into the rest area to get around the roadblock. The rest area was a total mess. Trash, clothes and heaps of debris were everywhere. The vending machines had been dragged out into the parking lot and stood up with sheets of plywood laid across the tops to create a shelter of sorts. A couple of rusting barrels sat by piles of wood. It was obvious that this location was manned for a long time.

"Look at that," Sarge said, pointing out the window.

He was motioning towards a large pile of clothes, shoes and assorted personal items. Several types of cheap backpacks and messenger-type bags were mixed in. "That doesn't look good," I said.

"That's nothing," Dalton called out. "Check out your eleven o'clock."

A tree at the edge of the parking lot was festooned with women's undergarments like some sort of garish Christmas tree. We all knew what it meant.

"There's been some evil shit going on here," Sarge said.

"Yeah. Just think of all those college kids trying to get out of here," I replied.

Sarge grunted. "I hope we run across the bastards."

"That's not our mission. We've got shit to do and it doesn't include trying to restore order to the city of Gainesville."

"I know, I know," Sarge replied, waving me off. He nodded forward. "Go on, let's get a move on."

I pulled past the MRAP and assumed the lead of the convoy again. But as bad as the rain was, it worked in our favor and kept people sheltered, which allowed us to make it through Gainesville without seeing another soul. And that was how much of the trip went. It was just mile after monotonous, rainy mile.

"Wish we had a radio," I said as Lake City was coming into view.

Dalton, who was back in his seat now, leaned forward and asked, rather excitedly, "You want me to sing?"

He started to clear his throat as Sarge pointed over his shoulder at him, replying, "Don't even think about it."

Dalton slumped. But he perked right up and said, "Yeah. You're right. You're a much better singer than I am. You go."

Sarge turned slowly in his seat. I had to laugh, because as the old man swiveled in his seat, Dalton leaned away, at the same speed. And Dalton was nearly as bad as Mike. When the old man started to turn around, Dalton again leaned forward. Sarge quickly looked back over his shoulder and Dalton instantly sat back. I laughed out loud and Sarge shook his head.

"Why am I always surrounded by assholes?" He asked.

"You're just lucky that way," I replied as I swung the truck onto the I-10 ramp.

Sarge nodded. "At least we're on I-10 now. Getting closer."

I looked at my watch, it was already after noon. "It'll be dark before we get there."

"What do you care? You wanted to drive in the dark."

"Just making an observation, you old prick."

Sarge looked at me for a minute. "We can move faster now. Speed up."

"Why is this piece of asphalt any safer than the one we just got off of?" Dalton asked.

Sarge rocked in his seat. "Because the Army is in full control of this piece." He pulled a fluorescent orange marker panel from a pocket and handed it to Dalton. "Get your ass up in that hole, Gulliver. Hold this up so we don't get out asses shot off."

Dalton wormed his way into the turret and held the panel over his head with both hands. It flapped in the wind as we rolled forward.

We were still coming around the ramp as it swung to the west. As the interstate proper came into view, so did a couple of armored vehicles. I instantly slowed. Staring down a large caliber gun will do that to you.

Sarge pointed and said, "Keep going. Just take it slow. They're expecting us."

As we approached the overpass of the southbound lanes of I-75, I saw several uniformed men standing under it. They were all armed, but non-threatening, as they waved us forward. As we rolled up to them, men approached the Hummer from both sides. Sarge opened his door and the young man standing there nodded at him, and greeting him, "Afternoon, Top."

Sarge got out and shook the man's hand. "How's it going?" He asked.

I got out as the two men talked and looked around. A large tent was set up under the overpass, banked with sandbags. There were several other sandbagged emplacements as well. It looked to me like a well-prepared defense. The young soldier standing on my side was rocking back and forth on his heels. I looked at him and asked, "How's it going?"

He shrugged and looked up. "Rain keeps the shitheads away."

"You guys see a lot of action here?"

"We take a lot of pot shots. Thankfully, these dipshits can't shoot for shit. There was one guy that was pretty good. He'd come out every day at the same time and crack off a round. He hit a couple of people. Thankfully, we all wear these." He rapped his knuckles on the Kevlar helmet sitting on his head.

"What happened to him? He just quit coming out to play?"

He smiled. "No. He came out at nearly the same time every day. We finally just laid an ambush and shwacked his ass."

"Shwack em!" Ted shouted from where he stood by the MRAP.

After a moment, Sarge was twirling a finger in the air and shouting, "Mount up!"

I nodded to the young soldier I was talking to and climbed back into the Hummer. Once Sarge was in, we pulled off as the soldiers waved.

"So, the road is clear all the way?" I asked.

Sarge nodded. "Yep. Put your foot into it. Let's roll."

And so, while it was a long ride, it was a completely uneventful one. I marked the trip by noting the passing of landmarks I recognized. Exits to places like Live Oak, Madison, Monticello and then Tallahassee. Getting to Tallahassee always gave a false sense of coming to the end of your trip. But Eglin was still a very long way ahead, just a stone's throw from Alabama.

As the road signs told me we were getting closer to Tallahassee, I started looking for exit 217; it wouldn't be much farther ahead. Passing the 216 mile-marker, I slowed a bit and used the sleeve of my shirt to wipe the window. The sky was still gray, and the falling rain made everything outside look like the sky. But after passing the exit, I saw the little Ford sitting right where I'd left it, its silver paint blended into the surrounding murk; but it was there.

"What are you looking at?" Sarge asked as he grabbed the wheel and pulled the Hummer back into the center of the road.

"That's my car back there. That's where I was when this shit all started."

Sarge looked over his shoulder, "No shit. Damn, you were one hell of a long way from home."

"Want me to shoot it?" Dalton asked from the backseat. Sarge swiveled in his seat, giving Dalton a look and shaking his head. Dalton shrugged, "Just offering."

We passed several other checkpoints on our travel. But in Tallahassee there was a much larger presence. Here too, we were waved through, not bothering to stop. As we came out the other side of Tallahassee, I slowed to a stop in the road. Sarge looked at me and asked, "What's wrong?"

"I need a break," I said.

"I'll spell you," Dalton said as he climbed out.

Sarge got out and stretched, then told Ted to fuel all the trucks. "No sense in wasting the stop."

"Roger that, boss," he replied as he headed back towards the MRAP.

I walked to the front of the truck and took a long piss. When I turned around, Sarge was leaning on his door and asked, "You done now?"

I lifted my leg and farted loudly. "Am now," I replied with a smile.

He just shook his head. "You're getting as bad as Mike."

"We've had this discussion already," I replied, then looked around. "You know. This makes me feel good."

"What? Pissing and shitting yourself in the rain?"

"No," I waved a hand at the road. "Being out here knowing there's nothing to worry about. That the military has taken control of this area."

He nodded. "I'm honestly surprised they've come out as far as they have."

I laughed. "Hell, I wish they'd come a little farther. Well, a lot farther."

Sarge grunted. "Why? You've got *us*."

Now I grunted. "Yeah. You really instill confidence."

Sarge looked sideways at me before looking back over his shoulder. "I'm going to go supervise this goat rope or we'll never get out of here."

"Get 'em in line," I replied as he walked off.

It didn't take long for me to hear Sarge shouting and cussing. It made me laugh. The sounds of his old ass raising hell, Mike and Ian cussing him back and metal drums scraping and banging, making enough noise to wake the dead. It made me wonder if he really was helping. I heard an empty drum hit the road and turned back to see it rolling into the median.

I walked back to where the chaos was taking place and asked Sarge if we should keep the drum.

"Naw," he replied. "We need the room. We're going to be bringing a fuel tank back with us."

"How the hell are we going to pull that?" I asked.

Sarge looked at me quizzically and asked, "Who said anything about pulling it?" He looked back at the guys and Jamie and shouted, "Saddle up! We still got a long way to go!"

In a deep sing-song voice and mimicking an air guitar, Mike replied, "And a short time to get there!"

Sarge just shook his head and stomped off. I followed him back to the truck with Dalton. He was wiping his hands on a rag. "Damn, diesel fuel stinks."

"Not as bad as gasoline."

Dalton got into the driver's seat and I climbed into the backseat and pulled my bag over as he pulled off. I fished around inside and found the Biltong that Mel had packed for me. I was starving and quickly unwrapped the dish towel she had placed it in and took out a piece and took a big bite. It looked like she packed all of it, as there was a lot. I handed a piece up front. Dalton quickly grabbed it and I handed another piece up.

"What's this?" Sarge asked as he took it.

"Biltong from that cow."

"No shit? I remember you talking about it." He took a bite and nodded. "Not bad. Pretty close to the real thing."

"It is the real thing. How can it not be the real thing," I asked? "It's dry meat."

He clamped his teeth down on the piece of meat and pulled. Getting a piece, he replied, "Cause it ain't the same."

"You'd bitch if you were hung with a new rope."

"I'd bitch if I was hung with a rope made from the pubic hair of virgins!" Sarge barked. "The result is the same. Dead."

I chewed on the dried meat and stared out the window. I was thankful I drove as far as I did and that it had not been necessary for me to climb up into the turret. Not that it was that different as rain dripped and spattered in through the opening as it was. But it was still better than sitting in that web sling.

The sun was beginning to set when we rolled into Destin. I was surprised by the number of people I saw on the streets. The reason was revealed when the gates to the base came into view and I saw a stream of civilians coming out. I guessed they were working on base in some capacity.

It only made sense. With so much of our military forward-deployed, to use the preferred term, overseas, there was a lack of manpower. And with so many able-bodied men and women around who would happily work for food for themselves and their families, it was an easy choice. Not to mention the only one.

Two Stryker fighting vehicles flanked the gates to the base as well as a number of large Hesco barriers preferred by today's military. These pre-formed concrete wall sections could be interlocked to form a solid wall. And here they did just that. We had to zigzag our way up to the gates as the Hescos prevented a direct approach.

Dalton pulled up to the gate and stopped. An MP in full battle rattle leaned in when Dalton opened the door. "First Sergeant Mitchell here to see General Fawcett."

"We've been expecting you, Top. Glad to see you made it without any issues. I'll have someone escort you to the General."

The MP looked at Dalton and said, "Please turn off your headlights." and he promptly stepped away, shouting orders.

Dalton closed the door and looked at Sarge, asking, "You haven't used the radio all day. How did they know when to expect us?"

"Cause I told 'em when we'd be here. We were maintaining radio discipline."

"Why'd they have us turn the headlights off?" I asked.

"So, no one can see us in the dark. Good way for aircraft to mark you as a target."

I rocked my head against the bulletproof window. The old man never ceased to amaze me. He did some things as if by magic. Just made them happen. I guess he was always operating behind the scenes. But that would make sense. An NCO of his rank would be used to such methods.

There were no lights on anywhere. The base was blacked out. But since it wasn't fully dark, Dalton could easily see the truck in front of him. We weaved through the base for a while before coming to typical government-looking buildings with a brick façade. The truck in front of us stopped and the driver quickly got out. Everyone piled out and started stretching. Sarge told them to hang out by the trucks and told Ted and me to follow him.

We went inside the building and down a hallway past an open door. It appeared to be a conference room crowded with people leaning over a large table covered with maps. A large map of the state of Florida was projected on a screen at the head of the table as well. I noted the General was there, but we weren't invited into this particular meeting.

Instead, we were led to a small reception room of sorts and asked to take a seat. Sarge immediately spotted a coffee pot sitting on a small cabinet and helped himself without asking.

Ted did likewise, and I figured what the hell, when in Rome, and poured myself one as well and sat back down.

"What? No training wheels?" Sarge asked.

"It's been a long day. Shouldn't your old ass be tired?" I asked.

"I am. That's why I'm drinking this," Sarge replied, holding the Styrofoam cup up.

I spent a minute marveling at the cup in my hand. It'd been a while since I'd seen one. Something so common, so nondescript. But at the moment, it was kind of nostalgic.

"It's the cup, isn't it?" Ted asked, apparently reading my thoughts.

I looked up and nodded. "Yeah. Just trying to remember when the last time I saw one was."

Sarge looked at his and said, "This thing? This ain't nothing. I'd drink coffee from my boot right now."

I let out a loud breath. "You're missing the point."

"And just what is the point?"

"When was the last time you saw one of these?" Ted asked.

Sarge shrugged. "Hell, if I know. I don't remember the last time I saw dog shit either."

That got a laugh from Ted and me both. And the more we laughed, the more we laughed. Until even Sarge was laughing. When the General finally walked in the room, he stopped in his tracks and looked at all of us. No one bothered to get up. I didn't expect Sarge to, but thought Ted might. But he kept his ass firmly in his seat.

"Do I want to know?" Fawcett asked.

Sarge held the cup up and replied, "Cups. Just cups."

"And dog shit," I added.

Fawcett shook his head and replied, "You guys have been

in the wilderness too long. Come on in," he added as he went into his office.

We followed him into the office where I slumped into a chair in the corner while Ted and Sarge took the seats in front of the desk. Fawcett sat down behind his desk and stared at it for a minute. It was covered with paper. Forms, images, maps, all sorts of things were spread out. He rubbed his temples. The man looked tired. More than that. He looked drained, totally consumed. He was obviously overworked, and it was starting to show.

He looked up and smiled. "How are your folks fairing, Linus?"

"We're holding our own. It's harvest time, so we're bringing in crops. Things are starting to look up." Sarge shifted in his seat. "Or it *was*, that is."

Fawcett looked back at the desk and nodded grimly. "Yeah, that was unfortunate." Looking back up, he continued. "It was a calculated risk. We knew when we hit the Chinese, they would retaliate."

"What did we lose there?"

"A lot. But not as much as we would have had we not moved most of the resources. But it was still a tremendous loss."

Sarge nodded as Fawcett spoke. "Yes, it was. What's it look like on the ground in the Tampa area now?"

"It'll be uninhabitable for a hundred years," Fawcett replied. He then looked at his desk, sorting through the papers. Finding one, he held it up and read from it. As he did, he said, "Tell me about the run-in with the armor."

"We were out doing a recon and came across them sitting on top of an overpass. They had a good field of view. It was the perfect spot. We hit one with a Goose, but took a round into the ass of one of our trucks."

Fawcett looked back at the sheet in his hand. "One KIA?"

Sarge nodded.

"Do you know who they were?"

"Cubans."

Fawcett nodded. "Yeah, figured as much. The Russians are teaming up with them. Fortunately, there aren't that many Russians here. It's a long ride for them."

"One is too many," Ted added.

Fawcett dropped the paper to his desk. "Well, there shouldn't be too many more. The Navy has started sinking any ships approaching Cuba. The USS Albany and Helena are down there, wreaking havoc on shipping."

"What are those?" I asked.

Fawcett looked at me, smiled and nodded. "Good to see you again, Sheriff. They're Los Angeles-class fast-attack subs. Hunter-killers."

"So, what do you need from us?" Sarge asked.

Fawcett sat back in his chair and ran his fingers through his hair, that was probably grayer than he wanted it to be. Letting out a breath, he picked up a file folder and opened it. "Top, we've identified a few sites we'd like your people to prosecute. They're staging areas. We know there are Russian and Cuban forces there." He looked up, "But, as you can imagine, we're spread a little thin."

"Why don't you just bomb them with planes or drones?" I asked.

"All air assets are tied up flying CAP. Combat Air Patrol," he added, as though I didn't understand.

"I know what it means."

He brushed off my reply and continued. "We just can't support those kinds of operations. Only time a plane is used in a ground attack mode is if we have troops in contact. And even then, it has to be an emergency. The days of the unlimited use of force are over. Simply put, we have to triage what's more important. And at the moment, it's making sure that unfriendly aircraft are not in the skies overhead."

"Are we getting any support on that?" Sarge asked.

Fawcett nodded. "The Canadians are helping. They've stabilized their southern border that was affected and they've cranked up the aid now. We are literally getting tons of support from them every day. The Brits are helping as well, as are the Aussies. But that's about it."

"Sounds like a lot to me," I replied. Sarge shifted in his seat. I guess I was getting on his nerves, but I wasn't done. "That's good, General. Can you spare some for the poor people of Lake County? We need aid as well."

Sarge swiveled in his chair and looked at me. But Fawcett was unfazed, "It's ok, Top," Fawcett said before turning his attention back to me. "Of course, Sheriff. We will give until it hurts. What sort of things do you need?"

I reached into my vest and pulled out a Wright in the Rain notebook and tore a page out. I'd made a list of things while sitting in the backseat. No doubt, I had missed things; but it was a long list. I handed the paper to Fawcett. He looked at it and his eyebrows went up.

"You know I can't accommodate all this, right?"

I nodded. "Just give until it hurts, General."

He nodded and a thin smile cracked his face. Picking up a radio on his desk, he made a call. "Jim, can you come in here, please?"

There was a terse reply and moments later, a man with gold oak leaves on a pressed uniform came in. Fawcett held out the list and said, "Jim, can you go to supply and see what we can do about the Sheriff's shopping list?"

Taking the list, he replied, "Of course." He looked at me and held a hand towards the door, "After you, Sheriff."

"Take the truck, leave the MRAP here," Sarge said as I got to the door. I nodded and followed Jim.

"Just follow me," Jim said as we went outside. "Keep the headlights off."

Jamie and Ian were standing beside the truck talking. "Let's follow him," I told Jamie.

I climbed up in the cab and sat in the middle seat and Jamie drove. She seemed to have a thing for driving. Maybe it was the novelty of it now. Jamie followed Jim's Hummer as it wound its way through the base, eventually stopping at a large warehouse-type building. Jim stopped his truck and ran back to tell Jamie to back up to a loading dock on the side of the building. She did as instructed.

As she pulled the air brake on, she asked, "What's this all about?"

Waiting for Ian to get out, I replied, "We're going shopping."

"Something you're good at," Ian joked as he opened the door.

"Really?" Jamie asked with a very serious look on her face. "That's what I'm good at? Shopping? Shopping is what I'm good at?" Her head bobbed with every word.

The joke faded from his face and he half moaned, "I'm sorry."

Jamie threw her door open and replied, "Oh, you just think you are now." She jabbed a finger in his face, "But I can promise you, you will be." She then jumped down from the truck.

Ian and I both looked at one another. "That woman is scary," I said. "I fear for your safety."

Ian nodded. "So do I."

We walked through a side door and into a cavernous warehouse. The space was brightly lit and was bustling with activity. I looked around, curious about why I didn't notice any light from the outside. There were windows high up on the walls and skylights in the ceiling, but all were covered to black them out.

Forklifts seemed to be everywhere, as well as people pulling pallet jacks around. The opposite side of the building from where we parked was a continuous line of large roll-up loading doors. At each one sat a large truck that was being loaded.

"I parked you on the unloading side. There are no deliveries coming in tonight. The events in Tampa have made it a little more difficult to get cargo here."

Jamie looked at the pallet racks that went nearly to the ceiling and asked, "Where is all this stuff coming from?"

"Canada, England and Australia," I replied.

Jim looked at me. "How the hell do you know that?"

"Fawcett told me."

Jim nodded. "Oh, of course. But yeah, our allies have begun shipping aid. Canada of course sends the most. But Australia and England are sending considerable tonnage too."

"What kind of stuff is here?" Ian asked.

Jim motioned for another man to join them. "This is Buck. This is his warehouse. Buck, can you share with them what's in here?"

"All this is humanitarian aid. Food, hygiene, medical supplies. That kind of thing."

Jim handed Buck the list, saying, "Here's what they're looking for."

Buck looked at the list. "We have all this," he looked up and asked, "There are no amounts here. How much are you looking for?"

"The general said you'd give until it hurts."

"What'd you bring to carry all this?"

"A five-ton truck with a five-ton trailer," Jamie said.

Buck shrugged, "I'll see what I can do."

"Anything we can do to help?" I asked.

"No, just stay out of the way. We'll get it. There's a breakroom back there. Go help yourselves."

"Anyone for a cup of coffee?" I asked.

"Coffee?" Jamie asked as she turned and started towards the breakroom.

The breakroom was just what you'd expect. There were several people there, mainly civilians from the look of them. They watched us as we excitedly poured coffee and, to their utter amazement, each of our group grabbed a double handful of doughnuts before taking a seat.

Jamie's eyes rolled back in her head as she took a bite of one she'd dunked in her coffee. "Oh my God," She said. "I never thought I'd see another one of these."

Ian stuffed an entire glazed doughnut in his mouth and replied, "Ah kna, fma naffer!" Blowing crumbs out as he tried to talk.

I took my time. I'd mixed creamer and sugar into my cup and luxuriously dunked the doughnut in and taken a bite. I savored every moment, every part of the act, dunking the pastry, then tapping it on the rim of the cup as a drop would fall back in. I took all of it in. Such a silly thing. But for me, it was the highest of treats.

A woman came and sat down at our table. She watched, smiling at us. I picked up another doughnut and dunked it. "They're good, huh?" She said.

I nodded as I tapped it on the rim of the cup. "Yes, they are. I'm amazed to see them."

"So was I the first time. I ate so many the first day, I got sick."

Jamie wiped her mouth with the back of her hand and asked, “How long have you been here?”

“Almost a month. Where are you guys from?”

“Lake County. Down south,” Ian replied.

“You kind of look like you’re in the Army,” she said. Then she looked at me and added, “But then you don’t.”

I was looking down at my cup and glanced up at her. “I’m not,” then I pointed with the pastry across the table at Jamie and Ian, “but they are.”

“Kind of,” Jamie said.

“Kind of,” I added with a smile.

The woman nodded at me and said, “You some kind of cop or something?”

“Something like that.”

“He’s the Sheriff,” Ian clarified.

“I didn’t think there were any of those around now.”

“We’re an endangered species,” I replied, causing her to laugh.

“That’s funny. You here for supplies?”

Ian stuffed another doughnut into his mouth and nodded. He chewed it and tried to swallow the ball of dough, but something went wrong. His face contorted and he stretched his neck out. Picking up his coffee, he poured it into his mouth and worked his jaw. After a moment, the mass managed to find its way down his neck. With watering eyes, he said, “Damn. I better slow down. That one liked to have killed me.”

“Good,” Jamie replied, looking sideways at him as she swirled her cup.

“Look,” Ian replied wiping his eyes, “I said I was sorry. It was a joke. Cut me a break.”

“Mmm hmm.”

“How are things around here?” I asked the woman.

"They're better now. The Army is providing a lot of supplies. It's changed everything. We work here and can use our pay to buy other stuff."

"What do they pay you with? I can't imagine anyone taking dollars for anything. Where we come from, they're useless." I added.

She smiled shyly and reached into a pocket and pulled out a silver dollar. "Everyone uses these. They pay us with them too."

"Well, that's good to know. It's real money, actually worth something."

"What can you get with that?" Ian asked.

"A lot." A devilish grin spread across her face. "*You* can buy about whatever you want," her eyebrows bounced to convey just what she meant.

"You better find some silver dollars," Jamie said to Ian.

I reached into my vest and pulled out a gold Maple Leaf. Holding it up, I asked, "What can I get for this?"

"Anything. And I do mean anything you want. Hell, you could buy a house with that. Why do you even have it? No one has enough change for a trade with one of those."

I shrugged and put it away. "I had it before."

"Oooh," she said knowingly, "you're one of those survivalists."

"Something like that."

She looked at her watch and said, "Well, I have to get back to work. It was nice talking to you."

I waved at her, "Nice meeting you too."

She then looked at Ian and smiled. "Try not to kill yourself with those doughnuts."

Ian just looked down at his cup, afraid to make eye contact with her because Jamie was burning a hole through the woman's head. "Nice chatting with you," he replied.

She didn't say anything to Jamie and Jamie made no attempt

to speak either. Once she was out the door, I said, "Well that was fucking awkward." Looking back and forth at them, I added, "Why don't you two go somewhere and have make-up sex now. It'll make the ride back a lot less tense." I knew Jamie hated that kind of thing and I was really, really hoping Ian would take the bait. But he just looked into his cup, even as Jamie stole a glance at him.

"Fuck you, Morgan," Jamie replied as she got up to refill her cup.

Ian chanced a glance at her and said, "Come on, man. Don't say shit like that."

I laughed, rocking my head back as I did. "Look at your whipped ass!"

I didn't see Jamie was returning. I only realized something was up when I noticed Ian look past me. Just as Jamie slapped me in the back of the head. "Mind your manners, asshole."

Rubbing the back of my head, I laughed. "Yes ma'am," I replied.

We spent another couple of hours in the breakroom drinking coffee, as none of us could stomach another doughnut. At the moment, I couldn't face the thought of eating another one. Ian went to a corner of the room and stretched out on the floor to sleep. Jamie waited a little before finally joining. I smiled when she lay beside him and he put his arm around her. Since they were going to snooze, I pulled a chair over to the wall and rocked it onto its back legs, folded my arms over my chest and dozed off.

There is no way I would put myself in such a vulnerable position if the old man were around. But he wasn't, and I thought I was safe. Fat chance. I woke up when the chair slid out from under me. I was on my back before I opened my eyes. When I did, I was looking up at the old man and Dalton. Sarge was looking down, shaking his head. He held a coffee cup in one hand and a doughnut in the other. Dalton stood beside him with a doughnut on each finger like a fat doughy ring.

Rubbing the back of my head as I got up, I said, "You really are an asshole."

"You make a shitty Indian. You know that?" Sarge replied.

Still rubbing my head, I said, "What?"

"Can't sneak up on an Indian."

"I'm not a fucking Indian!"

Sarge laughed. "I know you're not. Just told you."

Mike and Ted walked in and Mike's eyes went wide when he saw Dalton with the pastries.

"Dude! I want one!" Mike shouted.

Dalton looked at the doughnuts and licked the one on his middle finger before extending it to Mike. "You can have this one."

Mike didn't hesitate. He snatched it from Dalton's finger and stuffed the whole thing in his mouth. "Try me again," he mumbled with a full mouth.

Meanwhile, Ted had fixed himself a cup of coffee and was leaning against the counter eating one himself. When Mike looked at him, he said, "You could have just got one from the box."

Looking past Dalton and seeing the box, Mike pushed him out of the way and rushed it. He stuffed two into his mouth and started stuffing them in his dump pouch.

"What the hell do you want?" I asked Sarge.

"Can you drive a tractor trailer?"

"Yeah. Why?"

He nodded. "Good. You're going to drive a truck pulling a trailer. Come on, I'll take you over to it."

I nodded at the door into the warehouse and asked, "What about this stuff?"

The old man pointed at Ian and Jamie sleeping in the corner and replied, "They'll get it. Come on, we need to go get this truck."

I followed him out into the warehouse. The truck was being loaded and looked to be nearly to capacity. The trailer was also being loaded. I don't how much of my Christmas list I was going to get, but it looked impressive enough. We went outside, and I was surprised to see a large armored vehicle with an enormous cannon sitting beside the Hummer. Doc was leaning against it, trying to keep out of the rain.

"What the hell is that?" I asked.

"That," Mike replied from behind me, "is a Stryker M1128 Mobile Gun." He walked past me to the machine and hugged it, laying his head on it. "And she's all mine."

"What the hell are we going to do with that thing?" I asked.

Mike stood up and patted it, "Blow shit up of course."

"We're taking this back to Eustis, so we have a way to deal with armor like we encountered last time," Sarge added.

"Don't let them fool you, Morgan," Ted said. "That thing is a huge piece of shit. I hate em."

Mike climbed up on the machine and patted the cannon. "Don't worry, sweetheart. I won't let the bad man hurt you."

"Look at the size of that damn cannon," I muttered.

"Oh yeah!" Mike shouted. "This is a 105-millimeter rifled gun. And we've got a load of ammo for it."

"That's all fine and dandy," Ted said. "Until that shitty autoloader goes down and we have to climb out on top of it to fix it."

"Irene will not let us down!" Mike shouted back.

"Come on, Morgan. Let's leave these idiots so they can jerk off in private," Sarge said as he got in the Hummer.

"How the hell are we getting that thing back?" I asked.

Sarge hit the starter and replied, "Drive it, of course."

"Do we have enough people?"

"We're leaving the MRAP. We need something to deal effectively with the threat of armor. This is as good as it gets."

I looked over my shoulder at the hulking war machine as we pulled away and asked, "Can it do it? I mean, it's not a tank."

"No. It's not a tank. But that gun is a tank gun. It can knock tanks out. It just can't take return fire very well. But we ain't seen no tanks. Just armored personnel carriers. And it can knock the dog shit outta those."

We made our way through the base until we came to a fenced area. The gate was open, and we drove in. A tractor hooked to a large tank trailer occupied most of the area beside a metal building. "There she is," Sarge said as he shut the truck down.

Pointing at it, I asked, "That? You want me to drive that?"

"Yeah. What's the problem?"

I asked, "Is that thing full of fuel?" He nodded. "You want me to drive that rolling inferno all the way back to Eustis?"

"Yeah. We need the fuel. There isn't anything out there to worry about."

"What if some asshole takes a shot at it? I don't want to be burned up in that thing!"

Sarge shook his head. "A rifle isn't going to hurt it. It'd take something like an RPG, and we aren't going to encounter any of those."

I shook my head. "This is bullshit."

Sarge's face contorted. "Would you quit your bellyaching! You're driving it. End of story. And pull your fucking skirt down. Your mangina is showing!"

He walked away shaking his head and mumbling to himself and went into the building. I stood there for a minute, thinking of all the ways this could end badly. Seeing that there was no choice in the matter, I followed him inside.

The building was brightly lit and much larger than I first thought. Various trucks and fighting vehicles were being worked on by several crews. Things must be pretty intense for them to be working around the clock. Sarge was talking to a large man whose arms stretched the sleeves of his uniform. There was something familiar about him, so I walked over.

"Hey, Faggione!" I said.

He smiled, causing the large cigar in his mouth to turn up. "Hi there, Morg. I see you're still running with this band of merry misfits."

"Window-licking retards," I replied, looking at Sarge. "Glad to see you're alright. When I saw what happened in Tampa, I was worried about you."

He pulled a lighter from a pocket and lit the stogie, taking a long pull on it. "We're alright," he replied as smoke wafted out of his mouth. "We moved back here long before that mess."

"I see you've found a new line on cigars."

He held it out. Bouncing his eyebrows, he replied, "Finest Cuban leaf. Having those little bastards here isn't all bad."

I smiled knowingly, "Ah. War trophies?"

He smiled again as he tucked it back in the corner of his mouth. "Something like that." He pointed at Sarge and said, "Top tells me you're going to drive my truck home."

"Looks that way," I replied.

"You still got my babies?" I nodded, and he asked, "You taking care of them?"

"They're doing fine. But we could use some tires and oil filters. That kind of stuff."

Faggione nodded and pointed with the wet chewed end of

the cigar. "Already in your truck out there. Hope you weren't planning on having any passengers."

I looked at Sarge and asked, "I don't know. Was I?"

The old man shook his head. "Nope. You're riding alone. If that thing gets hit I don't want to lose more than one person."

"You're a dick," I replied.

"Don't let him get a rise outta ya, Morg. "You'll be fine. We've done a lot of recon and there isn't anything that can ruin your day between here and Eustis. Now south of you, that's a different story." He smiled and looked at Sarge, "But we'll be dealing with that shortly." He struck the lighter again and took another puff.

"I thought you didn't smoke those things. Just chewed on 'em," I said.

He took the roll of tobacco from his lips and spat a small piece that remained behind. "Usually not. But current conditions dictate I have a drag from time to time."

I shook his hand, "It's good to see you again, my friend."

Reaching into his blouse pocket, he removed several cigars and handed them to me. "For your ride home. It's against regs to smoke in the truck," he smiled, "but you're not exactly in the Army, now are you?"

I took the proffered Havanas and smiled. "Thanks, man. These will be a nice distraction." He then handed me a Bic lighter. Pocketing it, I said, "This will help," and I shook his hand again.

"Take care of my truck. I'd like to see it again someday."

"I'll treat it as if it were my own," I replied.

Sarge snorted. "Tony, if you saw his truck, that wouldn't mean shit to you."

"Not my fault the damn thing is a bullet magnet."

Faggione laughed. "Seems to be a lot of that these days."

"Enough of this bunkum. We need to get ready to hit the road," Sarge said. Then, in an exaggerated manner, he asked, "You do want to get home, don't you?"

"Yeah, yeah, yeah," I said dismissively and looked at Tony. "Thanks again. Take care of yourself."

"I'm safe as being in my momma's arms. You guys take care of yourselves. I hear it's pretty tough out there in the wilderness."

Sarge turned and headed for the door. "Nothing we can't handle. See you next time, Tony!"

I cocked my head to the side and looked at Tony. "You know, that's funny."

"What's that?" He asked.

"That's the second time today someone referred to the wilderness. Fawcett said it too."

Tony worked the cigar to the other side of his mouth. "That's what we call it now. Anything outside the wire is the wilderness, full of Indians, bandits, settlers and other trials. It's like being back two hundred years. You take care of yourself out there in that wilderness."

I followed Sarge back to the warehouse as I thought about what Tony said. *The wilderness*. I guess it did fit. Life was certainly a lot harder now. Maybe not as bad as trying to hack it from the wilderness, but a damn close second. The truck was heavy and slow; it would be hard to react to anything in this barge. But having thousands of gallons of diesel would be incredible, so I sucked it up. At the warehouse, the truck was sitting beside the Stryker with the trailer now reconnected. The rain had abated a bit, and everyone was standing around. I parked the truck and got out.

Sarge walked up and looked at his watch. "It's nearly 2:30. Everyone find someplace to grab a couple hours of sleep. We're going to leave at six. Jamie, you and Ian will be in the five-ton." He then looked at Ted, "You take those two misfits in the Stryker. Dalton, you're with me in the Hummer."

Dalton nodded. "I can drive."

"Only thing you're driving is that Browning up there. I'm driving. And Morgan will be in the fuel truck. I'll be at the head of the column and Ted, you're at the rear. Any questions?" There were none, and we all broke up to find someplace for a quick nap. I went to the truck. It wasn't particularly comfortable. But it was dry as the rain picked back up.

I lay in the truck listening to the pattering of rain. It was funny that this thing smelled like every other military rig I'd ever been in. They seemed to be issued with a particular odor. Not necessarily offensive, or pleasant. Just present in intense form. Eventually, I drifted off to sleep.

CHAPTER 5

THAD CAME INTO THE KITCHEN with a laundry basket full of tomatoes and set it on the counter, announcing, "Here's another basket."

"We'll get them washed. Thank you, Thad," Kay replied.

He went out the back door onto the porch. Mel, Bobbie, Jess and Mary were there tending two kettles sitting on a large two-burner propane camp stove. The top of the picnic table was covered in steaming jars. Thad paused and listened as some of the cooling jars made the telltale *tick* as the lids sealed. He smiled, "That sure does look good."

Mel lifted a large strainer from one of the rolling pots, holding it to allow water to drain. "It's hard work. But it'll be worth it," she replied as she carried the scalded tomatoes over to another table where Mary sat working a manual food processor to separate skin and seed. Thad stepped over to her and wrapped his arms around her from behind. She smiled and looked up at him.

"You got a pile of seeds there. We'll have plenty of tomatoes next year," he said.

"We have a lot this year," she replied as she dropped more fruit into the hopper.

"Remember, you have to let those seeds ferment. Squeeze a couple of tomatoes into the bowl. They need the fruit to mature."

"Mary stopped turning the handle and spun around to face Thad. She stepped on her toes and kissed him on the cheek. "I know." Then she turned him towards the door and said, "Now get. We've got work to do and so do you. Danny is out there waiting on you." She pointed to the garden where Danny was busy picking.

He and Thad had put up a large canopy, one of the types you see at the beach that deploys quickly. It allowed them to work in the rain without getting soaked. It was time to harvest the garden and they weren't about to lose anything if they could prevent it.

Thad smiled and replied, "Yes ma'am," and headed for the door with an empty basket.

"We're going to be eating squash 'till we're sick of seeing them," Danny said.

Thad went to the next row of tomato plants and started picking. "That's a good problem to have. Too much to eat."

"I wonder if Morgan will get anything from his list," Danny said as he piled more squash into a milk crate.

"He had a heck of a list," Thad replied.

"I bet they don't give us anything."

"Why would you say that? They've helped us before."

"I guess you're right. I'm just setting myself up for disappointment. That way, when he comes back with some supplies, I'll be really happy." Danny paused and looked over at the pond where the kids were fishing. Miss Kay told them if they caught any fish she would cook them for their lunch. So, they were giving it their best. "I'm just worried about the kids."

Thad straightened himself and looked towards the pond. "We're doing alright, Danny. I think we're actually doing pretty good. Compared to most folks, we're living in the lap of luxury."

As Thad spoke, Lee Ann walked up. She waited for him to finish and asked, "Is there anything ready to go up to the house?"

Danny slid the now-full milk crate out to her. "Here; you can take this."

She picked it up and said, "Kay says not to pick anymore today. She said we have all we can do today and it's better to leave it on the plants than to pick it."

"She's right. We'll get back to it when they get caught up," Thad said as he picked up the laundry basket. Carrying it under one arm, he put his other arm around the girl. "How you doing?"

"I'm good," she replied as they walked. She looked up into the dreary sky. "It's just kind of depressing out."

Thad pulled her in closer. "It's just rain, and we need it. It's a good thing. At least it ain't hot!" He laughed.

Lee Ann smiled, "I guess that's true. It is kind of nice out when you think about it like that."

They went up onto the porch and deposited their loads on the table. Danny went out to the pond and called the kids to the house. They came running back, looking comical in their makeshift rain ponchos of cut plastic sheeting. They laughed and jostled one another as they ran. When they came up onto the porch, stomping, laughing and making a ruckus, Bobbie told them to take off their wet stuff before they went inside.

Taylor was busy cutting squash and putting it into jars. She would fill a jar and place it on the table in front of Mel. Mel would then dip a measuring cup into a pot of boiling water and pour it into the jar. Then she'd place the lid and ring on top of the jar and give it a gentle shake to remove air bubbles. Once it was sealed, she would pass it to Bobbie, who was standing in front of the canner. She had a small wind-up timer and was monitoring the cook time of the water bath canner.

It was a smooth process and efficient. As a result, there was a huge amount of vegetables being put away. The dining table, kitchen counter and nearly every other surface were covered with jars. When Danny came up onto the porch, Bobbie looked at him, "We need to find a way to store all this."

"I'll figure something out," he replied.

"Why don't we just distribute it out between all the houses. It'll take care of the issue of space as well as not keeping all our eggs in one basket," Thad said.

"That's a good idea," Danny replied. "We'll know where it is and can always bring it back."

"I'll make a list of what goes where. I already have an inventory going," Kay said. She had a penchant for organization.

"I'll still build us some shelves here," Danny said.

"You want to go to the hardware store?" Thad asked. Danny nodded, and Thad said, "Let's take the little red truck. It's out front."

The hardware store was actually the shop behind one of the houses. It was the home of an older man who was found having shot himself in his recliner in the living room. That very pistol was now tucked into Jess's belt where she sat cutting zucchini. While the house wasn't fit to go into, the shop was a veritable treasure chest of useful and hard-to-find materials. From fasteners to assorted lumber, the shop was a constant source of supply.

The wipers bumped back and forth in a pathetic attempt at keeping the windshield clear of water. The little truck splashed through the water flowing down the center of the road. Since traffic was now so limited, the frequent summer rains had washed it out considerably. Thad did his best with the tractor to maintain it, but it was still a rough ride.

The truck bounced in a particularly large rut. Thad said,

"Soon as this rain stops, I got to get out here and do something about this road!"

Danny was clinging to the *oh shit* handle and agreed with him. "Good idea, I think. This is getting ridiculous."

When they got to the paved portion, the ride smoothed out. But they had to make an immediate turn into the driveway of the hardware store. Thad pulled to a stop in front of the large roll-up door. "What are you thinking of for shelves?"

Pulling the hood of his raincoat over his head, Danny replied, "I don't know. Let's go see what's in there."

Inside the shop was a dry refuge from the unceasing rain outside. Shaking off the water, Danny took his coat off and laid it over the workbench. Thad hadn't bothered to put one on and was just dealing with the wet. It was dark inside despite the large door being open, and both men put on headlamps.

"Let's check out the lumber," Danny said as he moved towards the back of the shop.

"Why don't we just take these?" Thad asked, pointing at a couple of the black plastic shelving units that can be had from any hardware or big-box store.

Danny shook his head. "I hate those things. They'll bow with any weight on them. And with the number of jars we'll be piling on them, they would certainly sag." Thad nodded in agreement. "But those," Danny said as he pointed at another set of shelves that were more industrial looking. Like pallet racking from a warehouse, only smaller scale. "Those are perfect."

Thad ran his hand over the plywood shelf. "Someone put some good wood on these. They'll hold some weight."

"Let's clean these off and take them."

They worked together to move the material from the shelves they wanted to other available space. Thad was simply moving things in as efficient a manner as possible and piling them on whatever surface was available. But that didn't sit well with Danny's OCD tendencies. He started rearranging the material. Sorting it according to type and size wherever possible.

Thad looked at him and laughed, asking, "What are you doing?"

"Just organizing it. That way, if we need to find it later, we can."

"We know where to find it. In this here building. It ain't going nowhere."

Danny picked up a couple peanut butter jars full of screws and replied, "I'm a little more organized than that."

Thad nodded. "Oh yeah. I think I remember Morgan saying something about you having OCD or something."

Danny laughed. "It ain't quite that bad. But you could say I'm the polar opposite of him. His idea of organization is throwing shit in a corner."

Thad laughed, covering his mouth. "You right about that. He seems to do a lot by the seat of his pants."

"You got that right."

Thad picked up a box full of metal framing straps and asked, "Where do you want these?"

They got everything moved and disassembled the shelves they were going to use and carried them out to the truck. It was still raining, and they decided to hang out in the open door for a minute. Thad stretched and wandered back into the bowels of the building, which had not been thoroughly searched yet.

Danny could hear him shuffling around as he looked up into the desolate sky and asked, "What are you doing back there?"

"I found something. Come help me," Thad replied.

Danny made his way back through the rows of shelves and found Thad stacking boxes of jars. "Look at all these," he said as he added another flat to the pile that was already four-feet tall.

"Holy crap. See any lids?" Danny asked.

"There's all kinds of stuff here," Thad replied as he slid a large box full of lids out. Picking one up, he inspected it, "These are Tattler reusable lids. This is a gold mine."

"I'll start loading it," Danny replied as he hefted the top three flats and headed for the truck.

They loaded all the canning supplies and got back in for the short ride home. As Thad pulled out onto the road, Danny said, "Be careful or we'll have a bed full of broken glass."

"Ain't that the truth," Thad grunted, then said, "Hey, did I tell you I found a greenhouse?"

Danny shook his head. "No."

"It's a little rough. Ain't been used in a long time. You care if I disassemble it and bring it to your place and set it up?"

"Not at all, I'll help you. That would be great to keep the garden going."

"And for starting seed. That's where it'll be really good."

Thad backed the little truck up to the back porch to make unloading easier. Aric and Fred were sitting in rockers, staying out of the rain, and they came over to help. They made a chain of sorts, passing items to the two of them.

"Look at all these jars!" Fred shouted.

"Yeah, you just made Miss Kay's day," Aric added.

"Now, we ain't got to use all them peanut butter jars and other weird ones we found," Thad replied.

Taking the last case from Thad, Fred replied, "Yeah, she didn't know how she was going to get them to seal."

Aric had a stack of jars in his arms and said, "Come on, babe. Let's take these in and surprise her."

He pushed the door open with his foot and stepped in, shouting, "Miss Kay, we brought you something!"

Kay was at the sink and turned around, wiping her hands on

an apron Jess had found in another house during the wedding dress search. "What is it?" She instinctively asked before seeing the cases of jars Aric and Fred were carrying. "Wherever did you find those?" She shouted as she started towards them.

"I don't know," Aric replied as he deposited his load onto the island. "Thad and Danny found them somewhere."

As he said that, Thad stood in the open door, wiping his wet feet on the rug. Hearing Kay, he looked up and smiled, saying, "I thought you would like these."

Kay picked up one of the jars and inspected it. "Where did you find them? We searched all the houses."

Thad shrugged and replied, "At the hardware store," as though it were as normal to say today as it once had been.

Kay looked up, "The what?"

Bobbie came in from the back porch with a large pot swinging from one hand. "We need more water for the canner," she said. Then she saw Danny coming through the door with another stack of jars in his arms. "What in the world?" She asked.

"Wait till you see what Danny has," Thad replied.

Danny slid the two cases of jars and the box sitting on top of them onto the counter. Thad took the box and opened it. Reaching in, he took out one of the Tattler lids and handed it to Kay. Her eyes immediately lit up.

"Reusable lids!" She shouted.

Thad pulled back one of the flaps and looked down into the box. "A whole bunch of 'em too."

Kay pulled the box over and looked down into it. Her excitement grew even more, and she hugged Thad. "I don't care where you found them! This is amazing! We've been trying to reuse lids and so many of them have failed to seal. This will really save us!"

Bobbie set her pot down and patted Danny on the ass. "Good job, babe. Where did you guys find them?"

"At the hardware store," he replied. Which naturally made Thad laugh as he shouted, "That's what I said!"

Picking up a case of jars, Kay said, "Well, I don't care where you found them. I'm just glad you did."

Bobbie gave Danny a sideways look, "What do you mean, hardware store?"

He leaned in and kissed her quickly before replying, "Just that. The hardware store."

Bobbie wasn't buying it though. "Hardware store my ass."

"Don't look gift jars in the mouth!" Kay shouted from the sink.

Jess and Mary walked in from the back porch. Though it was very overcast and relatively cool, Jess's forehead was beaded with sweat and her hair clung to it. Brushing it away with the back of her hand, she said, "Kay. These jars aren't sealing." She shook her head and looked at the ceiling in exasperation. "We're going to lose so much."

"Where did all these come from?" Mary asked, a smile beaming across her face.

Kay smiled and nodded her head at Thad. "Your man there found them."

Mary looked at him and gave him a timid smile. "You found all this? We looked in all the houses and didn't find them."

Thad jabbed a thumb over his shoulder. "Me and Danny found them. They weren't in a house though."

Mary stepped over to him and raised herself up on her tiptoes and kissed him on the cheek. Thad's face flushed as he was still getting used to the public affection, not that it was much of a secret to everyone. And to Thad's relief, the small act went unnoticed. Or at least, there were no comments.

Jess lifted a case of quart jars up, saying, "I'm getting these into some boiling water now," and she disappeared out the back door.

"I'll help," Mary called after her, grabbing another case as she followed.

I was startled awake by banging on the door of the truck. Sitting up, I rubbed my eyes and cracked the door open. "What?"

Mike was standing on the step up to the cab. He had a pile of something in his hands and asked, "What size pants do you wear?"

Still trying to come to my senses, I blinked and asked, "What?"

"What size pants?"

Fumbling for the answer, I mumbled, "Thirty-eight, maybe. Hell, I don't know."

Mike picked through the pile of pants draped over his arm and pulled two pair out and handed them to me. "Here, these'll fit you."

I took the MultiCam pants and said, "Thanks. Where the hell did you find these?"

Mike bounced his eyebrows and replied, "While you were sleeping, me and Ted were out getting our scrounge on. The old man said we're getting ready to pull out. But we're going to have to take another route home. All this rain has caused the Santa Fe river to overflow onto I-75. We're going to have to go around it."

Sitting up and stretching as best I could in the cab, I replied, "Great. Let's just drag this shit out for days."

"Aw come on, Morg. It won't be that bad. Little sightseeing."

He stepped down and I pushed the door open. "I've seen those sights before and don't really care to see them again. I'm going to go get a cup of coffee before we leave."

"Better hurry. His Royal Pain in the Ass is already starting to bitch."

"Let him," I replied. Mike headed for the Stryker to hide his loot and I had a second thought about the coffee. Reaching into my pack, I took out my stainless water bottle. There was still water in it and I poured it into one of the Platypus water bags and took the bottle inside with me.

The coffee pot was a large affair, as would be expected in such a place. I put the bottle under it and opened the tap. As the brown liquid flowed in, I held a can of sugar and a can of powdered creamer in either hand, shaking their contents into the bottle as well. When the bottle was full, I wrapped my bandanna around it and shook it to mix well.

Removing a Styrofoam cup from its plastic sleeve, I made a cup for the road and headed back to the truck. Everyone was milling about around the trucks as rain gently but steadily fell from the sky. I found the old man and asked, "So which route are we going to take home?"

He was shining a red flashlight at a map inside a plastic case. "I figured we'd take nineteen. Be the easiest route."

"That's going to take us through a lot of populated areas."

He tossed the map into the front seat of the Hummer and replied, "They're not as populated as they once were."

I grunted. "I guess not." I looked up into the spitting sky and said, "Maybe the rain will keep the Indians at bay. I'll be in the truck," as rain drops pelted me.

Sarge cupped a hand to his mouth and shouted, "Let's saddle up!"

As we were moving towards our vehicles, a Hummer came

racing up and skidded to a stop. Several men climbed out and looked us over. When they didn't say anything, Sarge asked, "Can I help you boys?"

"We heard you might be the folks that stirred a little shit up over in Crystal River."

Sarge nodded. "Maybe just a little."

The man looked back at those with him and replied, "We're with the 14th Brigade Engineers. We were there when the Russians showed up."

Sarge nodded, "Gong Mu Ro."

The man nodded and with a smile and replied, "Rugged. It's not often someone knows our motto."

Sarge pointed at Mike and Ted and said, "Me and these boys did some work with your people in Afghanistan back in '11."

"They were the guys doing all the route clearance," Mike offered.

The engineer held his hand out, "We just wanted to thank you guys. Name's Arnold"

Sarge shook the man's hand and replied, "I don't know why. We could see you guys there. But there wasn't anything we could do for you with the number of Ruskies. We just had to leave you fellers."

Another one of the engineers stepped up and asked, "What the hell did you guys do to that boat?"

Sarge jabbed a thumb at Mike, "Well. This one here," then he pointed at Dalton, "and Gulliver there swam out to the boat and planted a pile of C4 on the shafts."

The engineers laughed. "Yeah," one of them replied, "that really pissed the Russians off. They were caught completely off guard."

"They expected an attack from the air," another said. "Had all kinds of MANPADs ready to shoot down aircraft."

He laughed, "But when that boat erupted and sank. They shit themselves."

"What the hell did they want with that spent fuel anyway?" Ted asked.

"We don't know," Arnold replied. "They were really tight-lipped about it around us. I have to say though, they were decent guys. We had some wounded in their raid and they treated them like their own. Their medics were top notch."

"We watched you boys from the top of that coal elevator," Dalton said. He pointed to one of the men and said, "I remember you. Watched you while one of their medics bandaged you up."

The man worked his arm. "It's still a little sore, but I still have it."

"Once they realized what had happened, they figured you guys were up there," Arnold said. "They sent a team up there and found your hide. Followed your tracks to the water and out. Even back to where you exfilled to your truck."

The man with the injured shoulder said, "Yeah. The boat really torqued their ass. But whoever was on the trigger of that rifle up there, that really pissed them off."

Dalton nodded. "I'm sure it did. I went for the most important looking ones."

"You got him. You took out some scientist of theirs. He was the guy everyone looked to on the movement of the fuel rods. Apparently, their number one job was to protect his ass. They had no idea there would be an attack like that."

"Yeah," Arnold added. "They really wanted your ass."

"Better than they have tried and failed," Dalton said.

"How did you guys get out?" Ted asked.

Arnold took a deep breath. "Well, once the boat was gone, there was nothing else for them to do. Then they got word there was a force moving our direction and they decided to unass the AO."

"They just left you there?" Mike asked.

Arnold nodded. "Yeah. They didn't have the time or resources to deal with us."

"Not to mention they didn't want a fight," another of the engineers added.

"How did they get out?" Sarge asked.

"Boat," Arnold answered. "They had other boats."

"Just not the one they really wanted," Mike said with a smile.

Arnold smiled and shook his head. "No, they damn sure didn't have that one."

"I'd still like to know what they wanted that spent fuel for," Doc said, "but I was happy to see they took care of you guys."

Sarge patted Doc on the back. "Yeah. Doc here wanted to go over and help you guys. Thought I was going to have to tie his ass up." Sarge held his hand out to Arnold. "I'm glad to see you boys are alright and made it out of there. We were worried about you."

Arnold shook his hand, "We appreciate the fact someone knew we were there. We didn't know what was going to happen and were really worried. When your fireworks show started, we knew it wouldn't be long."

I'd stayed out of the way during their talk. Just listening. This was a time for fellow men at arms to talk. I didn't need to be sticking my nose into it. I occupied myself with my coffee. Then, remembering Tony had given me some cigars, I took one out and ran it under my nose. The tobacco had a spicy aroma and I decided, what the hell. A cigar before the sun came up seemed like a good idea.

After cutting the cigar, I rolled it between my thumb and

forefinger while holding the lighter to it. Once it was warmed up, I puffed it to life. The tobacco was intense and aromatic. Maybe a bit heavy of a smoke for this early in the morning, but it was a new world we now lived in, and I enjoyed it nonetheless.

I sipped my coffee and enjoyed the smoke while the conversation continued. I was eager to get on the road, but also knew I wouldn't interrupt them. Once their conversation wrapped up, we'd leave, and fifteen minutes either direction wouldn't much matter. Instead, I thought about our route home.

It would take us through the very path I walked, or much of it anyway. As the smoke drifted up before my eyes, I thought back to the car on the side of the interstate. Seeing it only hours ago, something I never thought I would ever do, brought that day back to me vividly. I could remember walking up and looking over the rise and seeing nothing moving. I remembered sleeping in the car and waking to fogged-up windows in the cold.

I remembered those kids walking down the side of the road, cold and shivering. The girl in nothing more than flip-flops and the kid in a t-shirt. His arms hugged tight to his side against the biting cold that morning. It was a surreal scene to remember, like something out of a Hollywood production. The cold, the heavy wet fog. The silence. Silence like I'd never experienced before. I could see how someone could go catatonic from the shock when you considered the noisy overload our senses were subjected to in our daily lives.

I was brought back to the present by Sarge snapping his fingers in my face. "What the hell are you thinking about? I was talking to you and you acted as though you didn't even hear me."

I shook it off. "Oh, yeah, I didn't. Was just thinking about the day all this started. Seeing my car out on the side of the interstate just kind of brought it back."

Sarge nodded. "Would be kind of odd, seeing it after all that time. We need to get on the road now though."

I puffed the roll of tobacco, that was threatening to expire, back to life. "It was. It's funny, you know. When I think back to that time and compare it to where we are today, it just doesn't seem like we've gone all that far."

Sarge leaned back against the fuel tank of the truck and folded his arms over his chest. "Oh, we've gone a long way, Morgan. Mainly backwards. But we've gone a long way."

"Yeah. I guess you're right. But at least we're all still here." I paused and looked at him. "Can you imagine how many starved to death, or were killed in any thousands of ways?"

He stood up and patted my shoulder. "I can. But let's not dwell on that. It's time to get on the road, ole buddy."

As he turned to walk away, I said, "I'm ready to get back home."

Turning his head to the side, he said, "I put a couple of MREs in the front seat of your truck. We'll eat on the road."

It was still dark when we rolled out the gates of the base. The roads were deserted and we were the only thing moving. It offered both comfort and concern. Comfort in that no one was out. Concern in that we were the only thing moving. But I was certain the presence of that Stryker would prevent any of the locals from even thinking of messing with us. It was the thought of encountering other armor I was worried about.

We started out the way we had come, going through Tallahassee as the sun began to rise, the only indication being the black morphing into gray. I was still nursing the cigar along, intent on smoking it as far down as possible. Between it and the caffeine from the coffee, I was sporting a healthy buzz. Probably not the best idea considering I was dragging several thousand gallons of diesel around behind me.

I watched the side of the interstate, waiting for the car to come into view again. It didn't take long for it to begin to appear, a vague apparition that slowly took on its true form. I thought I'd have a hard time picking it out amongst all the other cars. But as soon as I saw it, I knew. I slowed the truck a bit to get a better look. The doors were open, and it was covered in dust and grime, impossible to see into the windows. But as it slowly passed, I could see in the open driver's door for an instant. There was nothing to see. Other than a memory of a day long ago.

A thin smile cut my lips as Sarge's Hummer veered onto the same off-ramp I had walked down. When the litter-strewn parking lot of the truck-stop came into view, I saw the lowboy tractor sitting and wondered if the old boy ever made it back. The store had been abandoned for a long time, although it looked as if it'd had plenty of visitors. How many people had wandered into it to pick over the leavings of the countless folks before them?

It was like watching a film of my past as we turned onto Perry Highway. It wasn't long before I could see an intersection coming up that I couldn't forget. As we passed the run-down store, I could still see the old men playing dominoes and the kids running around. There was no body lying there, not that I expected to see one. I'm sure someone loved Gold Dollar and came to collect him. That made me think about the entire ordeal. I killed a man and never heard another word about it. But then, he was only the first. There have been many others since. It was a disturbing thought.

This trip was odd. Like Scrooge being guided by the ghosts through Christmas-Past, I too was touring memories from the beginning of our apocalypse. While things looked so much the same, they also looked different. The steady indifferent march of time and nature applied layer after layer of crap, crud and corrosion upon the memories until one day they would no longer resemble what they had been on that day. Vacant were the places, giving no indication of the people and the interactions between them. Some, life and death. Nothing would remain. Eventually, even their memories would be consumed by the steady progression of time.

I was refilling my cup with cold coffee when we passed a store that was like every other one we'd passed. The parking lot was filled with windblown trash. But this one had a memory attached to it. The memory of an old pickup and a fat sow in the bed. That meant James and Edith's place was coming up. It brought up several emotions at the same time.

Happiness at the thought of the old couple. And sadness about what could have happened to them. I decided to find the answer to that question. Picking up my radio, I said, "I need a piss break. Let's stop at this little house up here."

Sarge's Hummer slowing to a stop told me he agreed. I left the truck idling in the road, afraid to shut it down in case it might not restart. An irrational sort of fear that took on a deeper meaning in today's world. Taking my rifle, I got out and started towards the house.

"Where you going?" Dalton asked. "You look like a man on a mission."

I nodded at the house. "I know the people that live here," I replied. Dalton looked at the place, then back at me. I took another look and corrected myself, "that used to live here. I just want to check on them."

Dalton walked with me and asked, "You come through here on your walk home?"

"Yeah. I stayed a couple days with them. They were really nice folks. Reminded me of my grandparents."

I stopped at the edge of the driveway and looked at Mandy's

house. Dalton was in tune and asked, "What happened over there?"

"I stuck a hatchet in the top of a guy's head on that porch." Dalton didn't reply, but started walking towards the house. I followed him around the little fence that separated the two houses.

The yards were overgrown, the grass up to our knees. It was obvious no one had been here in a long time. We stopped at the edge of the porch where the blood stain was still quite visible. Though now it was just a large black stain that could have been caused by anything.

I looked at the front door and said, "In the bedroom back there, I shot his partner in the face. He was trying to rape a young woman. She had two little kids they'd locked in a closet."

I stepped up onto the porch and paused at the open door and looked in. Closing my eyes briefly, I could hear the flick of the Zippo and smell the cigarette as it caught. The couch I'd slept on was still there. Though it looked much worse for wear now. The house was littered with the possessions of one's life. All the things we accumulate during our time on this planet, scattered and, in many cases, broken.

We walked through the house. Stepping over and around things that had been inspected and discarded as either useless or not worth the effort to whoever had come through here. I wondered how many people had been through the place since I left it. I didn't go into the bedroom. But I stopped at the door and looked in. The room had a musty smell of mold that assaulted the nose. The wall was covered in black mold in the same pattern brains and blood had left. Dalton looked over my shoulder into the room. It was obvious to him what had happened. "Well played," he said as he stepped back.

We went outside and stepped through a hole in the fence.

Someone had pushed it down instead of walking around it. The door to Edith and James's house was open as well. Dirt, leaves and other detritus blown in by wind or carried in by both man and beast littered the once tidy entry. I pushed the door open fully, the hinges squeaking audibly as I did.

The house was dark and dank. Unlike Mandy's house with its numerous windows, there were few openings for natural light. I clicked on my flashlight and used it to guide my way into the house. Here too was more evidence of people, many people, having been through the house. I bypassed the living room and went straight to the kitchen. This was Edith's space.

The cabinet doors hung open or were broken off altogether. The oven door hung open slightly and something there caught my eye. A dish towel hung from the handle. I stepped over to it and touched it. It was stiff and rough. I thought for a moment about taking it. I could clearly see Edith swatting James with it. But I decided to leave it where it was, as a testament to the sweet old woman. Though no one would know it but me.

I did a quick inspection of the rest of the house, relieved when I found no bodies. "I want to go out and see if James's tractor is still here." I said as I went out the backdoor.

Here, the yard was like the front. Overgrown and weed-choked. I could see into the little shop behind the house and the tractor was not there. For some reason, it made me feel better. Thinking there was no way James would leave it behind and wherever it was, he must be as well. A naïve idea of course, but it made me feel better. I decided I would remember them as I knew them and not allow my mind to go to that dark place.

"We better get back before that old geezer out there loses his shit," Dalton said.

I nodded, and we started back around the house. "I prefer to think they're alright wherever they are."

Dalton stoically replied, "Better that way."

Sarge was holding court out on the road. Doc came towards us as we approached, asking, "Everything all right?"

"Yeah. I just wanted to see if these folks were still here. I stayed here when I was walking home. They were really nice people."

Doc looked past us to the house and asked, "You want me to go and see if I can find anything?"

I shook my head. "No. I'd prefer to think they moved on and not that they were left to rot in that house."

Doc stared at the house for a minute before replying. "They probably did move on."

I gripped Doc's shoulder and nodded, "That's what I thought too."

"You see everything you needed too?" Sarge asked. I nodded, and he added, "Good. Now if you don't mind, I'd like to get the hell out of this rain and on to the house."

I smiled, "I'm ready. You know, just this side of Perry is the rest area where I ran into Jess."

"Do you need to stop there and take a stroll down memory lane too?" Sarge asked.

I laughed and replied, "We can go as long as your old-ass prostate can hold out."

"Get your ass in that truck," Sarge snorted as he turned to go to the Hummer.

Slipping the truck into gear, I pulled out behind the old man. We continued towards Perry and it wasn't long before I saw the rest area. I thought it looked like shit back then, but damn. It was a real mess now. But there were no people. Seeing it again brought a smile to my face. I could see Jess standing there with that look of desperation. I could only imagine what would've happened to her had I not relented and let her go with me. Even if she was an annoying little shit at that point.

The roadblock into Perry was still there, though it was no longer manned and appeared it hadn't been for a very long time. We had to stop and wait for Mike to drive around us and push some of the cars out of the way with the Stryker. Something he did with way too much enthusiasm.

"Knock that damn caterwauling off!" Sarge shouted into the radio.

"Sorry, boss!" Mike called back. "But this is the most fun I've ever had with my clothes on!"

"That's enough, shithead!" Sarge called back. "Morgan could drive that truck through there sideways!"

Mike did as instructed, kind of. In his own way, he *stopped.* When the Stryker stopped moving, it was sitting on top of a Honda Accord. Mike came back over the radio, laughing, "Stopped, boss!" The howls of laughter from him, Ted and even Doc, I think, were clearly heard. I could just see Sarge's head hanging as he asked, *why me, Lord?*

Mike's handy work had drawn a few people out to see what all the noise was. They stood in the rain taking in the show. As I rolled past them, I waved and a young woman under a broken umbrella smiled and waved back. We didn't see anyone else as we passed through. But Perry looked as though it were inhabited. The Walmart parking lot still had the remnants of the relief efforts from back then. The big military tents were still there, a couple of them. Conex containers sat with their doors open, rusting in the rain.

In rapid succession, we passed the spot on the side of the road where Thad was camped when we came across him. The little lake where Thad had his snake encounter, which brought a smile to my face. And then the little patch of woods that led to the unfortunate encounter where Jess nearly shot my head off. It was a stark reminder of just how long it took me to walk this far. Days and days on the road. And this wasn't even half way yet. There were so many days yet to come when I had made it this far. And yet, here we were in mere hours.

As we passed through Cross City, I picked up my radio and called, "Hey, Sarge, you want to stop by your house?"

No. No reason. Nothing left there.

Ah come on! Mike replied. *Let's stop by for old time's sake!*

No, Sarge replied.

You never let us have any fun. Mike replied.

Mikey, kids are meant to be seen, not heard. Sarge said.

But, you can't see me.

Exactly. And I shouldn't hear your prepubescent ass either!

Prepubescent? Mike asked.

Look it up, Einstein.

We continued on our path in the constant rain. Both a hazard and a comfort. As we passed through Chiefland, I looked for signs of people. Much like in Altoona and Umatilla, I saw what must be the local market. But the soggy tables and tarps covering them sat empty. There'd been other signs of life. In a couple of places, I saw crops planted and some that looked as though they were either in the process of or had already been harvested. It was heartening to see. Life does indeed go on.

We took highway 27 out of Chiefland towards Williston, which would eventually take us to Ocala. From there, I imagined the old man would take highway 40 through the forest to highway 19 and home. It was nearly the exact same route I had taken home. And again, I was struck by the difference. We'd be home today. It took me nearly a month to make the same trip.

I started to think of all the differences. Like the day everything changed. I'd just left a drive-through where I grabbed a burger and a Coke. A burger that contained probably forty or fifty cows. Maybe more. And a Coke, which I do dearly love, made with shit no one should put in their bodies. Though I and millions of others did it daily.

I was riding in a car at seventy-five miles an hour. Just the thought of what it took to make that happen could vapor-lock your brain if you really got into it, and not just everything it took to build the car. But the fuel, the road, the GPS system used for navigation. Millions upon millions of moving parts. But of course, at the moment I was sitting in the cab of a massive truck hauling a load of fuel. So, these things certainly weren't gone. But the idea that everyone would again be zipping down the highway would be decades away, if ever.

And maybe it wasn't all bad. Life was certainly simpler in some ways and immensely harder in others. You didn't have to worry about taxes or light bills. But you had to worry about how to produce light. Budgeting for the grocery bill wasn't so much of a problem. But coming up with food was. And in most cases, the food we now ate was far better for us. It was certainly organic and free of pesticides and chemicals. But it took far more effort to produce.

Unlike the old world, to put calories in required putting calories out. But then, that's the way the natural system works. We perverted that, making it too easy to input calories. We created calorie-dense foods when at the same time we were reducing the need to expend them in every facet of life. And that is why we became so unhealthy.

Between Williston and Ocala, the rain stopped and for an instant, the sun peaked through the clouds. I leaned forward to feel it on my face. To look up and see the sun. It made me smile and brought me out of the funk I was wallowing in. It was kind of funny. When the sun was overhead and baking you,

you wished for it to abate. For some clouds to move in and offer some relief. But go without it for a day or so, and you longed for its return, knowing full well it was going to make you uncomfortable again.

Alright, everyone. Ocala is coming up, and with this break in the rain, things could get western. Keep your eyes open, Sarge called on the radio.

I saw Dalton pop up out of the turret of the Hummer and man the machinegun. This would be the biggest town we drove through. Of course, Tallahassee was bigger, but we never left the interstate. We'd be driving right through the heart of Ocala's south side. Not the best part of town, even in good times.

The rain picked back up as we crossed under I-75. I smiled to myself, watching Dalton as the rain pelted him. He didn't appear to take any notice and continued to scan the sides of the road. Since I wasn't in a position to shoot back if anything happened, I paid attention to the town itself.

Interesting things happen to an urban area once man no longer rules over it. Grass grows in the cracks of the road and sidewalks. Weeds take over everything. They climb buildings, utility poles and anything their tendrils can reach. Seeing grass pushing its way up through the road in large clumps was the most interesting to me, as it was just so improbable in normal times.

But there were other things that showed the presence of people if you looked carefully. Worn paths through lots that were otherwise weed-choked. Lines of drift changed from roads to the shortest distance between two points. As a result, you could tell where people were moving. Even in parking lots and roads, the paths used would be clear of debris. In that light, signs of life were everywhere, though subtle.

It made me wonder how many people were still living in urban areas after all this time. They'd certainly lost their appeal at this point. The entire reason to live in them was ease of life, proximity to work and shopping, and where entertainment opportunities were plentiful. Maybe not so much for Ocala, but cities in general. But all that was gone now. Food had to be grown or hunted, and that required open land. Not to mention, municipal water supplies were a thing of the past. And most cities, in their infinite wisdom, had banned the drilling of private wells. Can't allow people to have even a modicum of self-sufficiency.

In the end, Ocala was like every other urban center we passed. Nearly abandoned and virtually destroyed. In the early days after the *Event,* some people went on an orgy of looting and senseless destruction. That eventually morphed into the desire to simply survive, which sent people into every structure in search of sustenance. This led to further destruction, either from the search itself or possibly in frustration at coming up empty-handed.

In the end, it turned into a long car ride. There were no issues driving through Ocala and we were soon on the other side, headed into the forest once again. And it would be here that we would see the most people. We encountered several people on the road pushing carts or pulling wagons loaded with unidentifiable plant matter or covered loads. They would always move to the side of the road as we approached and watch as we passed with a look of shock or wonder. Some were afraid and took to the woods at our approach.

As the Ocklawaha bridge came into view, I saw Sarge brake. This was the same river I swam to avoid a Stryker company set up on top. And now, I had one following me over it. Granted, I didn't use this bridge on my trek.

What's up?" Mike called.

There's something sitting on top of the bridge, Sarge called back. *Mikey, come around and ease up there and have a look.*

I heard the big armored vehicle's turbine engine spin up as it lurched past me. I leaned forward, trying to see what the old man saw, but could only make out a faint blob. Whatever it was, Dalton was certainly watching it closely. Looking around at the sides of the road, I realized this would be a good spot for an ambush, and I pulled my carbine closer.

Nearly all modern military trucks were sufficiently armored against small arms. So, I felt I was safe in the cab. But one can never be too careful at such moments.

Do not use that main gun unless it's armor! Sarge barked into the radio.

Ah, come on! Mike shouted back.

Don't worry, boss. He's driving. I'm on the coax and Doc is on the deuce, Ted said.

Good. Don't let him near anything with a trigger, Sarge replied. *It takes three men to run that bucket. Make sure he stays on the steering wheel.*

I can do the work of three men! Mike replied.

Yeah, you can. Sarge replied, *Moe, Larry and Curly.* You could hear the laughter on the radio. Hell, I was laughing in my truck.

I'm sure Mike wanted to say something else. But before he could, the fifty-cal manned by Doc started firing on the bridge. It was quickly joined by the coax that fired 7.62 rounds. From where I sat, I watched as tracer rounds skipped off the bridge and whatever else they were hitting. But it was over quickly and everything went quiet except for the engine of my truck rumbling beneath me.

What the hell was it? Sarge asked.

It used to be a truck. They had a roadblock set up. They actually took a shot at us. Can you believe that?" Ted replied.

Did you get 'em all?

Couple of them. Others went over the bridge into the river.

Alright then, let's move out folks. We're too close to home to stop now.

I'll lead the way, Mike replied.

You couldn't lead yourself to a blowjob in a whorehouse with hundred-dollar bills stapled to your forehead. Get that thing out of my way!

Mike drove the Stryker to the other side of the bridge and pulled it off to the edge of the road so we could all pass. As I went over the bridge, I looked at the handy work they had left behind. There was a Toyota pick-up sitting at the peak of the bridge. A bad idea in military terms. Doc had done a hell of a job on it with the fifty. There was no glass left in it and the front fender was shot up. There was no way it would ever run again.

There were two men lying dead on the pavement where they'd taken cover behind the truck. An AK clone of some sort lay beside one of them. The other had a scoped bolt-action rifle. There were a few spent casings scattered around them. An utterly futile attempt against the Stryker. What would possess someone to take a shot at something like that with a damn rifle?

A sense of relief washed over me once on the other side of the bridge. Like some barrier had been crossed and I was now safe. Not that we'd encountered any danger on the entire trip. I couldn't count what just happened as danger to us. I put the rifle back in the middle seat and relaxed.

As we passed through the Mill Dam area, I saw Dalton duck in the turret. When he came back up, he immediately began firing at the sides of the road.

Someone must have just volunteered for the Darwin award

and taken a pot shot at Dalton. "Keep your eyes open", Sarge called out.

I didn't see anything and doubted Dalton had either. But he was certainly giving the vegetation at either side of the road hell because of it. I could imagine some redneck sitting under an oak tree seeing our convoy coming and, out of boredom, taking a crack at it. Just for shits and giggles. He was probably lying behind that tree now, laughing his ass off. But then too, ammo was a precious commodity today and one was not wanting to waste it for entertainment.

Dalton eventually stopped shooting as we continued eastward. Seeing a sign for Juniper Springs, I wondered if those dirty hippies were still there. It would really be an awesome place to stay. All the pure fresh water you'd ever need. Great woods that have never been hunted. Fish, gators, turtles and waterfowl in the river. A land of plenty. Made me want to go in and see. It'd be a great place from which to base operations. And it was for that very reason that I was sure it had to be occupied.

I soon got my answer when the entrance to the park came into view. A large truck, an old military deuce and a half sat blocking it. Several men in various patterns of camo boldly stepped out from behind it and stood watching us as we passed. They talked animatedly amongst themselves. Dalton kept his weapon trained on them and I looked in the rearview mirror to see the big gun on the Stryker moving around on them as well.

"Keep an eye on these clowns", Sarge barked into the radio.

But they kept their weapons slung, making no threatening show. Though, when I passed, they did point excitedly at the tanker. It made me uneasy. Even if they did nothing, now.

"That was one clannish looking crew", Jamie called over the radio.

"I was thinking the same thing", Sarge replied. "They was so inbred, they might as well be a sandwich".

It made me laugh. And he was right. They looked as though their family tree had a transformer hanging from the top of it. They would certainly be a group to keep an eye on. And my tension was ratcheted up when Ian called over the radio.

"A motorcycle just came out of Juniper Springs and is following us. He's staying pretty far back. But he's definitely following us."

"My guess is they're interested in the fuel." Sarge said. "When we make the turn onto nineteen, I'm going to pull off into the woods as soon as I can and me and Dalton will waylay his ass and figure out what he's up to. The rest of you keep going. Just keep it slow in case we need backup."

"Roger that, boss", Ted replied.

And that's just what happened. When we turned onto nineteen, Sarge swerved the Hummer off the road and into the light brush off the shoulder. He pulled into it, knocking it over before backing out, turning around and backing into the hole he created. I laughed at the thought of the ticket he'd be facing in the old days.

We slowed down, but kept moving enough to be making a little distance. It didn't take long before I saw the motorcycle make the turn onto nineteen. The rider was obviously surprised by how close he was to the convoy. He slowed down, which gave Sarge the opportunity he needed. The Hummer raced out of the brush. The rider looked over and saw it, but when he tried to speed out of the way, he lost traction on the wet road.

The truck slammed into the bike, sending the rider sprawling to the ground. I stopped the truck and walked back towards them, watching as Dalton scrambled out of the truck and pounced on the man. I could hear shouting but couldn't tell what was being said. Dalton grabbed something from the man and tossed it into the road. Then I watched as a rifle was likewise sent skittering across the asphalt.

When I got to them, Dalton was holding the man down in the road and Sarge was squatted next to him, talking.

".....to see where you were going is all," the man moaned.

"You said that already," Sarge replied. "But I asked you why?"

To emphasize the question, Dalton applied a little tension to the man's arm. He cried out in pain and said, "We were just curious who you were is all!"

Sarge ran his hand over the back of his neck. "You know. It ain't too neighborly to be following someone like that. Personally, I think you wanted to know where that tanker was going. I saw that deuce you had. Probably needs fuel I would imagine." He tapped the young man on the head and asked, "You were looking to try and score some fuel."

"No!" The man replied. Then Dalton torqued his arm again and he cried out, "Maybe! Maybe!"

Sarge patted his shoulder and replied, "That's what I thought." Then he looked at Dalton and said, "Let him up." Dalton released him, and he rolled onto his back, wincing at the pain in his shoulder as he worked his arm back and forth.

"What do you want to do with him?" Dalton asked.

Sarge looked down the road as he stood up. "He's no threat to us. Let him go. But make sure that bike don't run. I don't want him getting back to his people real fast."

"Aw come on. Don't mess up my bike," the man pleaded.

Sarge keyed his radio, "Mikey, come down here and run this motorcycle over."

"With pleasure!" Mike replied.

I walked over and picked up the rifle Dalton had tossed

away, as well as what turned out to be a Baofeng radio. It was on and I turned it off. "Dalton, did he make a call on this radio?"

He shook his head. "No. He was too busy for that."

The rifle was a nice SKS. I opened the box magazine on the bottom and dropped the rounds out of it before closing it and cycling the action to get the chambered round out. Slinging it over my shoulder, I said, "If you want your rifle and radio back, it'll be at the police department in Eustis. You can come there and try to convince me you weren't up to no good."

"Don't take my rifle. That ain't right. I didn't do anything to you," he complained.

"Maybe not," Sarge replied. "But I got a feeling that was the idea. You can walk back and let your people know, we know what you're up to."

"We'll be distributing some food in town," I said. "You're welcome to come in for some of it." He looked up at me, confusion painted on his face. "We're here to help people," I pointed to the truck and trailer. "We went and got all that to help people. Your folks are welcome to come and get some."

The Stryker came rolling past us. Dalton had pulled the motorcycle out to the far travel lane and Mike never slowed down as he ran over it. Braking, he reversed the huge beast back over it. The man on the ground shook his head, witnessing the destruction of something he couldn't replace.

"Why'd you do that? You offer me food, then crush my bike?"

"I ain't having you follow us to where we're going. You're welcomed to come to town. But not my house," Sarge replied.

The man looked down the road at the tanker. "So, you're taking all the fuel to your house, huh? Gonna share the food, but not the fuel."

Sarge looked up at Dalton, squinting against the spitting rain. "Told you it was about the fuel."

"So, it would appear."

"Look here, sport. That fuel belongs to the Army. Now, if you want to tangle assholes with that, then go for it."

The man looked at the Stryker. "You guys are with the Army?"

Sarge looked at me and shook his head before answering him. "Are you always this fucking stupid? Or is today a special occasion? Of course, we are! You can't buy those things at Walmart, shithead!"

Dalton reached down and pulled the man to his feet. "Time for you to kick rocks, bud."

The man paused for a moment, looking around. Dalton drew his pistol to encourage him and the man raised his hands and started walking away. Sarge looked at me and said, "You guys go on to the ranch. We'll catch up. I'm just going to give this shitbird a minute to get gone."

I nodded and headed back to the truck. Climbing up into the cab, I released the airbrake and put the truck in gear. Looking back, I saw Ian was right behind me and the Stryker was rolling to catch up. Home was less than a half hour away and I couldn't wait to get there. I wanted a nap. I wanted to see Mel and the girls. I wanted to get home, again. It was kind of funny to be returning along this same route again. At least this time I was driving.

I looked over at the Pittman Center as I passed it. A smile started to spread across my face as I saw my road ahead. It only grew wider the closer I got. Before I knew it, I was turning onto it. The tanker was huge, and it could easily become stuck back in our neighborhood. I could only think of one way to park it, so I could get it out.

Waving at the smiling Guardsmen as I passed the bunker, I stopped the truck and backed into the road Sarge and Thad lived on. Getting the trailer onto the road, I backed down it for a way before pulling forward and parking it on the right side of the road. That way, it would be easy to turn left and leave when the time came. The airbrakes applied with a hiss and I shut it down.

As I got out, a couple of the Guardsmen that were manning the bunker walked over. They were eyeing the truck up and down. "Where did you get this?" One of them asked.

"Eglin," I replied.

Wallner, one of the Guardsmen, whistled, "Damn, that's a long way."

"Yeah," his partner replied. "And, so you know, Sheffield is pissed. He came by to check on us, and when he found out you guys were gone, he got really torqued off. Told us to leave, but we told him we were staying."

Wallner laughed. "Yeah. We eat way better here."

"If you guys think this truck is the shit," I turned and pointed down the road, "Check this out." I could hear the Stryker; and in a moment, it turned onto our road.

"Holy shit!" Wallner exclaimed. "How the hell did you get that?"

I shrugged, "I don't know. Something the old man did."

The truck Jamie was driving was right behind the armored vehicle and turned onto our road as well. The Guardsmen were getting excited now.

"What the hell is all this?" One of them asked.

Wallner nodded at the tanker and asked, "Is that fuel?"

I smiled, "Damn straight."

He was laughing. "I can't believe you got all that! A Stryker! Diesel! I can't believe it."

"What's in that truck?" The other Guardsmen asked.

"That's all kinds of stuff. I'm not totally sure. I gave them a list of what I wanted. We'll have to open it up and see."

As we were talking, Sarge's Hummer rounded the corner as well. The rain had stopped, though the evening sky was heavily overcast. But the reprieve was nice. Word was getting around we were back and people began to show up. Perez was one of the first ones.

He went straight to Jamie and wrapped his arms around her. "I was worried about you, chica."

She patted his back. "I'm fine, poppie. It was a milk run. No trouble."

He smiled. "Good." Then he rubbed the stubble on his chin. He'd given up shaving. "You, ah, got anything for me in there?"

Jamie took a deep breath and let it out. "You know how hard those are to find? I mean. It's like looking for a virgin in a whorehouse." Perez's shoulders dropped. Jamie smiled and climbed up onto the side of the truck and reached in, retrieving a bag. She hopped down and handed it to him.

Perez opened the bag and his face lit up. "Holy shit!" He exclaimed as he pulled a carton from the bag and tore it open. In an instant, he had a cigarette clenched in his teeth, holding a lighter to it. He took a long deep drag, holding the smoke in for a moment before letting it out through his nose. "Thank you, chica. I was out. I was dying."

"You were an asshole," Wallner said.

"You were grumpy as hell!" Jess announced.

Seeing her, I smiled. She was with Taylor and Lee Ann. "I wish you'd been with me," I said to her. "We drove back on our route. I saw the rest area and Perry. The spot where we found Thad. All of it."

She was thinking about what I'd said. After a moment, she shook her head. "No. I'm glad I wasn't there. I don't need to see any of that again. But I'm glad you guys made it back."

I smiled at her. "Me too." Then I looked at Taylor and asked, "How's mom?"

"She's good. She's at home. She knows you're back."

"You guys got a lot of stuff," Lee Ann said. "That tank is super cool. Can I get in it?"

"You want to see inside?" Mike asked. With a huge smile on her face, she nodded. He waved them on, "Come on. You can check it out." Taylor went as well, and Mike opened the rear doors and started explaining the ammo storage system and showing them the inside.

I leaned against the truck as everyone talked. Doc walked up to me and leaned beside me. "Man, am I glad to be back here. I don't like doing shit like that anymore."

"Yeah, me neither," I replied.

He reached into a dump pouch on his belt and took something out, holding his hand out to me. "Here. Got you something."

I held my hand out and he dropped a can of Copenhagen into it. I was stunned. "Damn. Where in the hell did you find this?" I was inspecting the can. It was still sealed. Turning it over, I saw it had a manufacture date that was nine months old. But I didn't care, as I pulled my knife and cut the can open.

"Just a little horse trading. I saw it and thought of you. Guy that had it kept it stored in a freezer. They said they salvaged a truck off the road that was packed with product from the US Tobacco Company. He had a lot of it."

Putting a pinch in, I said, "I really appreciate it, man. Thanks. What do I owe you for it?"

He waved me off, "You don't owe me." He stood up and slapped me on the back. "Happy to do it."

He walked away towards the Stryker and was intercepted by Jess. Even from where I stood, I could see the excitement in her. She made a bad job of hiding it. She laughed and leaned in, bumping him with her shoulder. It made me smile. Doc was a good guy and I thought of Jess as another daughter. A step-daughter that was kind of annoying. But a daughter, nonetheless. For his part, it was obvious Doc was just as interested. But he was respectful and didn't do anything inappropriate, which increased my opinion of him.

I walked out to where everyone was gathered up. Sarge was talking to Wallner. I could hear him cussing about Sheffield's visit. I interrupted his tirade, "I'm going home. I'm tired. This shit can wait until tomorrow."

"I'm with you," Sarge replied. "We'll go through this load tomorrow, then take it to town."

"Sheffield's going to give you an ear full," Wallner said.

"That's alright. I got something for him. But he should be happy with everything we've brought. We've got food for the folks in town."

I didn't know what he was talking about and didn't care. I was tired and just wanted to go to bed. "Alright. Tomorrow then," I said.

The air smelled especially clean as I walked towards the house. With all the rain the last several days, the air was scrubbed clean. But there was also an earthy aroma as well rising up from the ground as my boots squished into the sodden earth. It made for a pleasant mix. It was also very quiet. The only sound was the drips from the trees thudding into the saturated ground.

As dusk fell early because of the cloud cover, the dogs came trotting past me on their nightly patrol. They paused for a moment as they strode by. Just long enough for me to pat their heads before continuing on their way. They may be useless, but they did manage to bring a smile to my face whenever I saw them. Even if it was just them lying on the porch.

There was a dim glow coming from the windows as I came through the gate. I thought it odd. Then I remembered it had been raining for days. The solar system was probably very low. Coming through the door, I was greeted by the dim yellow light of oil lamps. There were two burning in the living room. Little Bit was lying on the sofa with a stuffed bear in her arms, asleep.

Mel was sitting in the chair with her feet up on the ottoman, also asleep. She looked up at me, bleary eyed, and smiled. I leaned my rifle in the corner and went over to her, leaned down and kissed her head.

"Are you hungry? You want me to fix you something?" She asked, always willing to feed me.

I kissed her head again. "No, babe, I'm tired. I want to go to bed."

"I'll put Little Bit to bed and I'll join you."

"You get ready, I'll put her to bed," I replied.

As she got up, I went around and picked Little Bit up in my arms. She half woke up and looked at me, smiling and hugged my neck. I kissed her head and carried her to her bed and laid her down. "I love you, daddy," she said as I pulled the sheet up over her.

She rolled over on her side, facing away from me, already back asleep. I kissed her head, "Love you too, Little Bit."

I stayed to watch her for a moment before quietly leaving her room. Mel was coming out of the bathroom when I came into our room. She was carrying one of the LED lanterns. As I took my vest off, I asked, "Are the batteries dead?"

"They're really low," she replied as she placed the lantern on the nightstand. "I had to unplug the fridge."

"I'll hook up a generator in the morning to charge it back up," I replied as I sat down on the edge of the bed.

"How was your trip?" She asked as she slid under the cover.

Untying my boots, I said, "It was actually good. Very uneventful." I stood up and slid my pants off before lying down on the bed. "We drove back on the same route I walked to get home."

"Really?" She replied, leaning on her elbow.

I was staring at the ceiling and shook my head. "It was really weird. Seeing all those places again. I mean, I saw my car. It was still sitting on the side of I-10."

She reached over and rubbed my chest. "Really? What'd it look like?"

I snorted, "Like shit. The doors were open. It was dirty as hell."

"Well, you're home now."

"Again," I quipped.

She laid her head down on the bed beside me. "All that matters is that you're still here."

I leaned over and kissed her. "Yes it is. Yes it is."

CHAPTER 6

I SLEPT IN A LITTLE LATE. Mel was already up when I came out of the bedroom. Little Bit was sitting at the table eating a pile of pancakes. I had to take a second look to make sure I was seeing what I thought I was.

"Where'd those come from?" I asked.

"Mommy made them. I have honey on them," she replied as she stuffed an overloaded forkful into her mouth. Adding, "They're so good!"

I stepped into the kitchen to see Mel at the stove cooking yet more griddle cakes. "You hungry?" she asked.

I hadn't considered it, but the smell of them was indeed making me ravenous. "Yes, I am," I replied as I returned to the table and took a seat.

Mel slid a pile of cakes in front of me and I picked up the jar of honey and poured a generous portion on top of them. "Where did this come from?" I asked.

"From the stuff you got yesterday. Everyone is out there going through it. There's so much. Things I didn't think we'd see again."

I packed the hot cakes into my mouth and asked, "Like what?"

"Feminine pads. Disposable pads. I can't believe you remembered."

I looked at her sideways. "I'm married to you and have three daughters. Why wouldn't I remember?"

She smiled and replied, "I guess you're right. Want some tea?" With my mouth full, I couldn't talk, but nodded my head. She went to the fridge and poured me a glass.

Noticing the light was out, I swallowed the wad of dough and said, "I'll go out and start the generator in a minute."

"Finish your breakfast," she replied as she set the glass down in front of me.

I pointed with my fork towards the door. "Who's out there working on that?"

"Everyone. They're going through it to see what's in it, setting some aside for us and loading the rest to take to town."

"Why didn't someone wake me up?" I asked.

She shrugged. "There's enough people out there. You were asleep, so I left you alone."

"Daddy, I want these for breakfast every day!" Little Bit shouted.

"I told you," Mel replied to her, "we can't have them every day."

"But I love them!" Little Bit replied as she forced another forkful into her mouth, smearing honey on the side of her face as she did.

I smiled at her and rubbed her head. "They are good, aren't they?" She smiled broadly and her head bobbed up and down in an exaggerated display of agreement.

I finished my breakfast and carried the plate to the sink. When I turned on the water to rinse the plate, nothing happened. "Water's out too," Mel said.

"Alright. I'll go start the generator right now. Then I'm going to see what's going on."

Little Bit began to wiggle out of her chair. "I'm going with Daddy!"

I went outside and pulled the generator out of the shed. The gauge showed it was about half-full, enough to get the charge back up now that the sun was shining through scattered clouds. I checked the oil quickly, then started it, relieved when it fired up on the second pull. While it warmed up, I connected the cord to it and flipped the breaker on. The generator took up the load nicely and was soon running smoothly.

Back inside, Little Bit was dressed and ready to go. She had on a large straw hat, much too big for her small head. I smiled at her and asked, "You ready to go?"

"Yep!" She replied.

I went into the bedroom and put my shoes on. I didn't feel like wearing that vest, and instead, I put a holster on my belt and secured the Springfield in it. Walking back into the living room, I called out, "We'll be back in a little bit. The generator is running, so you should be able to run water."

"Okay," Mel replied, "see you later."

We walked down the road, holding hands. The sun felt good on my face after not seeing it for so many days. I hoped it meant the tropical depression had moved on. As we made our way up the road and the bunker came into view, I could see the trucks. And it was quite a sight. There were mounds of goods stacked around them. More than I thought could possibly fit in the trucks we carried it here on.

Pallets had been scrounged up from somewhere and all the supplies were being sorted and stacked. Sarge was sitting on the hood of his Hummer watching the work. It was Kay who was in the thick of it. She was directing where to put things and keeping a running tally on a notepad. And it seemed everyone was there.

I went over and leaned on the hood of the Hummer. Little Bit didn't hesitate and dove right into the work. "Damn," I said. "I didn't think there was that much."

Sarge looked over and said, "You told him to give until it hurts. Looks like he did."

"If they gave us this much, can you imagine how much they actually have?"

He pointed at a pallet of fifty-pound flour sacks. "This is a good sign, that there's this much coming in."

I looked at the bags. On the side of one of them, it read, A Gift from America. That struck me. It was the sort of thing you'd see on TV in disaster regions around the world. Or where a population was starving. And yet, here it was.

"Looks like that was already here."

Sarge nodded. "Maybe. It could also have been stored overseas someplace. But that rice," he pointed to another pallet full of huge sacks of rice, "that came from Japan."

"Kind of funny how things come full circle. After WW2, we helped feed them. Now they're doing it for us."

Sarge spat onto the ground and replied, "The world ain't all bad, Morgan ole buddy." I grunted in reply and walked over to see what all we'd been given.

The variety of items was impressive. I had asked for a lot of it, but some, I hadn't. There was yeast and baking powder from England, as well as beans. There was sugar from India that I was sure found its way here through England as well. In addition, there were sacks and sacks of beans labeled with India as the country of origin. It was interesting to see.

There were also sacks of Costa Rican coffee and Mexican corn. That one kind of confused me as I was sure they weren't in the mood to help us at all. But who knows how it found its way here. There were also stacks of boxes of diapers from Turkey. The boxes had a company label on them, Vora; but other than that, they were generic looking. The same label appeared on boxes of sanitary pads. And the amount was impressive. Obviously, they wouldn't last forever, but in the near term, they would make the women's lives in the area easier. Along the lines of diapers, there was also powdered baby formula. Something I'd thought of because of Fred.

Mike was cutting open a case and I walked over to see what was in it, as I couldn't read the writing on the outside of the box. He removed a can and looked at it, asking, "What the hell is this?"

I looked at the can. It was a little bigger than a tuna can and had a picture of a horse on it. I took one from the case and examined it. It was from Romania. There was no pull top; it would require a can opener. But I had a pretty good idea what was in it. "I think it's horse meat," I said.

"No shit?" Mike mumbled while he examined the can. "I've never had horse meat before."

"It's good. I had horse steak once in Wyoming."

He looked at me, "Really? What'd it taste like?"

I shrugged, "Kind of like beef. But it was way more tender. You could cut it with a fork."

He grunted and dropped the can into his pocket. "I'm going to try this shit."

And there was more. Doc and Jess were going through the medical supplies. Everything from bandages and bottles of alcohol to bags of IV fluids and infusion sets. Doc was busy sorting the items into different stacks. One for dry goods and one for wet.

"Hey, Ronnie, are these antibiotics?" Jess asked, holding a small box in her hand.

He took it and looked at it. "No. This is a steroid. Didn't expect to see any of this."

I reached into the open box and removed a package. It was made in Israel and was just the beginning of the drugs we found that had been made there. In the end, there were indeed antibiotics. As well as anti-inflammatory drugs, pain killers, muscle relaxers, anti-diarrheal medicines and one that surprised even Doc.

"Holy crap," he exclaimed, inspecting a small box.

"What is it?" Jess asked.

"It's chloroquine. A malaria drug."

"I didn't think we had malaria here in Florida," I said.

"There were a couple of cases back in the 90s. But I thought they had it under control. Kind of weird they sent this."

"Maybe they just had a lot of it. Sent it as a precaution," Jess said.

"Maybe," Doc replied as he tossed it into a box of medications.

"You know, with all this rain, in a week or so the mosquitoes are going to explode," I said.

"Yeah. But that doesn't mean there will be a malaria outbreak. It has to be here first, and I really don't think it is."

"Look at this!" Fred shouted as she looked down into a very large box. She reached in and picked up a pair of white sneakers. They were simple canvas shoes, much like the old school Converse All Stars. "Anyone need shoes?"

Sarge hopped off the Hummer and walked over to inspect them. "We need to look through there and get a pair for these youngins. A size or two up for growing years too."

"Good idea," I said and called Little Bit over. She still had good shoes and we had a couple sizes up for her as well. Hand-me-downs from her sisters. But they were valuable now.

I sat her down on a sack of rice and took her shoes off. Fred handed me what she thought was her size and I tried them on her. She jumped up and pranced around, happy in her new shoes. I wanted to box them back up, but she ran off.

"I guess she's keeping them," I said. "I wanted a couple sizes up, so she'd have some later."

Fred dug back into the box and pulled out another pair. "Here. These will fit her later."

I took the shoes and said, "I feel kind of bad taking two pair for her when so many others need them."

"Morgan," Fred replied, "If it weren't for you, no one would have new shoes. Keep them."

"She's right, Morgan," Sarge said. "You thought of way more than any of us would have."

"I'm amazed they had all this stuff," I replied.

"Fawcett said they're starting to get a lot of aid in now that the military had control of the ports. The biggest problem they're having is distributing it. He was kind of relieved you came. That's why they sent so much with us. He knew you'd get it out to folks."

"Are things getting back to normal, then?" I asked.

"Normal?" Sarge asked. "Normal will be a long time in coming. But they are starting to stabilize a little bit. Just as soon as they round up those Russians and Cubans, they'll be able to focus on getting the country restored. They have engineers working on some things now, but they just don't have the manpower."

"How are they deciding where to focus their efforts then?" Aric asked.

Sarge smiled. "They're looking for the spark, that's how he put it. Places that are trying to get back on their feet. So much of the country is a lawless land, wilderness as he put it."

"Are we a spark?" Fred asked.

Sarge nodded. "Indeed, we are." He swept his hand out over the mounds of supplies still to be sorted. "That's why all this is here. And there will be more coming."

A clapping of hands got everyone's attention. We all looked up to see Kay standing with her hands on her hips. "Come on now. This isn't going to sort itself. The sooner we get it sorted, the sooner we can take it to town."

"Back to work!" Sarge barked.

I wandered around, inspecting things to get an idea of all that was sent. I found Dalton stuffing cans of sardines into a backpack. He looked at me and grinned, "I love these things." Looking at a can in his hand, he lamented, "Just wish they had 'em in hot sauce."

I shivered. "Man, I had a bad experience with those once."

He laughed. "Yeah, it's always a good idea to eat ice cream afterwards so you have something to look forward to when you're sitting on the shitter."

With his bag full, he slung it over his shoulder and walked back over to where Ted was inventorying the trailer-load of ammo. I walked over to see what sort of goodies the old man had managed to get for us.

"Anything exciting over here?" I asked Ian.

"All this shit is exciting. You just don't want to be on the exciting end of it is all."

"The old man was thorough," Ted announced. "He got everything from hand grenades to 105 rounds for the Stryker. We'll never shoot all this shit up."

I looked around at the crates of ammo and replied, "I sure as hell hope not. If we do, it's a bad damn day."

Dalton chuckled, "Ain't that the truth." He opened a can

of grenades and took several out, then opened another can and removed detonators for them.

Ted wagged a finger at him. "Do *not* arm that shit standing here!"

"I'm not, I'm not. This is just for my personal collection."

Ted waved him off. "Close that can and get those out of here."

Dalton dropped it all into his pack and carried it off a distance where he set it down under an oak tree before returning to the inventory. Looking over the ammo cans, cases and crates, I saw one that caught my eye. While I didn't speak military shorthand, it was obvious it was full of smoke grenades. I opened it and indeed, it was red smokes. I took a couple out and stuffed them into my dump pouch.

With this task well in hand, I told Sarge I was going to take care of some other things. He said they had it under control and that we would be taking the supplies to town tomorrow. I told him I'd see him later and went over to Thad, who had been doing most of the heavy lifting. I asked if he wanted to go for a ride with me.

He looked around and smiled, "I'd rather stay here and finish this," he replied.

I patted his shoulder. "No problem, buddy. I'll get someone else. But I'm going to borrow your little truck."

"You're more than welcome to it. It ain't mine anyway."

I laughed, "It's as much yours, if not more than it is anyone else's."

"I'll go with you," Aric piped up.

"Cool. Let's go."

While I collected Little Bit, he went and gave Fred a kiss, telling her he'd be back. Little Bit protested, "I don't want to go. I want to stay here and help."

"I have to leave, kiddo. We gotta go."

"You can leave her here," Kay said. She patted Little Bit's head, adding, "She's my special helper."

"You sure?" I asked.

"Of course, I am. You go on. Tell Mel that I'll bring her home later."

Little Bit smiled up at her, "Thanks, Miss Kay."

"You be good for Miss Kay now."

"I will!" She smiled back.

"Where are we going?" Aric asked.

"I want to go up to Save-A-Lot and take some parts out of their light fixtures."

With a look of confusion, he asked, "For what?"

"I'm going to build something that might help keep the houses a little cooler. Create a little airflow."

He rolled his eyes. "Anything would be an improvement."

We walked towards Danny's house where the little truck was parked. On the way, I stopped by the house to tell Mel we were running to Umatilla real quick and that Little Bit was with Kay. She said she was about to walk down to see if she could help anyway.

"Ok, babe," I said. "We'll be back in a while."

When I came out of the house, I could hear the little truck running, and I walked over. At the back of Danny's shed, I grabbed a ten-foot step ladder and slid it up on top of the lightbar of the truck and tied it with a piece of rope from the bed. Aric was sitting in the driver's seat as I climbed in. "To the market, James."

"Right oh!" he quipped as he pulled out.

"How are you going to make something out of light fixtures to cool the house?"

"You take two-liter bottles and cut them in half. Then, you

insert the small neck through something, in this case, the lens from the fluorescent light fixtures. And then you secure them. When a breeze pushes air into them, it compresses it, cooling it."

He thought about it as he drove. Then he looked at me and asked, "Really?"

"Yeah. It's simple thermodynamics."

He shrugged. "If you say so, professor."

"Hey, let's stop by the Market in Altoona. I want to let them know to spread the word that we'll be giving out food."

"Good idea," he replied.

He wheeled into the market and pulled up beside Mario's booth and I waved him over to the window. "What's up?" He asked as he walked up.

"Do me a favor," I said, "start spreading the word that there will be a food distribution here in the morning. We're going to do one here, as well as in Umatilla and Eustis.

"I'm going up to Eustis later. I'll deliver the news," Mario replied.

"Food? What kind of food?" Shelly asked.

"All kinds of stuff," Aric replied.

"Everything from flour and rice to canned meat. Plus, baby formula, diapers and some other stuff," I said.

"No shit? Where the hell did all that come from?" Mario asked.

"We went up to Eglin Air Force Base and got it all there. I was surprised they gave us so much."

"So, are things getting back to normal?" Shelly asked.

"Not yet. But we're starting to get aid from other countries now."

Mario shook his head. "Imagine that. The US needing international aid."

"Does seem like we're in an alternate universe now, doesn't it?" I asked.

"To say the least," Shelly replied.

"We got work to do. I'll see you guys tomorrow," I said.

Aric gave the peace sign, saying, "Later, tater."

We rolled up into the parking lot of Save-A-Lot and parked the truck right in front of the doors. I told Aric to grab the keys. I didn't want to come out and find our ride home gone. He agreed, "That would suck."

We carried the ladder in and set it down to have a look around. The place was totally devoid of anything that resembled food. As a matter of fact, it was missing anything that wasn't nailed down. I had to laugh when I looked at the busted cash registers. The thought of someone trying to break into them for something as useless as cash.

"What in the world were they going to do with it if they found any?" Aric asked.

"When was the last time you saw any?" I asked with a chuckle.

"Last night. I actually have a couple of bills in my wallet."

I stopped and turned to look at him and asked with a laugh, "What the hell are you doing with a wallet?"

"Sentimental," he shrugged.

I looked under the counters of the register stands.

"What are you looking for?" Aric asked.

"Bags, I'm looking for plastic bags. Check the others and see if there are any," I said as I pulled a full box of plastic shopping bags out and laid it on the belt that used to carry items to the cashier. It made me laugh, everything had to be made as easy as possible.

We found four and a half cases of bags and carried them

out to the truck. "What are you going to do with these? More thermodynamics?"

"No," I laughed. "We can use these to distribute the food and stuff. It'll make it easier."

"Good idea," he nodded.

After going through the store, partly to make sure no one was there, I set the ladder up and asked Aric to keep a lookout. "You're here for security," I said.

"I got your back," he replied as he turned to face the front of the store.

The bracket holding the lens in is held in place with two small clips. I used my Leatherman tool to open them because they can be a little stubborn and I wasn't going to close them, so I didn't care if I tore them up. Once open, the lens was easily pushed out. I let them fall to the floor. Moving from fixture to fixture, I removed about a dozen of them.

After carrying them out to the truck, I returned and picked up a few two-liter bottles I saw lying on the floor. Then I returned for the ladder and carried it out to the truck and secured it to the lightbar.

"You ready, boss?" Aric asked.

"I'm not your boss. But I am ready," I corrected him. "Let's ride over to the Umatilla market so I can let those folks know about the food tomorrow."

We rode up to the market. It was busy after so many days of rain. People were out looking for food. We parked, and I got out and walked over to the old fuel island where the majority of tables were set up. Getting to the middle of the island, I called, "Hey, everyone, listen up! Tomorrow before noon, there will be a distribution of food and other supplies here! Let as many know as you can to be here!"

I was bombarded with questions from the few dozen people

gathered. But I waved them off, "I'm not going to answer questions now! Just be here tomorrow!"

As I walked back to the truck, I was followed by the crowd as they continued to shout questions at me. I didn't respond to any of them. Instead, I climbed back in the truck and we left, headed back towards the house. We stopped where everyone was still at work on the supplies. I grabbed a couple of boxes of the bags and carried them over to where Kay was still working on her inventory.

Setting them down on a stack of boxes, I said, "Kay, I thought we could use these to break the food down. People probably won't have bags or anything to put the rice and flour in, so I thought this would be a way we could hand out smaller portions."

Kay picked up one of the bundles of bags. The tops of them had a tab that was heat-sealed together. She pulled one loose and shook it open. "This is a great idea! We can actually prepare individual bags. This will make it a lot easier to pass out prepackaged bundles."

"That would take a lot of work," Sarge said.

"Maybe," I replied. "But I stopped by Altoona and Umatilla to tell people we'd be handing out food tomorrow. I was bombarded with questions and chased out of the parking lot."

"What in the hell would you do that for? We're taking all this to Eustis," Sarge replied.

"And just what good does that do the people out here? How the hell are people supposed to get to Eustis? Then back with the food? Sure, they can walk. But why not just stop on the way and hand it out?"

"He's right, Linus," Kay said, supporting me.

He shook his head. "You know how long it will take to put that together?"

"Are we on someone's schedule?" Kay asked. Her question caught him off guard and he didn't respond immediately. "We have all the time we need."

Sarge thought about it for a minute, before nodding his head. "You're right. We can take some time to organize that. But we need to go through this stuff and separate a portion out for Sheffield's people before we start portioning it out."

"That's a good idea. We can separate theirs out first. Then the rest we break up," Kay replied. Then she looked at me and asked, "Can you find more of these bags? We'll need a lot of them."

"Maybe. We can go look for sure," I replied.

She smiled, "Good. The sooner, the better." She made me smile. As though it was just a matter of fact that I was going to be able to go out and get them. She clapped her hands, "Alright, everyone. We're going to start preparing bags of supplies. We need to put flour in one, rice in another. Those can go into a separate bag into which we put other things, like the canned meats, beans and bottles of cooking oil."

"I think we should make a separate one for the hygiene stuff," Jess said. "Put in a bar of soap, tube of toothpaste, shampoo, that sort of thing."

"And another bag with diapers and formula," Fred added. The reasoning obvious, coming from her.

Sarge ambled up beside me. His arms were folded over his chest. "You realize how long this shit is going to take, don't you? What a can of worms you just opened?"

"You think Sheffield would've done a better job?"

Sarge scratched his beard. "At least it would have been his problem."

I laughed. "Lazy ass. I'm going to go see if we can find some more bags for Kay."

The work shifted. The group started setting up stations to divide the foodstuffs and other items up. I found Aric and asked him if he wanted to go for another ride. He was more than eager. As we walked back towards the little truck, I stopped to talk to Mel.

"Hey, we're going back up to town to look for more bags."

She was working with Mary. They were opening boxes of hygiene products and setting them out in a row to make preparing the bags expedient. She looked up and smiled, "Okay."

Aric was in the driver's seat when I got to the truck. As I climbed in, he asked, "Why don't you drive your Suburban anymore?"

As he started the truck, I replied, "The batteries are dead."

"Aw, that sucks. No way you're going to find a replacement."

"No, probably not. But I'm going to try and restore them. It'll last awhile anyway."

As we pulled out of the neighborhood, he asked, "How in the hell are you doing that?"

"You can do it with Epsom salt."

"Didn't know that."

We rode up to the Publix on the outskirts of Eustis and parked on the curb. The automatic doors stood open and we went into the dark store. Using flashlights, we went through the register stands just as we did in Save-A-Lot. We found several bundles of bags, many scattered on the floor. Putting them in a pile by the door, I suggested we check the back of the store. I had worked for Publix when I was in high school. Of course, in those days we used paper bags. But the extra bags were always stored in the stockroom.

Naturally, the stockroom was even darker than the store. "This is like something out of a horror movie," Aric said as he held his rifle at low-ready.

I chuckled, "You afraid of Jason?"

"That shit ain't funny. Never did like horror movies."

In the stockroom, we found a grocery cart and I pulled it along with us. It banged and squeaked as we moved through the darkened corridor. There was light at the far end, and as we got closer, it was obvious it was natural light. Rounding the corner, we saw the rear roll-up door where the trucks were unloaded was standing open. This part of the stockroom was littered with debris, both natural and trash. Animal tracks were everywhere in the dust which made me immediately think it would be a good place to set up traps if one were really hungry.

In the Before, there were numerous books, websites, YouTube channels and other outlets dedicated to bushcraft and primitive skills. I was a part of that community as well. But I also realized there were a lot of manmade environments out there. Even in the post-apocalyptic world, such as we're living in now, there would be a whole lot of it left behind that could be useful to the savvy survivor. Fortunately, we were not living such a hardscrabble life and not relying on trapping rodents in grocery store stockrooms.

But, it made me think of the countless posts on forums. The numerous online articles, as well as those in magazines that promoted the idea of bugging out to the wilderness when the SHTF. But seldom was there one talking about surviving in the urban landscape; and even those that were, I thought, approached it from the wrong angle.

I often thought about surviving in an urban area. This grocery store, for example, could be a lifesaver to the cunning survivor. The roof of this store was probably holding numerous pockets of fresh water from the recent rains. Not to mention, it was also where the air handling units were, and they were probably large enough to use as a shelter. Utilizing the roof access ladder inside the stockroom, you could get to the roof and have water and shelter. A stove could be fashioned to keep a fire above what I'm sure was a rubber membrane roof. It could offer shelter, water and security. But it could also be a trap with only one access and exit, pros and cons.

We found a stack of bags still in their boxes. We piled them onto the cart and rolled them to the open door. "I'll go get the truck," Aric said as he turned and headed for the front of the store.

"I'll go with you. We should stay together. Safer that way."

He nodded. "Good idea."

As we walked out to the doors, I saw someone looking through the truck. Aric saw him as well and I grabbed his arm. "Let's just wait a minute and see if he's alone."

The man sat in the driver's seat of the truck. He was going through the glovebox, pulling the visors down and checking them. Finding nothing, he sat there for a minute looking around. Then he got out and lifted the seat to inspect behind it. That was when I told Aric to move. We'd not seen another person, and while his head was buried behind the seat, we quickly moved out the door.

With our weapons shouldered we stepped wide around the truck, getting a clear view of him. A rifle was leaning against the side of the truck. I hoped he didn't reach for it. Satisfied with his inspection behind the seat and coming up empty-handed, he stood up and flipped the seat back. Then he saw us. The look on his face said it all. We had the drop on him and he knew it.

"Step away from the truck," Aric said.

"And don't think about reaching for that rifle," I added.

He half raised his hands and stepped back. "Easy, fellas. I didn't mean no harm."

"Maybe not," Aric replied.

"But I would imagine that if the keys were in that thing, we'd be walking home," I said.

The man shrugged. "I was just checking it out." He nodded at me, "You the Sheriff?" He asked.

I nodded, "I am. Now keep backing up. You got any other weapons on you?"

"I have a pistol."

Aric and I both moved in behind the truck. "Turn around and put your hands on your head," Aric said. He did as instructed and Aric looked at me, "Cover me and I'll go get it."

I nodded and called out, "Don't move and there won't be any trouble. He's going to come get that pistol off you. We'll give it back when we leave."

The man half turned his head and asked, "You promise?"

"I do, now face away." Again, he did as instructed.

Aric moved quickly to him. He pushed his carbine around to his back to hang from the sling, and drew his pistol. Keeping it close to his body, I heard him ask, "Where is it?"

The man dipped his chin, "It's in my waistband."

Aric reached around him and removed what turned out to be a snub-nosed revolver, stuffing it into a cargo pocket. Using his free hand, he did a quick pat down on the man before looking over his shoulder and announcing, "He's clean now." I relaxed and stepped out from behind the truck.

The man looked over his shoulder and asked, "Can I put my hands down now?"

"Yeah. You're good," Aric replied as he holstered his pistol.

"What are you guys doing?" The man asked.

"We're getting grocery bags," Aric replied.

"What in the hell for?"

"We're putting together food bags," I replied as I walked up. "We'll be giving them out tomorrow."

"Food? Where'd you get enough food you can give it away?"

"Aid is starting to come in from around the world. The Army is distributing it. We're putting together bags to make it easier to hand out."

"Where are you going to be doing that?"

"Tomorrow in Eustis, at the armory," Aric replied.

The man scratched at his scruffy face. His clothes had a sheen of grime on them and his skin was oily looking. Hygiene was not a high priority for him. His shoes were tattered and I could see his sockless feet through them. "We've got shoes too," I said.

He looked down. "That would be nice."

"What's your name?" I asked.

"Alex Mackinnon," he took off his hat and mopped his forehead with a filthy rag. "I was down here for an IT conference. I'm from Canada."

Aric whistled. "Damn. That would suck. From what we hear, most of Canada is fine."

Alex nodded his lament. "I figured. No one wants to do anything to Canada. We're almost like Switzerland. And here I am, stuck in hell. And this damn heat!"

The scattered clouds from the morning had burned off and the sun was now blazing high in the sky. It was burning off the rain from the previous several days. You could virtually see the humidity in the air. Looking out across the parking lot, steam rose from the puddles. It was going to be miserable.

"Where'd you get the guns?" Aric asked.

"I acquired them over time. America is not a place to go unarmed. Especially now."

"Acquired them, huh?"

"I didn't hurt anyone to get them. This country is overflowing with guns. I don't have many bullets though, so I try real hard not to use them. Not to mention, I don't want to hurt anyone."

"Well, Alex," I said. "We're going to drive around back and load up the bags we have. Then we'll come back and give your guns back."

He nodded. "Fine by me." He pointed to the covered entry of the store. "I'll be waiting up there. In the shade."

Aric ran in and grabbed the cases of bags we'd left by the front door as I took Alex's guns and put them in the cab of the truck. We rode around back and loaded all the cases from the cart into the bed of the truck. We found Alex sitting under the entry when we returned. He stood up and walked out to the truck. Aric had already unloaded his guns. The rifle was a Ruger 10/22 with only four rounds in the rotary magazine. The Taurus revolver had two .38 special rounds in the cylinder. I felt bad for Alex, wandering this world with only six bullets.

We handed him the guns back. I told him I'd put his ammo on the curb and asked he not load them until we were completely out of sight. He laughed, "I'm not about to try and shoot it out with you two. You've got more ammo in that rifle than I've ever seen."

I laughed, "I appreciate that. Come to the armory in Eustis tomorrow and we'll give you some food. What size shoes do you wear?"

He looked down at the tattered loafers on his feet and replied, "Nine and a half."

"I'll bring you a pair of shoes too. You going to try and make it back to Canada?"

The pain on his face was obvious. "There's no way that will happen. It's a couple thousand miles and I've only managed a couple hundred so far. I was in Miami when all this started."

Aric snorted, "Shit, if you made it out of Miami alive, then there's nothing to stop you from making it back to the Great White North."

Alex smiled halfheartedly. "Maybe. But finding enough food is really hard. Plus, I have to hide every night to try and sleep. I've had some bad experiences. I was beat unconscious twice, everything I had was stolen, and it wasn't much. I've learned the hard way not to trust anyone."

"Alright, Alex, we'll see you in town tomorrow," I said as I got back in the truck.

As we pulled away, Alex stood in the sun watching us go. I imagined he was thinking of how that truck could easily transport him to Canada. If he could get gas for it, which he wouldn't be able to. So, in reality, all it would do is make him a target for others that weren't thinking it all the way through either.

"I feel bad for the poor guy," Aric said as he drove us back towards Altoona. "Imagine coming from a country where things are probably still normal and being caught here in this shit."

"I would imagine there are millions of folks like that."

"Never really thought about it. But you're probably right."

As we were approaching Umatilla, I pointed to a couple of Hummers sitting on the side of the road and told Aric to pull over. There were three Guardsmen standing under the shade of a large oak tree on the side of the road. Stopping the truck, I walked over to a power pole and looked up. Terry, the engineer, was on it towards the top. He'd used climbing hooks to get up there and was cutting a sideline loose from the mainline.

Scott was under the pole acting as his groundman. I looked around and asked, "Where's Baker?"

Scott glanced up at Terry before answering. "She's over at a SECO yard trying to get a bucket truck running. They took a couple of mechanics with them. Damn thing won't start."

"Having the truck would be helpful," I replied.

"You're damn right it would be! I got spoiled with it." Terry shouted down from the top of the pole.

We stepped back as he unhooked his belt from around the pole and started to climb down. This was always the hardest part. Getting up was far easier. Getting down had its own unique problems. Improperly setting a hook on the way down would lead to a fall, as you didn't know it wasn't good until it cut out. At least going up, the other hook would still be set, and you could test your weight on the next one. Most falls happened while coming down.

He was breathing hard and sweating like a seeing-eye dog at a Korean barbeque when he got to the ground. "It's hotter'n a cookout in hell in July up there!" He exclaimed.

I laughed. "That's pretty damn hot. How goes the work?"

He pointed up the pole. "One down. Several hundred to go."

"He's just pissed it's his turn to climb today," Scott said. "There aren't that many more we need to cut. We may be able to have power into Eustis next week."

"No shit?" Aric blurted.

"Yeah. We're going to get power to the armory and the courthouse for now, but that's it," Scott said.

"That's plenty for now. We'll be able to move the clinic out of those tents and into the courthouse building as well," I said. "Now, for the important question. What's it going to take to get it out to us?"

"That'll take a while longer. But we'll get there. It's a long run of wire that will need to be cut free," Terry said.

"Well, I'm looking forward to it," Aric replied.

"Got some good news as well," I said. The two engineers

looked at me expectantly. "We went up to Eglin and picked up an ass-load of food."

"What?" Terry asked.

"You went all the way to Eglin Air Force Base?" Scott asked.

I nodded. "Yeah. We took a couple of trucks and brought a load back. Ammo too."

"What kind of food did you get?" Terry asked.

"All kinds of stuff," Aric replied.

"Flour, rice, canned meat and vegetables. There's hygiene stuff. All kinds of shit," I added.

"Where the hell did all that come from?" Terry asked.

"According to the Army, it's coming from Europe, Canada and Australia."

"Damn. It's about time," Terry said. "Me and Scott were talking about that. Wondering when we'd start to see the international community helping us."

"Yeah," Scott added. "We sure as shit did it long enough. It's about time those countries helped us out a bit."

"Well, it's starting to come in. We'll be bringing a bunch of it to town tomorrow."

"Sheffield know about this?" Scott asked.

I shook my head. "No. We didn't tell him about it. We also got a load of fuel. Between that and the ammo, he should be happy."

Aric snickered, "You forgot about the Stryker."

"You got a Stryker too!" Terry shouted.

"Yeah, the one with the cannon on it," Aric replied with a laugh.

"Sheffield will definitely like that," Scott added.

"I don't think it's for him," I replied. "I think the old man is going to keep it. He said he had something for Sheffield if he showed his ass. Not sure what he meant by that, but he has no plans of giving up the tank."

Scott let out a whistle. "That's going to go over like a fart in church."

I shrugged. "I don't much give a shit. It's between him and the old man. We're dealing with the food, making up bags to hand out."

"We'll be sure to be in town tomorrow for the show," Terry said.

"Alright, guys. We're going to head to the ranch. Y'all need anything?" I asked.

"Naw, we're good. Thanks," Scott replied.

"Alright, we'll see you guys tomorrow."

Aric and I got back in the truck and made the quick trip back to the ranch. As we passed the Umatilla market, there was a bit of a crowd gathered. It looked as though word was starting to spread about the food. I was sure it was spreading like wildfire. We'd have to be careful with this as it could get out of hand fast.

When we got back, the progress that had been made was impressive. There were piles of bags tied up and waiting. We unloaded the bags we'd collected from Publix and they were immediately put to use. A couple of feed scoops had been found and cleaned and were being used to scoop the flour, beans and rice into a bag that would be tied up and dropped into another bag.

There was an assembly line of sorts where the bags would be passed from person to person and additional items were added. There was a separate line putting together bags with hygiene products. It was efficient and getting done quickly. Danny and Thad were putting the bags in the back of the truck with the help of some of the Guardsmen.

Everyone was upbeat and in good spirits, with an air of excitement to the whole process. Aric wandered over to help Fred, who was putting together bags for babies and mothers. As she was dropping a pack of diapers into a bag, she said, "We need to get some of these too. We're going to need them."

Mel wasn't far from her and replied, "Don't worry about those. I have a bunch of cloth diapers that I used for the girls."

Fred looked up, "That would be great. I know we won't have enough of these. It's so sweet of you."

Mel stood up and wiped her forehead with the back of her gloved hand, "They're not doing me any good. You may as well use them."

With this process well under way with plenty of help, I told Mel I was going to work on another project. There was plenty that needed to be done. I stopped by the water keg and got a drink. It was so hot out, you needed water, and this was ice cold. It hurt my teeth, but I relished it and drank until I couldn't hold anymore. I thought about Alex, who'd we met earlier. I could only imagine what this heat was like for him. I was born in it and hated it, but at least I was accustomed to dealing with it.

And it was the heat that was on my mind. I took the little red truck to the house. It still had the lenses from the light fixtures in the bed and I needed them for my project. I pulled around behind the house and parked by the shop and carried a couple of the lenses inside. The girls had collected bags and bags of two-liter bottles. I went around to the front of the house and grabbed one and carried it back.

The lenses were almost two-foot by four-foot. I went to the house and measured one of the windows, as this would fit into the bottom open half. With that measurement in hand, I went to the shop to cut one down. The lens would sit on its side, giving me a two-foot-high area to work with.

I took my skill saw and removed the blade, turned it around backwards, and put it back on. This was a way to cut the plastic without it shattering when the teeth hit it. After cutting the lens down, I measured a bottle and decided to have six across and four down, twenty-four bottles per lens. I could put one more on either side, but I wanted to make as many units as possible. The neck of each bottle was about 7/8ths of an inch, which was perfect because I had a paddle bit that could drill the holes.

Using a framing square, I laid out the grid on the lens for the holes and drilled one to make sure it would fit. The bottle fit through easily and I proceeded to drill the rest of them out. With the lens done, it was time to prepare the bottles. I needed to cut the bottom off of them; and having so many to do, I needed an easy way to do it.

I took a couple pieces of scrap two-by-four I found under the bench and screwed them together at a right angle. Then I decided how long I wanted the bottles to be and made a mark on the longer of the two pieces. Taking a utility razor blade, I hammered it into the wood at the mark. Now, all I had to do was lay the bottle into the L created by the boards, push it against the blade until it pierced the bottle, and rotate it to cut the bottom off. It was fast and made a perfect cut.

I ran through the twenty-four bottles I needed for the first lens. Once they were all ready, I had to prepare the caps before I could install them. I needed to cut the top off the caps. The caps, once open on the end, would be used to hold the bottles in place. I looked at the tools trying to find something that would be both easy and fast. I looked at the Sawzall, then the hacksaw. While both of these would get the job done, it wouldn't be clean or easy.

Then I saw the belt sander. I had an eighty-grit belt on it and decided to give it a shot. Laying it upside down on the bench, I pulled the trigger and held a bottle, cap down, against the belt. It ground the cap off quickly, and in no time, I had all twenty-four bottles ready to mount. This whole process was going faster and smoother than I had thought it would.

With all the caps now ready, I mounted the bottles into the lens. When it was done, it looked like some kind of a middle-school science fair project. But it would work. I carried it to the house and removed the screen from a window and put the lens in and lowered the window until it rested on top of it, holding it in place with the bottles pointed outside.

Having the process down, I got to work making more. I spent the rest of the afternoon making them until I ran out of bottles. That was definitely going to be the issue. But, I figured the world was awash in old bottles; I'd just have to find more. At least, I had enough to make nine sets.

I'd lost track of time and it wasn't until Taylor came into the shop to tell me it was almost dinner time, that I looked at my watch. "Wow, where'd the day go?"

"The time flew by today," she replied.

I dusted ground plastic off my shirt and replied, "Yeah, it definitely helps the day move along when you're working."

"I'm starving and can't wait to eat."

"Well, let's go get us a seat," I replied as I grabbed two of the lenses to carry over to Danny's.

"What are those?" She asked.

Stepping out the door I replied, "Come on and I'll show you."

We walked together over to Danny's, where the front porch was crowded with people. Mike was lying on the porch with a leg hanging off, and he said, "Hey look, it's Bill Nye the Science Guy."

"What in the world is that Rube Goldberg-looking contraption?" Sarge asked.

"I'm hoping it will help cool the house a little."

"How in the hell is that going to cool the house?"

I stepped up on the porch. There was a light breeze blowing, which was relief in its own right. I went over to one of the windows and removed the screen, then went inside with the lens. Inside, I put the lens in and lowered the window to hold it in place like I had done at my house. With it in place, I held my hand in front of the small opening. There was airflow coming through it and it was noticeably cooler.

Mel walked over and asked, "What are you doing?"

I took her hand and held it in front of the lens. "Hey, that's really cool! Literally! It's a lot cooler than the air. How does it work?"

Sarge and a couple others came in from the porch when they heard Mel. Each of them held their hand in front of the lens and all agreed it was cooler.

"How does that work?" Sarge asked.

"The air being compressed to go through the neck speeds it up and that cools it. That's all there is to it. Simple."

Everyone came over to check it out. While they were discussing it, I went and put another one in. Dalton was standing behind me and said, "This is interesting."

I straightened up and replied, "Yeah. It's pretty neat. These can actually reduce the inside temp by ten degrees. But this place is pretty big, so it probably won't reduce the temp that much in here."

He nodded, "But it will help. Ten degrees would be impressive."

The statement made me laugh. "Yeah, ten degrees. Kind of funny getting excited over ten degrees. Not much of a difference with the level of heat we have here in central Florida; but it will definitely help."

"It's the difference between ninety and eighty."

With mock surprise, I replied, "No shit? Wow, did you do that math in your head?"

"Bite me."

Since Miss Kay had been busy all day sorting the food and other supplies for distribution, Bobbie had prepared supper. And with the addition of some of the food stuffs, it was amazing. She made a stew with beef from the cow and large pot of rice. We all gathered on the back porch of Danny's house and feasted like we hadn't in a long time. It was a perfect example of feast or famine.

We'd spent so long, going with so little, that having both the garden come in and the relief aid at the same time made for a true bounty. And knowing that tomorrow we would be passing much needed food and other items out to the people of North Lake County, only made the evening better.

We were sitting around after eating, talking about the task for the next day. Sarge was relaxing with a cup of coffee. The old man sat reclined in a chair with his feet up on a bucket. He'd actually unsnapped his pants he was so full. I smiled when I looked at him and said, "You should take your boots off too."

"Hard to run barefoot," he replied.

"Hard to run with your pants around your ankles too." I replied with a smile.

"I don't plan on running." He replied. All I could do was shake my head.

"Are we taking that tank with us tomorrow?" I asked.

He nodded. "Yeah. I figure it'll keep folks from getting out of hand. I've participated in relief efforts before, and things can go sideways quickly. We're going in heavily armed so no one even thinks about acting up."

"So, you're going back to town tomorrow?" Wallner interrupted.

I looked over and nodded at him. "Yeah, why?"

He looked at the two other Guardsmen he was sitting with, then down at the plate on the table in front of him. "That means we have to go back to the armory." He looked up and added, "We don't want to go back to the armory." The way he said it made me laugh.

"No, we don't want to go back. It's better out here," another of the Guardsmen added.

"Why not?" Sarge asked.

"Because barracks duty sucks!" Mike shouted.

"Michael!" Kay admonished him, "watch your language!"

He whimpered, "I didn't say anything bad." Kay glared at him and he sank back even further into his chair.

"What's wrong at the armory?" Sarge asked.

Wallner shrugged. "Look, the Captain is a good guy, but he's in the reserves for a reason. He's not active duty, never has been. Never wanted to be."

"He's a military hobbyist," Sarge replied, getting a snicker out of the Guardsmen.

"He means well," Wallner said, "But he just does not have the leadership skills to inspire the men. Morale at the armory is really low. Livingston tries…"

He was cut off by another of the Guardsmen, "In all the wrong ways."

Wallner nodded, "Yeah. He tries to be all spit and polish military. But it just doesn't come off right with him. I like Livingston, he's a cool guy to talk shit with. But when he puts on his LT hat, you just can't take him seriously."

"He's a dick," the other Guardsmen added.

"Language!" Kay shouted. She stood up and shook her finger at the uniformed men, "You will watch your language! There are children here! Not to mention, I don't want to hear it!"

In unison, they all nodded," Yes ma'am." Kay then looked at Mike, who looked away as he chewed on his fingernail.

I chuckled and looked at Sarge, "And she's with you?"

"I have manners," he replied. Then he looked to make sure Kay wasn't looking at him and added, "dipshit." I laughed out loud and Kay looked back at me. I smiled and winked at her. She looked at the old man, then back at me. She knew something was up, but didn't say anything and sat back down.

Bobbie got up and started collecting the dishes. Mike was quickly on his feet to help her. As he was picking up bowls and plates, Bobbie looked at him and said, "Looks like you may get dessert after all."

"Dessert?" Was echoed across the porch. Most loudly by the kids.

Little Bit stood up on the bench of the picnic table and asked, "What's for dessert?"

Bobbie raised her eyebrows at her and said, "If you want to find out, you better sit down!" Little Bit quickly took her seat and giggled with Edie and Jace as they discussed the possibilities. They rubbed their hands in excited anticipation.

Once the dishes were cleared, Mike returned from the kitchen carrying a large pan. He smiled from ear to ear as he held it up to his face, eyes closed, inhaling deeply the aroma wafting from it. "Oh, my Lord, this is heavenly," he said.

"Well, what is it?" Sarge asked.

Mike deposited the pan on the picnic table as Bobbie announced, "It's peach cobbler."

Sarge jumped to his feet, catching his pants and buttoning them up. "You don't say?"

He stepped over to the pan where Bobbie was just digging a large spoon into it. He stretched out a finger, as if he were going to sample it. But Bobbie slapped his hand, "You will not!" She shouted.

His hand recoiled and he looked at her with a look of pain and longing. She nodded at his chair, "You just have a seat and I'll bring you some. The old man looked down at the pan, then back at Bobbie. "Go on, sit" she said.

Mike laughed as Sarge retreated to his chair. He handed Bobbie a bowl, in which she placed a scoop. Mike was giggling and rubbing his hands together as she did so, then held his hands out in anticipation. But the bowl passed right over them and his smile vanished. Bobbie handed the bowl to Kay, who then handed it to Sarge.

Slack-jawed, Mike muttered, "Whaaaat?"

Sarge snorted at him and held his bowl up as he scooped a bite into his mouth, "You're missing out, Mikey. This is really good, Bobbie." Mike glared at him as he watched bowls bypassing him.

Bobbie then made several more bowls, serving the very excited kids. Once they had theirs, she then handed one to Mike. Relief washed over him and he smiled once again, quickly taking a seat. I was in no hurry and waited as everyone was served. Mel helped pass them out and eventually brought me a serving. And it was indeed good. Really good. It was such an intense sweetness, it hurt my teeth initially. But I savored every bite. It had been so long since we'd had something this sweet.

As I chewed a bite, I pointed at the kids, who were already practically vibrating in their seats, "It's going to be fun trying to get that bunch to sleep tonight."

Danny looked over at the kids and asked, "Hey, you guys want to sleep over at Ashley's house tonight?"

There was an immediate, *Yes,* shouted back at him from all three of them. Mel was quick to reply, "*Pffft,* I don't think so, Danny."

"Awe, come on mom!" Little Bit implored.

Mel dropped her spoon into an empty bowl and replied, "Not tonight. Another time."

"Come on, mom, we'll be good!"

"I said no," she replied in that mother's voice that tells every kid the conversation is over. And it was. Little Bit returned her attention to her dessert.

I laughed, "Nice try, Danny."

He was grinning as he chewed, "It was worth a shot."

"Bobbie, how did you come up with this?" I asked.

"There were cans of peaches in all that stuff. Just used those and some of the flour. We had other stuff, like vanilla," she replied.

"Good job on it." Everyone agreed with me, thanking her for the effort. Because it was a real treat.

"Thanks." She nodded at Thad, "Thad helped with it."

He smiled, "I didn't do nothing, Miss Bobbie."

"You made the crust! That's the hard part. All I did was open cans and pour them in."

Wallner held up an empty bowl, "Another reason we don't want to go back to the armory. We don't get to eat like this."

"Neither do we," Thad replied. "Usually."

Another of the Guardsmen snorted, "Everything we've had here was better than anything we've ever had at the armory. I mean, this is fantastic."

"It's been good having you fellas here," Thad said. "We appreciate your help the last few days."

"It was our pleasure, really," Wallner replied.

"Do you guys do patrols out of the armory?" Sarge asked.

"It comes and goes. They'll get full of piss and vinegar and we'll patrol for several days. Then the fun wears off and it fades away."

Sarge listened and nodded. "Well. There's some changes coming."

I looked at him, curious as to what he meant. "Such as?"

"You'll find out tomorrow." His reply didn't help my concern any. "We got a big day tomorrow. Everyone should get some sleep."

I looked at Thad and asked, "You want to take a shift at the bunker with me?"

He nodded, "Sure."

Wallner stood up, "No, no. We've got this. Our way of saying thank-you for all the hospitality. You folks have been real good to us."

"I figured we'd give you the night off before heading back tomorrow."

Wallner shook his head. "No, that's alright. We'll take it."

"If you're sure," I replied.

"We are. You guys get some rest."

Mel and I collected the girls to head home. We said good night to everyone and left. Little Bit was pretty wound up from her sugar high. It was an interesting thing to see how the sugar affected her. We no longer consumed it in the quantities we used to, let alone the kids. So, getting something like a cobbler, dense with refined sugar, really spun her up.

But fortunately for Mel and me, sugar highs crashed as fast as they came on. So, I smiled watching her run around in front of us chasing a solitary lightning bug. I held Mel's hand as we walked. Lee Ann and Taylor flanked us on each side.

"Can we go to town tomorrow to help hand out the food?" Taylor asked.

I nodded. "Sure. We'll need the help." Both girls lit up, excited at the thought of getting out of the neighborhood for a while. "I doubt it will take long. I'm sure we'll be cleaned out quickly."

"All those bags?" Lee Ann asked, "You think it won't take long to hand them out?"

"I'll bet it takes less than two hours."

Mel looked at me sideways, "What?"

"People are hungry. We're giving them things they haven't seen in a long time. They're going to want it. I just hope they don't get out of hand."

"You're taking that tank too, aren't you?" Lee Ann asked.

"Yeah. But it won't be a lot of good. More of a visual deterrent."

"I wouldn't mess with that thing," Taylor said. "It's kind of scary looking."

"Oh, I'm sure it's nothing to be messed with," I replied, "But hopefully we don't have to see it in action."

The dogs were not on the porch when we got to the house. Little Bit paused and looked back, "Where are the dogs?" She asked.

"They're out on their nightly patrol. They run off every night," I replied.

"Will they come back?"

I smiled and patted her head, "Of course they will. They do every day. Come on, let's go inside and get ready for bed."

As she pushed the door open, she replied, "But I'm not tired."

I laughed, "Oh, you will be. You will be."

CHAPTER 7

Everyone was up early getting ready for the day's task of handing out the food and other supplies. While they were getting prepared, I went out to the shed to look for a pair of boots. After the raid on the Elk's Camp, we'd taken the boots from all the dead and I had stored some of them in my shed. I'd lain in bed last night thinking about Alex's shoes. Sure, we could give him a pair of the cheap shoes, but I thought a pair of boots would better serve him.

Don't know why I was so concerned for him. I didn't know Alex and would probably never see him again after today. Maybe it was getting close. It's one thing to see someone from a distance that is suffering. But to get face to face with them gives one an entirely different perspective. Maybe that's why I was looking for a decent pair of boots for him.

Finding a pair in his 9 ½ size, I carried them out to the porch and set them down. Going inside, I grabbed my kit and started putting it on. The girls were having breakfast, fresh biscuits and honey. Mel had the little camp oven on the Butterfly stove with a plate of biscuits sitting beside it. I love biscuits. So, I paused for a moment and cut one in half and put a dollop of honey on it and put it back together.

The sweet golden honey soaked into the fluffy biscuit, making for a delicious breakfast. I finished my biscuit as I put my gear on. The girls sat at the table, chattering away. There was an air of excitement ahead of the day's activities. Everyone was dressed and ready to go by the time I was geared up. For this project, I actually wore long pants, just in case things got sporty.

"Alright, guys, let's go over to Danny's," I announced.

"We get to give people food today!" Little Bit shouted.

"Are you going to help?" Mel asked her.

Her head eagerly bobbed up and down, "Yep!"

"Should we bring our guns?" Taylor asked.

"You're leaving the house, aren't you? What do you think?" I replied.

"Told you," Lee Ann said to Taylor, adjusting the sling of her H&K on her shoulder.

I glanced at Mel and smiled. She had her holstered Glock on her hip. She wasn't a fan of the Springfield. The grip was too large for her hand and the .45 caliber recoil was too punishing. But the 9mm, she really liked. The Glock 19 grip fit her hand and the recoil was far more manageable.

Danny, Bobbie, Thad and Mary were in the yard when we arrived. "Y'all ready for this goat rope?" I asked.

"Should be fun," Thad relied.

I shook his hand, then Danny's, asking, "You going too?"

He nodded, "Yeah. I'm going. Bobbie and the kids are coming too."

I smiled. "Cool. Little Bit will have a good time with them."

"I'm going to drive the truck. Y'all hop in the back," Thad said.

But the little truck was too small for all of us. We let the kids get in the back, and Danny, Mel and I walked up the road behind the truck. Lee Ann and Taylor kept the kids down inside the bed of the truck. As we made our way to where all the trucks were waiting, Mel asked, "You don' think there's going to be any trouble today, do you?"

I shook my head. "No. There might be some pushing and shoving, but that's about it."

"I'm a little nervous taking all the girls with us. We'll all be in the same place, you know."

I wrapped my arm around her. "We'll be fine, babe."

Sarge was busy getting everyone in order, sorting out who would drive what. Just like on our trip to get all of this, I would drive the fuel truck. There were three seats in it, so I told Mel to grab Little Bit and put her in the center seat. She thought that was the coolest thing ever, riding in the *big Army truck,* as she put it. Lee Ann and Taylor would ride in Sarge's big War Wagon, with Aric, Fred and Jess.

Perez was leaned against the side of the five-ton truck, smoking cigarettes of course. He was going to drive it with Ian and Jamie along for the ride. I walked over and kicked the toe of his boot. "You know you can't smoke in that truck. Army regs and all," I couldn't help but smile.

He laughed, showing his yellowed teeth. Pointing at me with a cigarette, he replied, "You're funny."

Sarge called everyone together. "All right, everyone, gather 'round!" We all grouped around him. "This shouldn't be a big deal today. We're going to stop in Altoona, then move to Umatilla, before ending up in Eustis. At each stop, we're going to hand out supplies to the folks there. We have supplies dedicated to give to the Guard troops in Eustis. Kay knows who's getting what."

"We also have special packages for certain people," Kay added.

Sarge nodded. "We put together packages for Cecil, the Eustis PD and Judge Mitch." Sarge pointed to the civilians in our group, "You people will be doing the distribution." He then circled his finger over his head and pointed to his guys, "We'll be providing security. We will not tolerate any violence from these folks. I know they're hungry, but we're here to help them. If things get out of hand, we'll fire warning shots in the air. You folks just hunker down. If, and I seriously doubt this will happen, there is any sort of an exchange of gun fire, you will be inner security. Let us handle it, unless someone gets through us and to the trucks. Then it's up to you to stop them." He looked around at the faces gathered around him and asked, "Any questions?"

There probably were, but no one asked any and we quickly climbed into our trucks and got ready to go. I was sitting in the truck, the engine idling, when Wallner walked up. I opened the door so I could talk to him, "What's up?"

He paused for a minute before answering. "Uh, me and the guys have talked. We're not going back to the armory. We're staying here. We're providing security while you guys are gone today and will from now on."

I was surprised. I knew they didn't want to leave. But it seemed kind of like desertion to me. But then, these weren't normal times and just because they were here didn't mean they were shirking their duty.

"Well, that's not up to me, buddy. We like having you guys here. But I'm sure Sheffield will be a little pissed about it."

He shrugged. "He's still got over forty people there. Besides, we've already talked to Top. He said we can stay."

"I guess the old man will take it up with Sheffield," I replied.

He patted the door of the truck, "Good luck today."

I smiled back at him, "This'll be a milk-run, buddy. We'll see you in a couple of hours"

Sarge pulled out and all the vehicles fell in behind him.

When I finally made it to the county road, I found the line of trucks stopped. Sarge came over the radio, "Y'all wait here. I'm going to take a package to Gena real quick."

"That's really nice," Mel said. "I'd like to go visit her."

"We can do that," I replied. "Once we get back, we'll take a ride over there."

"I like Miss Gena," Little Bit shouted.

We waited on the road, trucks idling for Sarge to get back. The radio broke again, it was Ted.

"Pull up the Guard's net. They've got something going on." He announced.

I pulled the radio from my vest and switched to the frequency.

.....know where they went.

Sandbag Four, Big Town Six. What was their last known location?

Moving west on citrus from our current position.

Big Town Seven, Big Town Six. You copying this?

Affirmative, Big Town Seven. I'm putting together a patrol now to go find them.

Suddenly, Sarge's voice came over the radio. "Big Town Six, Stumpknocker. SITREP?"

There was a long pause. "Stumpknocker, we're looking for an OPFOR recon unit spotted on citrus, moving west."

"Big Town, we'll be at your location shortly."

"Unnecessary, Stumpknocker. We'll handle this."

"Teddy, switch back to our freq," Sarge said.

"What's going on?" Mel asked.

I shrugged. "Sounds like the guys in Eustis saw something. I know they have an observation post out on the trail, on the other side of Mount Dora. Maybe they saw something over there."

"Is it still safe to go to town?"

"Oh yeah. There wasn't any shooting or anything. He said it

was a recon unit; who knows what that was exactly. But a recon unit isn't designed to fight head to head." I didn't tell her they could be the lead of a larger force. But there hadn't been any word of anything larger headed our way. I switched my radio as well to hear what Sarge had to say.

"Teddy, you keep an ear on that net. Let me know if they come up with anything else."

"Roger that, boss."

Then Sarge made another comment, "Big Town. What a jackass." I had to laugh. He cracked me up.

"What's he talking about?" Mel asked as we started moving again.

Smiling, I replied, "He's mocking Sheffield's call sign." I glanced over at her, "Just being Sarge."

When the market in Altoona came into view, I said, "Alright, babe. I'm going to hang out near this truck. But I'll be keeping an eye on you guys."

She was craning her neck to see where the vehicles were going. "Okay. Look at all those people. I didn't know there were so many around. You never see them."

She was talking about the crowd gathered at the market. There had to be close to a hundred. It was the most people I'd ever seen out here. The trucks and trailers with the food pulled into the parking lot as the crowd parted like a wave. They immediately started trying to climb into the truck and trailer. But Dalton had been riding in the back of the truck, lying on the bags of food. He started pushing, kicking and throwing people off the truck.

The radio quickly came to life, "Teddy, get some rounds out of that deuce! Put their heads down!"

The Stryker pulled out into the entrance of the parking lot and the big machinegun started to thunder. It sent the people scattering. Dalton climbed up onto the cab of the truck and started shouting.

"That's enough of that shit! You're not animals! Line up like damn adults! There's enough here for all! But the next person that tries to climb onto this truck, I'll shoot in the face! Now, line up!"

Between the warning shots and the image of an AK-wielding mad man standing on top of the truck, the crowd calmed down and started to form a civil line. It was then, once things were settled down, I told Mel to go over and help. But I decided the truck was fine. The Stryker was sitting close by, no one would mess with it. I wanted to be close to Mel and the girls.

We moved into the crowd, making our way to the back of the trailer connected to Sarge's Hummer. There were enough people at the truck. Danny and Bobbie were working from the Hummer, so we went to help them. The people were eager, very eager, and peppered us with questions about what was in the bags.

I stood watch as bags were handed out as fast as they could be. Some people tried to take more than one, but were quickly pushed along and they didn't resist. I don't blame them; if you don't try, you can't succeed. But I think it was the presence of the kids that contributed the most to keeping things under control. We had the kids in the trailer handing the bags out to the people. As hungry and desperate as they were, they were still struck by the sight of little kids handing them food.

Little Bit handed a bag to a woman. She looked at it and asked, "What's in it?"

"Pancakes and biscuits! We had biscuits this morning!" Little Bit shouted.

The woman looked at me, the question painted on her face. "There's a lot of stuff in there," I said. "Flour, rice, canned meat.

All kinds of stuff. Be sure to get a hygiene bag too. They have soap, toothbrush and paste. Stuff like that."

As she was being pushed by those behind her, she asked, "Where did all this come from? What took so long to get it?"

I gently gripped her shoulder, ushering her along as I replied, "It's coming from other countries. They're starting to help."

She looked at the bag with tears in her eyes, "God bless 'em!"

It only took about thirty minutes to hand bags out to everyone there. In most cases, as soon as they had their precious loot, they quickly left for home to inspect their packages in private and relative safety. In a couple of cases, people simply moved to the edge of the crowd and immediately tore their bag open. Word quickly spread about what was in them. People were at the same time happy and befuddled by the contents.

Things like canned meat, fruit and veggies were eagerly accepted. The flour though, caused some to complain. Asking, "What are we supposed to do with this? We don't have ovens?"

I was asked this question by a man and quickly replied, "Make pancakes. Cook them on a griddle. Make bannock, wrap it around a stick and cook it over a fire."

The man looked at the bag of flour, turning it over in his hand. Then replied, "I remember doing that as a kid in the Scouts."

I smiled, "Then you remember how good it was."

The man smiled back, "It was good. My boy's never had it. He's going to get a surprise tonight." He then looked at me and asked, "Are there going to be more deliveries like this?"

I shrugged with uncertainty, "I really can't say. It wasn't easy getting this. Don't plan on it. If it happens, then all the better."

He thrust his hand into mine, "Thank you for getting this, Sheriff. If we ever get to vote again, you'll have mine for life."

I shook his hand and laughed, "Thank you. But it ain't a job I want for life."

As soon as it looked like we'd passed all the bags out, I went to the trailer and grabbed several bags and took them over to Mario and Shelly. They'd been watching the show from the seat of their UTV. "Well, that was interesting," Mario said as I walked up.

I placed the bags into the bed of the UTV and laughed. "Yeah. Once they settled down, it wasn't too bad."

"The way they swarmed the trucks when you first got here, I thought it was going to go a lot different," Shelly said.

"Me too," I quickly replied.

Shelly picked up one of the bags. Holding it up, she said, "Thanks for this."

I nodded. "You guys do a lot for everyone. Only fair you should get some too."

"Yeah, but we're doing better than most. We have something everyone wants. Unlimited supply of it," Mario said.

"I was thinking about that. How's security out there?" I asked.

Mario rolled his eyes. "It's never ending. Like I said, everyone wants it. We give a lot away, trying to help people. But some people try to sneak in and take it."

"We've lost some hives," Shelly added.

I nodded. "I'm going to see if we can help you with that. Your hives are a huge benefit to the community. We need to support you guys."

"How?" Mario asked.

"We could put some Guardsmen out at your place. You've got forty acres out there to secure. You could use some help."

Shelly looked at Mario, "John would appreciate the help."

Mario shrugged, "It would make things easier."

"Yeah," Shelly laughed, "we could actually get some sleep."

"That would be nice," Mario agreed. "Most of the trouble comes at night."

"Come on, Morgan!" Sarge shouted. "We got shit to do!"

I rolled my eyes. "I'll catch you guys later," I said as I headed for the truck where Mel and Little Bit were waiting.

Once I was up in the truck, Mel said, "That was kind of scary."

"Maybe in the beginning. But things calmed down quickly," I replied.

"I thought it was fun!" Little Bit added.

"I hope the next time is less fun," Mel replied.

We did things differently in Umatilla. There were more people here. Sarge had the Stryker pulled right into the parking lot. I told Mel to wait in the truck and got out and walked over to the parking lot where Dalton, Ian and Perez were making a visible show of force. It worked and the people backed away, to wait under the old gas canopy. There was no trading going on today, everyone was waiting for the promised food delivery.

Once we had the people out of the way, I addressed them. "Alright, we will do this in an orderly fashion. You will form a line and act like adults. There's enough here for everyone, so there's no need to push and shove. We will not tolerate or allow this to get out of hand. Are we in agreement?" Many of the faces nodded back as they whispered amongst themselves.

I turned around and waved the trucks in. They moved into the parking lot and parked. As things were getting set up, I walked back over to the truck and told Mel that she and Little Bit could go over and help. This time, things did go differently. The initial show of force had the desired effect as everyone lined up in an orderly manner and patiently waited for their turn.

There was a lot of excitement among the people when they

received their package. Some tore them open immediately, just as in Altoona. Others quickly spirited theirs away. Here too, we were peppered with questions about what was in them. Was more coming? Where did it come from? We answered the questions as best we could, telling them we didn't know if there would be more.

I stepped over and looked into the back of the truck, surprised to see the amount of supplies that still remained. Despite the amount we'd already handed out, which was considerable, there was still a mountain remaining. But that was a good thing, because we had not yet been to Eustis where there were the most people.

This stop at Umatilla went much faster, despite the fact there were more people. Altoona provided a couple of lessons that we quickly learned from. Umatilla provided more, which was good, as the main show was about to start when we moved down highway nineteen towards Eustis. As we drove, Sarge called Ted on the radio, "Keep an ear on their net. Let me know if anything else comes up."

"Roger, boss. I've been monitoring it. They say a couple of thin-skinned trucks came through. Doesn't sound like much to worry about."

"Just keep me updated."

We rolled into Eustis and parked on the road in front of the armory. We never came to town to deliver the message that food was coming, but we did tell Scott and Terry to pass the word. It must have made it because there was a large crowd gathered at the park down the road from the armory. Before we were even stopped, Sheffield and Livingston were stomping their way out of the armory and towards the trucks.

"Keep her in the truck," I said, referring to Little Bit. "I have a feeling this is going to get ugly."

"We'll wait here," Mel replied.

I got out and made my way up towards the old man's Hummer. Livingston pointed at the Hummer, saying something. I saw Sheffield nod his head as he stepped into the street.

He immediately stepped in front of Sarge, jabbing his finger in his face, and started shouting. "You fucking lied to me! You said you needed my people for something up your way, some bullshit you made up! Just so you could sneak off!"

Sarge held his hands up, trying to calm him. "Now calm down, Captain. Just relax and let me explain where we went."

But Sheffield wasn't about to give him the time. "I don't give a shit! You lied through your ass! Did you forget who's in charge around here?" He gripped his collar, holding his insignia out, "In case you forgot, I am, asshole!"

"Look, I'm trying to be nice here," Sarge said.

Sheffield started to laugh. "I don't give a shit what you think you're trying to do."

"Where the hell did that come from?" Livingston asked, pointing at the Stryker.

"You know he stole it from someone!" Sheffield smarmily replied.

"Actually, I didn't...." Sarge replied before Sheffield cut him off.

"I'm sick of your shit and don't want to hear another word out of your fucking mouth."

Sarge wagged a finger at him, "You really need to relax a little and listen to me."

Sheffield was looking a little unstable. He laughed again and shouted, "No, I don't!" He looked at Livingston and said, "Take his ass into custody!"

Sarge and Livingston replied in unison, "What?"

"I said, take him into custody!"

"Look, Captain, that's not going to happen," Sarge said.

Sheffield raised his carbine, pointing it at Sarge's face. The old man didn't flinch, but everyone around him did. I had been standing off to the side and took a couple of steps towards Sheffield, who was focused on Sarge, and I stuck the muzzle of my rifle into his ear.

"Sheffield, you really need to relax. I don't know why you're so spun up, but it ain't that big a deal," I said quietly.

He cut his eyes towards me, "You're just as bad as he is!"

While Sheffield was looking at me, Dalton walked up behind him. Livingston was still in shock at the sight of Sheffield pointing a gun at Sarge. Once Dalton was behind him, Sarge gave a very slight nod and quickly pushed the muzzle of Sheffield's rifle out of his face. Dalton grabbed Sheffield's head in a sleeper hold. Sheffield released his rifle, more focused on the large man that was trying to squeeze his head off. Dalton cocked his head to the side, his lips close to the man's ears and whispered, "Shhh, just go to sleep."

And he did just that. Sheffield's eyes rolled into the back of his head and he passed out. Dalton stepped back and deposited him face down on the ground and removed his weapons. Then, he pulled Sheffield's hands behind his back to secure them.

"Don't do that, Dalton," Sarge said. Then he looked at Livingston and said, "Come on, help me get him woke up and on his feet."

Once they had Sheffield up, Sarge looked at me and said, "Go ahead and move to the park and start handing the food out." Looking at Livingston, he said, "Send a bunch of your people too, for security. But you stay here. We need to have a talk."

Livingston nodded and gave a couple of quick orders. Sheffield was coming around now and had a look of disgust on his face. One, he made sure Dalton could see. But Dalton ignored it, doing his best to look disinterested.

I stepped up onto the side of the truck Perez was driving and pointed to the park, telling him to head that way. He nodded and started it up and pulled away. Aric got into the driver's seat of the Hummer, and all the trucks, except mine, moved to the park. I was waiting to see what Sarge and Sheffield were going to do.

"Look, Captain. I know we don't get along. But I'm not your enemy. I'm here to help you. We went to Eglin Air Force Base and got all this food for the people here. We got fuel and ammo for you." He pointed at the Stryker, adding, "Hell, we got us a tank! Kinda," he added with a smile.

Sheffield ran his hands over his face. "I'm sorry. I'm sorry."

Sarge patted him on the shoulder. "I know you are. I know this isn't what you wanted to be doing. And I'm guessing it's starting to wear on you a little."

Sheffield nodded. "It is," he twirled a finger in the air, "there's some assholes running around out here right now. We don't know who they are or where they are. I have to take care of all these people."

Sarge held his hand up. "I get it. Trust me." He reached into his blouse pocket and removed a piece of paper and said, "but I'm going to do you a favor," and handed him the paper.

Sheffield looked at it, then at the old man. Sarge nodded, "Go ahead, read it."

Sheffield unfolded the piece of paper. Holding it up, his lips moved ever so slightly as his eyes scanned across the sheet. Sarge stood, watching patiently. After a moment, Sheffield shouted, "What the fuck!" A smile spread over the old man's face and he looked down at the ground as he rocked back and forth on his heels.

Sheffield looked at Sarge and said, "You've got to be shitting me."

Sarge shrugged. "Wasn't my idea," he innocently replied.

Sheffield looked at the paper again, shaking his head. Livingston asked, "What is it?"

Sheffield handed him the sheet, still shaking his head. Livingston quickly scanned the print and looked up. He too was in disbelief. "Sarge, they made you a Colonel?"

"Like I said," Sarge replied, "it wasn't my idea. But you two can see it for yourselves."

"So, this means, you're in charge now," Livingston said flatly.

Sarge slowly nodded. "It appears that way."

"Wait," I said. "You're telling me they made you a Colonel?"

Sarge cocked his head to the side and asked, "And why is that so hard to believe?"

I started laughing loudly. Leaning over and holding my stomach as I howled.

"What the hell are you bawling about?"

I stood up, wiping my eyes. In a deep tone and with a heavy southern accent, I said, "Lawdy, lawdy, Colonel I do declare! I can just see you in a white three-piece suit!"

He stared down his finger at me, "Keep it up and I'm going to shove three pieces up your ass!" Then he turned his attention back to Sheffield. "As you can see, you can relax now. It's not all on your shoulders. Now, it's all on my head. You just do what you're instructed to do and let me worry about the rest."

Sheffield looked off into the distance. "So now, I work for you?" Sarge shook his head, confirming the new pecking order.

Sarge gripped his shoulder. "Look, nothing is going to change. We're going to move some folks around so there's not so many people here. It'll make your job easier because you're going to still be in charge here. I'm not going to meddle in your business here. I will, from time to time, need your help. But overall, you're still in charge here. And no one needs to know about this either. I'm not here to undermine your authority."

Sheffield listened, and when Sarge finished speaking, Sheffield clucked his tongue. After thinking about it, he shrugged and replied, "Fine by me." He took a deep breath and said, "So what's the order?" There was a short pause and he added, "Colonel."

"Don't start that shit. We've got to get your fuel bladder refilled right now. The rest of the fuel we'll be taking back with us. With Russians and Cubans sneaking around, I don't want to keep all of our supplies in one place. There's also ammo for you and I got a couple of Mark Nineteens for you as well."

"I'll get some people on it," Livingston said.

"We're going to step up patrols," Sarge continued. "I want to find any Commies that may be sneaking around. We need to find them, before they find us."

Sheffield nodded, "I've got a patrol out now. They were told if they found them, not to engage, but to call it in." He nodded at the Stryker and continued. "Now that we have that, we can deal with their armor."

"We've also got a TOW launcher that can be mounted on a Hummer. I'm leaving that here as well. You need to get it mounted. There's only eight rockets for it. So, use it with discretion. I'll be coming back up here tomorrow so we can draw up a plan to deal with these assholes. In the meantime, do not engage them if you find them. We'll have to coordinate things carefully. We don't have the manpower or equipment to go off half-cocked."

Sheffield nodded. "I agree. It's been worrying me."

"Me too. That's why we'll pick the time and place. Not them. We'll stack the deck in our favor before we put the boots to them." Sarge looked over at the park where the food was being handed out. "But for now, we're going over there to help out. Have your people unload the stuff in the Hummer, it's all for you."

"I'll get it done. Livingston and I will be ready when you get here tomorrow."

Sarge nodded and patted him on the back, "Don't worry, Captain. We'll be fine." Then he looked at me and said, "Bring you ass. Let's go to the park."

I walked with him towards the park. I couldn't help but smile. He noticed and said, "Go ahead. Get it out of your system."

I laughed and replied, "I just can't help but have the image of the *southern colonel* in mind when I think of this. I can't believe they made you a Colonel."

"Wasn't my idea. But Fawcett said, desperate times call for desperate measures. I asked to be made a Major or something. Anything but a Colonel." He stepped in front of me, stopping me. Jabbing his finger in my chest, he said, "You keep this shit to yourself too! If Mikey finds out about it, he'll make my life hell. This changes nothing here. Got it?"

I pushed his finger away and replied, "Don't worry, Colonel. Your secret is safe with me."

He shook his head. "It's hard to get the big picture when you have such a small screen, ain't it? Work with me here."

"I won't say anything. I promise," I said. But I was already thinking about getting Little Bit to start calling him Colonel. "But, I gotta admit, you handled that way better than I expected you would."

"Sheffield is a good man. He's just out of his depth. Some people know how to lead. Some know how to make their way through the system, punching their ticket. Sad thing about the military, you do that long enough, you get promoted. Nothing against him. He's just a different kind of officer."

We made it to the park and I found Mel and Little Bit helping in the distribution. Things were going smoothly. But there were a lot of armed men making sure it stayed that way. I nudged Sarge and said, "I told you it'd go smoothly."

"Yeah," he grunted back. "Altoona went *real* well this morning."

I was thinking about something smart to say back when Aric walked up. He tapped my shoulder and pointed, "You see that guy over there working on that net?"

I looked in the direction he pointed and saw a man sitting in the grass. A net was piled beside him. He was working on a section in his lap. "Yeah. What about him?"

He studied him for a minute and said, "I think that guy worked in the camp."

I shrugged. "So?"

"For the DHS. I think he was their interrogator."

I looked at him, "Really?"

I looked back at the man. He was focused on his net. Another man walked up to him and knelt down. This one, I did know. Something about Micha always rubbed me wrong. I couldn't figure out what it was about him I didn't like.

"Well, if you're right, then so am I. That guy that walked up, never have cared for him either. Don't know why." I watched as the man working on the net handed something to Micha. It was small, too small to see from where we were. But Micha nodded and quickly walked off. I told Aric to keep an eye on the him.

Dalton was standing by the front of the truck. I walked over to him and bumped him with my shoulder. "You see that guy over there. On the other side of the park, walking towards town?" Dalton nodded. "Can you follow him and see where he goes?"

"Will do. I'll be in touch," he replied and started after him without question.

"Just find out where he's going. Give me a call and let me know."

He gave me a thumbs-up and continued his pursuit. I made my way back to the truck to watch the progress. Little Bit was up in the back of the truck with Edie and Jace, carrying bags to those handing them out. Each child could only carry one at a time. But they were keeping up. Lee Ann and Taylor were helping to hand the bags to the people as they passed.

As I stood watching the work, Shane ambled up and leaned against the truck beside me. "How the hell did you pull this off?" He asked.

"We went to Eglin. I asked the Army to give until it hurt."

"Looks like they did."

I nodded and changed the subject. "Have you seen Micha around lately?"

He shrugged, "Sometimes. He doesn't come around as much as he used to."

"He's not helping you guys out anymore?"

Shane snorted, "He's never really been any help. More nosy than anything else."

"What? Asking questions?"

Nodding, he replied, "Yeah. Always asking questions about what was going on. Where people were. That kind of thing."

I pointed to the man with the net. He was on his feet now, piling it up. "You know that guy?"

He shook his head. "No. Can't say I do. Who is he?"

"I was hoping you knew. Aric here thinks he worked for the DHS out at the camp."

"I'm almost certain," Aric replied.

Shane looked at the man who was now walking away from the park. "You want me to go roll him up?"

I shook my head. "No. Not yet. But could you go follow him, see where he's going? Dalton is following Micha. The two were just talking, so I'm curious what's up. I don't trust Micha, never have. And with Aric thinking this clown was with the DHS, I'm just curious what they're up to."

"Sure," Shane replied. "I'll keep an eye on him."

"Take someone with you," Aric said. "If he's who I think he is, he's pretty dangerous."

"I'll grab Shawn. He's on that side of the park anyway."

I saw Mitch and Michelle working their way through the crowd and made my way over to him. He smiled when he saw me and I shook his hand. "How's it going?" I asked.

He shook my hand and replied, "Going great. Thanks for the food."

I nodded. "You're a big part of things now. It's only right you get your share."

"We really appreciate it. We ran out of flour, now I can make some bread," Michelle said.

We hung out in the park, chatting and watching as the crowd moved through the distribution line. I found my way over to Sarge and asked if he'd seen Cecil. "He's out at the farm. There's still a lot of work going on out there."

"You got his stuff set aside?"

"Yeah. We put his aside and enough for the folks working out there." Sarge peeked over the side of the truck. He looked surprised and said, "Still quite a bit in there. We may have leftovers."

"Good. We'll hold onto it."

As I was speaking, the radio crackled to life. Dalton's voice came over it, saying, "You're about to have incoming."

I looked at Sarge and asked, "What'd he say?"

But Sarge was already on his radio, "Repeat that!"

"You're about to have incoming!"

Sarge raised his carbine and fired a long continuous burst into the air. People began to run, some dove to the ground. The burst of rifle fire was interrupted by the sound of the air tearing apart, followed immediately by a thunderous explosion in the park. Dirt flew high into the air as shells exploded like a thunder clap.

I was on the ground and crawling towards Mel and the girls. They were all pressed to the ground under the truck. Another shell landed with a roaring explosion, this time closer to the truck. I made it to Mel, and she had her hands pressed tight over her ears and her eyes clenched tightly closed. I grabbed her hand and pulled it from her ear, screaming, "We need to move!"

She stared back at me, her eyes wide with fear. I ducked as another shell landed. An unidentifiable piece of pink meat slapped into the truck and fell to the ground. I grabbed Mel's hand and jerked her out from under the truck. Little Bit was beside her and I pulled her out as well. I didn't see Edie or Jace. Another shell landed and I saw a body fly into the air, high into the air and land in a tree. I pushed Mel, screaming for her to run towards the band shell at the opposite end of the park.

"When you hear the sound in the air, get flat on the ground!" I screamed as I pushed her again and told her to run.

I moved back to the truck and found Lee Ann and Taylor. The air wailed again and I fell on top of them as the shell slammed into the park. It landed near the gallows and sent splinters of wood flying in all directions. There were screams and wails. But they sounded far away as my ear drums felt as though they'd ruptured from the explosions. I stood up and pulled the girls to their feet and pointed at the band shell and screamed, "Run!"

They didn't hesitate and took off as fast as their feet would carry them. I saw the Stryker moving, Mike was getting out of the strike area. The air tore apart once again and I fell to the ground. It hit the truck, sending pieces of it flying and igniting the fuel from the ruptured tanks. A person, fully engulfed in flames walked slowly away from it, hands held over their head. A living pyre.

I looked around for anyone I could recognize and saw Danny. He was on his feet and running towards the burning truck. I started towards him and the air screeched again. The earth spewed up, sending both of us flying. I came to with the sensation I was moving. But that couldn't be. I knew I was on the ground. I looked to my left and saw Danny beside me. Then, looking back over my shoulder, I realized Thad had us both by the collar and was dragging us, much faster than I would have thought possible.

Another explosion rocked the park. But it sounded farther away. Or maybe it was just my shot-out ears making me think it was. Thad deposited us both against a concrete wall. Mel and the girls were there, as well as Jace and Edie. Mary, Jess and Fred were also there, huddled against the wall.

But there were also cries of anguish. I tried to regain my senses and started to look at everyone. I ran my hands over Mel and the girls. Little Bit had some scratches, Mel was fine. Lee Ann had a gash in the top of her head, but I couldn't see bone, so I told her to hold pressure on it and moved on. Thad was doing the same as I was. He was checking Mary when I looked over to see blood on his hand.

But a cry of pain got my attention and I looked to the

source to see Danny holding his left wrist. The hand was a bloody mess. Blood ran freely from it and I quickly moved to him and ripped the med kit from my vest.

"Hang on, Buddy!" I tore open an Israeli bandage and tried to sort out just what was going on with his hand. Determining most of the damage was to the lower three fingers, I wrapped the bandage around them and secured it.

The park was full of screams, wails and shouts. People were running around looking for loved ones, friends. When they'd discover them, dead or mutilated, they would add their voice to the chorus of anguish. It was hard to distinguish any one sound from the cacophony filling the air.

I saw black smoke suddenly pour out of the Stryker as it lurched forward. It began to build up speed as it raced through the park. I found Sarge, shouting into his radio. I hadn't noticed the traffic and cocked my head to the side to hear it.

"...ing now and will be moving pretty quick. I got nothing to try and stop them." Dalton said.

"Mike's on the way to you. Try and keep them in sight." Sarge replied.

"Grab that little bastard Micha!" I shouted into the radio.

"I already have him," Dalton replied. "He ain't going anywhere."

"Bring his ass to me when you can." I said. Then I looked around the park. There were so many hurt it was hard to find a starting point. But seeing Doc working on a woman, I ran over to him to help as best I could.

The park was a surreal scene. Smoke filled the air, mixed with the smell of blood, dirt and torn vegetation. Leaves from the trees in the park blanketed the ground, covering body parts that were scattered across the lawn. Tables that the traders used were turned over or smashed. In a couple places, they were burning. The truck that I'd pulled Mel and the girls from under was a ragging inferno. All the food and supplies in the back of it, now gone.

But that small loss paled in comparison to the loss of life. It would take some time to tally the dead and wounded as the death toll would surely climb in the days to come. I could see a woman being carried away, missing her left leg from mid-thigh. A woman carried a small blond toe-headed boy, his body limp in her arms. His bright blond hair matted with blood.

We applied a tourniquet to the woman Doc was helping. A severed artery in her right arm spurted bright red blood with every beat of her heart. Her right side was riddled with shrapnel as well. As soon as we stopped the arterial bleed, Doc grabbed two people and told them to take her to the clinic. We moved on to see if we could help others.

As we moved through the park helping those we could, we found an elderly man lying on his stomach. His lower back had a hole big enough to put a can of soup in; he was still conscious. Doc spoke to the man, he was alert and calm.

"Are you in pain?" The man shook his head affirmatively. Doc patted his shoulder, "Ok. We'll get you moved to the clinic soon."

"Alright," the old gentleman replied with a nod.

Doc pulled a Sharpie from his pocket and leaned over, writing the word BLACK on the man's forehead. As we moved through the survivors, that became the routine. Doc would evaluate the patient quickly and we would mark their forehead with a color. Red for immediate, meaning they needed immediate care and were a priority. Yellow for delayed. These cases could wait and were next in line. Green for minimal; these were usually the walking wounded. And black for expectant. Those people were too injured to help and were expected to die.

If all others were helped and there were time and material, they would be seen last. If they were still alive.

We stopped by a couple, the man cradling his wife in his lap. She had head wounds that looked worse than they were. Her face was covered in blood, her hair matted as well. Doc looked her over and removed a couple of sponges from his kit and wiped her forehead and face to give him room to write, DELAYED.

The man seized Doc's hand, asking, "What does yellow mean?"

"It's alright," I replied. "It means her injuries aren't that bad. She's going to be okay."

The man pulled Doc over to him, "Is that what it really means? You are going to help her, aren't you?"

Doc patted his shoulder, "Yes we are. She'll be fine. Might have a nasty scar, but that's it."

The man looked down at his wife, tears in his eyes. "See, baby. I told you it wasn't that bad. You're going to be fine."

The worst part was the children. We found many of them dead. Others, we were forced to mark with BLACK. Their little bodies simply could not deal with the trauma caused by modern military-grade high explosives. I saw Thad carrying the body of a teenage girl. She was obviously dead. He gently placed her in a row of other bodies in the shade of the trees. He was covered in blood, but didn't seem to notice. After laying her down, he immediately went to look for another. And, so it went for more than an hour.

The walking wounded made their way to the clinic. Those not mobile were aided by their friends, family or neighbors. The more severely wounded were carried on makeshift stretchers until proper ones arrived from the clinic. Once the wounded were removed from the park, we were able to survey the damage. Twenty-three people lay dead throughout the park.

In the distance, I heard a loud boom, followed by an explosion. I hoped Mike had found whoever did this. I hoped they would be brought back alive.

Dalton knelt on the side of Micha's face as he bound his hands. He'd placed a stout oak limb into the crook of his elbows, behind his back, and bound his hands together in front of him. It was a very uncomfortable restraint. Having secured his prisoner, Dalton stood up and looked to where the small Jeep-like vehicle was sitting, its crew still lobbing rounds. Micha sat up and started to say something. Dalton looked down at him, drew his Glock and gripped it by the barrel. He grabbed Micha by the hair and pushed his head to the side. Using the Glock like a mallet, he struck hard, once behind the ear. Micha collapsed to the ground, unconscious.

With that taken care of, Dalton stepped into the small cinder block home where he'd caught Micha nearby. Going through the house, he came to a bedroom that faced the small field the mortar team was working from. The window was broken out, so he wouldn't need to open it. He stepped back into the closet of the room to obscure himself and raised his carbine. It would be a fairly long shot, in excess of three hundred meters. He was glad that today he had the AR with the ACOG. While the AK could shoot that far, this was much better suited.

Resting the rifle against the doorframe of the closet, he steadied it and used the hashmark on the vertical reticle for three hundred meters and squeezed the trigger. The rifle thundered in the closet, it was a miss. The mortar crew instinctively ducked when the round cracked as it passed them. The intensity of the crack gives a good indication of the proximity of the passing bullet, and this one was damn close.

They all ducked behind the Jeep and looked for the source of the shot. But not knowing where it came from, they had no idea they were still in Dalton's line of sight. The second round did not miss as one of the men crumpled to the ground. The remaining men moved to the far side of the Jeep and pulled their stricken comrade with them. They began firing wildly at any place they thought the shooter could be. But they still did not have a line on Dalton.

He took his time, waiting for one of them to poke his head out. Dalton could clearly see the mortar set up behind the truck. It was large and had a single axle to allow it to be towed. To fire, it had to be disconnected from the truck and allowed to pivot back. The mortar was then lifted from its cradle and the base and bipod planted firmly in the ground.

Dalton kept an eye on the men. His radio crackled, "You still in the same place?" Mike asked.

"Roger that."

As he spoke, a second light duty Jeep came racing up and slid to a stop. The three men in this truck began shouting and gesturing to the others, who remained behind their cover. *Bingo*, Dalton muttered to himself as he settled the optic on the man in the passenger seat and squeezed the trigger. The man was mid-sentence, leaning half out of the vehicle when the bullet struck him and he fell out, landing facedown with one foot still in the truck. The others began to fire wildly again.

Dalton heard the Stryker before he saw it. It came racing up the street he was on. Leaving his cover, he went back out through the house to show them where their target was. Micha was awake now, struggling to get to his feet. As Dalton passed him, he delivered a butt-stroke with the carbine to the top of his head, sending him sprawling to the ground again. He wondered, for an instant, if poor Micha was going to have any brain damage from the repeated blows. He shrugged, soon it wouldn't matter anyway.

Dalton jogged out to the street. He couldn't see anyone topside, but the turret did turn towards him quickly as he came out. But the top hatch popped open and Ted's head came out. Dalton shouted to him, pointing to where the now two trucks were sitting. Ted popped out of a hatch and gave him a thumbs-up before disappearing back inside. The Stryker jerked as it gained speed down the road, the turret rotating to have the gun in position as soon as the targets came into view.

The big fighting vehicle stopped abruptly once it passed the house Dalton had used for cover. It rocked back and forth, but the gun stayed level. Almost immediately, the gun fired with a deafening blast. A spent shell ejected from the rear of the gun, landing on the road with a loud clang as the huge piece of smoking brass rolled towards the gutter. At nearly the same instant, the mortar truck exploded, sending pieces of it and bodies cartwheeling into the air. The mortar, that weighed more than five-hundred-pounds, also cartwheeled through the air. The second truck that had pulled up was also knocked onto its side and caught fire.

Dalton started running towards the scene as the Stryker also began to move. Ted popped out of the hatch and manned the fifty-cal, pulling its charging handle back twice to get the weapon into battery. A couple of the men who had survived the Stryker's main gun staggered to their feet in obvious shock. One was holding his head as he stumbled about. Another of the men began firing at the approaching Stryker, a futile attempt, but the last great act of defiance. Ted opened up with the Browning and cut him down as dirt and sand shot up in geysers.

Dalton made it to the overturned truck as a man was trying to crawl out. He grabbed him by the collar and pulled him out. He was bleeding and his face was burned. Throwing him to the ground, he searched the man, stripping a pistol from him and tossing it aside. Mike quickly joined in the search and the two checked both the living and the dead.

There were only two men left alive by the time they finished the search. The one Dalton pulled from the overturned truck had succumbed to his wounds, and the others were all dead. Some lay in the sun naked, or nearly so, their clothes having been blasted from their bodies by the force of the explosion. The two prisoners were both wounded, one more so than the other. The two were herded to the back of the armored vehicle where Ted tended to their wounds.

Neither of the men spoke, though the one did moan in pain. The man that survived relatively unscathed sat staring at the ground.

"They're Cubans," Dalton announced as he searched their pockets.

"Yeah, they look like it," Ted answered as he wrapped the head of the more severely wounded of the two.

"You guys got these two? I got another one I need to go get." Mike nodded, keeping his eye on the man sitting on the ground.

Dalton walked back to the yard of the house and found Micha awake again. He cowed at Dalton's approach, certain another bash to the head was coming. Dalton grabbed his arm and pulled him to his feet. "What's going on?" Micha mumbled.

"Let's go over here with your friends," Dalton replied as he dragged the bewildered Micha along.

"What friends?"

Dalton shoved him out in front of him, announcing, "Walk. Your buddies from south of the border are waiting for you."

Micha tried to turn and say something, but Dalton shoved him with the carbine. Micha didn't want another blow to the head so he kept quiet and walked. When they got to the Stryker, Dalton told Micha to sit. He looked at the Cuban sitting on the ground. The guy made eye contact with him before quickly looking away. Micha looked at the burning trucks and the bodies scattered about. Then he looked at the wounded soldier Ted was still doctoring.

Dalton was leaned against the Stryker and nudged Micha with his foot, "You speak Spanish?"

He nodded, "Yeah. I took it in high school like everyone else."

"Mmm," Dalton grunted.

"What's going on?" Micha asked.

Mike stepped up in front of the seated man and squared off with him. "You know damn well what's going on. Don't pretend you don't."

Micha looked at the ground, "I don't."

Dalton reached into his cargo pocket and took out a small green radio and dropped it into his lap. "That refresh your memory?"

Mike looked at Dalton and asked, "He had that on him?"

"Yeah. I followed him and heard him talking on it. That's how I knew it was coming. He posted up a short distance from the park and gave a fire correction before beating feet to meet up with these guys. As soon as he did that, I followed him until I saw the mortar team; then I jumped his ass."

Mike looked down at Micha and asked, "Still wondering what's going on?"

"Morgan said he didn't trust your ass. Guess he was right," Dalton said.

"We need to call in transportation for these guys. This one won't be able to walk that far," Ted said.

CHAPTER 8

Danny was nearly inconsolable. Once we took stock of our people, the ugly truth was revealed. Bobbie had perished in the fire. It haunted me to know that she was the one I'd seen on fire. Out of shame, I didn't say I'd seen her though. Not that there was anything I could have done to save her. At that point, even had we managed to extinguish the fire, the short time she would have lived would have been agonizing. As horrible as it was to say, it was for the best.

Jess had a broken arm. Doc had it in a Sam Splint and was urging her to go to the clinic. But she was refusing to leave our group. Aric had shrapnel wounds in his right leg. None of the wounds was life threatening at the moment, but Doc was worried about infection.

Doc stood up, having just cleaned some cuts on Little Bit's face. The man looked tired. He surveyed the group that had moved to the pool behind the band shell. "Good thing we got those antibiotics on the trip."

I was sitting beside Mel with Little Bit in my lap. I looked up and nodded. "Are we going to have enough?"

He shook his head. "Probably not. I thought I was stocking up. This will wipe It all out."

Mel wiped sweat-matted hair from Little Bit's forehead and

replied, "At least we have it." She'd been crying. She and Bobbie had known one another their entire lives. Bobbie's loss would affect Mel for years. I gripped her hand and smiled at her. She tried to smile back, but it wasn't in her.

Sarge walked up with Kay. He'd taken her to the clinic to have her wounds treated. She was on crutches. A piece of shrapnel had hit her foot. Jess got to her feet and went to assist the older woman, but Kay shooed her away.

"I'm fine, Jess. There are plenty more hurt a lot worse than I am," Kay said.

"I tried to get her to stay at the truck," Sarge said. "But she wouldn't hear of it."

Kay held her hand out and Sarge steadied her as she took a seat. "Like I said, I'm fine."

"Is anything broken?" Doc asked.

Kay shook her head. "No, just a laceration."

"Where are the prisoners?" I asked Sarge.

"On their way back to the ranch. The boys will keep them *comfortable* till we get there."

"Good," I replied. I wanted a word with Micha. "Has anyone seen Shane or Shawn?"

Sarge stabbed a thumb over his shoulder. "They're at the clinic. Had to kill that ole boy you sent 'em after. He worked 'em over pretty good from what they said, until Shane shot his ass."

I looked at Aric. He was lying on the ground with his head in Fred's lap. "Looks like you were right, buddy."

"I only wish I'd seen him sooner. We may have been able to prevent this," he replied.

"We did the best we could, man."

Mel squeezed my hand, saying, "I want to go home."

"That's a good idea," Sarge said.

I helped Mel and Little Bit back to the armory where all the trucks were. As we walked, I saw Thad coming from the clinic. I hadn't seen him since watching him carrying the dead. His clothes were covered with blood. He looked like someone in a zombie movie. We stopped and waited for him and Mary.

"How you doing?" I asked, looking him up and down.

"I'm fine," he replied. "Not a scratch on me."

I looked at Mary, "How about you? You alright?"

She nodded meekly. "I'm fine. We took a couple of the wounded to the clinic." She clenched her eyes closed and shook her head. "There are so many people hurt so bad."

I patted her back. "I Know. I'm just glad we're alright."

She went over to Mel and hugged her. "I'm so sorry about Bobbie."

Mel held her for a moment, taking comfort in the embrace. After a pause, she replied, "Thank you. I'm just glad no one else was really hurt."

As we walked back to the armory, I talked with Thad. He looked down at himself and said, "I can't believe nothing happened to me. One shell exploded right in front of me. I mean, right in front of me."

"You've got an angel watching over you," I replied. I put my hands over my ears. "I thought my ear drums ruptured. But my hearing is coming back."

Thad half smiled, "I'm really surprised you didn't get hit. You know, you seem to have a knack for it."

He made me laugh and I slapped his back, "It's because you were there. I was collaterally protected." I cocked my head to the side and looked up at him, "It was purely by accident, mind you."

As we walked, Alex, the man Aric and I had met at the abandoned Publix, walked up. "What the hell was all that?"

"I believe it was a mortar attack by some Cuban soldiers," I replied.

"But why?"

I shrugged. "I don't know. Target-rich environment maybe. But we've got a couple of them and we'll find out."

He looked at the ground as he walked and asked, "I don't mean to sound like an asshole. But you said you'd bring me some shoes. I was headed to the park when it started. I'm guessing the shoes were in the truck that burned?"

I nodded. "All the shoes were in the truck. But not yours." I pointed at the fuel truck sitting in front of the armory. "Yours are in there."

We walked over to the truck and I took out the boots and handed them to him. Then I took out the bag of food I'd set aside for him as well. "I had your stuff in here."

He looked at it all and said, "Wow. This is more than I expected. Thank you is not enough, but thank you."

"No worries. I hope they help you."

He sat down on the ground and pulled off his tattered shoes and put the boots on. Mel and the girls were getting into the truck. It would be a little crowded, but we'd manage for the short ride home.

Standing up, Alex looked at the boots and announced, "These feel amazing. Again, thank you."

I looked over my shoulder as I helped Mel into the truck. "No problem. Good luck to you."

Aric walked up as I was getting into the truck, "I'm going to go find Shane. I want to see the body, to see if it is him."

I nodded. "Alright. Let me know."

We convoyed back home. There was a lot of work to do. Many graves needed to be dug. But in today's world, you buried your own. Bobbie's body was in a body bag in the bed of the little red truck. Danny sat in the back with her as Thad drove. I was really worried about him. They'd been together for better than twenty years. It was going to be hard on him.

I parked the truck and we walked home together in silence. As we came through the gate, Little Bit said she wanted to watch a movie. I imagine she needed to distract her mind. Can't blame her, I'd like to as well. Inside, Lee Ann and Taylor piled onto the couch with Little Bit to distract themselves.

"Are you ok, babe?" I asked Mel.

She was sitting on the foot of the bed and nodded. I sat down beside her, putting my arm around her. "Are you sure?"

She wiped her nose with a rag she fidgeted with in her hand. "I'm so very thankful my family wasn't hurt." She broke down and started to cry, "But I can't believe she's gone."

I rested my chin on her head. "I know. Of all the people. I would never have imagined this kind of thing would happen to her." I thought back over the years. Danny and Bobbie had been a constant part of our lives. For as long as I'd known Mel, I'd known them. Our kids grew up with the two of them and were thought of as part of our family. Their house was always a safe and happy place for our girls.

"I'm going to go check on the girls," I said as I stood up.

Mel nodded and crawled up onto the bed. "Okay. I'm going to lie down for a while."

I looked back at her from the door and saw her holding the rag to her face as she cried. I felt so horrible for her, but the only thing that could help this was time. I quietly closed the door and went into the living room. The girls were sitting closely together and I leaned over the back of the couch.

"You guys ok?" I asked.

Little Bit looked up, her eyes red and swollen from crying. "Is Aunt Bobbie dead?"

I gently rubbed her head. "I'm afraid so, sweetie." Lee Ann and Taylor both sniffled.

Little Bit started to cry again. "I don't want her to be dead."

I leaned over and kissed her head. "I don't either, baby."

"Am I going to die?"

"No baby. We all die eventually, but you're not going to die, not anytime soon." Trying to get her mind off it, I asked, "What are you watching?"

Sniffling, she replied, "The Sponge Bob Movie."

I tried to smile, but it was forced. "I like that one. I have some things to do and I'll come back and finish it with you."

"Okay," she whimpered.

"You guys take care of her," I said to her sisters.

Taylor looked up; she'd been crying as well. "We will. Where's Mom?"

"She's resting."

Turning her attention back to the cartoon, she replied, "Okay."

I went outside and stood on the porch, wiping my eyes. The dogs could sense something was going on and whined, thumping their tails on the porch. I sat down on the bench and all three tried to put their heads into my lap. I patted their heads and scratched their ears for a minute. But there was an unpleasant task that needed to be addressed, and waiting wouldn't make it any better.

Going over to Danny's, the porch was crowded with people. The mood was naturally depressed and I didn't speak to anyone as I went into the house. Danny was sitting at the dining table as Doc tended to his hand. It was a mess. The pinky and ring finger were gone, as well as part of the palm. Doc was trying to stitch it up as best he could.

But Danny wasn't there. He was someplace else entirely. I

know what Doc was doing had to hurt, but he never so much as flinched. Maybe it was shock. Of course, it was shock. Who wouldn't be in shock after something like that?

I could see Thad on the back porch with Kay and Mary, and I went through the door. They were talking when I came out and looked up at me. I nodded at Thad, "I think we need to take care of this right away."

"We were just talking about that," Kay said.

"I'll get the shovels," Thad said as he stood up. I was happy to see he'd changed clothes.

"Where is she?" I asked.

"Still in the truck," Mary replied.

I nodded and went back into the house. Doc was finishing what little he could do and I pulled a chair out and sat down beside Danny. "Hey, buddy. Thad and I are going to take care of Bobbie. Is there any place you'd prefer?" There was no *right* way to ask such a question.

He looked at his bandaged hand and stood up, "I'll show you. I'm going to do it."

Doc reached out and grabbed his arm, "You can't use—" he paused and rephrased what he was about to say. "Your hand needs some time for the wound to close."

Danny looked at his hand again and replied, "I have to do it."

Doc looked at me and I shrugged. He shook his head and said, "Let me take another look at it afterwards."

I went out the backdoor with Danny and into the yard. Near the pond was a birdfeeder that had been there as long as they had lived in the house. It was one of the first things Danny had put up, so Bobbie could watch the birds when she was in the kitchen or sitting on the porch.

"Right here," he said, pointing to the ground in front of the feeder.

I nodded, "It's a good place."

Thad came around the house with a couple of shovels. He held one out to me, but Danny took it, Thad looked at me, and I replied with a look that didn't require any further explanation. He set to work breaking the ground. Initially, Danny tried to break the earth as well. But with only one hand, he couldn't very well. Instead, he and Thad got into a rhythm of Thad breaking the new ground and Danny scooping it out as best he could.

I offered once to give him a break, but Danny refused, determined to bury his wife. So, I left them and walked over to the shed where I found a flat shovel and returned to help. By the time I got back, Danny's bandage was soaked through and blood from his hand dripped into the grave we were digging. It was almost symbolic in a way, part of him would be there with her.

We worked for some time to get the hole deep enough and perfectly shaped. The sides were clean and the corners nearly perfect. It was more than a hole after all. When we were finished, Thad and I went to the truck and slid the OD green bag out and carried her back to the spot, laying her down for a moment so Thad could get down in the hole. Danny interjected, "I don't want her in this. I want something better."

"This is the best, Danny. Really," I replied.

But Danny was insistent and wouldn't let up until Thad reached out and took him by the shoulder. "Danny, my friend, trust me when I say this. You do not want to see her like this. Remember her how she was. Not like this."

Danny hadn't seen her body. We had quickly put Bobbie into the body bag before he could see her for this very reason. I didn't want to see, but as his friend, I really didn't want him to.

It was a horrible sight that I wouldn't wish on anyone. Especially someone I cared for.

Thad's words had an impact on Danny. He knew Thad spoke from personal experience. He knew he'd buried not only his wife, but also his son in the same condition. And he'd done it alone. At least Danny wasn't alone. We couldn't change Thad's past, but at least we could help Danny deal with it.

As tears began to run down his face, Danny nodded, "You're right. You're right." He knelt down and put his hand on the bag, running it back and forth. I was struck by it, for I knew what Bobbie looked like under his hand. My stomach began to protest, the whole image threatening a loss of control. But I fought it. I didn't want that as the memory of his wife's burial either.

Thad stepped gently into the grave and Danny, with his good hand, and I helped lower her down. Once she was in her resting place, Thad carefully climbed out and we stood there for a minute in silence, giving Danny the opportunity to say whatever he needed to. He didn't utter anything aloud, but I was certain he was saying what he needed to silently.

When Danny stood up and grabbed a shovel, Thad and I did likewise and we filled the grave in. When the work was done, Danny's shovel was completely covered in blood, all the way down to the spade. Doc sat on the porch and watched the process. Once he saw we were done, he came out and put an arm around Danny. "Come on back to the house so I can clean that up," he said.

Danny didn't protest and the two of them went back to the house together. Thad and I carried the shovels back to the shed, stopping by the hose to clean Danny's shovel. But his blood had stained the wood; it would be a lasting reminder of the day.

"Tomorrow, we'll have a service for Bobbie," I said as I used my hand to scrub the handle of the shovel.

"That'd be good. We needed to get this done as soon as possible," Thad replied.

I nodded. "It needed to be done."

"How's Mel taking it?"

Turning off the water, I shook my hands as we walked towards the shed, "Rough. They've known each other their entire lives. The kids grew up with them their entire lives. It's tough on all of them."

Thad leaned his shovel into a corner of the shed. "I can relate to how they feel."

"I know you can, my friend. I'm sorry for everyone."

Thad looked up into the sky and ran his hands through his hair. "Maybe someday it will calm down."

"Maybe. But in the meantime, you really need a haircut."

Thad smiled weakly. "Yeah. Mary said the same thing."

"I've got clippers, you know."

"I'll come over later and let you sheer me," he replied, again with a weak smile.

"I'm going to go over and talk to Sarge. They've got those three prisoners. I want to see what they've found out."

"I'll come with you."

We went back to the house. The smell of cooking filled the air as we stepped inside. Jess and Fred were preparing supper, under Kay's supervision naturally. She sat at the bar, keeping watch over the goings-on in her kitchen. The thought of *her kitchen* struck me. It was Bobbie's kitchen. It *was* her kitchen before today anyway.

Aric was sitting at the table. I looked over and asked, "Hey, we're going to see the old man. You want to go?"

He was immediately on his feet. "Damn right I do."

Thad stepped over to Kay. "How you doing, Miss Kay?"

She reached out and touched his arm. "I'm fine, Thad. Thank you for asking."

"If you need anything, be sure to let us know."

She patted his arm, "I will."

We left the house and headed down the road. It was getting late and the sun was starting its final descent. With the sun closer to the horizon, the temperature dipped ever so slightly. It was a refreshing change, little as it was. Pulling my bandanna from my pocket, I mopped my forehead and said, "Damn, I can't wait for winter."

"Then you'll be looking forward to spring," Thad replied.

"Nope," I replied as I stuffed the cloth back into my pocket. "I love cold weather."

"What the hell are you doing here then?" Aric asked.

"I have no earthly idea. I've left several times. But I always came back for some reason."

"I couldn't wait to get here," Aric replied. "I grew up in the Midwest. Snow is pretty to some people. Usually, it's people that don't have to shovel that shit before school in the morning."

I looked up into the fading sky where countless insects darted to and fro. "I wish three feet would fall right now."

Aric howled. "That'd make this walk real pleasant!"

I laughed. "We wouldn't be sweating like we are!"

"I'll take the heat," Thad said. "I like the heat. Never was a fan of the cold. Winter here in Florida isn't too bad. I like it."

As we passed the bunker, Wallner stepped out. "Hey, guys."

I smiled, "Looks like you're still here."

He smiled broadly. "Permanently now, thanks to Top."

"I'm glad to have you fellas. But I feel bad you always have to be out here."

He waved me off. "We're good. We work in three eight-hour shifts. Believe me, we're all good with it. The food is better here. We're in a real house, which we've cleaned up nicely now." He nodded at Thad, "And thanks to Thad here, we even have running water now. This is great!"

"Glad to do it for you fellas," Thad replied.

"So, don't worry about us." His tone shifted. "I'm really sorry about your loss. We didn't know Bobbie very well. She brought us supper here while you guys were gone and when we went to the house to eat, she was always very nice. It's terrible."

I nodded. "Thanks. We're on our way now to see what the old man's got out of the perpetrators so far."

"We saw them when they brought them in. What are you going to do with them?"

"Remains to be seen," I replied.

"They're an invading force. What do you think we'll do with them?" Aric asked.

Wallner nodded. "There were lots of rumors about what happened out here. Sheffield was always ranting about it."

I snorted. "Yeah. He's a peculiar sort."

"Now that Top is running things, it's going to be different," Wallner replied.

"What?" Thad asked.

I looked at him. "He doesn't want a big deal made of it. But he has just been promoted to full bird Colonel."

"What!" Aric shouted. "Are you serious?"

I nodded. "But don't say anything. He really doesn't want anyone to make a big deal about it. Sheffield still runs things in town. But he now has to answer to the old man."

"I'll bet that didn't sit well with Sheffield," Thad said.

"Actually, he was fine with it. Relieved, actually."

"I can see that," Wallner said. "He was always stressed out. He may be a Captain, but he's no officer."

I smiled. "Yeah, Sarge said he was a military hobbyist."

Wallner laughed and pointed at me, "That's it! That's it exactly!"

"Alright, buddy, we gotta go check on him," I held my hand out and shook his. "We appreciate what you guys are doing."

He gripped my hand tighter. "It's our pleasure. Really."

As we headed down the lane towards Sarge's house, Aric said, "I can't believe they made him a Colonel."

"I laughed out loud when I heard it. Pissed him off, but all I could picture was an old southern Colonel, ya know."

"Like Colonel Sanders?" Thad asked seriously.

I nodded and wagged a finger at him. "Yes. But don't start on the chicken thing. We've already had that discussion." Thad smiled in reply.

"What chicken thing? Which one is best? Hands down, Bojangles."

Thad and I both looked at him in horrified shock. "You need to stop talking now. Your Yankee is showing," I replied as Thad laughed.

"I'm not a Yankee!" Aric grunted.

"Were you born north of Tallahassee?" I asked. He didn't answer right away and I added, "Then you're a Yankee."

That didn't sit well with Aric and he mumbled, "North of Tallahassee, my ass." It got Thad to laughing. And I was glad to see it. This silly-ass little conversation pulled us, even if just momentarily, out of the darkness that was closing in around us.

The Stryker was sitting in front of Sarge's house, and as we walked around it, we saw the garage door was open. It revealed what had become an all too common sight. Micha was hanging from the ceiling, naked. Beside him hung one of the Cubans. The other one was too injured for such treatment. But he was strapped to a chair where he could see everything that was happening.

Sarge was sitting in a chair facing the men. He was leaned back with his feet outstretched and his hands stuffed into his pockets. Doc, Ted, Mike and Dalton were all there as well. Doc, being a man of medicine, was off to the side. He generally didn't take part in interrogations. Mike and Ted stood on each side of the two men and Dalton was behind them, a length of hose in his hand that I recognized. It got Thad to laughing. And I was glad to see it.

Micha didn't look well. He hung limply from the ropes, his full weight on them. His body glistened with sweat and his breathing was heavy. I could see red welts on his sides that I was sure extended across his back as well. The Cuban was in a similar condition. Both men looked as though it had been a long afternoon.

Walking into the garage, we looked the scene over. "Does that one speak English?" I asked, pointing at the Cuban.

Dalton nodded and Sarge replied, "Just like a cue ball. The harder you hit him, the more English you get out of him."

Micha looked up weakly. I stepped up in front of him and looked into his eyes. "You know, I never did like your ass." I turned and walked away from him. Sliding another chair over beside Sarge, I sat down. "So, what has he had to say?"

"Oh, you know, the usual shit. He doesn't know what we're talking about. Has no idea who these hombres are. Never seen 'em before."

"Really?"

"That's how it started out," Dalton said. Then he ran the piece of hose down Micha's flank, who recoiled at its now familiar cold touch.

"He's starting to come around. He's been a busy boy. He

was working with the DHS before we pushed them out. He's the one that was spraying the farm with herbicide. He was responsible for a number of things," Sarge said.

"I knew it," Thad said.

I shook my head. "Why the hell did they spray the farm?"

"They didn't want us to succeed," Sarge replied. "They wanted suffering. Thinking the people would beg for the Fed's help. But that ain't all. He was also involved in the bombing at the park." Sarge looked at me and said, "His partner was a tough bastard for not telling me that."

Micha looked up and I caught his eye. "Don't worry," I said. "You'll join him soon."

"What about that one?" Aric asked, pointing at the Cuban.

"He's more willing to talk. Just a soldier. They were told they'd be able to walk across the country. Apparently, the Russians and the Cubans got together to carve up the east coast. The Ruskies also had a deal with China, giving them the west."

"Was he spotting for them?" I asked.

Sarge snickered, "Yeah, he was. Still won't admit that." He nodded to the beleaguered Cuban and added, "But he did. They were working together."

"What about the guy working on the net?"

"Oh, the Chinaman." Sarge looked at Aric, "You were right about him. He was who you thought he was."

"I knew it was him. I saw his body. If he was still around here, then others probably are as well," Aric replied.

"Well, he ain't around anymore," I said. "Shane and Shawn put his ass in the dirt." Micha looked up briefly before dropping his head again. "That's right, asshole. We bagged him too."

"What do you want to do with them?" Sarge asked.

I thought about it for a moment, considering the options. I thought back to the bombing in the park. About what happened there. The stinging smell of alcohol mixing with the acrid smell of smoke and metallic odor of blood and flesh. The crunch of glass under my boots as we walked around the scene. It was so much like the last scene at the park, the one that killed Bobbie.

It was almost like stepping back in time. Like revisiting a nightmare in troubled sleep. The image of Bobbie's charred and smoking body as I slowly pulled the zipper up over her face. I remembered the image of Danny's hand, the missing fingers and the rivulets of tears cutting through the black dirt and filth on his face. Then of my girls sitting on the couch and Little Bit looking over her shoulder and asking me if she were going to die too.

As I was considering all this, my radio crackled. It was Shane. "Morgan, we've got issues."

"What's going on?" I asked.

"People are gathering; they're saying the attack was the Army's doing. They're nearly rioting."

I looked at Sarge, "What the hell are they thinking? That we did this to ourselves?"

"Someone is stirring this up. I don't think they came up with it on their own," Sarge replied. Sarge scratched the stubble on his chin. "Ask him to get Cecil to calm them down. He'll be able to handle this until we can get there tomorrow morning."

I nodded and relayed the statement to Shane, telling him to get Cecil to try and calm them down. He agreed and said they could handle it until tomorrow. "It hasn't gotten out of hand yet," he replied.

I looked around the room. At the men hanging from the rafters, the others, Mike, Ted, Doc and Dalton watching them from the perimeter. Settling my eyes on Micha, I said, "We'll take them to town tomorrow and hang them in the park."

Sarge's head bobbed as he processed this. "It's good. It's good and proper."

Then Micha's raspy voice broke the silence. "And what good will that serve?" I looked over to see his eyes cast up as he was too weak to lift his head. He shook his head from side to side. "We," he started to say, then glanced at his Cuban compatriot before correcting himself, "I am worth more alive than dead." A slight smile cracked his lips. "I know what's going on. Where," he jerked his head towards the Cuban, "the rest of them are." His smile spread, "where the Russians are." He was playing his ace, or so he thought.

Sarge's cackling cut the weight of the moment. I was thinking about what Micha had said. But Sarge wasn't impressed. Instead his head rocked back and forth. "Thank you!" He shouted. "Thank you for giving me that. I was wondering just where the limit was. Just what you did indeed know." Sarge rose to his feet. "But now I know." Sarge looked over at me and said, "Don't worry. By dawn, **we'll** know what **he** knows."

Fear washed over Micha as he asked the question for the answer he already possessed. "What? Why? Why not keep me alive?" He seemed to find strength and started to fight against the bindings. "You can't kill me! You need me!"

I stepped past Sarge and close to Micha's face. I leaned over and looked into his eyes. I knew how he'd managed to this point. How he would so easily, quickly, cast his allegiance to the strongest.

"You know the problem with selling your morals?" I asked. "Eventually there are no more buyers. I always wondered why you bothered me." I wagged my finger at him, "Something about you always ate at me. Watching you slink around, and now knowing you were making deal after deal to keep yourself safe and comfortable." I grabbed his chin and lifted his head.

"But there are no more deals. You cannot take this and turn it into a better situation for yourself. You've burrowed your way in for the last time. Tomorrow, you will hang."

Micha glared back at me. I could see he was trying to formulate his response. But he wouldn't get the chance to issue it. Sarge stepped past me, clapping my back as he did. "Tomorrow is a long way off and we've got a lot to do," he said as he gripped my shoulder and turned me away from Micha. "Go on and get some rest. Tomorrow, in town, he's yours. But tonight," Sarge said as he looked at Micha and added, "but tonight, his ass is ours."

A fear washed over Micha's face and his tongue flicked out of his lips as a lizard would. "I've already told you everything I know."

As I stepped away, Sarge snorted, "Well now, we know that's not the case," Sarge looked past Micha to Dalton and added, "don't we?"

Dalton nodded grimly, "Indeed."

"And I believe you are well acquainted with my man Dalton," Sarge said to Micha as he spun him around to face the big man. "And all we've done to this point was with the aim of keeping you alive." Sarge laughed and patted Micha's shoulder. "But that's no longer an issue. Now is it?" The last words Sarge spoke directly into Micha's ear.

Panic gripped the naked man as his new reality swept over him. "But I can help you! I know where they all are! I can tell you!" Micha pleaded.

Sarge stepped behind Micha and tussled his hair. "Oh, you will. See, now, we know you have more to tell us. And we know you want to." Sarge stepped back in front of him and asked, "you do want to, don't you?"

Micha nodded, "Yes, I'll tell you everything."

Sarge stepped back over to his chair and took a seat. He chewed on his thumbnail as he made a show of thinking. "That's good. It'll make all this easier. But," he paused and looked at the nail, "we have to be sure you're telling us the truth. We have to believe you."

"I'll tell you the truth!" Micha shouted, believing he'd found his salvation.

Sarge looked past Micha to Dalton and asked, "Do you believe he'll tell us the truth?"

"I'm not sold," Dalton replied.

Micha was reinvigorated and now stood on his tip toes. He tried to spin around to see Dalton, but Dalton prevented him from doing so. "I will! I have no reason to lie now!"

Sarge leaned back in his chair and smiled. "Good. That's what I wanted to hear."

I listened to the exchange with little interest. Whatever the information we could extract from the little slug paled, at least in my mind, to the value he would serve swinging from a rope on the gallows in the park. His death will serve a couple of public purposes, and a private one as well. The people of northern Lake County have not yet forgotten the evils of the DHS and what they did to people here. While we thought we vanquished that particular evil, this will demonstrate that the threat still exists. It will also demonstrate the fact that we are still very much fighting it, and will not shrink from the threat.

On a personal level, it will be vengeance for Bobbie. For the pain her death has caused my friend, my wife and my daughters. She was someone who never caused harm to another person. Innocent in the evils of the world around her. But just another tick mark in the column for those that, still it would seem, seek to oppress or rule over us.

It was this last thought I had the hardest time with. It's only natural that there will always be those that seek to subjugate others. To lust for power and control. But control over what? Our society has so little now, of anything. What good is it to rule over a wasteland, other than to serve one's own ego perhaps? Because, with the power, even if sought vindictively, comes responsibility. And it was the latter I sought to avoid, not covet.

I willingly accept my responsibility for myself and family. But I damn sure didn't want it for everyone around me. It was as foreign an idea to me as space travel at the moment. Our once soft lives were now hard, and the thought of willingly, wantonly, trying to complicate it further through conquest was unfathomable to me. But the fact remained there were those that didn't think this way and it was because of them, we, I, had to stand where I did.

"You want to live then?" I asked Micha. He nodded eagerly, his eyes wide with the thought of saving his skin. "Then you need to give a full accounting of your actions, since the beginning. You will read them aloud tomorrow in the park, before the community, so all will know your scheming."

Micha nodded enthusiastically. "I'll do it!"

Sarge looked up at me and didn't say anything. I could see he was thinking. "Good. Then you can make your confession tonight. Dalton will be here to make sure your memory doesn't fade." I replied. I looked around at the guys. "Tomorrow morning we're going to have a service for Bobbie, before we go to town." Solemn nods were the only reply. "I'll leave you to it then. I've got other things to attend to," I said as I headed towards the open garage door.

Sarge got up and followed me outside, waiting until we were out of earshot of the others. "Then what?" He asked.

"Then what, what?" I asked.

He stuffed his hands into his pockets and looked at the

ground. "Tomorrow, after he reads his confession, as you call it. Then what?"

"We hang him," I replied easily.

Sarge nodded. "I figured that's where you were going with it. Having him list his dirty deeds in front of everyone is a good idea. They'll never believe us if we just say, *it wasn't us.*"

I nodded. "That's what I was thinking too. We need the folks in town to know we're trying to help them at best and not trying to kill them at the least. This will serve to do that."

"And him swinging from a rope will also send a message that we aren't going to tolerate this sort of bullshit."

I let out a breath and looked up as a mosquito buzzed in my ear. "We'll let Mitch look at his confession in the morning. Have Micha sign it in front of him to keep up the appearance. But in the end, we will stretch his neck. I, we, can't tolerate people that don't want to work for the benefit of everyone. And we certainly can't tolerate those that will actively conspire against it."

Sarge laughed. "Careful, your commie is starting to show."

I grunted, "Whatever. We're not forcing anyone to do anything for the benefit of others. If you want to benefit, you have to provide, labor, something. We're not making anyone work so others don't have to. It's not the same thing."

"I know," he replied. "But when words like, *the greater good*, start getting tossed around, it's a short trip to Marxism."

I stopped and turned to face him. "What we are doing is so far from that twisted logic as to not even be on the same plane. We're simply trying to save this community, lives. What we did yesterday was for the greater good. We handed out food. We try to provide some semblance of order. But we're not forcing it on anybody. Everyone is free to stay or go. Participate or not. I don't give a shit either way."

"And I'm with you on that. But those other systems, they

exist because those men believed it was easier to achieve their idea of community through force. And in a way, it is. It removes responsibility from the individual; and in times like this, people will willingly accept it. I just want to make sure you know how easy that is. How fast people will beg for it."

"You don't have to tell me. Just look at what the country was like before this happened. Decadence is the last stage of a crumbling empire," I laughed, "and we are a hell of a long way from decadence at the moment."

Sarge pinched his nose and blew a snot rocket into the dirt. "Damn straight. We'll get a full accounting out of him tonight," he looked back over his shoulder into the garage. "I don't think we need anything from the Cubans. They'll just say they were soldiers following orders."

"And they are. But they're invading soldiers on a sovereign nation's land. They can swing with him. But, that's up to you. Micha is a civilian and Mitch and I will deal with him. They are soldiers and therefore your problem, so you can sort out what's right for them."

"It's the same in the end," the old man replied as he arched his back, stretching it. "The rope."

I left them to their work and headed back towards the house. As I walked, I plucked the mic from my plate carrier and called, "Hey, Shane."

In a moment, he responded. "What is it, Morgan?"

"You still have that Jap's body?"

"Yeah, we're getting ready to bury him now."

"Don't. Bring him to the park tomorrow."

He didn't hesitate in his reply, probably relieved he didn't have to dig the grave in the heat. "No problem. I'll have him there."

"How's it going? People still grumbling?"

"There's still a lot of talk that the Army did it on purpose. But Cecil got a lot of them calmed down. Something more needs to be done though or it's going to get out of hand."

"We're going to do something tomorrow that should take care of it."

"Okay, good. We'll see you tomorrow."

As I continued towards the house, I thought of what needed to be accomplished. Of course, the service in the morning was weighing heavy on my mind. I'd never considered the possibility of having to bury one of the women in my life. It may be Bobbie this time, and that's horrible, but it could have just as easily been Mel. And that thought was one I couldn't bear. But there was one small project I could work on that would keep my mind off things.

As I passed the shop, I saw the roll-up door open and could hear someone inside, so I wandered over to see who was in there. I found Thad working on a piece of wood sitting on two sawhorses. He had a chisel in hand and was carving into its face. I stepped up and looked over his shoulder. He didn't pause his work, simply asked, "What do you think?"

I put my hand on his shoulder and replied, "I think it's really nice. Danny will appreciate it."

Thad laid the chisel down and took up a small propane torch and lit it. He ran the flame back and forth over the words he'd carved, charring them to a deep black. The rest of the wood, he singed to a light brown. I helped him for a bit as we fit the two pieces together. He had the idea of drilling through the back of one into the back of the top piece and fitting a dowel. Using some wood glue, we clamped the two pieces together for the glue to dry.

"I think everyone will appreciate it," I said. "It's a nice cross."

Thad looked at the cross and said, "I wanted to build her

a casket. But it would take a lot of wood and more time than we have."

I patted his back. "I think the body bag will have to suffice for now." I nodded at the cross, "This will give everyone something to look at and remember her."

"I'm going to varnish it, I think," Thad said as he inspected his work.

"Sounds good," I nodded. "I've got a couple of things I want to do. I'll see you later."

"Thanks for the help."

I nodded as I left him to finish his monument. Both sad and noble at the same time. The dogs were lolling in the driveway when I came through the gate. Their tongues hung from their mouths into the dirt and pine needles as they tried to cool themselves. They must have been out running after something. I stopped to scratch heads and pat flanks. Their tails thumped the round, kicking up small clouds of dust. I envied them. To be a dog and have no concern, let alone knowledge of the bigger powers at play around them. Most people didn't look twice at a dog today. Unless they were hungry of course. Then, being a dog could be a real liability.

I went over to the old Suburban. It was covered in leaves and pine needles and looked as though it'd been sitting there for years when it'd only been a couple of weeks. I popped the hood and looked at the two batteries. I wanted to try to restore them. Even if they only lasted a short time. I'd need some tools, so I headed to the house.

The house smelled wonderful and I found Mel and the girls gathered around the dining table. "What smells so good?" I asked.

Mel got up and went into the kitchen and returned with a plate for me. "Here. Made you one too."

I sat down, leaning my rifle against the wall. "What is it?"

"It's a bar-b-que sandwich. Kay baked rolls and I slow-cooked some of the beef in a crockpot. It came out really well."

"It's really good, Dad," Lee Ann affirmed. Her sisters both nodded their agreement.

I picked the sandwich up and sniffed it, "This smells amazing."

And it was amazing. "Wow," I said as I licked sauce from my fingers. "This is terrific."

We chatted around the table as we ate. Normal talk, nothing morbid. Nothing about Bobbie. Sad as it was, life had to continue. Our lives had to continue. So, we talked about how good the food was. About the cookies Kay was baking for dessert and about the coming weddings. Bobbie's death put a damper on the coming nuptials, but they were still going to happen, and it gave us something positive to focus on. Well, for some to focus on. I rarely thought about it.

After eating, I told Mel I was going out to work on the truck. Little Bit said she wanted to help and carried her plate into the kitchen before meeting me at the back door. I used the moment to remove the plate carrier, any reason to get out of the damn thing. Before heading out, I grabbed a box of baking soda and bag of Epsom Salt. We walked out to the shed while she told me a story about a squirrel she had watched earlier today as he buried acorns. She said every time he would bury one, another squirrel would run over, dig it up and steal it. I laughed when she said they should be nice to one another.

"That's critters, kiddo. Only the strongest survive," I said.

Her lip curled and she replied, "Or the sneakiest."

"Or the sneakiest," I agreed with a pat to the head.

"What are we going to do?" She asked as I put tools and other items I'd need into a bucket.

"We're going to fix the batteries in the truck."

"You going to charge it?" She asked.

"Yeah, but we've got other things to do first."

Once I had everything I'd need, I carried the bucket out to a small yard cart and set it down. Naturally, Little Bit wanted to pull the cart. I only had to help a little. At the truck, I asked her for the wrench in the bucket. She handed it to me and I removed the two batteries from the truck. I asked her to set out a dish-pan type container I'd brought as well as I popped the caps from the batteries.

"What are you going to do?" She asked.

"We're going to pour this old acid into there."

"Can I do it?"

I smiled, "No, sweety. The batteries are very heavy and this acid can burn you. We have to be very careful."

I slowly poured off the first battery, ending with it held upside down over the tub to get as much of the acid out as possible. Then, I drained the second one. Once the batteries were empty, I mixed up a solution of baking soda and water.

"Grab that little funnel and stick it in one of those holes," I said.

"What's that for?" She asked as she placed the funnel into one of the open cells.

"We're going to clean the battery with this."

"The inside?" She shouted.

I smiled and nodded, "Yeah, the inside."

We filled the cells of both batteries with the solution. Then I capped the batteries and rocked them back and forth. Little Bit tried to help, but discovered just how heavy the batteries were. After agitating the solution in the batteries, I poured them out into the tub. The baking soda would help neutralize the acid already there.

"Now what?" Little Bit asked.

I rubbed her head. "Now we need to go inside for the next part." I picked up the Epsom Salt and handed it to her. "Can you carry this?"

She cradled it against her chest with both hands. "Yep. It's heavy, but I'm strong." She made me smile and we went back inside.

I told her to take the salt to the kitchen and I'd be right there. I told Mel I was going to use the stove for a minute before taking out a Pyrex container. I measured out four cups of water from the Berkey filter and poured it into the bowl, then lit the stove. Setting the measuring cup on the counter, I told Little Bit to fill it with the salt.

"Is it safe? Can I touch it?"

I nodded, "Yep. It won't hurt you."

She reached in and grabbed a fist full of the crystals and let them fall through her hand into the cup. She repeated this until the measuring cup was full, and there was quite a mess on the counter. I tested the water with my finger, it was getting hot, so I started slowly pouring the Epsom Salt in while Little Bit stirred it with a spoon.

"This is fun. It's like we're cooking," she said with a smile.

"We are cooking. We're cooking up science!" I replied with an exaggerated smile as I tickled her sides, getting a squeal out of her.

I added another two cups of water and we measured out another two cups of salt and continued the heating and mixing process until all the salt was dissolved. I was using a two to one ratio of water to salt and the process went faster when the water was heated. With the solution ready, I told Little Bit it was time to go back outside. We walked back over to the truck and she held the funnel while I poured the solution into each cell until both batteries were full.

"Now what?" She asked.

As I was placing one of the batteries on the cart, I replied, "Now, we have to charge them. We'll take them to the shop and put the battery charger on one of them tonight."

After setting the batteries on the bench, I connected the charger to it, on its lowest setting. The needle jumped up, showing it was taking a charge. "Now, we wait," I said.

"That was fun," Little Bit replied as we walked back to the house in the dark.

"You're a good helper," I replied. "But it's time for you to get ready for bed."

She yawned. "But I'm not tired."

I smiled as we went inside. Mel and the girls were sitting in the living room. The house smelled of soap and Taylor was mopping at her hair with a towel. Mel intercepted Ashley as she passed by, "You need a bath, stinky girl. The tub is already full. Go take a bath."

"Awe, Mom, I don't want to take a bath," Ashley moaned in protest.

Mel got up from the couch, pointing down the hall, "I don't care what you want. You need a bath and you're going to take one."

With her shoulders slumped, Ashley slogged down the hallway as she peeled off her clothes. Just as I sat down, there was a knock at the door. I looked over and called out, "It's open!"

Jess came in, holding a plate covered with a dish towel. She came in and sat down on the ottoman. "Here's some of Miss Kay's cookies. I thought you guys would like some."

I flipped the towel off the plate and took one, "You thought right!"

"You didn't have to bring them over," Mel said.

Jess shrugged. "I was on my way home anyway."

Pushing a crumb into my mouth, I asked, "How's Danny doing?"

She considered the question for a moment before answering. "He's still very sad. Not saying much."

I held up the last piece of the cookie before popping it into my mouth and asked, "Did he eat a cookie?"

She smiled, "Yeah. He had one."

"That's good. Danny has a soft spot for cookies. It'll take some time for him."

"How are the kids?" Mel asked.

"They're taking it pretty hard too. Edie is really sad. But Mary is staying close to her. Jace is staying with Danny. He won't leave his side."

"Probably the best for both of them," I replied.

Jess looked at the floor for a moment and she asked, "We're going to have the service for Bobbie in the morning?"

I nodded. "Yeah. First thing in the morning."

"Then what?" Mel asked.

I let out a slow breath. "Then we go to town and hang the men responsible."

"How many are there?" Jess asked.

"We have three of them. A few others are already dead. But there are more of them out there. I think the old man will know where they are after tonight."

"What's he doing?" Mel asked tentatively.

"Let's just say, he has a way with words," I replied, not wanting to go into details.

A breeze kicked up once the sun went down and we spent the evening in the living room listening to music on the iPad. The coolers I made were drawing air into the house, and that lowered the temps inside noticeably. Not to mention, just the introduction of fresh air; the house smelled good. It was comfortable, and lounging on the couch as the song, "American Pie" played made for a sleepy setting. I woke up around nine, according to my watch, and carried Little Bit to her bed. The older girls were asleep on the floor and I left them where they were.

Mel was in the bed when I returned. She looked up and said, "Why don't you take a shower?" And she patted the bed.

"Oh, really?" I asked with a smile. Stretching, I said, "I was thinking about it."

"Stop thinking about it and get in there."

"Good thing I took a nap," I said as I flipped on the bathroom light.

CHAPTER 9

We stood silently, gathered around the bird feeder. The earth was still fresh there. The smell of it filled the air. Its broken surface sparkled in the early morning sun as countless drops of dew glistened and shimmered in the growing light. As was sadly becoming our custom, each was left to themselves to say their piece. A dry eye was the oddity as most were wet with grief.

Little Bit hugged Mel's leg and wouldn't look at the place. Kay stood close to Sarge, holding his arm as he patted her back and she dabbed tears from her eyes. Aric stood behind Fred, his arms around her. Jess stood with Doc, the two holding hands. Jace and Edie were with Mary, and Thad stood behind her, offering them all strength. Dalton, Ted and Mike stood off to the side, more stoic than the rest.

After a moment, Thad's deep voice filled the air. "He will wipe every tear from their eyes. There will be no more death, mourning, crying or pain, for the old order of things has passed away." Then he stepped forward and took up the cross he'd made and gently pushed it down into the soft dirt. Bobbie's name ran down the vertical with the dates marking her life on the horizontal. It was a tasteful adornment to her grave with its surface darkened by the flame.

Danny looked up and nodded at Thad. Thad walked over

to him and firmly gripped his shoulder. The two shared a look, but said nothing. It was often the way of men. Men who were not prone to speaking their thoughts could readily share them in this manner. And here they did.

"O my love, my wife!

Death, that hath suck'd the honey of thy breath

Hath had no power yet upon thy beauty." Dalton belted out in a voice that possessed surprising strength. I could visualize him on a Roman stage. He could project his voice so well, he didn't need speakers. It naturally carried and seemed to echo throughout the woods behind the pond.

Danny said nothing. He stood, looking down at the grave of his wife. It caused a fear to well up in me. An all-consuming and nearly insurmountable fear of having to do the same. It terrified me more than anything my mind could conjure. The thought of having to scrape away the earth to lay Mel or one of the girls into a pit, it made me physically ill and my head started to spin. I had to get control of myself and push the morbid thoughts from my mind. We were here for Bobbie and I would remember her. But as I pushed those thoughts away, I promised myself that I would do whatever it took to prevent having to perform this for my own family.

Danny knelt down and placed his good hand on the softly mounded dirt. His head hung and he began to weep. His fingers clenched into a fist around a knot of dirt and he softly pounded the ground with his fist. Dalton stepped up beside me and nudged me with his elbow and nodded at Danny. I knew what he was saying and we stepped up on either side of him and gently raised him to his feet. He didn't resist, as his body shuddered from the sobs. We guided him back to the house, still clenching the fist of dirt.

Everyone said their personal goodbyes and one by one,

they drifted away from the scene. I looked out from the porch to see Mel still at the grave, the last to leave. Mel had known Bobbie the longest. Actually, longer than Danny, Mel was there when they started dating. I walked out to the grave as she wiped her eyes.

"You OK, babe?" I asked.

She shook her head. "I just don't get it. Why her? We were handing out food. We were doing good. Why would someone do that?"

"You can't explain evil."

She looked up at me, her eyes red, swollen and wet. "How much more suffering must we endure? What's the point? The world doesn't make any sense."

I wrapped her in my arms. It was easy to fall into the trap of thinking the world was against us now. There always did seem to be a new disaster or threat to be worried about. I took it day by day, trying not to focus on the distant future or past, but dealing with the issues of the immediate. But everyone had to come up with their own way of coping with it.

"I'm not leaving here anymore," she said as we walked back towards the house.

"Okay," I replied. "But I'm going to town today. We're going to hang the men responsible for this."

She nodded. "Okay. One more trip to town. I want to see their faces when they hang. I want them to suffer."

I pulled her in and kissed the top of her head. "Don't let the hate consume you, babe. It doesn't go anywhere good. Believe me."

"Well, I'm going to watch."

"I don't blame you. But Little Bit can't go. The girls need to stay here."

She nodded her head. "I was already going to tell her sisters to watch her. I'll go with you. When are you going?"

"I was planning to go over to Sarge's place and see where they're at on the interrogation. When I'm done with that, I'll let you know."

She stopped and stepped in front of me, to face me. "Do **not** leave without me."

I leaned in and kissed her forehead. "I won't. I promise."

I made my way to Sarge's house. The garage door was open, and I was met with a curious sight. Micha was still tied up and hanging from the ceiling, albeit in a creative fashion. His legs were tied together and his hands were likewise tied together, but under his legs. A stout piece of oak was run under his arms across his chest and this piece of wood was suspended from the ceiling. It looked uncomfortable as hell.

"Whose creation is this?" I asked as I came into the garage.

Mike pointed at Dalton, "It's that sadistic fuck. I've never seen anyone like him; and I thought I was bad."

Micha's body was racked with obvious pain. "How long has he been like that?" I asked.

"Oh, since last night," Dalton replied. "I wanted to make sure he didn't have anything else to tell me."

"And?"

Dalton gave Micha a push, spinning him. "I think we're good."

I walked over in front of Micha and grabbed a handful of hair and lifted his head. "You ready to confess your sins in public? If you want to escape the rope, it's your only way out."

He nodded and croaked in a raspy voice that I was sure was raw from a night of screaming, "I'll read it. Please, please, cut me down. I can't take this anymore."

I looked around. "Someone got all this shit written down?"

Ted tapped a notepad with a pen. "Yep. Got it all right here. This one's been a naughty boy."

Looking at the two Cubans, I asked, "What about these two?"

"They won't say anything," Mike said. "The one is nearly dead and the other just says he's a soldier following orders. Typical shit. He seems to be under the misguided assumption the Geneva Convention is somehow in play."

"Funny how animals like that will commit untold atrocities against civilians and then, when they're captured, fall back on perceived protection of the Convention," I replied.

"Let's get them all loaded up and headed to town," I said.

Dalton produced his Kukri and in one fluid motion severed the ropes holding Micha up. He crashed to the concrete floor, landing on his hands. But they were so numb from being bound all night, he hardly noticed. We pulled him to his feet and gave him clothes, which he couldn't put on without assistance. Dalton and Mike roughly helped him into a pair of pants and pulled a shirt over his head. His hands were once again bound behind his back and he was stuffed, along with the two Cubans, into the back of the Hummer.

I told Sarge I would meet him in town and left to go get the little red truck. The Hummer was full as it was, and I wanted to see if anyone else wanted to go. Wallner was at the bunker when I walked by and expressed his condolences again. I thanked him and asked if they needed anything.

"No, we're good. You taking him to town?"

Watching the Hummer and the Stryker turn out onto the road, I nodded. "Yeah. They've got to pay for what they've done."

"Should've just shot them."

"Hanging them in public will do far more good. For everyone. If we just told the people we shot him and put him in a hole, they would never really know. There are already some rumblings in town that the Army was responsible for what happened at the park."

"That makes sense. Let everyone see it," Wallner replied.

I told them I would see them later and headed for the house. I went to Danny's to see if he wanted to go. He was already on the porch when I walked up. Thad was there with him.

"You guys want to go to town?" I asked.

They both stood up, the answer clear. I nodded and said, "Let me get Mel and we'll head that way."

The girls were sitting on the porch with the dogs. I told them we'd be back shortly and to stay around the house. Little Bit asked if she could go to Danny's house to play with Jace and Edie. I said she could, but that they needed to stay within sight of the house. She said they would and jumped up and ran off.

"How long are you guys going to be gone?" Taylor asked.

"Couple of hours," I replied.

"Can we come?" Lee Ann asked.

I shook my head, "No, kiddo. You need to stay here and keep an eye on your sister, help with the kids." I thought she'd protest, but she didn't.

I went in to find Mel. She was ready to go and I didn't even shut the door before we were heading back out. Thad pulled up in the little truck and we hopped into the back. The air rushing by felt good. It was still warm, but it was moving. The market in Altoona was bustling with people, and even from the road, I could see people were trading the goods we'd just given them. It made me wonder what they were trying to get. Why they didn't just eat the food. But it was bound to happen. The sudden influx of items no one had seen in a long time made them valuable, and therefore, they were defacto currency.

The Umatilla market was also busy, with more people out

than usual. It was good to see so many people out and about. I'm sure word had spread about what happened in Eustis. But it didn't seem to deter folks from getting out and gathering. As we passed the Publix, I saw Alex on the side of the road. He had a bag over his shoulder and waved as we passed. I waved back, noticing the boots. He watched us for a moment before turning and continuing his trudge down the road.

As we passed through the barricade, I saw the old bucket truck on the side of the road. Terry and Baker had apparently managed to resurrect it. I thumped the roof of the truck. Thad slowed and pulled up behind the big truck. Baker was on the ground looking up.

"How's it going?" I asked. "You're making better time than I thought you would."

She nodded. "It's going faster now. We've almost got the line to the armory ready."

I looked up at the bucket where Terry was cutting a sideline lose. "That's great. How long do you think?"

"We might have it today if everything goes alright," she replied.

"How about getting it out to our place?" Mel asked.

Baker's head rocked side to side. "That will take a little longer."

"But you can do it, can't you?"

"Babe," I said, "don't get your hopes up for power to the house."

"We'll get it out there. It's just going to take a while. We'll have to clear all the lines out there. But we've got a system now," Baker replied.

I nodded up the road, "So this will power the armory, the clinic and the county building?"

Baker wiped her forehead with the back of a gloved hand.

"Yeah. We're going to bring up the armory first, then the clinic, then the courthouse. The guys are up there testing the transformers now."

It was a major step. Real progress everyone could see, and I hoped it would be a boost for the entire community. Not that it would affect their daily lives, but just seeing that it's coming, that things are returning to normal, would reinforce people's will. Maybe pick their spirits up after recent events.

The Stryker was sitting in the park, not far from the burned-out hull of the five-ton truck. The bodies were all gone, though the park still smelled of death. The acrid stench of the fire, the putrid smell of the dried blood and other organic matter mixed into a nocuous funk. Sarge and the guys were standing on the ground in front of the gallows with the prisoners. I hopped out of the bed of the truck and told Mel I was going to look for Mitch. She gripped my hand and said she was coming with me.

We made our way through the crowd until I found Mitch and Michelle by the side of the gallows. He was watching the goings-on and asked, "What's this all about?"

"We're about to hold court," I replied.

"What do you mean?"

I nodded at the three bound men. "They're the ones that attacked the park. We caught them in the act. The one in civilian clothes there, he's caused a lot of problems here. He's going to read an accounting of his crimes and you'll decide his fate."

"Here? Like this?"

I nodded. "Look at these people. They think the Army, that we, attacked the park. That's we're the ones responsible for all this."

"I've heard people saying that," Michelle said. "There's lots of talk about it."

"Well, it wasn't us of course. But we need the people here

to know that, so we're going to do this in public in front of everyone. Otherwise, things are going to get out of control."

"And they're close to that point now," Cecil said from behind me. I turned to look at him and he continued. "People are really upset. There was a lot of folks killed. Little kids even. And they want vengeance and they're about ready to take it into their own hands."

"And we can't allow that," I replied.

"But is this the right way?" Mitch asked. "Is this the way to do it? Is he really responsible?"

I nodded. "Yes, he is. He was spotting for a mortar team. Him and another guy. The other one is dead, but we have his body here to show everyone. There were a couple other soldiers in the mortar group, but they were killed in the fight."

"I think it's the right thing," Michelle said. "By doing it this way, no one can say it wasn't proper. Everyone will see the same thing. There can be no confusion."

Mitch thought about it for a minute. "I guess you're right. It's being done out in the open." He nodded, "It's for the best."

I clapped him on the back and we walked around to the front of the gallows. The crowd was full of whispers and murmurs. There was the occasional finger pointed in our direction, accompanied by hushed words. The crowd was obviously on edge and it wasn't certain where they stood on things at the moment. But we were about to find out.

I leaned in to Dalton and said, "Let's take them up the platform."

"Why are we going up there?" Micha asked.

"So everyone can hear what you have to say," I replied. "And to make sure they can't get to you."

He obviously hadn't considered the possibility of the crowd wanting to tear him apart. He quickly turned and headed for the steps. Dalton followed him up, with Mike and Ted bringing the two Cubans up.

The crowd began to hush as I stepped up to the edge of the platform. I looked out across the crowd, then down at Sarge. He was standing at the bottom of the steps, preventing anyone from rushing up the steps. I looked back over my shoulder at Mitch and he nodded. I nodded back and cleared my throat.

"I know there are a lot rumors going around about what happened here." Heads bobbed and words were exchanged throughout the crowd. "But we're here to set the record straight on what happened."

"How are we supposed to believe you?" Someone shouted from the crowd.

"Because I'm not the one that's going to tell you what happened." Surprise swept over those gathered. "The men responsible for that horrible event will tell you themselves what they did."

I nudged Micha with an elbow. He hesitated and I pushed him towards the edge of the platform. Leaning in close, I whispered, "Start talking or I'll throw you off here and tell them what you did myself."

Fear covered his face as he looked out across the park. But he started to speak, softly.

"My name is Micha," he began weakly.

"We know who you are!" Someone shouted from the front of the crowd.

"Speak up! We can't hear you!" Another voice shouted.

"Tell us what you did!" Yet another shouted.

"I was with these men, and others, who bombed the park the other day," Micha managed to say.

The crowd erupted with shouts of *why? Terrorist,* and others. Micha shrank from the shouts, then a rock flew out of the crowd and hit him in the chest. He turned to shield himself as other things started to fly from the crowd. Sticks, pieces of concrete, blackened pieces of metal from the truck. The end of a mortar round with the stabilizing fins still attached.

I drew my pistol and fired two rounds into the air. "That's enough of that shit!" I shouted as the crowd pressed away from us. I leaned over to Ted and asked for the piece of paper with the notes. He handed it to me and I stepped to the edge of the platform.

"As many of you know, the DHS ran a camp out in the forest before we kicked them out. Many atrocities were committed there. The DHS members were being sent to a prison after being captured by the Army. Micha here helped them escape. He is also the one that sprayed herbicide on our farm in attempt to deny you food. He also worked with others to plant the bomb at the park earlier this year. He consorted with the Russian and Cuban forces that currently are causing trouble. Which leads us to what happened here. Micha and another man acted as spotters for the mortar team that launched the attack on the park where so many were killed and injured.

"Which brings up another point. Some of you are starting rumors that the Army committed this crime against us. And I say us because that's what I mean. We were here when the attack started. We lost people, both killed and wounded as well." I looked down at Danny standing in front of the platform. "We were here handing out food for crying out loud! How could you think we were the ones to do something like this?" I paused for a moment as the crowd shared some guilty glances. "That sort of thinking is exactly what the enemies committing this violence want you to do. They want to splinter us, to separate us. Cause division. But we have to stick together!"

I stopped, trying to think of what to say next when someone shouted, "Now what?"

I looked down at Mitch. He nodded and walked up the steps. I looked out over the crowd and said, "We'll let Judge Williams decide his fate."

All eyes were on Mitch as he made it to the top of the platform. He looked out across the crowd, then at Micha, who wouldn't make eye contact. I think he was starting to get the idea he wasn't getting out of this.

Mitch turned to face the crowd and licked his lips. "These men have committed grave crimes against the community. Murder, maiming and sowing distrust." Mitch turned to face Micha, "You've admitted your crimes, and on behalf of our community I sentence you to death by hanging."

Shock filled Micha's face as he started to cry out, "You said if I told the truth you wouldn't kill me!"

The crowd erupted with shouts of, "Hang him! Hang them all!"

Micha, still trying to talk his way out of this, struggled. But he was no match for Dalton who roughly pushed him into position on the platform and pulled the rope over his head. Micha tucked his chin into his chest in a last-ditch effort to keep the rope from tightening around his neck. But Dalton gave him an open palm slap to the groin. It let the air out of Micha and Dalton was easily able to cinch the noose tight.

Sarge came up on the platform as this was being done. The two Cubans began to understand just what was happening and one of them, the less injured of the two, began to pray in Spanish.

"As the highest ranking military official here, I sentence these two soldiers to death for war crimes committed against civilians. They'll share the same sentence as Micha, hanging by the neck until they are dead."

All the while, Micha was still blubbering, sobbing and cursing us for lying to him. He'd spent his days since The Day aligning himself with those he felt were stronger. He was happy to do whatever he was told, with no thought or consideration for those he was helping to harm, so long as it meant he could eat and live comfortably. But that time was about to run out, at the end of a rope.

Mike and Ted moved the Cubans over their trapdoors and placed the nooses around their necks without protest. They were resigned to their fate. Or maybe they decided they would go out like men and not like a coward. I couldn't imagine what was going through their minds. I know I wouldn't stand patiently by while someone hanged me. They'd surely get the job done, but by God, I'd make it a challenge for them.

Once the men were in position, we stepped back from them. I looked down to see Danny holding the rope for Micha's trapdoor. He had it wrapped around his wrist and was staring intently at the man. Thad had the other two ropes, one wrapped around each wrist as well.

Danny sneered at Micha and said, "May you rot in hell!" And he gave the rope a violent jerk. The trapdoor fell out from under Micha's feet and the rope caught him. But it didn't break his neck. Instead he writhed against his own weight, slowly suffocating him. Danny stepped towards him, Micha's upturned face only a foot or so higher than his own as the two Cubans fell through the platform, snapping their ropes tight.

Danny watched with morbid intensity as Micha kicked and jerked. As the blood vessels in his eyes burst. When the man finally stopped moving, Danny studied him for a moment longer. Then he drew his pistol and shot Micha in the face. There would be no doubt about whether he was dead or not.

The crowd was silent. The blood lust leading up to the act drained away as they watched life leave the three men. Their limp bodies turning slowly from their ropes. The crowd started to drift out of the park, the spectacle of dying men, and the rush of morbid excitement that comes with it, now spent. Leaving those that witnessed it feeling an uncertain shame in the pit of their stomachs.

We walked down off the platform where Cecil was waiting. He nodded approvingly as we passed him. "It was done good. Done right." He said.

"It's never good, Cecil," Sarge replied.

Cecil looked at the three men as they twisted slowly. "Maybe not good. But some men, some men just need killing. Micha was a sneaky little shit willing to sell his soul to the highest bidder. He was a constant source of distrust and trouble. I bet things calm down a little around here now." He nodded at one of the Cubans, "As for those two poor bastards, war sucks. It's the price you pay to play that game. I've seen worse done to men who were captured."

"But we aren't like that. We're not going to torture them just for the sake of inflicting pain. To extract information?" Sarge asked, "Sure. Anyone who says torture doesn't work during interrogations has never properly employed it. But that's the end of its usefulness. Beyond that, it's just bloodlust; and that's where we have to draw the line. Lest we become like them."

Cecil nodded. "It's a dangerous line, that's for sure."

"It needed to be done, and it's done," I replied.

"It seems to have calmed people down," Ted said as he watched the crowd slowly plod away from the park. "Looks like all their piss and vinegar is spent."

"When pressure builds, you have two choices," Sarge said. "You either vent it. Or you don't and it explodes." He jabbed a thumb over his shoulder towards the men on the ropes, "This was the vent."

"That's a fucked-up way of looking at it," I said.

"Why? You saw these people when we got here. Only thing missing was the pitchforks and torches. Now they're calmed down. They got their blood."

"I'd hate to think we hung those men just to satisfy some group bloodlust," I replied.

"We didn't," Danny's voice caught me off guard. "We hung them because they killed Bobbie. And many others. You saw the bodies. You saw what they did. They needed killing and we killed them. Period."

I nodded. "You're right, my friend. They deserved it for Bobbie."

The bodies were cut down and loaded into the bed of the little red truck. We took them over to the police department, I wanted to see the other man, the one Shane killed. I asked Aric to ride over with us to verify it was him since he knew the man best.

We parked in front of the roll-up door and Shawn came out. He looked over the side of the bed and nodded. "It's done."

"Where's the other one?" I asked. Then I noticed his face. Both of his eyes were blackened and his nose looked broken. "Damn, dude, you look like you were hit by a truck."

He jerked his head towards the roll-up door, "The truck's in there. Hang on, I'll open it." And he went inside the building.

We waited out front as the metal door clanged and banged as it rolled up. As the door rose, the feet of man came into view. I watched as the view slowly crept up his body until the man was revealed. The man's shirt was stained with blood and flies buzzed about his open mouth and hazy eyes. Shane was standing beside him. He too had a black eye and was holding his left arm close to his chest.

I jutted my chin at him, "You alright?"

He kicked the form on the ground, "This fucker broke a rib I think."

"You seen the docs yet?"

He nodded, "Yeah, we've both been to the clinic. Nothing time won't fix."

Aric stepped into the dim bay and looked down at the body. He knelt down and grabbed the man's chin and turned his face up. Looking up, he said, "This is him. His name's Niigata. He was their torturer. Of course, they called him an interrogator. But he was a sadistic bastard."

Shawn snorted, "He's not going to torture anyone else."

"How'd it go down?" I asked.

"We were following him. He went behind the old Ace Hardware. When we walked around the corner, he jumped us. Sum bitch was quick and hit like a damn mule," Shane said.

"He was enjoying it. He smiled the entire time." Shawn said. "It was no contest trying to fight him. He hit me in the face, then went after Shane. I drew my pistol and shot him in the back. He actually turned around to look at me. Started walking towards me. So, I kept shooting him until he fell."

"And this one?" Aric asked, pointing to a bullet hole over the man's left eye.

"Insurance," Shane grunted. "I didn't want the bastard getting back up."

"It was worth it," I said. "The old man knows where they're operating out of now. The Russians and Cubans have teamed up with the remnants of the DHS. They're holed up in the auto auction off the 429. He's working with the DOD guys up at Eglin to deal with them."

"What do you want us to do with him?" Shane asked.

I pointed at the truck, "If you don't mind, I'll leave these three here for the night. Tomorrow, take them to the farm and bury them there. Let them fertilize the field."

"Will do."

"I'll get with Cecil. He'll have a hole dug for them."

We unloaded the bodies from the truck into the bay. It was surreal seeing so many bodies piled up as they were. But it was the reality. Dead bodies didn't faze me anymore than seeing a road-killed opossum now. It was just another part of the fabric of life. We shook hands and said we'd get with them later before Aric and I loaded into the truck and drove back to the park.

We found everyone gathered around Sarge's Hummer. Cecil and the old man were talking when we walked up.

"Was it him?" Sarge asked.

I nodded, "Yeah, it was him. One less vermin to worry about."

Sarge nodded. "Good. I'll get with the General and we'll put together a plan to hit those pricks at the auto auction."

Mike clapped his hands, "You mean I'm going to get to blow some shit up with that big ass gun? Goodie, goodie, goodie!"

"Stop acting like a damn snot-nosed runt for cryin' out loud. Act your age for a change."

"He is," Ted quickly replied, "he is acting his age. He stopped aging at thirteen."

The old man snorted, "Explains why yer nuts ain't dropped yet." He said it quickly and without thought. Then he looked at Mel and said, "Sorry, Mel."

Mel didn't miss a beat. "It's alright," she replied. Then she looked at Mike and said, "Don't worry. They'll come down on their own."

Mike blushed and adjusted his crotch, mumbling, "They did a long time ago."

Mel patted his shoulder, saying, "Sure they have." And she walked towards the little red truck. Naturally, this got a big laugh out of the old man, and Ted. It made me smile too. Mike looked at me and I shrugged.

"How's that field of corn coming, Cecil?" I asked.

"'Bout ready. I checked a couple of ears earlier today. They're drying out nicely."

"You got security on that field?" Sarge asked.

Cecil nodded with a laugh, "You're damn right! You think you could plant acres of corn and expect it to be there when you come back? Not hardly. We've run a few people off. Mitch sentenced a couple we caught in there poaching corn to labor at the farm. But for the most part, it's all there."

"That's going to make a shit ton of corn meal," I said. "How's the mill coming along?"

"We got it working. Have to run a generator, but it'll turn out some corn. We even found a Burrall corn sheller at Renninger's and got it working. We'll be able to shell the corn out a lot faster," Cecil replied.

"We'll be up to our eyeballs in grits and cornbread," Sarge said.

Cecil smiled and patted his belly, "I ain't going to complain none. Cornbread will go nice with the beans we got in those supplies."

"Cecil, we're going to be having a wedding out at the ranch here shortly. You should come out," I said.

He smiled a broad toothy smile, "Who's getting married?"

I put a hand on Thad and Aric's shoulders. "These two are."

The smile vanished and Cecil's face turned sour. "Not to each other, I hope."

The surprise on Thad's face was instant and Aric muttered, "What? Fuck, what?"

I cocked my head to the side and gave each of them a quick glance. "Now Cecil, I thought they made a fine couple."

"What?" Aric shouted. Apparently, it was the only thing he could manage.

Thad started to laugh, slapping his knee. "You a mess, Morgan!"

Cecil broke out into a broad smile again and started to laugh. Mike was standing behind Thad and in as deep a voice as he could muster, which wasn't much, he said, "You wanna be the husband or you wanna be the wife?"

Thad was still laughing, but Aric was slightly shocked. "I wanna be the husband!" He shouted.

Mike started to laugh and slapped Thad on the back and shouted, "Then get over here and suck yo wife's dick!"

The joke made Thad laugh even harder. Sarge got a chuckle out of it as well, but he shook his head at the same time. "You just don't know how to be a grown-up do you?"

With a blank stare, Mike replied, "No. I'm a Toys R Us kid."

"No, you are without a doubt, the posterchild for infanticide," Sarge snorted back.

Cecil cleared his throat and stepped towards Thad, "Thad, I'm happy for you." He stuck his hand out and shook Thad's. Cecil then turned to Aric, "You too, my friend. This is good news. Seeing that people can still fall in love in all this." He smiled again. "Maybe we'll see some youngins soon."

Aric looked down at his feet and hesitantly replied, "Well, uh, Fred's pregnant."

Cecil broke out into a loud raucous laugh. "That's great news! When's this wedding to going to take place?"

"Day after tomorrow," Thad replied.

Cecil smiled, "I'd be honored to be there."

CHAPTER 10

EVERYONE WAS UP EARLY. THERE was still a lot to do. With the loss of Bobbie so fresh, everyone was looking for something to cheer them. A little bright spot in the darkness. So, the ladies, all of them, even Jamie, were busy in the kitchen. Naturally, Bobbie's absence was felt. But she was with them in spirit as her name came up often.

Danny was spending his time with the kids. He had the entire troop out at the pond fishing. He was hurting, but so were they. Jace and Edie already lost their parents. Now they've lost Bobbie. Danny had always wanted to have kids. But Bobbie was reluctant. When the kids lost their parents, he seized on the opportunity. He was good with kids, having helped raise all three of my girls, and they loved him.

So, I assumed it was a coping mechanism for him to spend so much time with the kids. And it was the best method for him too. He knew there was still someone depending on him. He couldn't just sink into a pit of despair and not look up. He had to take care of them; and they were the anchor holding him in place. Not to mention, he had a large and very concerned group around. But we didn't hover over Danny. He was given his space. He needed to grieve, and we allowed him the time and room to do so. But everyone made sure he knew we were thinking about him.

I was sitting on the back porch watching the kids be frustrated by the little bait stealers in the pond. They were keeping him busy baiting hooks. Except Little Bit; she would pinch her own bread balls onto the hook. Miss Kay gave them a heal of bread that Danny dampened with a little water to make it sticky so it would stay on the hooks.

Doc strolled past me, his medic pack over his shoulder, and pushed the screen door open and went down towards the pond. He was constantly checking Danny's hand, changing the dressings and inspecting the sutures that closed the large wound. He was diligent in ensuring infection didn't set in.

Seeing Doc approach, Danny took a seat in one of the plastic chairs, ready for his exam. Doc dropped his pack and pulled another chair over. "How's the hand feeling?" Doc asked.

"No better, no worse."

Edie missed another fish; and with her bait gone, she was excitedly asking for another bread ball. Danny told her she'd have to wait for a minute. "You gotta wait, sweetie. Doc here wants to poke and prod me first."

She cocked her little head to the side and scrunched her nose. "Is he taking the Band-Aid off?" Danny nodded and she leaned her pole against a young cypress tree. "I want to see it."

Little Bit and Jace quickly joined her. They all stood watching as Doc unwrapped the gauze and removed the sponges that absorbed the drainage from the wound. Edie moved closer and looked over Doc's knee. "Where's your fingers?"

Danny turned the hand over, "They're gone."

"But where'd they go?"

"The bomb took them," Little Bit said as she watched Doc work.

"Can you get them back?" Jace asked.

"No, they're not coming back," Danny said with a hint of sadness in his voice.

"That's true, but Mr. Danny will be alright," Doc said as he cleaned the wound. "He'll be back up to speed in no time. He just won't be able to give you a high five." Doc leaned in close to Edie and added in a silly tone, "it'll have to be a high three!"

The kids all laughed. Even Danny half chuckled at the comment. Doc smiled and rubbed Edie's hair.

"It's ok," Edie said as she took Danny's other hand with both of hers. "He still has this one." She pulled the hand up to her face and rubbed it on her cheek."

Doc smiled and looked at Danny and the little girl. "Like I said, Mr. Danny will be just fine."

As I watched this, Mel walked up and leaned against me. I looked up at her. Her arms were crossed over her chest and she was looking down at me. "What?" I asked.

"Have you got those flowers yet?"

I rolled my eyes. I'd been selected to fill buckets with the bright pink Azalea flowers that grew in huge numbers at our old house. "No, not yet."

Mel leaned down and whispered in my ear. "Don't you think you should get that done? You know the wedding is tomorrow, right?"

I rocked my head side to side, "Yeah, yeah. I'm going." I replied as I got to my feet.

"Remember, it's a secret," Mel added.

I waved over my shoulder at her as I headed for the screen door. "I know."

Walking out to the shed, I grabbed a couple of empty five-gallon buckets and headed for the gate. It was nice out, for a summer day, and I was going to walk down to the old house. As I got closer to the bunker, I saw the National Guardsmen standing their watch. These guys were very diligent and never complained about having to be on duty. It said something about what it must be like in town at the armory.

Wallner stepped out from under the tarp. I smiled at the sight. He was starting to get comfortable out here. Gone was the body armor and the heavy BDU blouse top. He was in a t-shirt and boonie hat and even had the legs of his pants rolled up to his knees. A rather funny sight with the boots he was wearing.

"You guys look like you're getting into the groove," I said.

He looked down at himself and smiled, "Someone once told me, conditions are what you make them."

I laughed, "Indeed, my friend."

He turned to the north and pointed to a small house that sat off the road in a five-acre field of grass. A scattering of oak trees grew in front of it. "What's Thad doing over there?"

Looking at the house, I replied, "I do believe he's getting the place ready for his soon-to-be bride."

"I thought that was it. It's a nice little place. It's just separated from everyone else."

I nodded. "Yeah. But I think Thad is looking for a little separation. Somewhere he can begin to rebuild his life."

"He's been hard at it. We've offered to help several times, but he always turns us down."

I reached out and gripped Wallner's shoulder. "That's because you guys do enough for us. I'll go over and check on him."

"We're happy to be here. Anything you guys need, just ask."

With a smile and nod, I replied, "I know, my friend."

I looked over at the house Thad was preparing for himself and Mary. He appeared in the door as I crossed the yard. He was working a broom and a cloud of dust erupted from the open door.

"You'll make someone a fine wife one of these days with domestic skills like that," I said.

Thad looked up and smiled. "You think she'll like this?"

I nodded and poked my head in the door. "I think so. We need to get a couple things going over here for you guys, but I think she'll be happy."

We walked through the house that had once been owned by an old man. He lived there alone and kept to himself. I had never even spoken to him. But he disappeared shortly after the event and I never saw him again. The house was in pretty good shape, though it was obvious it had been gone through many times. I know our group had raided it on several occasions. But unlike others, we didn't trash the places we looked through.

The little house had lots of windows and it was bright inside and surprisingly cool. Thad had the rear sliding-glass door open, revealing the small pool out back." It was nearly full of water, but was green now of course.

"I'm going to build another water tower here and fill it from the pool," Thad said. "It'll allow us to flush the toilets at least."

"I'm sure we can sort something out. I wish we had more solar panels to get you some power," I replied.

"We can live without the power, but having a flushing toilet is really nice." I nodded and Thad said, "I need a favor, Morgan."

I looked at him and replied, "Anything, buddy."

He rubbed his hand through his hair. "I really need a haircut before the wedding."

I agreed, "Yeah, you do," and laughed. "But I only know how to do one kind."

He smiled again. "I know. That's the kind I want."

"Let me take care of a little project real quick and then we'll get to that haircut."

Thad looked around the house and nodded. "I have a little more to do here and I'll meet you at your place."

"Sounds good to me," I replied as I headed for the door and grabbed my bucket.

As I continued towards the old place, I saw Mike coming from the direction of his house. He waved me down and I stopped and waited for him. "Hey, Morg," he greeted me.

"What's up, Mikey?"

"Hard dicks and helicopters."

"Not anymore," I replied with a laugh.

"Oh, sorry to hear that, man. You know, you used to be able to get a pill for that. Gonna be kind of tough now though."

I shook my head. "I meant the helicopters, asshole."

He looked around and stretched. "I know."

"What do you want?" I asked, trying to get to the point.

"Oh yeah. Hey, I need some ice."

"For what?"

He cocked his head to the side, "Oh. I didn't tell you?"

I waved him off. "Yeah, yeah. How much?"

"A few big blocks would be nice."

"I can put some into the freezer in a little while. When do you need them?"

"Tomorrow."

I knew he was up to something. And that was always worrying when it came to Mike. "You aren't going to do anything stupid at the wedding, are you?"

He looked shocked. "I am an asshole. But even I ain't that big an asshole. No, this is just my little gift. You'll like it, I promise."

"Oaky. It'll be ready in the morning."

He clapped his hands together. "Perfect." He hopped

backwards and pointed at me. "You're the man, Morgan." Then he spun around and trotted back towards his house.

I shook my head, smiling as I headed down the road. Finally making it to the house, I started to pluck the bright pink flowers from the azalea bushes. Once the bucket was full, I headed towards home. When I came out onto the road, Meat Head and Drake came trotting up. They were panting heavily and whining. I stopped and patted Meat Head.

"What's wrong, buddy?" I looked down the road and asked, "Where's your sister?"

Drake looked down the road, then back at me. He trotted down the road towards the highway, then stopped and looked back at me. Meat Head licked my hand and whined again. I stood up and started towards Drake. Meat Head took off at a run towards Drake. The two dogs waited as I walked towards them, then ran off as I got closer.

I'm not one to think dogs are of superior intellect, but you certainly build a relationship with the animals over the years. You get to where you can read them, and they can read you. And it was obvious they were trying to tell me something. And the fact Little Sister wasn't with them was very worrying. I thought she could be hurt. For an instant, the image of her being hit by a car flashed into my mind. But I dismissed it just as quickly. There'd have to be cars on the road for that to happen.

The dogs turned north, running up the center of the road. They were moving way faster than I was. But they would stop and wait for me to close the distance before taking off again. They turned west and headed into the woods. Bad memories rushed back to me of Reggie's niece. We were headed towards Baptist lake.

I tried to avoid further memories of Reggie by thinking of the dogs. I always wondered where they went when they ran off, and they obviously roamed further than I imagined. They continued to lead me into the woods. They seemed very anxious, almost desperate for me to follow them. I was getting a little annoyed. We were far from home and no one knew I'd left. No one knew where I was.

As that thought began to form in my mind, I started to hear voices. The dogs' attitudes changed as well. They slowed down and began moving stealthily through the woods. It was then I realized I didn't have my rifle. All I had was my pistol. *Shit,* I muttered to myself as I pulled the .45. It was pure instinct when the weapon came from its holster that my fingers would run over the chamber and striker indicators. Both were positive, the pistol was ready to go.

The smell of wood smoke started to drift through the air. Then, the smell of cooking meat. My stomach started to churn as a fear crept up in me, the sudden realization of where the dogs were taking me and what I was about to see.

The dogs stopped and looked back at me. I slowly moved up to them, pausing to rub Drake's ears. I picked my steps carefully as I closed the distance between myself and what I now knew was two men. Moving closer, they came into view. The two men were sitting on a log, their backs to me, with a fire burning in front of them. A large piece of meat was on a spit over the fire.

They looked like all the scavengers I had seen since the Event. Unlike people in town who tried to keep some semblance of appearance, the people who wandered the woods were always ratty looking. Both had long, wild hair and beards to match. Their clothes had a sheen of grime to them, and experience told me they'd smell like hot garbage.

I looked around their camp and saw a skinned carcass hanging from a tree. Below it was a pile of offal and white fur. I nearly puked and my head began to spin as the realization of that terrible thought I'd had while walking in set in. They were cooking my dog.

Restraining myself for a moment, I looked the camp over. There was a .22 rifle leaned against the tree that the carcass swung from. I didn't see any other guns. I slipped the ASP from my vest and gripped it tight. I was about thirty feet from the men, a long distance to close. I wanted to just shoot them. And yet, I didn't. I started to close the distance to them as fast as I could, while trying to be quiet.

But it wasn't enough. About ten feet from them, they both turned to look over their shoulders. Both men immediately jumped to their feet. One was holding a large knife, like a big kitchen knife. The other looked at the rifle. I dropped the ASP and raised the pistol in a two-handed grip.

"Don't even fucking think about it!" I shouted.

The one with the knife gripped it tight. I could see in his eyes he was ready to fight. "You toss that blade into the woods before I kill you," I said as calmly as I could.

The other two dogs came running into the camp. I heard them come past me and saw when the two men noticed them as well. I could see the recognition in their eyes. The one man still had the knife, and I told him again to throw it into the woods. His friend looked at him, and as yet, neither man had said a word.

The one with the knife nodded at me. "You the Sheriff?" I nodded and he took another look at the knife before tossing it into the woods.

I motioned with the pistol. "Sit down on that log."

The two men shared a glance, then reluctantly sat down. The dogs were sniffing around the hide of their friend piled on the ground.

One of the men with a thick shock of red hair and beard to

match asked, "Them your dogs?" He spoke with a thick drawl that reminded me of Appalachia. I'd walked around in front of them, keeping their fire between us.

"Yes, they are."

"Shit," he muttered and shook his head.

"It's just a dog," his partner practically spat.

"No, it's not. It's **my** dog. And my little girl is going to be very sad you fuckers killed her."

"We gotta eat too. You shouldn't let your dogs run around like that. You're lucky we didn't kill the other ones."

"Lucky? I'm lucky you didn't kill my other dogs?" I asked.

He shrugged and spat into the fire. "It ain't a crime to kill a dog." His red-headed partner glanced up at him, but didn't say anything and turned his gaze back to the fire.

"I guess that depends on who you ask. Didn't see the collar on the dogs?"

The man shrugged. "That don't mean shit."

I wasn't sure what to do. Yes, they killed my dog. But they were obviously starving as well. Would it be right to kill a man that simply needed to eat? These thoughts were roiling in my head when the man reached out to what I now knew was a hind quarter from my dog roasting over the fire. He ripped a piece from it and stuck it in his mouth, then looked up, glaring at me as he chewed.

It wasn't a conscious decision to pull the trigger, and I jumped when the Springfield barked fire. He fell backwards, landing on the ground with his mouth open and his tongue pushing the half-chewed meat around. The bullet hit him high in his chest, nearly dead center. From the sound of it, the round hit his trachea. He was gurgling and clutching his neck.

His partner rolled to the side, curling into a ball on the ground. I looked down at the pistol in my hand, then back at the stricken man. He was still struggling as blood pooled in his mouth and he coughed it out onto his chin. It mixed with the chewed meat, making for a disturbing scene. Then he looked at me and reached a hand out towards me.

I shook my head and said, "You shouldn't have killed my dog. And you damn sure shouldn't have started eating her in front of me." I raised the Springfield, the front sight between his wide, wild eyes; and this time, I consciously pulled the trigger.

The bullet struck him in the corner of his left eye. His head fell back and blood bubbled in his mouth with his final exhale. The red head, hearing the release of his friend's final breath rolled over and looked at him, then at me.

"Look, I'm really sorry. We were hungry. I didn't want to kill your dog. I really didn't. But what else were we supposed to do?" He pointed a trembling finger at me. "An, and you're the Sheriff! You can't just kill me!"

I looked down at the star pinned to my chest. I plucked it off and stuck it in my pocket. "Right now, I'm not the Sheriff. To you, it's just a dog. But she was more than that to my family and you took her from us."

"But, it's just a fucking dog!"

"Not to me," I replied as I raised the pistol and fired two quick rounds into his head.

I sat down on the log beside the dead men. The leg was still roasting over the fire and I kicked it off. Holstering the pistol, I looked around. Drake and Meat Head were gone. They never did like gunfire. I imagined they were probably already back at the house. Standing up, I walked over to examine Little Sister's hanging carcass. I shook my head and looked down at the .22. I snatched it up and gripped the barrel like a bat and smashed the rifle against the tree. The stock splintered into pieces. I looked at the barrel and action and swung it two more times until the barrel was bent nearly ninety degrees before throwing it to the ground.

Going back to the two men, I found a grubby backpack and dumped it out onto the ground. An old blanket was in the pile of filthy clothes and other crap. I took the blanket over to where the dog hung and laid it out on the ground. I piled her entrails, hide and head into the blanket. It was then I saw she'd been shot between the eyes at what was obviously point-blank range. I could see the powder burn in her fur.

The scene was clear. The dogs, being friendly, probably came up to these guys. When they saw the rifle, I imagined Drake and Meat Head ran. But Little Sister was always more tolerant of guns and wouldn't have been scared. And the bastard pointed it at her head and shot her. I looked back at the two dead men and suddenly didn't feel as conflicted as I had. I cut down the rest of her carcass, dropping it onto the blanket. Then I picked up the quarter the bastards were cooking and placed it into the blanket before folding the corners up.

I picked her up and slung her over my shoulder and started back towards the road, pausing to kick the fire out. It was a long walk home with the weight of the dog over my shoulder. The longer I walked, the worse I felt about it. Sure, I always said the dogs were lazy and useless, but they were part of my family. A part I would now have to tell the rest of my family was gone. This hurt more than anything.

Little Bit and the kids often played with the dogs. On really hot days, the dogs would go to Danny's and get into the pond to cool off. The kids would often be there with them as they splashed around. Her loss would certainly be missed by everyone.

As I came to our road, Sarge's Hummer skidded to a stop.

Ted was in the turret with a SAW. Sarge was behind the wheel and looked as though he was ready to kill me.

"Where the fuckin hell have you been!" He screamed as he climbed out of the truck.

I swung the blanket off my shoulder and laid it on the ground. "Getting my dog back."

Sarge looked at the blanket, then at me. "Come again?"

"The other two dogs came home; and obviously upset, they led me back to where two assholes were cooking her," I said, pointing at the blanket.

He looked at the blanket again, then back at me. "Shit, Morgan. I'm sorry." He looked down, shaking his head and asked, "Where are they?"

"Out in the woods," I replied as I reached down and picked up the blanket again. "Buzzards got to eat too."

"They shouldn't have shot your dog," Sarge replied.

"That's what I said."

The old man opened the rear door of the truck, "Lay her in here and I'll take you home."

In the truck, Sarge looked over at me. "Don't ever do that shit again, Morgan. We've got plenty of people and enough firepower to take care of any problems we encounter like this. But you wandering off into the woods alone," he looked around the truck, "and without a damn rifle, will not happen again."

I nodded. "Yeah, I realized that once I saw them. I was just following the dogs to start with. I thought maybe she was hurt, snake bit, or something. But when I saw her hanging there like that, I lost it." We were coming up on my bucket of flowers that still sat in the road. I pointed at it and said, "Stop here and let me get that." Sarge rolled to a stop, and I opened my door, leaned out and grabbed the bucket.

"What the hell is that for?" Sarge asked.

I shrugged, "Something Mel is doing for the wedding."

He reached over and grabbed my shoulder, "Really sorry about the pup, Morgan."

I nodded. "Thanks. I need to get her home and get her buried before anyone sees her."

"We'll help you," Ted said from the back seat.

Over my shoulder, I replied, "Thanks, Ted."

We made it to the house and I told Sarge to pull around to the back, behind the shed. There was a large oak tree back there, on the edge of the woods I wanted to put her under.

"You got shovels?" Ted asked as he stripped his plate carrier off.

I nodded. "Yeah. I'll be right back."

I walked back to the shed and grabbed a couple of shovels and headed back. Ted took one immediately and asked for me to point out a spot. I did, and he set to work immediately. I was surprised when I went to set my spade into the dirt by Sarge snatching it from my hands.

"We got this, Morg," he said.

It didn't take the two men long to dig a hole large enough to hold her. Ted stepped out of the hole and Sarge asked, "You going to leave her in the blanket?"

As I picked it up, I replied, "Yeah. She's whole in here and I don't want to see her again."

The old man patted my back, saying, "Good call."

I laid her in the hole and they began shoveling the dirt back in. It didn't take long before the spot was nothing more than a place of disturbed earth. I studied it for a minute before remarking, "You know, I'm getting kind of tired of digging these holes."

Sarge took a noisy deep breath and blew it out. "I know

what you mean. But we'll all end up in one." He looked up at me and said, "None of us gets out of this alive."

I nodded and looked back at the house. "I need to go in and tell Mel what happened." I thought for a minute and added, "but I think I'm going to lie to the girls."

"I was hoping you would," Sarge replied. "They don't need to know what happened."

"Especially Little Bit," Ted added.

"Agreed," I said with a nod.

"We'll leave it to you then, Morg. Holler if you need anything," Sarge said. As I turned to walk to the house, he grabbed my arm and said, "Don't ever do any dumb shit like that again or we'll be digging your hole. And I don't want to do that."

When I got into the house, I couldn't bring myself to tell Mel what happened. When she saw me, she asked, "Did you get them?" Fred was in Mel's wedding dress, standing on a chair so Mel could pin it up to make some alterations.

"Sure did. Bucket full."

Fred had her arms up in the air, holding the position Mel needed. "Bucket of what?"

Mel stuck a pin in her teeth and replied, "Don't you worry about it."

"Where are the girls?" I asked.

"They're over at Bobbie's," Mel replied without thinking. I saw her flinch when she said it. But she carried on.

"I'll go check on them in a little bit." But before I left, I filled several large plastic containers with water and put them in the freezer.

"What's that for?" Mel asked as she pinned another piece of the dress back.

"No idea. Mikey needs it."

Once the water was in the freezer, I left the house. Meat Head and Drake were lying on the front porch. They weren't panting now, but they looked listless and unenthused. I sat down on the bench and both their tails thumped the porch. Rubbing Meat Head's ears, I said, "I'm sorry old, buddy. I did my best. But she's home now." As I spoke, his tail thumped a little faster. There was no way in hell he understood what I was saying. But I suppose in some way, he knew that I was talking about his little sister.

I left them lounging on the porch and headed for Danny's. The kids were out back playing. It looked like bows and arrows were back in. Palmetto stem arrows flew back and forth across the yard. I smiled at them as I climbed up onto the porch. Perez was sitting in a rocker watching them. A pile of trimmed palmetto fronds were at his feet.

"You the official arrow maker?" I asked.

He looked down at his feet and replied, "Someone needs to keep ‘em in ammo."

I looked out at the yard. It was cluttered with arrows and squealing and wheeling kids. It made me smile. Fortunately, they weren't shooting at one another. They were shooting at several palmetto fronds stuck in the ground. I patted Perez on the shoulder and said, "Don't let ‘em kill one another."

"It's under control," he replied as I walked into the house. The house was busy. Mary was in her dress, just as Fred was next door. Jess was trying to follow Kay's instructions on how to pin the dress for modification. All the while, Kate was busy on a cake.

Jamie was helping Jess pin the dress up. I looked around and asked, "Where's Danny?"

"He's out back behind the pond," Kate replied without looking up from her mixing bowl.

I didn't reply and quickly left the way I came. Nothing good was going to come from me being in there. I walked out to the pond and could see Danny on the back side of it swinging a weed-eater. I shook my head because he shouldn't have been doing that. I walked out and he shut the machine down when he saw me.

"What the hell are you doing?" I asked.

He looked around, as though the answer to my question were obvious. "I'm cleaning up back here so we can have the wedding here, near the pond. I thought it would look nice."

I nodded at the Stihl in his hands and said, "You shouldn't be doing that. Your hand isn't ready for work yet."

He shrugged. "It's been doing fine today."

I looked around at the brush piles he'd created and asked, "Want some help?"

He handed me the Stihl and I went to work cutting the brush down. We worked the rest of the afternoon together. By the time we were done, the back side of the pond looked nearly as good as a manicured lawn. My girls came around the house in the little red truck. Danny had sent them out earlier in the day to find chairs. He wanted the plastic type of lawn chairs that nearly everyone had a couple of.

The girls helped us set the chairs up, forming two neat rows. Danny said he had an idea and went to the shed. He returned with a piece of rolled-up carpet on his shoulder. It was a chunk of green indoor/outdoor carpet, and we laid it out in front of the chairs.

"This looks really nice," Taylor said.

I wiped my sweaty forehead and looked at the product of our efforts. "It's not bad. Not bad at all."

"I think they're really going to like it," Lee Ann said.

I looked at Danny, "You ready to call it a day?"

He looked tired and nodded. "Yeah. I think we've done everything we can. It looks pretty good."

We piled the tools we'd used, the Stihl, rakes and pitchforks, into the bed of the little truck. The girls drove it back over to the shed to put everything away while I walked with Danny to the house. Mary was out of her dress and she and Jess were sitting on the sofa stitching up the adjustments on the dress. They were laughing and talking as they worked.

Danny headed upstairs, saying he was going to get cleaned up. I sat down at the bar. Kay was still in the kitchen, but it appeared the baking was done. Not only from the wonderful smell in the air, but the fact that the kitchen was cleaned up. She was always so fastidious about cleaning up as soon as she was done cooking. Only thing in the kitchen now was a large pot sitting on the stove, slowly simmering.

"What's in the kettle?" I asked.

"Tonight's supper. I just made a goulash. Something easy," she replied.

"Cool. Have you seen Mel?" She shook her head. "I'm going to go back to the house," I said as I headed for the door.

Perez was still on the porch, his hat pulled down over his eyes and his feet stretched out in front of him. I slapped his shoulder as I passed him and said, "Keep up the good work."

He adjusted in his chair and mumbled, "I'm on it."

Mel was sitting on the couch when I came in. I looked around and asked, "Where's Fred?"

"She went home. We finished the dress and she took it with her."

I sat down beside her. "It's really nice you gave it to her."

"It's not like I'm going to wear it again."

I patted her leg, "I sure as hell hope not!"

She smiled and stood up. "It's hard to meet people today. You want some tea?"

"You're not funny," I replied. "And yes, thank you." I landed a playful kick on her ass as she passed me.

She returned from the kitchen with a glass of tea for me and an ice water for herself. "What's with all those tubs of ice in the freezer?"

I took a sip before replying. "I don't know. Mikey is up to something."

"That's what you said before. You still don't know what he's up to?"

"Nope," I replied. Then I figured this was as a good a time as any to break the news to her. "I've got some bad news."

She looked at me with genuine concern. "What?"

"Meat Head doesn't have a sister anymore."

She sat up and looked at me. "What do you mean? What happened to her?"

I told her the story of the dogs coming home and the way they acted. Of how I followed them into the woods.

"What happened to her?"

I took her hand and said, "Someone killed her."

"What? Why?"

I couldn't tell her why. "I brought her home and buried her out back."

Mel got to her feet and went to the kitchen window. "Why didn't you tell me? Why did you bury her already?"

"You didn't want to see her like that," I said as I came up behind her. I pointed out the spot where she was resting. "She's right there."

She turned around and looked at me. "Who did it?"

"Don't worry about them. I took care of them."

"You kill them? How many were there?"

I took her hand. "Look, I don't really want to talk about it. Just know it's done. It's over."

Mel looked back out the window. "What are we going to tell Ashley?"

"I was thinking of telling her she was bit by a snake. I don't want to tell her she was shot by someone."

"I don't like to lie to her. But, it's probably better that way."

"Come on. Let's go get some dinner. I want to go to bed early tonight. Tomorrow is going to be a busy day."

By the time we made it back to Danny's, the place had changed. Everyone was there, even Wallner. He said his guys were on duty and he wanted to come down and collect their dinner. We stopped in the yard to talk to Doc. He had the Geiger counter out and was taking readings.

"What's it look like today?" I asked.

"Not much. Just barely above background."

"That's good, isn't it?" Mel asked.

Doc nodded. "Oh yeah, real good. It's what we want to see."

"You heard any more about that unit they were sending to Tampa?" I asked.

"No," Doc replied and nodded towards the porch. "Grumpy up there probably has. He's been talking with Eglin on the radio quite a bit."

I looked at the porch and asked, "What's up?"

Doc shrugged, "Got no idea. He don't tell me and I don't ask. Less shit I have to worry about." Doc then looked at Mel, "Sorry, Mel."

Mel laughed, "Ronnie, I live with him. I can handle a little shit."

Doc snorted, "Living with him, you gotta be able to handle truckloads of shit."

"Thanks, buddy," I replied, "thanks for that."

As he started to roll the cord up for the remote sensor on the Geiger counter, he said, "What are friends for?"

As we walked towards the porch, Mel asked, "Who's performing the ceremony? If Sarge is giving the girls away, who's actually going to perform the service?"

"I have no idea," I replied.

"Don't worry about it. It's all taken care of," Sarge barked from the porch.

"Ok, then who's doing it?" I asked.

"I just told you! Do you ever pay attention?"

I looked at Mel and palmed my forehead, "That's right, don't worry about it; *he's* coming. I love that guy."

Mel shook her head and said, "I'll leave you boys to your games." Then I headed inside.

I went up on the porch. Perez was still snoozing in the rocking chair with his feet stretched out, the heel of one boot resting on the toe of the other. I kicked the top one off as I passed him.

From under his hat, he muttered, "Aye, carbon!"

Sarge looked over at him and asked, "Has he done anything today?"

"Yeah," I replied with great exaggeration. "He's been riding herd on the kids all day."

Sarge snorted. "Only person better for that would be Mikey."

"Mmm, yeah, I'm gonna have to go ahead and disagree with you there. He's been acting really flaky lately. Did I mention he's been having a problem with his TPS reports?"

The old man cocked his head to the side and looked at me, "What the hell are you talking about?"

"You don't watch many movies, do you?"

"No. Hollywood is full of fruits and nuts."

As we talked, Dalton and Mike walked up. Dalton was

filthy, covered in sweat and smelling like a forest fire. "What the hell have you been doing?" I asked.

"Been working, my precious."

I laughed, "That's funny."

"What's funny? Him calling you precious?" Sarge asked. "Seems a little quirtzy to me."

Mike looked at Sarge and said, "You really need to get out more. You're like a troop of the seven dwarfs, but they're all Grumpy."

Sarge cocked his head to the side and asked, "Ain't you got some crayons that need eatin' somewhere? Or maybe some windows to lick?"

Mike puffed out his chest, "I'll have you know, I prefer paste. Now, if you'll excuse me, I smell something wonderful coming from the house."

Wallner came out the door as Mike was going in. He carried a large pot and several bowls. "Man, this smells so damn good!" He announced as he came onto the porch.

"You guys coming to the wedding tomorrow?" I asked.

"Someone needs to be down at the bunker."

"We can let it go for a little while tomorrow," Sarge said. "You and your boys come on up here in the morning. There's going to be cake and everything."

"No shit?" He asked with genuine surprise. "That woman of yours sure can cook, Top."

"She ain't my woman!" Sarge barked back. Catching Wallner off guard.

He looked at me and I mouthed the words, *yes, she is,* while I nodded my head. He smiled and said, "We'd love to come up. I'm just worried about leaving the place unsecured."

"Don't worry about it. It won't take more than an hour or so," Sarge replied.

Wallner nodded, "Alright then." He looked at Dalton and said, "You look like you been working hard today."

"The fires of the forge are hot, my friend."

I looked up at Dalton and asked, "What are you forging now?"

He winked at me, "You'll see."

"I'm gonna take the guys their supper," Wallner said as he headed off.

Sarge got up from his chair and stretched, in the way old men will do, and said, "Let's go get us some supper before that window-licker eats it all."

"Smashing idea, old chap!" Dalton shouted, "I'm simply famished!"

Sarge looked him up and down for a moment before deciding, "You're one weird fucker."

"Mmmm, indeed," Dalton replied.

I kicked Perez's feet, "Come on there, poppie. Supper is ready."

He lifted his hat and rubbed his eyes, saying, "Call me what you want. Just don't call me late for supper."

As usual, dinner was a raucous affair. Maybe a little more so this time because of all the excitement about the forthcoming weddings. I sat at the table with the kids, delighting in their infectious happiness. These kids were always happy. Despite the loss of Bobbie, Jace and Edie were doing well. Maybe it was just a fact of the new life. That loss was inevitable. Maybe so much had happened to them that it just didn't affect them the same. But sitting here at a table with bowls of steaming goulash, they laughed and fidgeted in their chairs as they ate.

I asked about their bows and arrows. Little Bit said she was the best shot, of course. And of course Jace disagreed with her. But I talked and played with them at the table. I looked around to see Thad and Mary sitting together, along with Fred and Aric. Miss Kay and Jess were also at their table. Mel was sitting with Jamie, Danny, Mike and Doc. Perez was also at the table.

The old man sat with Miss Kay and Dalton and Ian at another table. All the talk was about tomorrow. Even the kids were talking about the wedding. I was beginning to wish I'd never brought it up. But it was a good thing. I was making people happy. Adding a bright spot to our world.

I got up from the kids' table, tickling Jace and Little Bit as I did and getting ear-piercing squeals from them. Carrying my bowl into the kitchen, I bumped into Mike coming out the door. He asked about the ice. "It's at the house. What the hell are you up to?"

He gave me a wicked smile. "Oh, dude, you're going to love it. I promise, no bullshit, really."

"Well, it's at the house when you need it."

"Can we go get it real quick? I need to get it back to my place."

I shrugged, "Sure. Let's go."

"I'll meet you at your place with the truck," he said as he clapped his hands and headed for the door.

I told Mel I was going home, she said she'd be along shortly with the girls. I headed back to the house and Mike was already in the driveway when I got there. He had the old man's Hummer and was pulling a couple of large coolers from the back of it.

"Let's put it in here," he said as he slid one onto the porch.

I went into the house and started carrying the containers out. Some just released their ice into the coolers, while other containers simply had to be tossed into the cooler because we couldn't get the ice loose. Mike promised to return the containers.

"That's all of it," I said as I dropped the last piece in.

Mike looked into the two coolers, "That's perfect. It'll be awesome."

I still didn't know what the hell he was up to and asked, "The old man know what you're up to?"

"Sorry, bro, this is top secret, need to know only kind of shit."

I waved him off, "Whatever there, Cloak and Dagger."

Mike quickly left, eager to complete whatever sort of skullduggery he was up to. I was now alone in the house, and I didn't feel like going back to Danny's, so I just flopped onto the couch. I stretched out and closed my eyes, intending to relax until Mel and the girls came home. And I must have really relaxed. Because I was out when they came through the door. Mel was complaining it was dark and called for someone to turn on a light.

I sat up and rubbed my eyes. My head was a little thick and it took me a minute to realize what was going on. Getting up, I said, "Sorry, babe. Guess I fell asleep." And I clicked on a lamp.

"You girls get ready for bed," Mel said as she closed the door. "That means take a bath!"

"Ah, come on, Mom. Do I hafta?" Little Bit asked.

"Yes, you do. You're not wearing that pretty dress tomorrow unless you do."

"Okay," she grumbled as she headed down the hall.

"What are you girls wearing?" Mel asked.

"I have a nice pink dress I'm going to wear," Taylor said.

Lee Ann held her hands out and said, "This."

"Uh, no you're not. Find something nice to wear," Mel replied. With a groan, Lee Ann headed towards her room. Mel looked at me and said, "I can't believe she hasn't picked anything out yet." Then her eyes narrowed and she asked, "What are you wearing?"

I looked down and said, "I guess, not this?"

She shook her head. "No. Not that. I'll pick something out for you." *Great,* I thought.

Once everyone was cleaned up, me included, we went to bed early. Tomorrow would be busy and I was already tired. Climbing in under the sheet, I asked Mel, "What are you wearing tomorrow?"

"I've got a cute little outfit picked out. I need to get up early so I can get ready."

"Don't wake me up," I replied.

The morning came quickly and I was awakened by a sound I hadn't heard in a long time. A hair dryer. I looked at the bathroom door; it was closed, but I knew Mel was in there getting ready. I decided not to bother her and instead went out to the kitchen. Our chicken flock had been growing. So much so that Kay was starting to talk about culling them some. Chicken would be a nice addition to the menu. But in the meantime, they were producing incredible amounts of eggs.

We had all the eggs we wanted. And eggs in all their varieties were usually available for breakfast. And with the addition of the recent supplies, I was able to whip up a batch of breakfast burritos, kind of. If you call scrambled eggs in a tortilla a burrito. What I would give for some cheese. But it must have been enough, because it wasn't long before the girls were rising from their beds with the aroma in the air.

As they ate, I went to check on Mel. She was in the process of putting on her war paint. Something she hadn't done in a very long time.

"All my makeup is drying out," she complained as she fussed with a bottle of some potion or another.

"I doubt you'll be seeing any more, any time soon, babe."

"All the stuff we stored and I never even thought about it," she lamented.

I laughed, "Because it wasn't important."

"To you," she grumbled back at me.

"Besides, you don't even need it," I said as I leaned in to kiss her.

Her hand flew up and she shouted, "Do not touch my hair! There's no more hairspray and it took me forever to get it to look like this."

So, I patted her ass instead. "And it looks amazing."

She paused from putting on eyeliner and looked at me in the mirror. "You really think so?"

I stepped up behind her and grabbed her butt. "Oh yeah. You're hawt," I said, using the term humorously. Then I leaned over her shoulder and whispered, "You know. Since you're all dolled up, it'd be a waste to not take full advantage of it. If you know what I mean."

She was back to putting on her eyeliner and replied, "Oh I know. Go get dressed and we'll see. Your clothes are hanging in the closet."

I went out to find a pair of khaki pants, a button-up shirt and a pair of dress shoes. It'd been so long since I'd worn anything like it that I immediately said, *nope.* I kept the shirt, it was nice enough in the generic way of button-down dress shirts. But instead of the khaki pants, I pulled down a pair of blue jeans. But, pulling them on, I quickly realized they were a no-go. I could pull them down to my knees even when they were zipped up.

So, I pulled out a plastic bag I kept older clothes in. From back when I was skinnier and younger. In there, I found a nice pair of Wranglers. And I stood in the closet laughing when they fit, perfectly, and looked pretty good. I grabbed my cowboy boots, another thing I hadn't worn in forever, and carried them out to the bedroom. Once I was dressed, which required drilling a new hole in my leather belt, I stepped into the bathroom.

Mel looked at me in the mirror and said, "That's not what I picked out."

I held my arms out and made a little pirouette and replied, "I think I look pretty good."

She turned from the mirror and studied me up and down. After considering me for a minute, she replied, "Not bad. I haven't seen you in jeans in a long time."

I slapped her on the ass and said, "You look pretty good too." Then I gave her a kiss and turned to leave. I smiled when she slapped my ass as I headed out.

The girls were all busy getting dressed when I came into the living room. Little Bit was already dressed and looking adorable. She was in a little white dress, complete with pantyhose. Lord only knows where those came from. She had a little headband on with silk flowers. She was the perfect picture of a little girl about to participate in a wedding.

"You're really pretty today!" I said to her.

She bounced on the sofa and smiled. "You look really pretty too, dad." I leaned over and kissed the top of her head.

Meanwhile, the older two were busy arguing in the bathroom. I walked down the hallway and poked my head around the corner. "You two knock it off and get ready."

"Wow, Dad, you look great," Lee Ann said.

"Have you seen Mom?" Taylor asked. "She looks amazing."

"Yes, I have," I replied. "And yes, she does."

"We're almost ready," Lee Ann said.

"If you'll get out of my way!" Taylor shouted.

Lee Ann rolled her eyes and stepped out the door. "There, now you can finish."

I put my arm around her and said, "You look good, kiddo. I haven't seen you in a dress in a long time."

Lee Ann looked down at herself and said, "Yeah. Well, as soon as this is over, I'm taking it off."

I went out to the kitchen and poured myself a glass of tea, then went out to the living room and sat down with Little Bit. She was holding a basket full of flowers and practically vibrating with excitement.

"You ready to do this?" I asked. I wasn't involved in all the planning, but I'd picked up on what was going to happen today. Little Bit was going to be the flower girl as both brides walked down the *aisle*, for lack of a better word. Jace was going to be the ring bearer. But he was only going to carry the brides' rings, as the guys didn't have rings. Not that it was that big a deal.

Mel came out of the bedroom and announced, "Alright, everyone, let's go."

Taylor came out of the bathroom, still brushing her hair. "Give me a minute."

"Hurry up," Mel replied. "We need to go."

Once she finished brushing her hair, we were ready to go. I had everyone gather in the living room. My family looked really amazing. After so long of not seeing anyone dressed up, it was incredible to see them all decked out and ready to go.

"I wish I had a camera," I said. "You all look so good."

Mel looked at the girls and said, "One thing we didn't prepare for. Family photos after the apocalypse."

"Alright," I said, "let's get this show on the road."

We walked over to Danny's house and could hear voices

out back. The back porch was crowded with people. Thad was dressed in a suit and I had to do a double-take.

"Where in the hell did you find a suit to fit you?" I asked in amazement.

He held his arms out and said, "It wasn't easy and Miss Kay had to make some adjustments. But it fits."

"You look amazing," Mel said, and she stepped up on her tip toes to kiss him on the cheek.

Thad blushed and smiled. "Thank you, Mel."

I shook his hand and patted his shoulder. "Looking good, buddy." He smiled and nodded.

Aric was sitting in a chair against the wall. He was leaned forward on his knees as they bounced rapidly up and down. I walked over to him and he looked up. "Nervous much?" I asked with a smile.

He sat up and bit his thumbnail. "Kinda."

I laughed and patted his shoulder. "Don't sweat it, buddy. You got this?"

He smiled nervously. "Yeah."

The ladies were all inside and much chatter leaked through the door to the house. I was informed no men were allowed inside. I looked around the porch and saw Ian and Jamie sitting on a chase lounge on the far end of the porch. Perez was in a chair beside them.

"Where's Sarge and guys?" I asked.

"They'll be here soon," Ian said.

"Anyone seen Dalton?" I asked.

All I got in reply was blank stares. I shrugged. "Maybe he'll show up."

I heard a truck roll up out front and walked around the porch to check it out. Sarge's Hummer was idling in the yard. When the door opened, I was surprised when Mitch stepped out.

"Mitch!" I called out. "Hey, man, great to see you," I said as I stepped down off the porch. Then Cecil got out, dressed in a suit no less. It was such a shock to see these guys dressed like they were. When Michelle got out, she looked amazing as well. I greeted each of them and hugged Michelle.

Then the old man got out and I nearly passed out. He was in a suit as well, tie and all. As soon as our eyes met, he pointed at me and said, "Say one fucking word and I'll break your legs."

I blinked and shook my head. "Uh, no. You look really sharp. I genuinely mean that."

Then Ted, Mike and Doc piled out of the back of the truck. Ted and Doc were both likewise decked out in a nice suit. It made me scratch my head. *Where in the hell did all these suits come from?* I wondered. Then I took a second look at Mike. He was wearing a jacket. But it was over a pair of Multi-Cam pants and combat boots. I had to shake my head and laugh.

Mike looked at me and asked, "What?"

Still shaking my head, I replied, "Nothing. You look exactly like I'd expect."

Mike grabbed the lapels of the coat and looked himself over. "I think I look pretty sexy myself."

"You look like some kind of retard that dressed himself," Sarge shot back.

"Nailed it," Ted added.

Mike smoothed the coat and said, "Y'all are just haters." And he headed for the steps up to the house.

We all filed up onto the porch. Sarge opened the door and started to go in. Mike went to follow him, but the old man stopped and pushed him back, "Nope," he said as he slammed the door in Mike's face.

"What the hell?" Mike asked.

"No guys in the house," I replied.

Mike pointed at the door and asked, "What the hell's he doing in there then?"

I shrugged. "He's giving them away. Guess they're working out how that's going to happen."

Ted grabbed Mike by the shoulders and said, "Come on. Let's go out back and I'll get you some juice and cookies. And we can put your helmet on before you hurt yourself."

Mike shrugged him off and replied, "I'll stick my helmet up your ass."

Mitch and Michelle went into the house as well while the rest of us waited on the back porch. We were doing this early, trying to beat the heat. We were sitting on the back porch shooting the shit when the old man came out and said everyone needed to go out and grab a seat. Mel and the girls came out, along with Jess and Kay. We all made our way out to the back of the pond. But I saw Mike dip out and head around the house. I really hope he's not up to anything nefarious.

Mitch was standing in front of everyone, a huge smile on his face. I looked at him and asked, "What are you doing?"

He smoothed his coat and said, "I'm performing the ceremony."

"Where the hell did you figure out how to do that?"

"I have the analog internet."

"What's analog internet?" Lee Ann asked with a hint of excitement in her voice.

"Encyclopedias," Mitch replied.

I laughed. "That's a hell of an idea. Having a set of them."

"We've had them for many years," Michelle said. "I used them when I was a kid and took them when we got married."

"Awesome idea," I replied. I looked over my shoulder at Lee Ann and said, "Sorry, kiddo. Not what you were expecting, I know."

Thad and Aric walked up and stood in front of Mitch. He shook both their hands. There were a couple cat-calls from the crowd, which got a smile from Thad and nods from Aric. Suddenly, we began to hear a guitar and everyone looked back.

Sarge was heading towards the pond, Fred on one arm and Mary on the other. Behind them was Mike, like a strolling troubadour, except, thankfully, he wasn't singing. But he quietly strummed something like the wedding march as he followed the brides towards their grooms. Little Bit led them as she dropped handfuls of azalea blooms onto the ground.

The crowd fell silent as they made their way towards where Mitch waited for them. It was quite the sight to see the old man in a suit with Mary and Fred on either arm. Each wore a beautiful dress, and I glanced at Mel and saw her wiping tears away at seeing her wedding dress again. The three made their way up the small aisle created by the arrangement of chairs. Fred and Mary were both smiles as they made their way to the front.

I caught Danny's eye. He was watching Mary. She wore Bobbie's wedding dress and I'm sure a lot was running through his mind. But he had a slight smile on his face. Bobbie may not be here physically, but she certainly was in spirit.

Mike stepped off to the side and kept the chords going on the guitar as everyone got into the position. Sarge hugged and kissed each of them before stepping back and clasping his hands behind behind his back. Mitch whispered a couple of things as Mary took Thad's hand and Fred took Aric's. Then Mitch nodded and cleared his throat.

"Friends, we are gathered here today to join these two couples in holy matrimony in the eyes of God and their community. Who gives these women today?"

Sarge held his hand up, "I do," then he looked at Thad and

Aric and added, "and they better take damn good care of them." A little laugh spread through the crowd.

Mitch looked at Thad and asked, "Thad, do you have any vows prepared?"

Thad nodded and Mitch motioned for him to continue. Thad brought Mary's hands up before him and said, "I never thought I'd find happiness again. I was in a deep and dark place. Then you brought the light back to my life. I promise you before everyone here, I will protect and provide for you. I love and laugh with you and together, we will help strengthen our community."

Mitch nodded at Mary and she flushed. Very nervously she started. "I've watched you for a long time, Thad. You are a good man, noble, honorable and strong. I've thought of this day for a very long time. Like you, I was in a dark place and you thought I was the light. But you were mine. I promise to love you, to provide for you and to be by your side until the day I die."

Everyone was getting teary-eyed. The words they offered one another expressed exactly how everyone sitting here felt for one another. This marked a change in our lives. No longer were we simply trying to exist. It was the first step, the first real step, to making our world anew. Not to what it once was, but maybe, what it always should have been.

"Thad, do you have a ring?" Mitch asked.

Jess ushered little Jace up the aisle. He had a small pillow with a ring on it. Thad knelt down and took the ring from the grinning boy, patted his head and stood up.

"Thad, do you take Mary to be your wedded wife?"

"I do," Thad replied with a smile.

Then repeat after me," Mitch said. "With this ring, I thee wed."

Thad took Mary's small and delicate hand into his massive

strong hand. Positioning the ring in front of her finger, he looked into her eyes and said, "With this ring, I thee wed." And he slipped the ring on her finger. Tears rolled down her cheeks as he slid the band on.

Mitch leaned in close to the couple and asked, "Do you have a ring for Thad?"

Thad shook his head. "No. But that's alright."

Suddenly, from the woods behind us, came a thundering voice. "And one ring shall rule them all!"

Everyone looked up to see Dalton come strolling out of the woods. He was dressed in jeans and a polo shirt. I had to do a double-take. Then another. I'd never seen him in anything other than what most of wear on a daily basis. He walked towards the brides and grooms as everyone stared at him.

He walked up to Thad and gripped his shoulder. "I know I haven't been here long. But I consider you all family. And it's just not right for you not to have a ring on your wedding day. Dalton reached out and took Mary's hand. He pushed his clenched fist into her hand, leaned over and kissed her on the cheek, saying, "Congratulations." Then he opened his hand and dropped a simple gold band into her hand.

She looked at it and began to cry, then looked up at Dalton and reached out to hug him. He had to lean over so she could. She thanked him, over and over. Then Thad hugged him too. Dalton patted his back and congratulated him as well. Then he stepped out of the way.

Mitch looked at Mary and asked, "Mary, do you take Thad to be your wedded husband?"

"I do," she replied.

Mitch smiled and said, "Mary, repeat after me. With this ring, I thee wed."

Mary smiled as she held Thad's big hand. As she slid the

band on, she excitedly shouted, "It fits!" We all laughed and she blushed as she looked at Mitch, then back at Thad. "With this ring, I thee wed." A round of claps erupted from the crowd and the couple stood before us, smiling and holding one another close.

Mitch took half a step forward and said, "We're only half-way done!" And once everyone settled down, he stepped up to Aric and Fred.

Mitch looked at Aric, then Fred. "Have you prepared any vows?"

Aric shook his head. "No. I love her with all I am and ever will be."

"And I love him with all I am and ever will be," Fred replied.

Kay ushered little Jace back up with Fred's ring on the pillow. Aric knelt down and took it from the smiling boy, tussled his hair and stood back.

"Aric, do you take Fred to be your wedded wife?" Mitch asked.

"I do."

"Fred, do you take Mitch to be your wedded husband?"

"I do," she replied.

Mitch then turned to Aric and said, "Repeat after me. With this ring, I thee wed."

Aric repeated the verse and slipped the ring onto Fred's finger. She wiped a tear away as she held her hand up to look at it. It was the same ring she'd been wearing since the announcement. But, now it meant more. Dalton stepped up and pushed another gold band into Fred's hand. The tears flowed from her when she looked at the simple gold ring and she reached up and hugged him.

Mitch gave her a minute and said, "Alright, Fred, repeat

after me. With this ring, I thee wed." And she slid the ring onto Aric's finger.

He looked at it and asked, "How did you size these? It fits perfectly."

Dalton smiled. "I pay attention to detail."

Mitch addressed the crowd. "Alright, everyone. If there are no objections—"

I'd been waiting for this moment and stood up. To Mel's obvious shock and horror as she grabbed my hand.

"I wasn't going to say anything. But now that you mention it—" I trailed off, not intending to say anything. But everyone was collectively holding their breath.

Sarge cut his chin over his shoulder and said, "Shut up and sit-down, Morgan."

I laughed, and it broke the tension. When I sat down, Mel asked, "What the hell was that?"

Patting her hand, I replied, "Just having a little fun. It'll be a story for them to tell later."

Mitch stepped forward, putting his arms around the two couples, and moving them with him, he announced, "By the power vested in me by, well, you guys, I now pronounce you husbands and wives!"

A collective cheer erupted as everyone leapt to their feet, clapping and whistling. I noticed Mike took off at a sprint and disappeared. A procession line of sorts formed as everyone made their way by the newlyweds to shake hands and offer hugs. When I got to Thad, he pointed at me, shaking his head, "You a mess, Morgan. You a mess."

I laughed and hugged the big man. "I was just having a little fun."

"You scared the shit out of me," Aric said.

I clapped him on the back and laughed. "I thought it might get a rise out of you."

"Rise, hell. I nearly shit myself. This was your idea!"

Dalton was standing off to the side and I waved him over. "Where did the rings come from?" I asked when he approached.

He reached into his pocket and took out a gold eagle coin. "I made 'em out of these. It wasn't hard and didn't take long. I just wanted the guys to have a ring."

"We really appreciate it," Fred said as she looked at the ring on Aric's finger.

"Very much," Mary added.

As we all talked, music suddenly erupted from the house. It was the Jimmy Hendrix "Purple Haze". I looked up towards the house and saw Mike standing on the rear steps. "Are we going to have a reception or what?" He shouted across the yard.

"Looks like we should move to the house," I said.

As the group started towards the house, Sarge came up beside me. "Real funny there wise-ass," he said.

"Awe, come on. It was funny."

"That's the kind of shit I'd expect from that pecker-head up there on the porch."

I patted his back. "Come on. It's like I told Mel. Gives them a story to tell later." I patted his chest and added, "You look really sharp too. It was a cool thing you did for them."

"It wasn't shit and I'm getting out of this burin' suit as fast as I can."

Everyone made it up to the porch where the cakes were waiting along with a selection of things to eat. The two jugs of blackberry wine were also set out. I looked around for the music and found Mike standing beside an old record player. It had amazing sound and he was thumbing through a stack of records. His suit jacket was gone, and he now looked like the Mike we all knew.

Mike turned his attention from the turntable and looked at the gathering crowd. "Alright. We ready to kick this party off?" He asked. There was a cheer from the crowd and he clapped his hands. "It's not much, but I have a contribution for the reception. He reached down to a cooler sitting at his feet and opened it. It was full of beer bottles floating in water with blocks of ice. Reaching in, he grabbed one and tossed it to the old man. "Here."

Sarge caught it and looked at it suspiciously, asking, "What the hell is this?"

"What's it look like? It's an ice-cold beer!"

"Where the hell did you get beer from?" I asked.

"I found a brewing kit and a lot of supplies in the garage of the house. I've been saving it. Figured this was a good time, so I brewed it all up. This is all there is, so you better enjoy it."

Sarge still eyed the bottle with suspicion. Mike shook his head and took the bottle from him, twisted the top off and took a long swig." Ahh, damn that's good!"

Soon, beers were being passed around and everyone was enjoying a cold one. And it wasn't bad! Not the best, but considering how long it'd been since we'd seen a beer, it was the best I'd ever had."

Despite his reservations about Mike, Sarge couldn't take it any longer and tried the beer. I watched as he took a long pull and swished it around in his mouth. Swallowing it, he started to nod. "Just when I think you can't possibly be any more worthless, you go and do something like this." Sarge saluted Mike with the bottle, "That's a fine oat soda there, Mikey."

Mike smiled and replied, "I told ya." Then Sarge turned his bottle up, draining it.

The Hendrix record was taken off and Otis Redding put on. I grabbed a couple of beers from the cooler and went outside. I pulled a folding camp chair over and set it up where I could watch the merriment on the porch. It was quite the contrast to what I was used to seeing. Music blared from the turntable and people milled about with beers in their hands. Then there was the way they were all dressed. That thought made me look down at my own clothes. It's been a long time since any of us dressed this way. And tomorrow it would all go back to *normal.* Our normal at any rate.

I drank my beers and watched the brides and grooms dance. I watched as Sarge danced with each of the girls. There were a lot of cat-calls. Lots of laughing and hooting and hollering. No doubt that this night no one was worried about anything. For tonight, we would be carefree. I drained the bottle in my hand and got up to go find my wife. She was in a dress today and I was out of uniform. I was going to get the most out of this situation that I could. Tomorrow would have to wait.

PROLOGUE

BAKER WAS LEANING ON THE open doors of the big green transformer. "What do you think?" She asked.

"Well," Terry replied. "One of two things is going to happen. One, the lights will come on. Or two, the doors will blow off this thing and it'll burn like a damn torch."

"Only one way to find out," Scott replied. "I trust it. I megged it out and it looks good. I think it's going to be fine."

Terry stood up and closed the doors to the transformer. "Like I said, only one way to find out," he said as he walked away from it.

Baker and Scott moved with him, and once they were at a comfortable distance, Terry waved to Eric. He was standing up the power pole where the wire from the transformer dropped underground. He had a long telescoping pole in his hands. At the top of the pole was a peg that came out at ninety-degrees from the head. This peg was in the eye ring of the fuse holder on the pole. Eric saw Terry wave and he braced himself. He gripped the pole, took a quick look up and quickly slammed the switch closed with an upward thrust of the pole.

The pad-mount transformer that supplied power to the armory began to hum as the lights on the outside of the building came to life. A cheer erupted from the assembled Guardsmen. Sheffield ran over and grabbed Terry in a hug, lifting him off the ground. "You did it! You actually did it!"

80937604R00195

Made in the USA
Lexington, KY
10 February 2018